The Four Symbols

A former journalist for *Le Parisien*, Eric Giacometti spent several years uncovering some of France's biggest medical scandals. He also spent the end of the 1990s investigating Freemasonry, a subject he then explored in fiction with his writing partner, Jacques Ravenne. Together, they form a bestselling author duo, and have written over fifteen books together, including the several million-copy bestselling Antoine Marcas series.

GIACOMETTI
RAVENNE

The Four Symbols

Translated from the French
by Maren Baudet-Lackner

HODDER

First published in the French language as *Le Triomphe des ténèbres.*
Le Cycle du Soleil Noir by Editions Jean-Claude Lattès in 2018

First published in Great Britain in 2020 by Hodder & Stoughton
An Hachette UK company

This paperback edition published in 2020

I

A CIP catalogue record for this title is available from the British Library

Paperback ISBN 9781529359398
eBook ISBN 9781529359411

Typeset in Plantin Light by Palimpsest Book Production Ltd,
Falkirk, Stirlingshire

Printed and bound in Great Britain by Clays Ltd, Elcograf S.p.A.

Hodder & Stoughton policy is to use papers that are natural, renewable
and recyclable products and made from wood grown in sustainable forests.
The logging and manufacturing processes are expected to conform to the
environmental regulations of the country of origin.

Hodder & Stoughton Ltd
Carmelite House
50 Victoria Embankment
London EC4Y 0DZ

www.hodder.co.uk

To our readers and friends

The structure of the SS was designed by Himmler according to the principles of the Jesuit Order. The rules and spiritual exercises outlined by Ignacio de Loyola were a model for Himmler, who did his best to reproduce them.

General Brigadeführer SS Walter Schellenberg, head of the intelligence and counter-intelligence division of the RSHA, the Reich's central security service. (From *The Memoirs of Hitler's Spymaster* by Walter Schellenberg, A. Deutsch Editions, 1956.)

Prologue

The coal-burning stove swathed the mostly dark room in a thick blanket of warmth. Standing in front of the tall windows with polished wood frames, Professor Otto Neumann contemplated the city lights. His city. He loved it passionately, and yet this was the last night he would spend here.

His last night in Germany.

The bookseller, who had never left Berlin, still hadn't fully realized that by this time the next day he would be in Paris, and after another twenty-four hours, he'd be in London. He had never taken a plane, but his wife had been enthusiastic on the phone. "It's incredible. You feel like a bird up in the sky."

Hearing the mischievous voice of his beloved Anna had restored his hope. She had left the week before, with a tourist visa, to avoid raising suspicions. And now it was his turn to head for Tempelhof Airport. He glanced annoyedly at the clock on the wall. It was almost ten thirty and his friend still hadn't arrived, though the English Embassy was only fifteen minutes away by car. Maybe he'd been held up at an overzealous SA checkpoint. Over the past few months, the ruthless Brownshirts had begun playing traffic police in town—an ideal pretext to beat up Jews and steal their cars.

"Mr. Neumann, can I go? The boxes are all put away. I have a date with my Greta."

The weak voice of his apprentice made its way up the spiral staircase.

"Yes, Albert. Leave the door open when you go. I'm expecting someone," answered the bookseller. "See you next week."

The bell on the front door jingled as it shut. Neumann didn't have the courage to say goodbye to the young man. He sat down and bowed his head for a minute, lost in his thoughts. He would never see the boy again. Officially, he was closing the shop for a week's holiday in France, but he knew that when the authorities discovered he had fled, the bookstore would be confiscated by the Aryanization of Business office.

Since the Nazis had come to power, he had become a *Mischling*, a half-Jewish, half-Aryan mutt, an ex-professor run out of the university turned bookseller. For the learned men behind the racial laws in force, he was part superhuman, part subhuman. The product of race pollution.

Five years earlier, in Heidelberg, the president of the university, a mathematician and Nazi enthusiast who also served as vice-president of the Reich's science association, had used the law to motivate Otto's dismissal from his position as chairman of the comparative history department. Neumann had tried to appeal against the decision, arguing that the "super-" and "sub-" prefixes cancelled each other out, meaning he was just a simple human. He was perfectly fine with that. Unfortunately, the university president was immune to his humour and failed to change his mind. Three months later, the eminent Professor Neumann became a bookseller specializing in antique editions—his passion.

He stood up from his chair and closed a small box full of invaluable volumes.

My precious books . . .

He couldn't take them all with him. Only three boxes full of his most cherished texts, his treasures, would be quietly sent to a fellow bookseller in Switzerland. The rest of them—over a thousand titles—would be left behind. The very thought that they would fall into the hands of backward, overzealous fanatics was revolting, but there was nothing more he could do.

He would bring just a single jewel with him. For the moment, it was hidden away in the safe. He couldn't let the Nazis get their hands on that. He couldn't even dream of the consequences of such a sacrilege.

Through the window, the city seemed peaceful. But evil was coursing through its veins, infiltrating stones and minds alike, poisoning even the air. He couldn't bear to turn his head to the right anymore because, just beyond the first row of buildings, was the massive silhouette of the neoclassical headquarters of the Gestapo on Prinz-Albrecht-Straße. The giant banner bearing the malevolent swastika was lit every night by vertical projectors. The symbol was black like an overfed venomous spider, its four legs grown stout. A spider turned flag. "Swastika: ancient symbol of peace and harmony in Asia, and particularly India."

Those were his words, written over twenty years ago in his book on pagan symbols.

Peace and harmony! What sinister irony. He should have added, "for an Indian swastika, which turns to the left." Hitler wasn't one for eastern wisdom. He set his swastika spinning in the other direction. A full reversal of Asian traditions.

He had sucked all the good out of the swastika to turn it into the symbol of infamy—at least for the Reich's so-called inferior races, Jews first in line. Germany was delirious in its veneration of the evil gammadion.

He looked at the clock on the wall again. Time was running out and his visitor still hadn't appeared. He walked across the room and knelt down in front of the wall safe. The dial turned quickly under his fingers, freeing the armoured door from its slumber.

Just as he slipped an object into his fawn leather bag, the bell on the door to the bookshop rang again. Neumann sighed with relief. His friend had made it. The bookseller put the bag down on his desk and headed joyfully down the stairs.

"At last! I've been waiting for you for nearly an hour," he said as he landed on the last step. "You clearly—"

His heart jumped.

Three men were standing on the other side of the counter. Three men wearing the same uniform. Brimmed cap adorned with a skull symbol, perfectly tailored black jackets and trousers, a red armband showcasing a swastika on their right arms, and shiny leather boots. And each of them had a pistol in his belt. The face of the oldest one in the group brightened. A thin scar ran the length of his cheek, up to his temple.

"Hello, Professor," said the SS officer, bowing his head. "It's an honour to meet you."

He was tall and thin, around forty years old, with short grey hair, and a narrow, intelligent-looking face. His light eyes wielded a penetrating gaze.

"My name is Colonel Weistort. Karl Weistort," he added.

The bookseller remained still, unable to respond. The two other officers had moved away from the counter and were browsing the shelves.

"I . . . Delighted to make your acquaintance . . . I was just about to close up for the night," he finally stammered.

The colonel looked disappointed.

"Could you make a little exception? I've come all the way from Munich to meet you. Look what I've brought you," he said, placing a yellowed book on the counter. The worn cover featured a statue of a bearded man sitting on a throne.

Neumann adjusted his glasses and instantly recognized his biography of Holy Roman Emperor Frederick Barbarossa.

"A magnificent work," continued the SS officer. "I happened upon it when I was young, at the university in Cologne, and it's been the star of my library ever since, sitting alongside your other book on sacred symbols, of course. Such a fount of knowledge!"

"Thank you," the bookseller replied awkwardly.

"No, you deserve it. You must know that the Führer has an unbound passion for this extraordinary emperor."

"I didn't."

"However, I disagree with you as to the importance of the legend of Barbarossa. You know, the one that claims the emperor isn't dead, but lies sleeping in the bosom of a magic mountain. And when he wakes, the Reich will reign for eternity."

Neumann frowned in confusion. The SS officer tapped his index finger on the cover of the book.

"You say it's just a story for children, but it's a powerful myth, capable of galvanizing the hearts of all Germans. The imagination, professor! That's the real source of power over men. Whoever captivates their imaginations is stronger than ten armies combined. But I suppose you have too much Jewish blood in your veins to understand . . . It's not your fault."

The bookseller's pulse was racing. The colonel placed his palms flat on the counter.

"Because, if you think about it, isn't Adolf Hitler the reincarnation of the old sleeping emperor? He's awoken the people and will establish a new Reich to last a thousand years. He's been sent by providence. You should understand that. Haven't the Jews been waiting for their messiah for millennia? We Germans have found ours first."

"Yes . . . Probably."

The SS colonel's eyes sparkled with excitement.

"And as such, we are now the chosen people. What an immense responsibility!"

"I'm delighted for you . . . What is it you're looking for exactly, Colonel?" asked Neumann in a forced neutral tone.

"I'm sorry, I got carried away. I'm sometimes such an incorrigible romantic. First, an autograph would make me very happy," he replied, suddenly strangely jovial.

The bookseller noticed the other two officers opening one of the boxes destined for Geneva.

"Those books aren't for sale," said Neumann.

The colonel tapped the counter with the book.

"Let it go, Professor. My deputies are naturally curious. It's a sign of intelligence. Grab a pen and get to work!"

Neumann did his best to contain his annoyance. He had to get rid of these visitors before his friend turned up. If he walked into the shop at this time of night, he'd be taken into custody immediately, and the bookseller with him.

"I'll get something to write with."

"No need," replied Weistort as he handed Neumann a big black-and-silver fountain pen bearing the SS insignia. "A gift from Reichsführer Himmler himself."

The bookseller took the pen as if it were a venomous snake.

"'For Karl', plus something nice," the colonel continued affably. "That will be perfect." Then he turned towards his deputies. "The Reichsführer would faint if he found out a half-Jew was using his pen."

The other two burst into laughter.

Neumann remained impassive and did as he'd been told.

"There you go. Can I do anything else for you?"

One of the two Nazis walked over, his arms full of books with ornate bindings, and placed them on the counter.

"Look at these hidden treasures," exclaimed the tall blond as he went over the covers spread out before him. "It's incredible! I found a *Stéganographie* by Abbé Trithème, the original edition, and the *Mutus Liber* prefaced by Paracelsus."

"I found two gems as well," chimed in the second deputy, his hands deep in the box. "An *editio princeps* of the *Malleus Maleficarum*! I thought they had all been burned in the 1635 Hamburg book burning. And a copy of the *Codex Demonicus* by the Grand Inquisitor of Bavaria."

Neumann couldn't believe it. These men had perfectly identified the books. Where did these learned brutes, interested in and know-ledgeable about symbolism, come from? Members of the ranks usually stuck to lowly police jobs or protecting dignitaries.

The colonel intercepted the bookseller's surprised look and took back his signed volume.

"How silly of me. I forgot to tell you about our positions. We work at the Ahnenerbe, the Ancestral Heritage Research and Teaching Society, of which I'm the head. Don't mind our SS uniforms—we're scholars like you, intellectuals, but of pure blood."

Neumann frowned. Nazi intellectuals. What a sinister oxymoron, he thought.

"Really . . . From which universities?" he inquired prudently.

The colonel bowed.

"I graduated from Cologne with a doctorate in ethnology. My two deputies both attended the University of Dresden. The captain is chairman of anthropology at the University of Munich and the lieutenant left his job as a professor of medieval literature to take up his new position at the Ahnenerbe. We are drowning in work at the moment. We're always hiring. If you can believe it, Himmler has asked me to create more than fifty research groups! I'm a little overwhelmed."

One of the SS officers was carefully piling books up on the counter.

"These works would have a select place in our Society's library. Unfortunately, our budget is quite tight. Maybe our friend the professor could give us a good deal?"

Neumann watched them without a word. Despite their degrees, these three weren't worth any more than any other Nazis. They too were taking advantage of the reign of terror to steal from Jews. His mind started racing: refusing would get him in trouble but accepting would mean losing his treasures. He made up his mind. This was no time to hesitate.

"Since you like these books so much, I'd be more than happy to donate them to your Society."

The colonel nodded in satisfaction.

"How kind of you. If I may take advantage of your generosity, I'm also looking for one work in particular: the *Thule Borealis Kulten*, from the Middle Ages."

The bookseller's eyes narrowed and his heart raced.

"I don't believe I've heard of it. I'll check my register to be sure. What was it again?"

"*Thule Borealis*," answered Weistort, carefully articulating each syllable.

Neumann flipped nervously through his catalogue.

"No, I don't see it. You'd have more luck with my specialist colleagues."

The colonel put on a sad expression.

"Come now, Neumann. Are you sure? It's about purely Aryan esoteric teachings. Extraordinary teachings . . ."

"Is it? That must be very interesting," the bookseller lied carefully.

The colonel turned to his deputies. "What was the name of the Jew we interrogated yesterday?"

"Rabbi Ransonovitch, a charming man, though a bit gruff," answered the lieutenant. "It's a shame he didn't survive the interrogation."

Neumann's blood froze in his veins.

"That's it, Ransonovitch. He told me you had a copy."

"I'm sorry, but I don't know this rabbi," murmured the bookseller. "If you wouldn't mind, I should close up shop now."

The colonel shrugged and took two bills out of his wallet. "What a shame. I was eager to get my hands on that book," he said as he placed two hundred Reichsmarks on the counter.

Neumann's eyes opened wide. "That's too much. I told you I was happy to donate the books."

The scarred man raised his hand. "You've misunderstood. This is what I'm offering to buy your whole bookstore. I'm feeling rather generous."

"It . . . it's not for sale. This is ridiculous."

"Oh, Professor. It would have been so much easier if you had just handed over the *Thule Borealis* on your own. Given my admiration for you—I don't normally have many kind words for Jews—we could have stayed friends. And you would have escaped the purge."

"The purge?"

The colonel glanced at his acolytes and grabbed the bookseller by the shoulder. "You'll understand soon enough. In the meantime, let's go up to your office. Your friend the rabbi whispered in my ear, just before he died, that the book was hidden in your safe."

"The key to the safe is in the cash register," he mumbled. He bent down behind the counter, felt around a basket and found what he was looking for.

"Hurry up, time's running out," urged the colonel. "For you especially—"

He was cut off mid-sentence. Neumann stood up with a Mauser pistol aimed right at Weistort.

"Get out of here! I don't want you defiling my bookstore!"

The colonel didn't blink, though the two deputies backed away.

"Come now, Professor. Threatening an SS officer with a gun is punishable by death. Do you even know how to use it?"

Neumann smiled for the first time since they had walked into his shop uninvited. "I fought in the Great War. Iron Cross at the Battle of the Somme," he said. "I'm willing to bet I've killed more men than you, to my great regret. But for you I'll make an exception."

The Nazi backed away, fear appearing on his face for the first time. Neumann felt a wave of happiness wash over him. Scaring an SS officer was a rare pleasure—he would remember this for the rest of his life. But he knew that by executing the intellectuals bearing the skull insignia, he would only gain a short respite, because the rest of the pack would come for him. At least he would have time to flee and hide the book.

Suddenly the youngest SS officer unholstered his pistol. The bookseller had just enough time to react and pull the trigger. With a bullet in his skull, the Nazi fell backwards with a scream. Neumann didn't have time to return his aim to the colonel. The man with the scar was faster. His Luger already free of his belt, the colonel fired. The bullet went straight through the bookseller's upper chest and exited through his back, shattering his collar bone. Neumann crumpled to the ground, his shirt drenched in blood.

"You idiot!" sighed Weistort. "Let's take him upstairs."

"What about Viktor?" asked the captain, gesturing towards his fallen colleague.

"He's in Valhalla now. Tonight, he dines with Odin."

The two remaining Nazis dragged Neumann up the stairs. As they climbed, blood stained the steps. When they reached his office, they put him down in the armchair across from the window.

Weistort noticed a spool of packing string on the ground. "Use the string to tie him to the chair."

While the captain executed the order, Weistort rifled through the open safe.

"Where did you put the book?" shouted the colonel as he hurled stacks of bills to the floor.

"Go to hell!" answered the wounded Neumann, whose mind was becoming less and less clear.

Suddenly Weistort spotted the bag on the table. He opened it and brandished the thin, red, leather-bound volume. "The *Thule Borealis*!" He sat down on the couch and opened it carefully. As he turned the pages, his eyes filled with wonder.

"Magnificent. Absolutely magnificent."

"You have no right."

The colonel pointed towards the windows. "Tonight, Aryans have all the rights and Jews have none. Look!"

A red-and-yellow glow rose over the entire city.

"What's happening?" stuttered Neumann. It looked like a fire was ravaging the neighbourhood.

Weistort set the book down, opened his arms and raised them to the sky like a priest in church. "It's the purge, my friend. You should have listened to the radio, to the good Dr. Goebbels. He called the German people to take to the streets and express their justified anger with the Jews following the cowardly assassination of Ernst vom Rath in Paris."

He opened the windows wide. Screams shot up from below along with the sounds of breaking glass. Weistort crossed his arms behind his back, watching the flames dance across the synagogue to the south.

"But . . . the police . . ."

"They're not allowed out of the stations. Same for the firemen. Germans can enter homes and businesses, throw out their occupants, beat them, humiliate them, steal from them, and even kill them. The purge. This devastating force is barrelling across the land like an unstoppable wave. Berlin, Munich, Cologne, Hamburg, blood will fill the streets all over the country. Impure blood, the blood of Jews. And anyone who tries to help them will be considered an enemy of the people. There's only one law tonight: the law of pure blood."

"You are evil, pure evil."

Weistort smacked the wounded Neumann on his broken shoulder. "It's a question of perspective. For us National Socialists, you Jews are a foreign virus that has infected the German body. You have poisoned our country and our blood like a disease. You are evil. Since we are eliminating you, we are on the side of Good, of the people."

"You're crazy."

"But it's so simple. The majority is Good and the minority is Evil."

"The majority is Good! That's absurd. People will revolt."

"I doubt it. Do you think any of the brave Germans who are taking part in this night of purification will feel guilty tomorrow? Hardly. They'll feel a bit ashamed, like after a night of heavy drinking at Oktoberfest. But in the end, they'll see it as a salutary intoxication."

Weistort put the book back in the bag and opened the rest of the windows. The screams had made way for shouting, coarse laughter and patriotic songs, which now filled the air. He leaned out to see the street below. Outside a ransacked clothing store, three Brownshirts in caps chuckled as they dragged an old woman in her nightgown by her feet. A blood-stained old man lay motionless in front of the door.

"Those SA idiots," sighed Weistort as he turned around to face the bookseller. "If it makes you feel any better, I strongly disapprove of sadism."

"Your damn swastika has poisoned your soul."

"No, it's revealed us to ourselves. That's its power. Its magic. Oh, Professor, I do regret your *Mischling* heritage. I could have offered you a job at the Ahnenerbe. We could even have been friends . . ."

Neumann tried to look up, but pain burned in the back of his neck.

"Go to hell!"

The colonel laughed. "Sorry, but I only believe in the magic of our pagan powers, not that of the Devil. Satan is just a Judeo-Christian invention for simple minds."

The bookseller's strength was leaving him. The SS officer's voice sounded like an echo in his brain. He cried. Not from pain, no. From anger. With himself. He should have put that goddamn book somewhere safe.

Weistort prepared to leave.

"What do we do with him?" asked the captain with a glance at Neumann, who was losing the last of his blood.

"Let him die alone as he watches the events of this marvellous night."

"And the shop? Should we burn it?"

"No. Send a lorry for the books tomorrow. They'll make a lovely addition to the Reichsführer's library at Wewelsburg Castle. Tell them to pick up the body of our comrade, who lost his life in the pursuit of his perilous mission, murdered by a cowardly Jew. Make sure he's awarded the Iron Cross posthumously."

The scarred colonel leaned towards Neumann.

"Goodbye, Professor. Thanks to you and this book, Good will finally triumph."

The two SS officers left, leaving the bookseller to his fate. On the other side of the windows, heavy clouds reflected the red glow from the streets, as if drops of blood were about to start falling from the sky.

Hunched over on his chair, Otto Neumann was slipping into darkness. The synagogue had become a torch before his eyes. Now he knew that the fires outside were only the beginning.

Tonight, Germany was aflame. Tomorrow the world.

All because of a book.

A damn book.

PART ONE

All intellectual, natural and supernatural sources of power—from modern technology to medieval black magic, and the teachings of Pythagoras to the Faustian pentagram incantation—were to be exploited in the interests of final victory.
Wilhelm Wulff, Himmler's personal astrologer.
(From *Zodiac and Swastika*, Coward, McCann & Geoghegan, 1973.)

I

The storm was losing strength. The bellowing thunder echoed over the peaks in the distance as flashes of lightning continued their silver ballet to the north, near Yarlung Pass.

Standing at the entrance to the cavern, protected from the freezing wind that had been gusting through the valley for three straight days, a man in a white snowsuit stared intently at the last rays of light shining on the Himalayan peaks. Manfred wasn't afraid of lightning. On the contrary, he had learned to tame it with his mountaineering father as they climbed the sheer cliffs of the Bavarian Alps. His father's words came to mind every time he was in a storm.

Learn to love lightning. It purifies the air and forges the hearts of strong men.

But here, in this forgotten corner of Tibet, at the heart of the deep valley, there was something stale in the air that even lightning couldn't purify. The weather was like a faulty compass. It hadn't snowed a single flake, though the surrounding mountains were covered in a thick layer of fresh snow. It was as if an invisible, insidious force had imposed its laws on nature's most powerful elements.

Hauptmannführer SS Manfred Dalberg turned a hostile gaze to the foothills which formed the valley below. He was very far from the beauty of the Bavarian mountains of his childhood. The ground was grey and sterile and there was a total lack of vegetation. The rocky cliffs dotted with ridges sharp as knives were of an astounding size. The landscape seemed to have been crafted with a single goal: to annihilate all human and animal presence. He could feel it in his bones.

The Land of Screaming Skulls.

That was the name the Tibetan people gave this strange place forgotten by men. He hadn't seen or heard any screaming skulls, but the howling wind was grating on his nerves. All he wanted was to return to Germany and rejoin his combat division.

Manfred turned up the collar on his standard-issue SS Alpine snowsuit, then heard a familiar noise to his right. He grabbed the binoculars for a better view of the mountainside below. A lorry covered with a dirty canvas tarpaulin was speeding up the battered path that served as the only road. The tyres spewed dirt in their wake, leaving behind a trail of dust.

Schäfer is here.

A wave of relief washed over the SS officer. His boss had kept his word—he was here to take the situation in hand.

Manfred put on his hood and hurried down the stone steps that wound along the hillside from the cave to the edge of the road, taking them four at a time.

I have to get out of this Godforsaken dump.

He'd left Lhasa and the bulk of the Schäfer expedition almost two weeks ago with a small scientific unit made up of two archae-ologists, a linguist who also served as a translator, half a dozen Tibetan porters, and three Buddhist monks. In the beginning, things had gone well. He had followed his instructions to the letter and set up camp. At the exact place described in the sacred scrolls, there was a cave entrance set into a hill on the edge of the Sanshai slope, framed by two scarlet Tulpas—small, traditional Tibetan towers shaped like cones for housing prayer mills. But these didn't contain prayer mills, just sculptures of threatening horned demons.

It all fitted perfectly with the drawings reproduced in the scrolls of the Kangyur, the sacred book of the Tibetan people.

The door to the skull kingdom.

But as soon as they finished setting up base camp, two porters came down with an unknown illness that resulted in massive haemorrhaging, emptying their bodies of all their blood. Not long after, relations between the Germans and the "smelly monks", as his deputy called them, became tense. The Buddhist priests had ordered the porters to block the entrance to the crypt. They could go no further inside the cave. If it had been up to him, Manfred would have nonchalantly executed them, but he didn't want to jeopardize his country's diplomatic relations with the locals. Tibet had become a great friend to the Third Reich and had asked for Germany's help to fight the Chinese.

He had sent a messenger to ask for help from his superior, Hauptsturmführer Ernst Schäfer. The commander of the "Aryan Tibet mission" had become the confidant of Lhasa's leader, the fifth Rinpoche, after all. He'd even managed to convince the latter to give the Germans the eight hundred scrolls of the sacred Kangyur.

Manfred reached the road just as the lorry covered in moon-coloured dust came to a stop. A porter was cleaning a mule harness in front of the Tulpas. Manfred shot a dirty look at the short little man whose face was as wrinkled as a baked apple. He still didn't understand why Schäfer was always arguing that these subhumans were of the Aryan race.

When the two men in white coats got out of the vehicle, Manfred stood at attention, his right arm raised in their direction in the customary fashion.

"Heil Hitler!"

The men replied in kind. The tallest of the two, who was built like a boxer with a blond beard and a cheerful face, shook his hand exuberantly.

"Manfred, it's so nice to see you," exclaimed Schäfer in an exalted tone. Then he gestured towards his companion, standing a few steps behind him.

"Let me introduce Colonel Karl Weistort, Director of the Ahnenerbe and member of the Reichsführer's personal staff. He comes to us from Berlin."

The SS officer walked over to Manfred. A thin scar ran from his temple to his cheek. Manfred had seen this type of scar before on fencers he had met in Prussian student societies. Despite the scar, the man exuded a kind of benevolence he'd rarely seen in superior officers of the SS.

The colonel shook his hand and smiled warmly. "Congratulations, Obersturmführer Dalberg. If the information I've received is correct, we're on the verge of making an incredible discovery. Your future at the SS will be bright, my young friend."

The lieutenant frowned—it was as if no one had read his letter.

"I'm flattered, Herr Colonel, but I mentioned several issues we've encountered."

The officer placed his palm on his shoulder. "Tell me more," he said.

The lieutenant glanced disdainfully towards the inside of the cave. "Inside the cavern, there's a giant door with no lock that leads to the sanctuary, where we'll find . . . the object. But the monks are furious. They say they only ever intended for us to visit the cave, not to enter the crypt. They don't want foreigners to profane their sanctuary."

Weistort burst into frank, joyful laughter.

"Foreigners? Hardly. Though it's hard to see at first glance, we share the same blood," he said, watching the porter smoking a long pipe. "Let's go solve this problem with our cousins."

The three men climbed the stairs that led to the cave.

"How has your stay in Lhasa been?" asked Manfred.

"Excellent. I finished filming my future documentary and we've collected a wealth of top-quality scientific data. I'm only sorry we must return to Berlin so soon. This country is marvellous, and the Tibetans are remarkable people."

"I'm afraid I don't share your opinion, Ernst," replied the young lieutenant.

Weistort, who seemed to be in excellent spirits, raced up the steps.

"Come, come, Lieutenant. Let's be optimistic. You're an SS officer. What do the Tibetans call this area again?"

The trio was only about thirty meters from the entrance to the cave—a half dome dug into the rock of the bald hill.

"The land of the screaming skulls," answered Manfred. "According to the monks, some of the dead continue to live, unable to reincarnate. They wander the depths of the earth groaning in despair, searching in vain for new bodies to inhabit. If we open the door, hell will be unleashed on earth. And since we need at least ten men to force the door open . . ."

Colonel Weistort smiled. "Ghosts wandering as they await resurrection. How magnificent! It's like a parable of our people. The Germans, discouraged by defeat and betrayal, were awaiting their saviour: Adolf Hitler. The Führer has given Germany a new body. A stronger, more powerful body. I love these ancestral traditions. They help us come to understand the hidden meaning of the universe."

The colonel accidentally kicked a big empty can with remnants of food inside that had been lying on a step. It had rolled off a heap of waste piled in front of a big boulder off to the side. Weistort stopped short, picked up the can and threw it back onto the pile.

"Lieutenant, please have that trash buried immediately."

The young lieutenant opened his eyes wide. Weistort observed his reaction, shaking his head in disappointment.

"It is a crime to sully nature, Lieutenant. The earth provides us with so many marvels. The least we can do is take care of it. Didn't they teach you that in your ecology courses at the SS Institute?"

"No, Colonel, I joined the order just last year."

"Well, that's quite a shame. You should know that the word 'ecology' was invented by a fine German, biologist Ernst Haeckel, from the Greek *oikos*, meaning habitat, and *logos*, meaning science."

"Haeckel was a great precursor indeed! He believed the races fitted into a hierarchy and placed whites at the top of the ladder. He was a founding member of the German Society for the Hygiene of the Race at the beginning of the 20th century, before the rise of National Socialism," added Schäfer enthusiastically.

"That's exactly right. You should read his *Lebenswunder* again and again," added Weistort. "I'll lend you a copy."

Pleased with his speech, the SS colonel resumed climbing. It took the men several more minutes to reach the cave. Inside it was as large as a Bavarian pub, lit by torches set into the walls, which were the same grey as the valley outside. At the far end of the cavern, a group of men were sleeping around an acrid, smoky fire. The smell of hot grease wafted through the cold air. A tall blond man hurried over to them, his features drawn. He didn't even deign to salute the new arrivals.

"Lieutenant, one of the porters is not well at all. He's vomiting and spitting up blood."

Weistort and Schäfer quickly exchanged concerned looks.

"He's the third," added the young German. "They've put him in the other chamber."

"Take me to him, please," ordered the colonel gently.

They took a tunnel to the right towards an alcove filled with weak glimmers of light. A small group of people was sitting in front of a stone altar with an ember fire. Three monks in saffron robes were seated in the lotus position around a man writhing in pain on a frayed blanket. His face was dripping with sweat and blood oozed from the corners of his lips.

Weistort walked over to the monks and bowed.

"Translate everything I say. Tell them I've been sent here by Adolf Hitler, the Great Lama of Germany."

The translator did as he was told, but the monks remained impassive. Weistort squatted down and held his hand to the sick man's forehead.

"What's wrong with him?"

One of the monks looked up at the officer disinterestedly. A flood of choppy, biting words poured from his mouth. The translator listened attentively, then stuttered in a weak voice:

"The porter has been punished, like the others, for entering the sanctuary. He will die tonight and become one of the dead banging on the door to get out. If we don't leave, we will meet with the same fate."

Weistort nodded knowingly. "I'm very disappointed. We only wanted to pay tribute to our ancestors. Tell him that I have the utmost respect for his Aryan land and its customs. In Germany, we are re-establishing ancient traditions scorned by Christianity. Could we make an offering, a sacrifice, to show our respect for the dead?"

As the translator spoke, the monk became increasingly aloof. He shouted a few words, then spat on the ground. The translator opened his eyes wide and shook his head.

"We must slit the throat of a goat anointed by the superior lama of Lhasa. Unfortunately, we don't have any goats."

The German officer smiled. Then, without a word, he took the knife out of the scabbard on his belt. He brandished it in the weak light from the fire, his blue eyes a reflection of the steel's metallic shine. His voice echoed against the walls.

"Tell him I also belong to a spiritual order—the SS—and that this knife was given to me by my superior, Heinrich Himmler. The blade is engraved with a motto: 'My honour is my loyalty.'" He drove the knife into the embers. The steel began to turn red. "I don't know if the word 'honour' means anything in Tibet, but in my country, it covers three qualities: pride, courage and loyalty."

The colonel smiled and walked over to one of the monks, the incandescent knife in hand. Weistort's voice became more soothing, almost gentle. He knelt down next to the oldest of the monks, who hadn't yet spoken a word.

"My friends, I can't help but feel you aren't being very loyal to us."

As soon as the last word had left his mouth, he stabbed the old man in the throat. The blade made his glottis crack as it cut into his flesh. A spurt of light-coloured blood gushed from the wound, staining the colonel's immaculate coat. The monk fell backwards onto the ground, next to the sick man, whose eyes opened wide as he thrashed like a worm. The smell of grilled meat filled the air around them. The two other monks hadn't reacted at all. Their faces remained impassive.

Schäfer came over. "You've lost your mind, Colonel! They aren't responsible for this man's illness."

Weistort wiped the blade on the monk's robe and answered condescendingly, "Your naiveté is charming, my dear Ernst. But let me explain. Do you see the red stripe at the bottom of the monks' robes? It tells us they belong to the Ganpitra, an internal order of the Tibetan clergy whose mission is to protect the community. At all costs. They are authorized to transgress their laws and to kill when necessary. Wolves in sheep's clothing. Who would suspect kind Buddhist monks? Very practical, don't you think?"

"I still don't see the relevance," replied Schäfer, who didn't dare look at the unmoving old man.

"The Ganpitra never use blades or guns—too vulgar. They prefer poison. It's one of their order's specialities. Before coming here, I read the memoir of an Italian missionary who was admitted to the Potala over thirty years ago. I think they poisoned one of the porters to make us believe there is a curse and scare us away."

One of the monks spoke.

"He says the disciples of Buddha are not afraid of you or of death. Killing them will change nothing. The porters still won't do as you ask. They'll prefer to die than to face the screaming dead."

The scarred colonel nodded his head and picked up his knife again. He leaned over the body of the monk and cut out a circle of flesh about the size of a coin from the unfortunate man's forehead. Just above the top of the nose. He brandished his trophy, then threw it in the fire.

"Translate again, please. I practise their magic, as well. I've taken their colleague's third eye and burned it. His soul is now mine and I will make him suffer a thousand torments. He will never reach Nirvana."

The monks' expressions suddenly shifted. They exchanged frightened glances.

Weistort's voice echoed through the cave once more. "They know all about this sorcery since they use it now and again to terrorize the Rinpoche's enemies. I paid careful attention to the book written by the priest from the Vatican, who learned all their secrets. Now, tell them to motivate the porters to open the door to the sanctuary. Or I'll have to take charge of their souls, too."

The two monks scrambled to their feet before they'd heard the end of the translation. They ran to the chamber, shouting orders to the sleeping porters.

Weistort put his knife away calmly. "Why don't we go open this famous door?"

Two hours later, the entrance to the sanctuary was clear. The heavy bronze doors, which must have weighed half a ton, lay on the ground on either side of a gaping hole that gave off a pungent smell.

"The sweet smell of death," whispered Weistort as he entered a long corridor with a torch in one hand, followed by Schäfer, who kept his finger on the trigger of his machine gun.

The other Germans had stayed back near the entrance, and they hadn't needed to ask the porters to leave. They had all fled the cave in fear, shouting prayers. The two remaining monks were now sitting silently before the fire.

The German officers edged forward on the damp ground, the torch casting an unsteady glow on the almost blue walls, dotted with a myriad of metallic glimmers.

"It must be an old mine," whispered Schäfer. "Tibet is full of precious minerals."

"What we're looking for here is worth infinitely more than silver or gold," replied Weistort. "By the way, I haven't congratulated you on your initiative yet. It was a brilliant idea to develop a friendship with the Tibetan dignitary and begin translating their sacred book."

The tunnel became larger, like a subterranean avenue plunged into darkness. Schäfer listened attentively—strange muffled noises, like scratching, could be heard all around them.

"Do you really believe in the legend, Colonel?" asked the head of the expedition in a frightened voice.

"The undead? Not at all. The people who hid the object here wanted to scare away a superstitious population. The rats, on the other hand—"

Weistort stopped short, then moved forward again, more slowly this time. "My God!"

He moved the torch closer. Before them stood a rectangular, black slab. The huge monolith looked like the enormous monuments erected to honour the dead in Prussian military cemeteries. But there was something in the middle of the slab that set it apart from German headstones.

A statue.

The bust of a man whose deformed features expressed intense pain. The lower half of his body seemed to be encased in the slab. His arms reached forward and his hands held a metal basin. At the foot of the monument, there was a pile of skeletons.

The two Germans drew nearer, bones cracking under their boots. They were hypnotized by their discovery. Weistort's face lit up.

He pulled a red leather-bound book from his coat pocket. Gothic letters spelled out the title:

Thule Borealis Kulten.

"Such an enticing treasure hunt across continents and centuries," said Weistort. "Can you believe it all started with this book written in the Middle Ages in Germany, which belonged to a half-Jew? I found a passage in it that alluded to sacred scrolls in the Orient and to the existence of . . ." He opened the book to a bookmarked page. An engraving appeared. "This very statue!"

They moved closer to the strange sculpture. The basin contained a ruby-hued object that glimmered as it reflected the glow from the torch. It had been carved into the shape of a symbol. A symbol that enchanted the two SS officers.

A swastika.

Colonel Weistort handed the torch to Schäfer and took the gammadion in his hands. His voice echoed like a burst of thunder.

"Year 1 of the Third Reich begins today."

2

Catalonia
January 1939

"¡No pasarán!"

A group of soldiers along the side of the battered road that led to the front saluted the lorry with the Republican war cry. Casually seated in the back seat of the Ford, Tristan answered with a raised fist, all the while fiddling with a cigar. He hadn't had time to light it yet. Cigars take time. Just like a good cognac, you have to enjoy the aroma first, and feast your eyes on its fawn wrapper. The driver broke hard all of a sudden, jolting Tristan from his imaginary tasting session. A flooded river had blocked the road with black mud.

"Everybody out!"

Jaime's hoarse voice was like a punch to the gut. The short, stocky group leader with the unkempt beard of a feverish conquistador had jumped out of the lorry, rifle in hand. He gave Tristan a furious look, causing the latter to carefully store his cigar in an inside jacket pocket.

"You, *el Francés*, move it. We have to get there before dawn tomorrow."

A dozen soldiers had taken up posts around Jaime, as if awaiting inspection. One turned up his worn collar, another tightened the rope he used as a belt. The state of their uniforms was representative of the Republic's status: in tatters. Tristan was the only one with a fine jacket whose silver buttons shone in the winter sun. He had taken it from a corpse—along with the cigar.

"You're going to get us shot with those damn buttons," grumbled Jaime. "With the first light of the moon, they'll shine like Easter candles."

The Frenchman smiled and pulled a round box from one of his pockets.

"I've got it taken care of. A bit of shoe polish and they'll see nothing at all."

Jaime pulled hard on his moustache. He hated the Frenchman. Nothing seemed to bother him. Neither hunger nor Francoist bullets. A daredevil, that's what he was. And he always had something to say, with a smile to boot. The kind of man who ruined discipline! If it had been up to Jaime, he never would have bothered carting around a guy like him. But he'd had no choice. Tristan was to play a key role in this crucial mission—though no one had told him exactly what that role entailed.

"Attention!"

The sudden slap of palms on rifle butts rang out in the frozen air. Jaime liked that sound.

"Weapons check!"

The perfectly oiled breech slid silently. German efficiency, thought Tristan, who recognized the Mauser. The lack of weapons and munitions was so severe among Republicans that they didn't hesitate to steal from fallen enemies on the battlefield. Nevertheless, elite troops had priority for scavenged Mausers.

"Something tells me our mission isn't going to be easy," commented Tristan's neighbour, an Irishman with red hair who had joined the International Brigades in the spring.

Jaime gave him a dirty look. He couldn't stand these volunteers who came from all over Europe to defend the Spanish Republic. They all thought they were heroes and felt they were above discipline.

"Right turn!"

Across from them stood a curiously shaped mountain range. Hundreds of grey crests chopped up the horizon in a disorderly fashion, as if a stone-cutting wind had first whipped them, then frozen them in place for eternity. The dark silhouette of a steeple rose out of a recess in the rocks like the thin blade of a sword. Jaime pointed nervously.

"That's where we're headed. Montserrat Monastery."

★   ★   ★

They had waited for nightfall to slip into the foothills. A path travelled by mule drivers wound its way through the blocks of granite. Jaime made the wise decision to leave their helmets behind—the sound of metal scraping on stone would have set the whole mountain ringing like a bell. El Jefe, as the men called him, had done a thorough job preparing for the mission. Or rather, thought Tristan, someone had done it for him.

"They say the monastery was evacuated," whispered the Irishman. "I've even heard people say that most of the monks were killed. I can't help but wonder what we're supposed to find up there. There's nothing left but ruins and crows."

"Maybe we're on a hunt for ghosts—a new weapon to finally win the war."

The redhead crossed himself impulsively.

"Don't say that! At home, in Ireland, spirits aren't a laughing matter. Look at these bloody upright stones. They look like warriors petrified by a demon. Sometimes I'm afraid they're going to wake up . . ."

"Halt!" ordered Jaime.

They had just reached a small plateau with a cliff overhang. Under the stone canopy, the moonlight made the rushing stream water glimmer in the rock basin below. The men set down their weapons to quench their thirst. The climb had been rough. Jaime struck a match, illuminating his face. In the light of the wavering flame he looked even paler than usual.

"Light!"

One of the soldiers hurried over with a lantern for El Jefe. Brighter now, the light revealed the cliff wall, with a door set under an ogee arch crowned with the statue of a saint giving his blessing under a star. Jaime spat on the ground. He hated priests more than anything. They were the reason Spain was in this civil war. For centuries, they had ensured the people remained ignorant and afraid. Ignorant of freedom and afraid of hell. But a new wind had swept through the country, kindling the flames of revolt, and now Spain was on fire.

"Irishman," whispered Jaime. "Are you from a Catholic family?"

The fatalistic redhead nodded.

"So you know your way around a monastery, then?"

El Jefe had just pulled out a map and thrust it into the light from the lantern. A red dot was placed where the church met the cloister.

"That's where we're going."

The Irishman used his finger to trace a path, then commented on their route. "First we'll make our way past the gatehouse. Then we'll cross the central courtyard to reach the church. We won't have much cover. If no one's here, it won't be a problem, but otherwise—"

"The monastery was emptied of its population several months ago, except for two people, who were authorized to stay. The Father Superior and the building's caretaker. Two priests."

Tristan, who had finally found a moment to light his cigar, joined in the conversation. "I doubt they'll let us pillage the abbey without a fight."

Jaime jumped up, furious. "Who said we were here to pillage?"

"The red dot. It's located at the exact spot where we'll find the scriptorium. In the Middle Ages, that was where monks recopied ancient manuscripts, but since Gutenberg's invention, the calligraphers have all been out of work."

"Get to the point." El Jefe couldn't stand the Frenchman's carefree tone. His tendency to discreetly mock everything around him made Jaime want to strangle him.

"For the past four centuries at least, monasteries have stocked their riches in the former scriptoriums: religious objects made of precious metals, works of art, etc. In short, it's where we'll find the abbey's treasure. That's why I doubt our hosts will welcome us with open arms."

All around them, the soldiers were listening carefully to the Frenchman. Since they'd been assigned to this special mission, there'd been a lot of questions. They all knew of Montserrat Monastery, which had been a pilgrimage site revered throughout Spain. From Sevilla to Burgos, by way of Barcelona, people travelled here to pay tribute to the monastery's miraculous Virgin. The spiritual heart of an entire country beat on this mountain. Its mysterious aura kindled superstitious fears. Some of the soldiers already glanced anxiously towards the edifice on its plateau. Jaime could tell that if he didn't boost morale quickly, his men would lose faith in the mission. All because of that damned Frenchman.

"Soldiers! The Republic chose you for your courage and valour. Our mission is crucial if we are to vanquish our enemies! Tonight, the future of the Republic is in your hands! Let's get moving!"

The galvanized troops got back on the road. Only Tristan remained behind, contemplating the chapel's pediment. The moon shone brightly on the saint, who seemed to burst forth from the stone. Just above his head, the star twinkled brightly like a perfectly cut diamond.

"Hey, *el Francés*, if you keep shooting your mouth off, this won't end well for you. Take my word for it."

Tristan didn't answer. He picked up his rifle, checked the cartridge and headed out with a smile. He knew Jaime would need him before long.

The dark abbey sat between two rock walls like a sleeping beast, but it was hard to tell if it was from a dream or a nightmare. To be safe, Jaime had split his men into two groups, each of which made its way to the entrance while covering the other. You never knew. But when they met up in front of the entrance gate, they found it wide open, as if a distracted monk had forgotten to close it. This unexpected ease of entry troubled them, especially since they were right across from the huge central courtyard where thousands of believers celebrated religious holidays before the war. Now it was deserted, but not silent. A cold wind rustled the dead leaves fallen from the tall trees, which towered above, dark spots in the night. None of the soldiers dared step forward. The constant stirring frayed their nerves. Even El Jefe remained still. Though he would never admit it, he knew that once they crossed this sacred threshold, there was no turning back. An invisible wall—a secret fear of sacrilege, maybe—held him back. He turned to his men, who seemed to disappear into the night.

"I need a volunteer to go into the church!"

Not a step nor a voice broke the silence.

"We have to find the abbey's caretaker. That's an order!"

"Well, if that's all . . ." Tristan replied sarcastically. He slipped his Mauser onto his shoulder, aimed at an invisible target, and fired. Seconds later the abbey's heavy bell rang out like a cannon, amplified by the echo from the mountains. "They'll come out now."

Jaime clenched his fists to keep himself from breaking the Frenchman's jaw. He had to react quickly.

"Irishman, you hide behind the door. The rest of you, form a half-circle around the church. As for you, *el Francés*, wait here."

The door squeaked on its hinges. A shadow appeared, preceded by a wavering light. The redhead didn't hesitate. He came out of his hiding place and took aim at the man in a cassock. A silver cross shone on his chest. Jaime hurried over.

"Where is the caretaker? Speak or you're dead!"

The Father Superior didn't have to answer. A pleading man fell to his knees behind the priest.

"Jesus, Mary, protect us from these demons! Jesus, Mary—"

The caretaker's prayer never reached the heavens. A rifle butt split his lip.

The Republicans dragged the two priests into the church. With their backs to a confessional, they watched in horror as the soldiers attacked the door to the scriptorium. Following their anxious nocturnal climb to the abbey, Jaime's men were now out of control, as if trying to exorcise their fears. In this battle against superstition, they raced to see who would commit the most acts of sacrilege. Holy fonts were already lying broken on the ground, their marble fragments lost among the shards of glass from the stained-glass windows that had shattered on the floor. One soldier used his bayonet to mutilate statues of saints, chopping off their ears and noses. Jaime let them rage. Once their thirst for destruction had passed, he knew discipline would return of its own accord. And he needed order, because the mission was nearing its goal.

The old oak door cracked ominously. The Irishman was first to enter the scriptorium. It was a long, vaulted room of dark stone with Gothic ogival arches. The only openings were thin arrow slits that let in the freezing wind. If it weren't for the large fireplace near the entrance, the room would have resembled a tomb forgotten by the living. It was hardly empty though. Along the walls, enormous off-white canvases covered vast piles of hidden objects. Tristan felt like he had just walked into a castle where the servants had covered the furniture with sheets at the end of the summer, to protect it from a winter's damp. The wary soldiers kept their distance from the greying canvases, which looked like death shrouds.

"Bring in the abbot."

When the Father Superior entered the room, Jaime clicked his heels, unfolded an official document covered in seals, and handed it to the priest. "In the name of the Republic, I've been ordered to requisition all objects of worth contained in the monastery. Here is the order signed by the authorities."

"What authorities?" exclaimed the priest, who feverishly clutched his silver cross. "I recognize only one authority—God!"

Jaime turned to the Irishman. "Pull off those canvases so we can see what's underneath."

The redhead did as he was told, revealing a mountain of gold and silver. Shining wafer boxes, carved crosses, pearl-covered reliquaries, and invaluable paintings. There was so much, Jaime started to worry. "We'll never be able to carry it all!"

"That's why I'm here," explained Tristan. "To sort the genuine riches from the rest—to separate the wheat from the chaff, as they say in the Bible."

Jaime looked at him, dumbstruck.

"Take this candleholder, for example." Tristan picked up the shiny silver candelabra. "It looks nice, but it's made of a cheap alloy with a fine silver plating on top. It's junk."

He threw it to the ground.

"This beauty, however, is a lachrymatory, a tear holder," he explained as he showed them a pale-blue vase with a long thin neck. "Centuries ago, it held the tears of a saint. It will bring in a fortune at auction. Plenty of money to buy weapons for the Republic."

The soldiers began fetching works of art and bringing them to Tristan like trophies for a victorious general. With a wave of his hand, he let them know which ones they should take. The rest rolled to the floor in a din worthy of the end of days. The abbot fell to his knees where he prayed silently while the caretaker squealed like an animal whose throat had been slit. Jaime watched as the others looted. He looked disdainfully on the greedy hands as they filled the bags they'd brought with them. Standing next to Tristan, the Irishman inventoried each object taken in a notebook.

"A silver wafer box, a reliquary adorned with gems and turquoise . . ."

The Frenchman stopped in front of a series of dusty little paintings. Blackened landscapes depicting the Stations of the Cross. He removed one from its rickety frame. Beneath the cracked varnish, it featured a tall mountain crowned with an edifice over which shone a bright star. Tristan slipped it into his bag.

"Is that worth something?" asked Jaime, coming closer.

The Frenchman laughed. "Not a thing, but it'll make a great souvenir! Every time I look at this hideous thing, I'll remember it all."

El Jefe suddenly grabbed his arm. "Who are you, Frenchman? What are you doing here?"

Tristan shook loose defiantly. "I'm an art hunter. I follow and track, and when I find it— Look!"

One of the soldiers had just pulled off a canvas covering a tall cross with a life-size Christ. The Frenchman grabbed Jaime's arm this time.

"Baroque crucifix from the 16th century. The cross is made of ebony, the Christ of ivory. A unique work." El Jefe stepped closer, his face level with Christ's feet, pierced with rounded nails.

"Get him down off the cross."

The caretaker shrieked. Using a bayonet, one of the soldiers pulled the nails out one by one. The ivory statue slid to the ground, supported by Tristan and the Irishman. Jaime stared at the Christ lying on the floor.

"It's too heavy to carry. Chop off the head, rip off the limbs, and break the torso into pieces. We'll sell the ivory by weight," ordered El Jefe.

Tristan placed himself between Jaime and the statue. "That's a crime!"

He didn't have time to finish his sentence. The caretaker leapt up, a candlestick in hand. "Go to hell, demon!" he shouted. All that noise was a mistake. Jaime turned around and dodged the impact. Caught in his own momentum, the caretaker rolled to the ground.

El Jefe let out a diabolical laugh. "Thought you could save your Christ, did you? Well, now you'll end up like him. Nail him to the cross!"

A year and a half later . . .

As the summer of 1940 draws to a close, the lights of democracy have been snuffed out in Europe.

As summer draws to a close, Adolf Hitler has achieved his outlandish goal. Nazi Germany reigns supreme over the Old World.

To the east, it occupies Czechoslovakia and Poland. To the north, it has conquered Norway and Denmark. To the west, thanks to a bold and swift attack, the Netherlands and Belgium have been wiped out. And to the stupefaction of the rest of the world, Germany's Panzer divisions have crushed France—a country thought to be invincible since the First World War—under their tracks. The campaign ended so quickly that even the Germans are astounded by their miraculous victories. The people whisper that the Führer has been anointed by God.

To the south, Mussolini's fascist Italy has blocked off access to the Mediterranean and is preparing to invade Greece.

The remaining European countries are divided into two camps: the fearful and the benevolent. The former, like Sweden, have hunkered down, terrified into neutrality. The latter, mostly dictatorships like the Balkans and the Iberian Peninsula, express their contagious admiration for the Third Reich.

As summer draws to a close, the reds and the blacks are allies. The communist czar Stalin has concluded a pact of non-aggression with Hitler, his sworn enemy. He watches as the Chancellor ravages Eastern Europe.

Summer draws to a close.

And the swastika's master savours his triumph.

Only one country still dares oppose him.

Just one: England.

A weakened and humiliated nation. Day and night, Luftwaffe bombers batter the wounded island and a naval attack is expected any day now.

Summer draws to a close.

In these past few months of fire and steel, strange and cruel things have happened, but it's nothing compared to what the German conqueror has planned. In the name of the Good he dreams of for his people, he will spread Evil. An Evil unlike anything humanity has ever known.

Summer draws to a close.

3

The Reich's leader pounded his fist into the table.

"Why do the shortsighted English keep rejecting my peace agreements? They're determined to defy us. Their loss."

Everyone else was quiet around the oval table, made of light-coloured marble and adorned with a giant red swastika. The seven most powerful men in the new Germany were used to their leader's sudden outbursts. The volcano never erupted for long. They waited a few minutes for the lava flow to cool.

Adolf Hitler nervously opened a grey folder sitting in front of him, put on a pair of reading glasses, and spoke again. "Gentlemen, I hope you have carefully read the report on Operation *Seelöwe*." He stopped, took off his glasses and looked intently at each member of the council. "The invasion of England by sea."

The seven men had all read the Operation Sea Lion file. Seated around the table with the Führer, from left to right, were Hermann Göring, Commander-in-Chief of the Airforce, Joseph Goebbels, Minister of Public Enlightenment and Propaganda, Reichsführer-SS Heinrich Himmler, architect Albert Speer, and General Wilhelm Keitel, Chief of the Armed Forces High Command. Nazi party leader Rudolf Hess and the regime's official ideologue, Alfred Rosenberg, who orchestrated the theft of works of art in occupied countries, completed the assembly.

All of these ruthless and efficient men—the Führer's inner circle —had helped him rise to power in 1933. They were united in their unconditional admiration for their leader but had known each other for so long that they had grown to hate one another on more or less cordial terms.

At the back of the room, against the wall, was the only female attendee: Hitler's personal secretary, who was diligently typing away on her Torpedo typewriter. The Reich might worship women as mothers, lovers and breeders, but they were confined to lowly positions in the professional sphere.

A thundering voice echoed through the room.

"Not a moment too soon!" boomed Hermann Göring. "This is no time to delay. My Heinkel bombers are shelling cities and industrial sites. England will fall like an overripe fruit. We must launch the invasion now!"

The massive Airforce Commander was also Prime Minister of Prussia and second in line to the Führer. If Hitler died, Göring would take his place. As a great nature lover who was particularly fond of titles, he was also named Reich Master of the Hunt and of Forests. His wide, greedy smile was set between full cheeks and his midsection was so large that his personal tailor had to import stretchy fabric from the United States to make his extravagant uniforms.

He was nicknamed the Ogre because of his insatiable appetite for both food and works of art. Since his master had seized power, his sumptuous home in the Brandenburg countryside had become an incredible private museum filled with paintings and sculptures that German forces had stolen or bought at preposterously low prices from persecuted Jewish families.

"I wholeheartedly agree with the Commander. The English are exhausted and will be unable to push back our troops from their coast. We'll be able to get some wonderful footage in London!"

The man who had just spoken was sitting to the Ogre's right. As frail and skinny as his neighbour was massive, Joseph Goebbels, the very influential Minister of Public Enlightenment and Propaganda, crossed his arms across his chest in a haughty stance. His eyes—as dark as his slicked-back hair—sat above a mouth shaped like an upside-down sickle. He was the magician who oversaw the regime's gargantuan parades and ruled over the world of arts and culture with an iron fist. He lovéd nothing more than writing long speeches for himself or his master. He was a man of his time, fascinated by new communications technologies like radio, films, and most recently, television. He wore jackets with oversized shoulder pads and the last tailor who had suggested reducing their stature had been sent to a concentration camp. His many powerful adversaries within the party and the armed forces called him the Dwarf.

"I can see you, on the balcony of Buckingham Palace, mein Führer," Goebbels continued in an exalted tone. "Standing with the King of England as our troops march by. Leni Riefenstahl could film it all. The parade would end with a display of prisoners, hands tied behind their backs. That damn Freemason Winston Churchill first among them. Those Americans will think twice before declaring war on us."

Hitler's features tensed. He was in no mood to indulge his minister's cinematographic delirium. He turned towards the only career military officer at the table, Keitel, Chief of the OKW High Command.

"What is your opinion, Field Marshal?"

The soldier sat up straight and put on an arrogant expression that masked his total lack of interest. Hitler had chosen him for his remarkable submissiveness and his ability to pass on orders to the troops. Nazi leaders and even some superior officers mocked him with a delightful nickname: the Lackey.

"I've examined every detail of the invasion plans and they all seem perfect. But the British navy gives me pause. Their fleet is the best in the world. Perhaps we should delay the attack."

Albert Speer raised a finger to participate in the debate. He waited for Hitler's nod.

"I'm not certain it's feasible from a logistical standpoint. It is crucial we build up our stocks of ammunition and fuel spent during the French and Belgian campaigns. We should postpone."

Speer had climbed the ranks by winning over Hitler with his colossal Aryan architecture projects. His models of Germania, the future capital of the Reich, held pride of place in the Führer's office. He was an opportunist with no ideological principles and spent much of his time resisting the pull of alliances and cliques. In private, he compared the Select Defence Council to a snake pit—but more dangerous.

Speer's eyes met those of Marshal Keitel. The latter spoke up again, surer of himself. "I would add that our men need rest and—"

The Ogre pounded his fist into the table. "Rest? It's always the same story with the army! If we had listened to you, we never would have invaded France."

Keitel blushed with anger. "How dare you!"

Hitler tapped the side of his water glass with his glasses. "Quiet. I haven't heard the Reichsführer's opinion yet."

The man in the thin steel-rimmed glasses and black SS jacket, made by a promising young fashion designer named Hugo Boss, nodded. Of all the snakes around the table, he was the most venomous. The deadliest.

Heinrich Himmler held two positions that made him incredibly dangerous. He was the head of the SS, the country's most elitist institution, which had distanced itself from the Nazi party over the years to become a state within a state, with its own police, army—the Waffen—and parallel economy. He was also the minister responsible for domestic security and the Gestapo. He had files on all of the members sitting around the table and delighted in their respective deviancies. The terrifying technocrat nevertheless considered himself to be a warrior monk. For him, the SS was modern Germany's new order of knights, whose religion idolized pure Aryan blood.

His icy face was framed by a crewcut that left his scalp bare for a full inch above his ears. He was nicknamed the Wizard, though Göring enjoyed calling him the Chicken—the Reichsführer had worked as a chicken farmer in his youth. Himmler squinted, then removed his glasses. As usual, he spoke intentionally slowly.

"This may shock you, but . . . I like the English."

The hefty Göring turned red while Goebbels's features grew tense. Himmler continued calmly.

"The English are our Aryan cousins and I would be mortified to spill their blood while tens of millions of Jews and other sub-humans still infest Europe. Why the hurry?" His voice was gentle, almost warm. He paused for a moment and smiled weakly in a gesture of conciliation.

Rudolf Hess applauded. He shared the same vision.

"Bravo! I agree entirely with the Reichsführer. I have many English friends with top government positions. They deplore Churchill's ridiculous strategy."

Hess was exhilarated. In addition to his bushy eyebrows and pronounced forehead, which fell over his eyes like a drawbridge, his smile made him look inhuman. Behind his back, people said he looked like Quasimodo. He had been with Hitler since the beginning, but in private he was referred to as the Madman because he had spent some time in a psychiatric facility before the war.

"Nonsense," muttered Göring. "The English are at our mercy."

The Wizard acquiesced and continued. "I agree, my dear Hermann. Churchill is nothing more than a frightened, hungry bulldog without teeth or claws. His army was all but wiped out in the Dunkirk retreat. But on the other hand, our intelligence services tell us the English are calling their Atlantic fleet back to port. We cannot ignore their naval strength. I suggest we postpone the excellent invasion plans until we have opened a new front to weaken Albion's defences."

The other members of the Council looked on in surprise. Goebbels uncrossed his skinny arms, which were swimming in his oversized jacket, and leaned over the table. "You can't mean we should attack the Soviets. We've just signed a pact with Stalin," he said.

Himmler smiled. "Who said anything about Russia, Joseph? I was thinking of Spain."

Göring broke out into thundering laughter and raised his arms to the sky as if in prayer. "Spain! Are you serious? Might our dear Heinrich be hiding some other reason? We all know the Reichsführer sends expeditions all over the world to confirm his esoteric theories. Maybe he's trying to prove bull fighting is an ancient Aryan tradition? Or that flamenco was invented by the Vikings?" The fat field marshal hated the SS, which was too powerful, in his opinion. He never missed a chance to mock the Wizard's spiritual doctrines.

The Reichsführer glanced at Rudolf Hess and Alfred Rosenberg, the only two Council members who hadn't smiled at Göring's joke. His two unofficial allies, who shared his mystical vision for the Reich.

Rosenberg came to the rescue. He hated the Ogre, who orchestrated art theft on a grand scale. "I don't think the Marshal understands the subtleties of the Reichsführer's plan, which relies on General Franco declaring war on England."

Himmler nodded in thanks. "Exactly. The Caudillo needs to pay his debts. After all, we supported his uprising with a steady supply of weapons and soldiers. Without our Aryan Condor legion, he never would have won the civil war."

"What exactly are you proposing?" Hitler asked Himmler.

"Request an official meeting with General Franco," answered the head of the SS. "Preferably in Spain. Push him to declare war on England. He won't be able to refuse you."

"What vague pretext will you use to motivate the Spanish, who are exhausted from four years of civil war, to join in this operation?" Goebbels asked in a sickly-sweet tone.

Himmler answered gracefully. He made it a point of honour to hide his disdain. "Gibraltar, of course, Joseph. Gibraltar has belonged to the English for more than two hundred years, and it's an intolerable affront for the Spanish. The city is located at the far southern end of the peninsula, in Andalusia. The flamenco dancer cannot wear British shoes. If Spain declares war, Churchill will have no choice but to send part of his fleet there to protect his base, which will leave his coasts vulnerable. At least as long as he believes we've given up on our invasion plans."

Hitler closed his eyes for a second, then opened them again with a radiant smile. "Excellent, my dear Heinrich. Anything else?"

No one spoke. Göring and Goebbels could see that the Wizard had once again cast his spell on the Führer.

"Good! You're right, Heinrich. I will postpone Operation *Seelöwe*, but our bombing of London must intensify. Tomorrow I'll request a meeting with Franco. In my absence, Marshal Göring will be in charge. Council adjourned."

Himmler put his glasses back on and added in a cloying tone, "Mein Führer, I would feel better if I could accompany you to Spain. I could personally inspect their armed forces and ensure they can get the job done. I would never forgive myself if I gave you poor advice."

Hitler had already stood up. "Gladly," he replied with a flippant wave of his hand. "Goodnight everyone. I'm tired, that's a good sign."

The seven men stood up and offered their leader a deferential salute, then watched him walk away.

Himmler took back his file and politely saluted the other members of the Council. His gaze idled on the Ogre and the Dwarf. "I hope my suggestion didn't disappoint you too much. The invasion of England is only postponed, you know. What's another month or two?"

"Not at all, Heinrich," replied Göring mockingly. "I'm sure you and your SS rune experts will find the perfect date." Without waiting for an answer, he turned to Hess. "As for you, Rudolf, why don't you go and have a tarot reading to see if Franco will send his terrifying Spanish armada to fight England?"

The Ogre laughed crassly, enjoying the reaction he had provoked in the two men. Hess shrugged and left without saying goodbye, followed by Rosenberg and Himmler, who had put his cap back on.

As he watched them leave, Goebbels whispered to the Ogre, "Why is he going with our beloved Führer to Spain? He must have something in mind."

The Ogre made a disgusted face, as if he'd just swallowed a rotten sausage. "I don't know what he's up to. I am sure about one thing, though: the Führer has just made a monumental mistake by postponing the invasion of England."

Göring stood up with more spring than one would have expected from a man who weighed nearly three hundred pounds. He adjusted the baldric that circled his stomach and its immaculate white jacket, then added, "We'll never have another opportunity like this. The English will make us pay someday. And the price will be high."

4

In a corner of the deserted museum, a radio broadcast the daily news. All of a sudden, the presenter's hoarse, staticky voice soared to military music in the background. Tristan listened closely. This was important news: at the end of the month, General Franco was to meet with Adolf Hitler. The voice on the radio was ecstatic. The two heads of state were about to begin political and diplomatic negotiations that would play a crucial role in Europe's future. If you believed Madrid's propaganda, the man who had saved Spain from communism and anarchy was now going to meet with Europe's new master—as his equal!

Tristan's mouth turned up into a bitter smile. In truth, given the hundreds of thousands of deaths the country had suffered, the Caudillo needed to boost Spain's fallen prestige and give the exhausted population the impression that it was once again a great nation. Spain's national anthem rang out. Tristan turned off the radio. The Führer and the Caudillo were scheduled to meet in Hendaye, in French territory. This humiliating choice left a lump in his throat. Half of the country—from Dunkirk to the Limousin region and from Paris to the Pyrenees—had been occupied since June. Hosting the meeting in a town under Nazi control was a symbolic reminder of France's defeat.

To escape his sadness, Tristan looked out the window. The square in front of the cathedral was empty, though he knew a few women in black would appear for mass. Half of Castello's population—the half that had chosen the Republicans—lived in fear of police raids, arbitrary arrests and summary executions on street corners. Every week, elated Francoists paraded through town, puffing up their victorious chests to the cheers of the other half of the population.

Strangely, they had never come into the museum. History didn't interest them. As they passed by, they looked disdainfully on the Roman mosaic displayed on the façade, clicked their boots on the pavement and sang the party's anthem, "Cara al sol".

Their indifference suited Tristan.

In town, everyone knew him as Juan Labio. A young curator from the museum of Barcelona whom the misfortunes of war had flung into the streets of Castello. Sure, he sometimes had a light accent, but it disappeared when he was talking about painting or sculptures, with passion and flair. The likeable, devoted and competent young man had moved into the museum, which had been deserted by its guards, to protect the collections from looting. He then volunteered to catalogue them—something no one had ever thought to undertake. When the new authorities took the city in hand, they naturally confirmed Juan in his position and began paying him a salary before promptly forgetting him and the museum.

The real Juan would have been very surprised to learn about his new life, but since he was quietly rotting under a collapsed building in Barcelona, it wasn't much of a concern. All that mattered was that his identity papers happily ended up in Tristan's hands. It was true the photo was a little worn around the eyes and lips, but you could recognize his high forehead, dark hair, pronounced cheekbones, and determined chin beyond the shadow of a doubt. In short, Tristan had been Juan Labio for over a year, to the satisfaction of all around—especially Lucia.

Every Sunday before mass, Lucia came up the street that ran from the square in front of the cathedral. One day she finally noticed the arrogant-looking young man discreetly smoking a cigarette—undoubtedly contraband—at his office window. Over the course of a few weeks, she had listened to the women's gossip at the market to learn everything she needed to know about the newcomer.

People liked him, and so did Lucia. She had to find a way to meet him. When she learned that the new curator was cataloguing the collections, she remembered that her grandfather had given several religious paintings to the museum. She rifled discreetly through the family's old papers, found a few letters exchanged between her grandfather and the curator from the time and walked boldly into the museum, armed with this irrefutable proof. Tristan wasn't used to having visitors, much less women, come to call. He was confounded by the young woman in her ruffled dress as she lay the yellowing papers on his desk. He thanked her warmly, asked for a few days to study the correspondence, and invited the charming stranger to come back and see him again. Lucia didn't need much convincing. She visited again the next week, in a dress just as dizzying as the first, and asked for a guided tour.

The museum was housed in a medieval building. The first floor displayed historic artefacts from the region. Generations of amateur archaeologists had gathered carved stones, arrowheads and bones indiscriminately, without any concern for chronology or pedagogy. Lucia, who had never visited the museum before, felt like she had entered a store where you could buy flints by the dozen and get a good deal on pottery. Imagining Tristan as a salesman in a bric-a-brac store made her laugh, but she quieted down as they climbed the stairs to the painting exhibition. Now it was more like an estate sale than a knick-knack shop. Hanging crooked on the walls or covered in dust on the floor, dozens of paintings awaited better days. Tristan had nevertheless managed to showcase a few religious works on display behind a window. Lucia was delighted to see that one of the paintings donated by her family was among those selected for the protected space. She thanked the Frenchman with a smile and announced that, if he liked, she could come by once a week to help him with his work.

Now Tristan awaited Lucia's weekly visit.

In theory, the young woman was helping him catalogue the many pieces in the museum's collection. They had begun with the Roman ruins in the spring. While Lucia quickly became interested in the animals—owls and bulls—found in the mosaic fragments,

Tristan developed a passion for his new colleague's dresses. She wore them with elegance and a hint of mischief around the knee. Sometimes the lace hem would climb a few inches if the sky was clear and the sun warm, but when clouds graced the horizon, the fabric dropped all the way down to her ankles. This innocent teasing delighted Tristan. The secrets of the past and the uncertainty about the future that sometimes worried him were suddenly swept away with the wind when she was around.

At the beginning of summer, they started on the medieval collections, labelling dented helmets and rusted swords. Sometimes their hands touched over the top of a shield adorned with a coat of arms. And Lucia wasn't always the first to blush. When the heat grew stifling, the young woman wore a lightweight blouse with a neckline that revealed just a hint of cleavage. She wore her hair in a braid to keep her forehead and the back of her neck cool, but beads of sweat still formed on her chest. One afternoon, while they were filing old documents, Tristan stared at the tiny droplets as they made their way down Lucia's tanned skin. Captivated, he contemplated the delicate spring, which reflected light like a mirror. He moved closer and kissed Lucia where the two sides of her blouse joined. Her breasts heaved suddenly. Tristan was in ecstasy with the taste of salt on his lips. To avoid ruining the moment, the Frenchman slowly moved away and dived back into his reading, though the letters danced before his eyes. He wondered what sort of expression graced Lucia's face, but didn't dare look her way. He thought of Montserrat, of their nocturnal climb, of seizing the abbey. His courage never abandoned him there, but now he couldn't look Lucia in the eyes. She coughed lightly and held out her hand to take the document. He was desperate to grab her palm and place it over his heart so she could feel how it raced for her.

"Lucia—"

She placed her finger on his lips. She didn't want to jeopardize the moment either. A wave of joy washed over Tristan. His shoulders suddenly felt light, as if a yoke had been lifted. His former life, his mistakes, his aimlessness—none of it mattered anymore.

He smiled. From now on, he would be happy every day. Every day he saw Lucia.

With his elbows resting on the windowsill, he watched the street corner where she would appear. A military song made him jump. A group of men in blue shirts had just emerged from a corner of the square. With their shiny boots and riding trousers, the country's Falangists were doing their best to resemble Italy's Blackshirts, but they were more like a caricature. Visibly drunk, they shouted enthusiastic slogans to the glory of Spain the Eternal and to its leader, the Caudillo. Tristan looked anxiously up the street where he could already hear Lucia's heels on the pavement. He immediately crossed the room, jumped onto the landing and ran down the stairs. The door to the museum was open. The first whistle echoed off the surrounding façades, followed by a hail of laughter. One of the Francoists was unambiguously miming a certain act with his hips. A new wave of crass laughter crashed into the buildings. Lucia had slowed her pace, but the rowdy group had already caught up to her.

"So, *pequeña*, you're out alone in the streets?"

"Nobody told you a woman's place is in the home?"

"Are you looking for someone?"

"Look at her dress. Such a tease!"

One of the men grabbed her arm. "We know just what to do with *putas* like you."

"What about men, do you know what to do with them?" intervened Tristan.

The surprised Falangist turned around, then smiled disdainfully as he sized up his adversary. "*¡Un intelectual!* And one who's looking for a fight. We'll teach you a lesson!"

Before he could fully raise his black gloved hand, Tristan punched him in the face. A nauseating crack ripped through his chin and echoed through his skull, causing him to forget his own name. Thrown against a wall, Lucia screamed just before the pack attacked her lover. Terrified, she watched their fists rain down on him relentlessly.

"We're going to kill you, *hijo de puta*!"

"Let's end this traitor!"

Tristan backed away, drawing the group further from Lucia. His face was already dripping with blood. He gestured at her to flee. She hesitated, a crazed look in her eye, then ran. For the last time, he watched her dress dance around her ankles. For a moment, he thought he could hear her heels echoing on the pavement, but a club bashed into the back of his neck.

Everything went black.

5

The official convoy came speeding down the road that led into town, half of which was in ruins. The black armoured Mercedes gleamed like a beetle, protected by a swarm of soldiers from one of the Spanish army's motorcycle units. Two small flags bearing a black swastika on a white background flapped in the dusty wind.

One of the riders signalled to the driver to slow down. The convoy came to a stop on the square in front of the town hall, which was framed by mutilated plane trees and gutted homes. A crowd of Falangists enthusiastically saluted, their arms extended. Behind them, around thirty skinny, poorly dressed residents waved small German flags.

Sitting in the back of the car, the Reichsführer rolled down the window to study the face of Catholic Spain's saviour, plastered onto the façade of a grey stone building. Despite its gigantic size, the portrait was unable to hide the scars of bullet impacts on the walls. General Franco's tanned face was childlike beneath its suspicious eyebrows.

Himmler sighed as he took a handkerchief from his translator, an army captain who was as blond as could be. "The Caudillo doesn't strike me as particularly Aryan. I wouldn't be surprised to learn he has Jewish ancestry." The Reichsführer blew his nose, then continued in a doubtful tone, "It was nice of the Catalonian governor to send word of our trip to all the villages we travel through, but are the people real residents of the towns, or paid actors hired to create the desired atmosphere?"

The young captain shook his head. "The new Spain has freed itself from the disease of communism and Freemasonry. The people you see are proud, passionate Spaniards."

Himmler frowned. "They're smart, too. They expelled their Jews to the rest of Europe in 1492. And now the problem is ours to handle. In fact, I don't trust Franco at all—they say he's not even anti-Semitic."

"In any case, he is fervently anti-communist and anti-Freemason. You can rest assured." The Wehrmacht captain sent from the embassy in Madrid to serve as Himmler's translator had spent three years working as a liaison officer with the Spanish nationalists during the civil war. He had learned to love the country and its people—or at least those who had chosen to back the Caudillo.

The young man continued in the same tone. "I fought the reds alongside Franco's troops. And I can assure you, the man is a great friend of Germany."

Himmler sniffled loudly. "I spoke to the Führer on the phone just before we left Barcelona. He'd just spent two hours negotiating in Hendaye with your 'great friend'."

"Are they going to sign an agreement? Will Spain declare war on England?"

The car had left the square and was moving terribly slowly down a battered street. Himmler shook his head and looked straight at the captain, his eyes full of pity.

"It doesn't look like it. He told me he would rather have three teeth ripped out than negotiate with the Caudillo again. Your proud Iberian came to the table with a pile of frankly unreasonable demands. The Führer was furious. So, Churchill can sleep soundly tonight—Gibraltar will never be invaded by your Spanish 'friends'."

The convoy picked up speed as it left the town and headed down a winding road that skirted the foot of a mountain range.

"I don't understand," answered the captain. "Germany has defeated all its enemies. It's the future of Europe."

Himmler's lips formed a thin smile. "I've been visiting this country ravaged by four years of civil war for four days now. Franco has put on a show. He put his best-equipped soldiers on parade in Madrid, invited us to visit the Prado Museum, and introduced us to the aristocracy and nationalist elite at several sumptuous balls. New Spain's façade might be bright and shiny, but the reality looks more like the devastated villages we've seen. This country is in ruins, its population is at the end of its rope, and the army is exhausted. And Franco knows it. What's more, the religious fanatic wants to install some dreadful form of national Catholicism. I've never seen so many priests and bishops swarming in every corner. I can't stand them."

The car continued along the road as it began to gain altitude over the fields. The captain was like a dog with a bone. "Haven't you been impressed by the way he's cleaned up the country, though? The prisons are full to the brim. Subversives who escaped capture during the war are hunted down and reformed or executed. They say there are more than a hundred thousand in detention camps awaiting sentencing. That is, those who won't die of hunger or heatstroke first."

The car passed by a herd of skinny cows listlessly grazing on grass near the edge of the road. The Reichsführer turned to the captain. "Barbarians! How can they inflict such suffering and take such joy in it?"

The captain's eyes widened. Himmler had legalized the use of torture by the Gestapo and crowded tens of thousands of German dissenters into camps. "I'm afraid I don't understand," he replied.

Himmler watched the cows sadly. "I'm talking about bull fighting, of course! Such a vile spectacle."

Two days earlier, in Madrid, they had been invited to the Las Ventas arena to celebrate the "eternal friendship between Germany and Spain." Himmler had sat, quietly sweating and full of disgust, for two long hours, shaded from the sun but not from the stifling heat. When the mayor took him to visit the inside of the arena and meet the matadors, he almost fainted in front of the bulls' still warm corpses. Like his Führer, the head of the SS loved animals and couldn't bear the thought of them being harmed.

The Mercedes wound its way down a series of hairpin turns that seemed as if they would never end. The sun was beginning to set over the mountaintops. The heavy clouds took on an orange hue.

Himmler tapped on the back window with his signet ring, engraved with the SS runes. "The Iberian people are truly cruel. There's too much Moorish blood in their veins."

"Do you really think so?" asked the captain, surprised.

The head of the SS turned to his subordinate, clearly annoyed. "I get the impression you don't share my opinion. Maybe you should leave this country. I could find you a position in line with your unique views. We're always short on officers at Dachau."

The captain felt the hairs rise on the back of his neck. His heart suddenly started to pound. "You're right. The bull fighting was disgusting," he offered.

Himmler stared at him for a few seconds, then burst into something that resembled laughter—in reality, a succession of high-pitched spasms that irritated the ears.

"I'm only joking, my young Wilfred. Don't worry, I tolerate a certain degree of independent thinking in my subordinates. You can like bull fighting if you so choose, as long as I have your undying loyalty."

The convoy slowed after rounding a turn that overlooked a ravine. A crenellated peak appeared before their tired eyes. A cluster of rectangular buildings was set back into the mountain's sheer sides, which reached skyward like long fingers.

"Finally," whispered Himmler. "Montserrat Monastery."

"The ambassador told me you had extended your stay by a day to come here in search of . . . the Holy Grail. Is that true?"

Himmler's face twisted into a strange expression. His eyes became two tiny slits behind his steel-rimmed glasses. "The ambassador should learn to hold his tongue, but what's done is done. Have you ever read Wolfram von Eschenbach's *Parzival* or seen Wagner's opera, which it inspired?"

The captain preferred not to answer that he hadn't had the privilege of attending the opera during the civil war.

"Yes, but it's been quite a while."

The convoy approached rapidly. Two lorries with machine guns had been stationed on either side of the road as it widened near the monastery's entrance. The stone reflected the setting sun's gentle, almost pink light.

Himmler put on his formal black gloves.

"The Holy Grail was kept in a castle set into the sides of a mountain. The legendary site was called Montsalvaje and, according to Eschenbach, it was located in the Pyrenees. It could be Montserrat, which shares similar etymology."

The captain listened attentively.

"The Grail has always been my destiny!" exclaimed the Reichsführer as his face brightened. He entered a kind of trance and his hands shook as if he were about to grasp the sacred chalice.

"But isn't the Grail just a legend?"

"You're only seeing the bark of the matter, not the sap that lives beneath it. The real Grail is something else entirely. It's the black sun of the Aryan people."

The captain remained impassive, though he was shocked by the strange beliefs of the man second only to the Führer. A black sun? The head of the SS had lost his mind. He determined, nonetheless, that it was best to keep quiet.

The convoy drove up a road lined with pine and linden trees, which came to an end at a large paved area filled with a compact group of uniformed troops. A detachment from the Spanish Legion, a stout general surrounded by half a dozen officers and clergymen in black cassocks, all beneath two huge flags—one Spanish and one German—hanging from the walls. Off to the side, his back against a granite calvary, stood a tall, thin man in a suit as pale as his complexion. He wore his Panama hat cocked slightly to one side.

Himmler sat up straight and his frenzied expression disappeared. "I specifically asked for there *not* to be a welcoming committee. Thank goodness my dear friend Oberführer Weistort is here. He's a world traveller. He's visited many exotic countries and was part of the Schäfer expedition in Tibet, the one they reported on in the *Völkischer Beobachter*."

He pointed at the civilian who had just stubbed out his cigarette and was now looking their way. The scarred man nodded discreetly at them.

"Have you heard of him?" asked Himmler.

"Yes, of course," answered the captain in a neutral tone designed to hide his surprise. The embassy's intelligence services had not told him the SS officer would be here. He had heard about Weistort from his younger brother, who had joined the SS three years earlier. The Oberführer was one of Himmler's close friends and he determined the curriculum taught in the black order's officer training schools. Rumour held that he also organized strange ceremonies and that his hatred of Christianity had driven him to slap the Bishop of Cologne when he objected to the persecution of the Jews. His influence on Himmler was so powerful that he had made many enemies within the high command.

"Why isn't he wearing the SS uniform?" asked the captain.

"Uniforms aren't a good fit for men like him," said Himmler as he adjusted his black cap on his sweaty forehead.

The convoy stopped short in front of the welcoming committee, which snapped to attention in unison. A Legion warrant officer hurried over to open the door of the Mercedes. Himmler got out of the car, followed by the captain, and carelessly returned the Spaniards' fascist salutes. He listened politely to the general's expressions of gratitude, without understanding a single word, then turned towards the clergymen who bowed respectfully. One of the monks mumbled a few words, which the captain translated.

"Father Andreu is delighted to welcome you," said the German. "Much to his regret, the abbot is in Girona at the moment. He heard you were coming too late to return."

Himmler waved his hand wearily and lowered his head to whisper in the captain's ear. "Tell them I don't want to be bothered in the monastery."

"No need."

The two men turned around to find the scarred man standing there, his arm raised towards Himmler.

"Heil Hitler. I convinced General Ariagas to let us visit the site alone. I told him that you wanted to pray to the Black Virgin before returning to Germany."

Himmler feigned disapprobation. "Me . . . pray to the Virgin . . . You have such a sense of humour, Karl."

Oberführer Weistort smiled at his friend.

"I'm so happy to see you," continued Himmler. "Don't keep me waiting! Did you find the second swastika mentioned in the *Thule Borealis Kulten*?"

The Oberführer kept smiling. "The book says that it can be found in a place called Montseg, which could be an old version of Montserrat."

"Have you explored the buildings?"

"No, Reichsführer, I only arrived an hour ago. My plane had technical difficulties during the stopover in Toulouse, so I continued the rest of the way by car, driving through the night. I travelled across half of India and part of Tibet and never had any transportation problems, but here . . . But to answer your question, a monk is waiting for us in his cell. We just need your translator."

Weistort looked over Himmler's shoulder at the captain, who was in the middle of a discussion with the general. "Is that him?"

"Yes, the first one cancelled on me the first day. Food poisoning or something like that. This one is smarter, but a little too Hispanophile for my taste."

"He belongs to the Wehrmacht . . ."

"I know, but there aren't many SS officers who speak Spanish."

Himmler gestured to the captain, who climbed the stairs to join him. The young man executed a perfect salute for Weistort, who stared at him intently.

"We're going to need your talents, Captain."

"Yes, Sir!" replied the young officer, ill at ease with the new man's unrelenting gaze.

When the three Germans entered the main building, the sweet scent of orange blossom filled the cool, dark hall. They continued down a long corridor with blank white walls. Himmler walked quickly alongside Weistort while the captain followed at a respectful distance.

Himmler spoke in a low voice. "It's hard to believe the success of my trip to Spain is in the hands of a monk."

They passed through a sumptuous library and walked past the entrance to a chapel before reaching the doors to a group of cells. One of them was wide open. The neighbouring room let in a ray of light. A fleeting shadow appeared, then disappeared just as suddenly.

Himmler stayed in the doorway, while the other two Germans entered. Inside, a tonsured man with hollow cheeks and countless fine, dark wrinkles sat upright in a chair. He muttered prayers as he fingered a rosary with wooden beads the size of olives. He wore a dirty burlap robe that smelled of mould.

Weistort couldn't help but glance disdainfully at the crucifix hanging on the wall behind the monk and its pale, gaunt Christ. The blood ran generously from his feet and forehead.

The monk bowed his head when they arrived, though not in deference. His gaze seemed absent.

Weistort placed his hand on the captain's shoulder. "Ask him if he knows anything about a little painting with a castle and a star overhead."

The captain raised an eyebrow in surprise. "I thought the Reichsführer was interested in the Grail."

"Don't ask questions. Just translate!" scolded the Oberführer.

The captain did as he was told, but the monk shook his head. "He says the Republicans looted the monastery almost two years ago. But he remembers the painting, which was stored in the scriptorium."

Weistort remained impassive, but his reply was swift. "Does he remember any details? A name?"

The monk's vacant eyes rested on the scarred man as he spoke into the translator's ear. The captain nodded. "He says it was a group of wild reds, real devils. They crucified one of the monks. There was the leader, Jaime, and another, a Frenchman. He's the one who took the painting. The monk doesn't know any more."

Weistort punched the wall. His face was hard, as if his features had been carved from granite. Himmler, who had heard everything, didn't bother to disguise his disappointment.

"Two years ago . . . God. They must have been killed or fled to France by now. I fear this trip has been fruitless. And to think I convinced the Führer to meet with that idiot Franco so that I could come here!"

Slowly, they left the cell.

"I have nothing more to do in this country," groaned Himmler. "As for you, Weistort, get back on the trail. Immediately. We need that painting at all costs."

Weistort clicked his heels. "Yes, Sir!"

Suddenly, a priest in a cassock emerged from the neighbouring cell. A huge man with a large forehead.

"Reichsführer, it's an honour to meet you," he exclaimed in perfect German. He held his hand out to Himmler, who backed away instinctively. He never touched people. It was a question of hygiene.

Weistort intervened. "Who are you?"

The man flashed a broad smile. "My name is Father Matteus. I'm the head chaplain for the garrison in Barcelona. I come here often for spiritual retreats."

"You speak our language well," remarked Weistort.

The man ran a hand the size of a frying pan across his poorly shaven chin. "I spent six months in Munich during the civil war. I was part of a delegation from the Spanish church. I'm a great admirer of your Führer, although I've been told he doesn't attend mass as regularly as our Caudillo."

He glanced towards the cell they had just exited. "I'm afraid I overheard your conversation. Please forgive me . . ." He hesitated for a few seconds, then continued. "As part of my job, I'm often called to national re-education camps to guide lost souls and, sometimes, perform the last rites before executions."

Himmler studied the man, clearly interested in his story.

"I get to know some of them well," continued the priest. "And sometimes we talk in their cells. I try to save those who deserve a second chance. Pope Pius XII is the first to agree that—"

The Oberführer raised his hand to cut him off. "Our time is precious, Father. Get to the point."

The giant ran his hand across his chin again. "Yes, of course. Please forgive me. A few weeks ago, I met a man named Tristan. A rather unusual name in this part of the world. I don't remember his last name anymore, but I remember him very clearly. A Frenchman. He was extremely knowledgeable and knew the Bible like the back of his hand. Which is rather rare among the reds. He belonged to the cursed International Brigades, which have done so much harm. Maybe . . ."

Weistort's face lit up.

"At last, a clue! Do you know which prison he's in?"

"No, he was with a group waiting to be sent to a detention centre. There were too many prisoners after our victory. As I understand it, the new administration didn't have enough prisons. Hence the mass executions . . ."

The priest seemed truly saddened as he pronounced the last word.

"Nothing else?"

"No, I hope I have helped. I have a small request, if I may."

Weistort's face displayed suspicion, but he leaned in attentively.

The priest continued in an almost pleading voice, "In Munich, I had but one vice. Tannenberg beer. A delicacy. I know your ambassador has it delivered for his receptions. Could I possibly get a case or two?"

Himmler smiled. "It would be my pleasure, priest. I'll get you ten, even. I'll take care of it personally."

The three men headed down the corridor, leaving the delighted giant to himself.

Himmler seemed more relaxed. "If I were still Catholic, I would say that brave man is a sign from God. All you have to do now is find this Tristan, presuming the Francoists haven't shot him yet. Would you like to keep my translator?"

Weistort unconsciously touched his thin scar as he glanced at the captain, who was following them like a well-behaved dog. "Give me a few minutes and have a look at the altarpiece in the chapel. I need to speak to him for a moment."

Himmler shrugged and walked into the chapel as Weistort motioned to the captain. "Follow me. I'd like to show you something."

The two men entered the abbey's chapter house, which featured a large balcony.

Weistort crossed the room quickly and stepped out into the fresh air. Across from him towered the sides of Montserrat mountain, below was a steep precipice. He climbed onto the balcony's railing, which was just wide enough for his shoes, and contemplated the view with a victorious attitude.

"Join me, Captain."

The translator obeyed despite himself. He'd been terrified of heights since childhood but didn't want to reveal this weakness to a superior. He climbed up next to the Oberführer. He didn't dare look down. His head was spinning, but he let nothing show.

Weistort contemplated the mountain and opened his arms wide as if to embrace it. "I love the mountains. So full of truth. It's the best place for an SS man, don't you think? Above the rest of humanity?"

"Yes, Oberführer, but I'm not an SS officer."

The young man felt his legs going weak. It took all his strength to continue standing there. Beneath him was a three-hundred-yard drop.

Weistort spoke in a gentle tone this time. "The Reichsführer offered me your services, but I need to know if I can trust you. Understand?"

"Of course. I would be delighted to work by your side."

Weistort placed his hand on the captain's shoulder.

"Good. Relax and enjoy the view. Admire the glorious mountains around you. Nature is a sacred temple, which we must preserve."

"Yes."

"Exquisite! The mountains are the most perfect incarnation of beauty and harmony. Like our National Socialist design. The Führer himself has set up his headquarters at the Berghof. A magnificent and inspiring location. Legend tells us Emperor Frederick Barbarossa is buried in the mountain there, that he will someday wake."

The Oberführer looked down. "I always like to say that the last thing a person sees before dying should be something beautiful."

With a sudden movement, he pushed the captain into the abyss. For a fraction of a second the poor man flapped his arms like a clumsy bird. Then he fell into the steep ravine with a long scream. His body bounced on the rocks several times, like a rag doll.

Weistort waited for the last bounce, then climbed down off the railing, fully satisfied. It took him just a few minutes to join Himmler, who was waiting at the entrance to the chapel.

"Where is the captain?"

"Unfortunately, he fell. Such a shame, all that good German blood lost."

"What happened?"

The Oberführer's features hardened. "I had nothing against him, but we couldn't leave behind any witnesses. Our quest is too important."

"Yes, but you'll need a translator to find the Frenchman."

Weistort shook his head. *"No es un problema. Me gusta hablar en español aunque no es una lengua aria."*

Himmler smiled. "I had forgotten your talent for languages, my dear Karl. As for me, I would rather all of humanity spoke a single language: German."

6

Spring was in full bloom in Barcelona. Though it was still early in the year, the sun had grown relentless over the city. In the jumbled little streets that crisscrossed Las Ramblas, shade was a rare commodity. As rare as people. With the buildings still in ruins, ripped open by bombs, their façades covered in bullet holes, and rubble piled up to the windows, the city counted many more rats than humans. But the remaining survivors amid the debris, desperate though they may have been, had one ultimate consolation. Not God, who had abandoned them, but a shadow. The malevolent shadow cast by Montjuic Prison, which towered over Barcelona.

A mother whose child was hungry had only to lay eyes upon the angular fortress to feel thankful for the chance to die of hunger rather than be a prisoner within those walls of death.

Up there, parched by the blazing sun, whipped by the dry inland wind, thousands of Republican prisoners were packed into the building to rot.

Up there, the Irishman, Jaime, and Tristan languished in an underground dungeon.

Every morning, Judge Tieros, dressed in his black robes despite the heat, waited for the bus at the foot of Montjuic hill. Since the city had fallen to the Francoists, he was once again employed. He was responsible for handling difficult cases: flushing out communist and anarchist hardliners from among the multitude of soldiers held prisoner. For over a year, he had had all the prisoners come to his office one by one, to interrogate them in depth. And at the end of each week, he enjoyed the sight of several freshly filled graves below his window—proof he was good at his job.

However, after several rounds of weekly executions, communists had become a rarity, and the anarchists were history. So, he was given a new mission.

As he stepped off the bus and headed towards the bridge that crossed the prison's moat, Judge Tieros rubbed his hands together. His new file was intriguing. This time, it wasn't about burying political enemies, but uncovering a gang of looters. A few months before Barcelona fell, a Republican commando squad had invaded Montserrat Monastery and stolen its treasures. But the impious thieves hadn't stopped there. Before they fled, they had nailed a priest to a cross. The unfortunate man didn't survive his ordeal. The judge's forehead furrowed in anger. How dare they plunder the church's riches! And harm a man of God! They had chosen well by giving him this case. He would be merciless.

When he arrived in his office, his clerk handed him the file. The judge didn't open it. As usual, he preferred to interrogate his assistant.

"How did they identify the men?"

The clerk was a meticulous civil servant. He knew every open file down to the smallest details.

"The armed group that attacked the monastery was made up of fourteen men. Twelve Spaniards and two foreign volunteers. To find them, we compared testimony from the abbey's Father Superior and the Republican archives, which contained a list of members of the commando unit. Most of them died in the battles that followed. We are certain nine of them are deceased. Two are missing, unless they've escaped to the other side of the Pyrenees."

Judge Tieros's face curled into a disgusted expression. More than half a million Republicans had taken refuge in France.

Cowards! Traitors! The clerk waited respectfully for the judge's silent moment of indignation to pass, then continued.

"The three survivors are held here. Jaime Etcheverria, a Basque who was captured, weapons in hand, in Girona. Colman Flanders, an Irishman they caught trying to sell a silver chalice to escape to France."

"Foreigner, thief, and black-market salesman," muttered Tieros in a knowing tone.

"And a Frenchman."

"Where did you find him?"

"In a municipal museum in Castello d'Empuries."

"Was he on a cultural tour?" joked the judge.

"No, he had everyone believing he was the curator. During and after the war, no one paid attention to him. He spoke Spanish perfectly and had in-depth knowledge of the collections. And since the mayor, city council, and civil servants had all fled, except for him, he was even decorated as an example!"

"Is this a joke?" exclaimed Tieros.

"Never, Judge. He was captured in a fight with party members. Before that, he had everyone fooled with his fake identity. A real chameleon."

"You can count on me to eradicate his taste for metamorphosis. But one last question: what happened to the treasure?"

The clerk raised his arms over his bald head. "No one knows. When interrogated, the looters claimed they handed it over to the Republican authorities. Then—"

"Then, the greedy dogs took what they wanted; you can be sure of that! A gold reliquary for one, a silver chandelier for another. I'm sure it all ended up in a clandestine foundry. We'll never find any of it, unless . . . The Irishman, you told me he had tried to sell a silver chalice?"

"That's exactly right, Judge."

"Yet another quick-handed bandit. Have him interrogated by the Guardia Civil. And have him brought to me tomorrow morning. If he's still alive, that is."

"And the other two?"

The judge looked out the window at what used to be gardens. Four new graves had just been filled. His colleagues had been busy and were even pulling ahead. Losing was out of the question.

"We must make an example of the Basque for murdering a priest, sadism and sacrilege. The new prisoners arrive at eleven this morning, right? And they still come in by way of the upper terrace?"

"Yes, Judge. Two hundred prisoners from all over Spain, including some particularly stubborn cases."

"We'll quash their spirits! Have the guards line the wretches up on the terrace. I'll give them a show they won't soon forget."

The clerk shuddered despite himself. "Yes, Judge."

Tieros rubbed his hands together. The morning was off to a good start. "And now, send me the Frenchman."

When Tristan entered the office, the judge stared intently at a spot on his face, just above his eyebrows. Tieros had noticed that his intense gaze unsettled the prisoners, who thought the judge was looking at something behind them. They would turn around, wondering, worrying, which caused them to lose ground to the rapid-fire questions. They were fighting two adversaries: the judge and their imaginations, and they always lost.

As for Tristan, he was smiling. He had just caught a glimpse of his reflection in a mirror. Despite his hermit's beard and unkempt hair, he still looked like himself. A lot of prisoners were so gaunt from lack of food and so beaten down by the sordid conditions, that the light had gone out of their eyes. Not Tristan. The judge noticed him looking in the mirror.

"So Juan, do you fancy yourself a scarecrow or a ghost?"

"A ghost," answered Tristan. "They can walk through walls and doors. That would come in handy in prison."

The judge ignored the provocation. No one escaped Montjuic. Neither the living, nor the dead.

"Ghosts have another gift as well. They have perfectly clear memories of their past. But not you. You were arrested under the name Juan Labio—a rather Spanish name, for a Frenchman."

Tristan remained impassive and let the judge continue.

"But we've found another identity. Tristan Destrée. Unless that's also an alias. We also found a report on you in the former Republican army's archives," explained Tieros with a smirk that revealed one incisor. He instinctively made this carnivorous expression whenever he knew he had the upper hand. "I see that you studied art history in Paris, that you worked for the Bloch family. International financiers who developed a passion for paintings."

"They wanted to build an art collection. I advised them on acquisitions."

"Travels to London, Milan. You were in Madrid just before the outbreak of the civil war. What were you doing there?"

"I was evaluating a private collection from which my employer hoped to acquire a few pieces."

"Yes, the Marquess de Valdemossa's collection. An aristocrat with Republican convictions. He didn't fare well. He's dead and his paintings are now government property."

"He had some magnificent works by Velázquez," noted the Frenchman plainly.

"Then you were in Barcelona in the autumn of 1939. A city in the grip of chaos and anarchy is a strange place for an art lover . . ."

"The Marquess de Valdemossa had an estate on the outskirts of the city that housed part of his collection. He had asked me to have it moved to France."

The judge glanced ironically at Tristan. "A kind of life insurance of sorts. You could use one as well. Where were you on the night of January 12, 1939?"

Tristan turned towards the window. An unusual smell was coming in from outside. Or rather, two. First, the almost sweet scent of freshly tilled earth, followed by another, headier fragrance, which he couldn't identify. He closed his eyes to focus his sense of smell.

"Are you trying to remember? Let me jog your memory for you. That night, you and thirteen other looters broke into and ransacked Montserrat Monastery. Oh, I almost forgot, you also killed a man."

From experience, Tieros knew that when men were accused

of murder, they immediately started protesting, but the Frenchman didn't react. It was as if he didn't care about what happened next.

"To be exact, you crucified him, and he didn't survive. So, desecration of a sacred place, theft of sacred objects, the murder of a priest . . ."

The judge left off intentionally. The verdict was obvious, but he wanted to leave room for doubt. Men often become quite forthcoming when they think they're about to die.

"It smells like mignonette flowers," Tristan stated slowly. "The fragrance coming through the window."

Tieros pursed his lips in anger. He enjoyed the cruel cat-and-mouse game he played during interrogations and he hated being denied it. He loved striking fear into the heart of prisoners, loved watching terror appear on their faces, skewing their features. He loved listening to them admit their treason and humiliation. And now this Frenchman was trying to deprive him of his enjoyment. What a hapless idiot!

"Clerk, what time is it?"

"Nearly eleven, Sir."

"Did you pass on my instructions?"

"Yes, Judge. The Basque is already down there."

Tieros stood up. He checked that the Frenchman was properly handcuffed. He couldn't have him jumping out the window. "Follow me," he said to the prisoner.

Tristan did as he was told. Out in the garden, Jaime limped between two civil guards. His legs were one big open wound.

"The Guardia Civil has its own interrogation methods. Pouring salt into wounds is one of them. They say the pain is unbearable. I believe that, because your friend, El Jefe, has told us everything. He says you're the one who nailed the priest to the cross."

Tristan didn't answer.

"That said, I don't believe it. The abbot of Montserrat was very clear in his testimony: Jaime Etcheverria is the one who committed the unforgiveable crime. And that's why he must pay."

Tieros nodded twice. One of El Jefe's guards leaned down and removed a tarpaulin Tristan hadn't noticed. The dark earth of a grave appeared.

"Freshly dug," clarified the judge.

Just above where they were standing, Tristan could hear footfalls.

"Those are the newly arrived prisoners. They'll enjoy the show. Usually, we arrange a firing squad for condemned prisoners in town, and then we bury them here. But I've arranged a special treatment for your friend Jaime."

Under the window, the guards checked the prisoner's bonds. A garrotte around his neck, rope with a sliding knot tight around his wrists, and chains for his ankles.

"Throw him in."

Jaime's screaming body rolled into the grave face down.

"Turn him over," ordered Tieros. "I want him to watch as he dies." Then he turned to Tristan. "You wondered about the smell coming from the garden."

The first shovelful of dirt fell into the grave.

"The smell of an execution is never the same. A body riddled with bullets produces a repulsive, bitter smell that doesn't linger. Hanged men smell like the excrement that sullies them in the end."

Jaime's legs were already covered in black dirt. He had stopped screaming. His wide eyes stared at the blue sky as if it were an insufferable enigma.

"Men who are buried alive, on the other hand, produce a sour scent—the scent of fear. Can you smell it?"

Only his face remained free of the dark dirt. Around him, the two guards wielding shovels awaited the judge's order to end it. Tieros nodded. They dumped in a pile of dirt.

"Have you ever wondered what you will smell like when we kill you?" asked the judge.

Another, larger pile followed.

"You, Tristan Destrée—or whatever your real name is—will die in a puddle of blood. Your own blood."

7

His throat burned as his blood rushed through his arteries like a devastating torrent. He never would have thought his body could make him suffer like this. He slowed his pace and slumped against a moss-covered boulder.

He tried to catch his breath. The freezing air struggled to make its way into his lungs. He looked towards the grassy hill which began at the edge of the woods and caught a glimpse of the lights from Heisenberg below. The city was only about a mile and a half away. He could find refuge there. *Thank you, dear Lord.*

Renewed hope washed over him as he massaged his aching thighs. He had to keep going, he couldn't collapse. Father Breno had never run like this in his entire life. Except once, in Cologne over thirty years ago, to catch a rascal who had stolen a silver crucifix from the seminary chapel. Since he'd become a priest, his legs hadn't been used for more than the bare minimum. Saying mass, celebrating weddings and funerals, seeing parishioners on their deathbeds—none of these activities kept the body in shape.

His head was spinning, and his eyes stung. The priest glanced behind him, but the huge, dark trees danced before him. If he wasn't being chased, he would have stopped to appreciate the magnificent landscape before him. The forest was beautiful. Beautiful and cruel. It seemed to be on the side of his pursuers. He could feel it in his bones. In these dark woods, God was not welcome, much less his servant. Maybe he wasn't welcome anywhere in Germany anymore. Or even in Europe.

He wiped away the tears that coursed down his rough cheeks.
When the three Gestapo agents had come to take him from his
presbytery three days ago, he hadn't been surprised. The police
officers had been polite. Just a little interview at the central station.
But he wasn't fooled. He knew why they were bringing him in.
The week before, he'd stopped at a train crossing while riding his
bike home from delivering the last rites to a farmer. A freight train
was stalled there, its engine out of order. Another train was parked
further up the tracks. SS soldiers moved between the two convoys.

He had hidden in a thicket, afraid they'd assume he was a spy.
Then he'd heard metal clicking and screams, and the doors of the
train carriages had opened to release their human cargo. Men,
women, and children. The SS soldiers shouted at them, ordering
them to move to the other train. This was the first time the priest
had encountered true evil in his life. Of course, like many Germans,
he knew that the country was sending its Jews to "work camps",
but this, this was a reality beyond all comprehension.

He witnessed murders as well. An elderly couple fell out of the
carriage and struggled to stand. An officer walked over and shot
them both in the head. From his thicket, Father Breno hadn't been
able to take his eyes off the killer. He was hypnotized by his plump,
jovial face. Two soldiers had thrown the corpses to the side of the
tracks, as if they were rubbish.

Terrified, the priest had remained hidden for over an hour, until
the second hellish convoy made its way towards the setting sun.
Alone in the freezing dusk, he had come to understand two things:
Satan was real, and he was German.

Back in his church, he had knelt at the altar to pray for those
poor people. But it hadn't been enough. Remorse ate away at him.
He was just like the people who had done nothing as they watched
Christ climb to Golgotha carrying the cross. He couldn't let it go.

Three days later, from his pulpit, he had delivered an angry
sermon. The most eloquent one he had ever given, in which he
explained what he had seen. The parishioners' faces froze. After
mass, almost all of them disappeared, out of fear. Then their
cowardice turned into denunciation.

The officers hadn't taken him to the station, but to a forest lodge, lost in the middle of the woods and surrounded by huge grounds bordered by high stone walls. They had insulted him and called him a traitor to the Führer, but strangely, they hadn't beaten him. They had fed him and given him new clothes. Two other prisoners had been housed in small neighbouring cells, but they had disappeared one after the other.

Earlier this evening, one of the guards in a hunting outfit had come to his cell. "Father, they're going to transfer you to Dachau tomorrow morning. That's where we hold all priests and pastors who are disloyal to the Fatherland. It's the gateway to hell. I'm going to leave the door open."

"Why are you doing this?"

"I'm a Nazi, but I'm also a good Catholic. I can't let a man of God die. Leave right away. I'll tell them you knocked me out."

He had explained the way through the forest to Heisenberg. Just as he was leaving, Father Breno had asked where he was.

The hunter had replied enigmatically, "In the Ogre's den, Father. He has no pity for his prey. Run. Run like the Devil is on your heels."

It had been an hour since his escape. He forced himself to breathe more slowly, to steady himself and tamp down the fear. But it was still there.

A hoarse shout came from behind the trees. Then another, and a third.

He jumped up.

It wasn't shouting, but barking. From dogs trained to hunt and to rip the prey they hunted to shreds. He had seen them tearing apart live rabbits that the guards enjoyed tossing into their cages. And yet, their ferocity hardly matched that of their masters. They were the real sadistic beasts. The guard had tricked him with false hope.

He was but a game animal to be tracked and shot down. Nothing more.

The sound of a horn echoed through the forest. Flashes of light appeared here and there in the woods.

The pack was growing impatient.

Father Breno held the crucifix they had left around his neck as tightly as he could and began mumbling in a whisper.

He heard shouting. He recognized whinnying and the sharp clicks of hooves on the wet ground.

The pack was pleased.

He knew he would never reach Heisenberg in time. Christ had chosen this bright night to bring him home.

He raised his red eyes to the moonlit sky.

His fear vanished.

He would face his executioners as Christ had done two thousand years before. It was all so clear now.

His death was a gift. A gift from his creator, to pay for years of blind ignorance, submission and selfishness.

He picked up a fallen branch and broke it in half over his knee. Then he took off his crucifix and tied the two pieces together. The cross was a little lopsided, and the ends of the horizontal branch were twisted, but it was the most beautiful cross he had ever seen.

He slipped it into a crevice in the boulder and knelt before the makeshift altar.

"Our Father, who art in heaven, hallowed be thy name. Thy kingdom come—"

Before he could finish, the barking turned to growling. Nearby growling.

He turned around slowly. Five dogs had him in their sights. They were all crouched down, their eyes narrow and their lips curled up to reveal their teeth shining like blades in the moonlight.

The pack had come for its prize.

The monsters were the pictures of obedience. They would never attack until their master gave the signal.

The Ogre.

All of a sudden, Father Breno understood. The dogs, the hunting lodge, the men dressed like hunters. He was on the estate of the Reich Master of the Hunt and of German Forests.

Marshal Hermann Göring.

Behind the dogs, rays of light broke through the darkness. He could hear the hunters' excited exclamations distinctly.

Father Breno stood up and crossed his arms across his chest in a sign of resolution. He would grant them his pardon but would show no fear.

Two silhouettes appeared on horseback in a break between the trees.

One of them was disproportionate to his mount, which looked tiny beneath him. His body hung over the sides of the saddle. He was holding a rifle aimed right at Breno.

The Ogre on horseback. Father Breno smiled as a ridiculous image came to mind: Don Quixote's portly companion Sancho Panza perched on his donkey.

Next to the marshal, the other, thinner rider seemed better suited to his horse, whose coat was a ghostly white hue. He held a long crossbow in his right hand. The moment had come.

Father Breno raised his arms to bless his executioners. "Forgive them, for they know not what—"

A shot rang out and he was unable to finish his sentence. The impact threw him backwards onto the boulder. He crumpled slowly to the ground, his back sliding along the rock. Intense pain ripped through the right side of his abdomen. He placed his hand over the expanding red stain on his shirt.

Was the Master of the Hunt a bad hunter, or did he just want to prolong the experience?

"*Angriff!*" The marshal's shout echoed through the night. The pack hurled itself at the priest and the pounding of the horses' hooves rang out through the clearing.

Every inch of Father Breno shuddered and he closed his eyes. *Dear God, please let it be quick. I . . . I am not strong enough to be a martyr.*

His prayer was granted as an arrow from the crossbow drove into his chest. Just below his heart. He felt the first two dogs begin to bite their prey.

"*Leg dich schlafen!*" The Ogre's voice was above him. Their snouts covered in blood, the dogs miraculously let go of his legs and sat down.

Breno could see that the hefty Göring was angry with the rider, who was putting the crossbow back into its case on the saddle.

"Frau von Essling, the animal was theirs for the taking. You've frustrated my dogs and deprived me of an exceptional show."

The last face Father Breno saw was that of a beautiful blonde woman with almond-shaped eyes. She appeared like an Amazon on her horse as she watched his agony, her light-coloured eyes impassive.

That night, Carinhall—the Reichsmarschall's sumptuous hunting lodge located an hour from Berlin—was full of people. The Master of the Hunt was hosting his lavish end-of-season party, as he did every year. The impressive reception hall, its walls decorated with the heads of deer, bears, and boars, was bursting at the seams. Over two hundred lucky guests—hunters and their wives—were happily chatting away to the rhythm of a waltz played by the orchestra in traditional *Lederhosen* and hats with feathers tucked into the brim. The atmosphere was euphoric. Most of the men there had participated in the Reich's victorious military campaigns.

Unlike the regime's official parties, this event wasn't open to all high-ranking party members. Instead it was a strange blend of socio-economic backgrounds: the middle classes, aristocrats, influential Reich administrators, and Wehrmacht officers as well as local farmers who were enthusiastic hunters, and often the best shots in the country. For the Third Reich, hunting was a cherished institution with codes, rules, and clubs throughout the country. The powerful network was more democratic than fox hunting in England, but was still very elitist in terms of talent with a rifle. To get a job or obtain a favour, a solid hunting record opened doors just as readily as years of party membership. In Germany, hunting had held discreet sway even before Hitler came onto the scene. Though the Führer himself was disgusted by hunting and meat, the Master of the Hunt and of the Forests indulged out of passion. The Ogre ruled over this predatory fraternity with a remarkable appetite and an iron fist as sturdy as his Mausers. He even came up with a motto, which he had written in gold letters in his Berlin office: *Hunting is the art of shedding blood in good company.*

Suddenly, "The Blue Danube" stopped playing. The conductor had received news that the master of the estate was about to arrive. His baton jumped to and fro as the first measures of the "Eroica Symphony" pierced the smoky air and the evening's host appeared at the top of the monumental marble staircase.

The Ogre, who was unrivalled in terms of his eccentric outfits, was wearing a grey silk jacket and vest with a white scarf tied around his waist and leather trousers that matched his high boots.

Thunderous applause erupted in the room as the satrap made his way to the microphone on stage. Beethoven was now interrupted, like Strauss before him. Göring's booming voice filled the hall.

"Ladies and gentlemen, I am delighted to welcome you all to Carinhall, a temple devoted to hunting and all of its associated pleasures. This year, dinner will be entirely composed of choice pieces of game I shot myself. And given the turnout tonight, I must say you gave me quite a lot of work. Don't tell the Führer, though. He'll think I've deserted my post at the Luftwaffe and that the English won't be showered with enough bombs."

Laughter rang out here and there as the Ogre looked on rapaciously. He was the only Nazi leader who cracked jokes, whatever the circumstances. "If there happen to be any lost vegetarians in the room, you'd be better off at Reichsführer Himmler's house. He's holding an Aryan cucumber and pumpkin party next week."

The audience laughed riotously. Even the handful of SS officers and hunters present couldn't help but chuckle.

"My very dear friends, I officially declare the hunting season closed. Let the festivities begin!"

Göring made his way through the crowd, which was heading to the dining room, giving warm handshakes with his plump fingers bulging around big shiny rings. In addition to hunting, opium, fashion, and paintings, the marshal had a real passion for jewellery—like a 19th-century courtesan.

He located the young blonde woman with glowing skin who reminded him of Diana the Huntress, though she'd deprived him of enjoying his human prey. It wasn't hard—Erika von Essling was the only woman at the event wearing trousers and boots. It was bold, but unlike the other men at the head of the regime, he had always appreciated audacity and eccentricity. Göring had known her for quite some time as he'd been friends with her late father, Count von Essling. The Rhineland aristocrat had regretted his lack of sons and played an active role in his only daughter's education. He had taught her things women simply didn't learn in the upper classes: hunting, fencing, and shooting. In the new Germany, where women were celebrated for their beauty and their ability to produce Aryan children, Erika stood out. But she could— her family owned steel mills and arms factories that were at full capacity. Shells, armour plating, and bombs had become the family's specialities. Power had changed hands over the centuries, but they had remained. With every new chapter in history, they had managed to stay central to the story. Like many manufacturers, Count von Essling had financed Hitler's rise to power when it became clear he was their only hope of beating back communism. Unfortunately, the Count had died in a hunting accident the day before his protégé took office as Chancellor. The family business was now run by his widow from Berlin. As for his daughter, she had developed a passion for archaeology and enjoyed an excellent reputation in academia, where she often outshone her male colleagues.

The Ogre moved closer to the young woman, who was standing in a part of the room with fewer guests. She seemed to be fascinated by the enormous painting of a woman, with a gentle face and an outdated brand of elegance, sitting on a sofa.

"Proper women of the Third Reich must wear dresses to parties, you know," said Göring as he watched Erika.

She continued to stare at the painting and answered without turning around. "I've never been particularly proper."

Göring walked over and contemplated the painting by her side. A veil of sadness fell over his plump face. Two small tears pearled at the corner of his eyes.

"You must recognize her. Carin, my first wife, who died in 1931. She was the love of my life. She didn't much care for conventions either. I owe her so much. I named this lodge Carinhall in her memory. You'd never guess, but I'm a very sentimental person."

"A gorgeous woman. And how is Emmy?" asked Erika.

"Good, she's at a spa in Baden Baden. I don't like having her around during hunts."

He took her arm and continued, "Frau von Essling, you displeased me tonight. Why on earth did you kill the game like that, right at the beginning? I bestowed quite an honour on you by inviting you to participate in my last private hunt of the year. Most guests are never afforded the opportunity to participate in such a hunt."

The young woman turned towards him calmly. "You didn't tell me we would be hunting a man. That's a little surprising for someone so sentimental."

"Apples and oranges. Not all men have the same worth. Plus, I like surprises. You are one of the rare women in this country who knows how to hunt. You have a kill record many men would envy. I thought you would enjoy it. But you haven't answered my question."

She stared at the obese man. "Let's blame it on my Protestant upbringing. I felt pity for the poor priest. Why did you choose him?"

Göring chuckled and his cheeks undulated as if water ran beneath his greasy skin. "I didn't know who it was until the last minute! Every year, the Chicken—excuse me, Reichsführer Himmler—sends me three prisoners for the hunt. They're usually Jews or communists. This time he slipped a priest into the bunch. It must be his idea of a joke."

Erika gave him a frigid look. "I don't see anything funny about hunting poor, terrified people through the forest to kill them."

The marshal squinted. "Come now, my dear. Given the way you deftly ended our prey's suffering, it wasn't the first time you'd taken a life. It surprised me. I was sure you would let me finish him. You would be surprised how many of my guests have backed down when the time came to pull the trigger."

Erika didn't answer. She had learned to hide her emotions in the new Nazi order. But Göring was an unsettling specimen. The man she was talking to could shed genuine tears before the portrait of his late wife, and enjoy hunting people at the same time. He was as ruthless as her father. It wasn't surprising they'd become friends.

Göring took an insincere tone and placed his hands on her shoulders. "Erika, if I understand correctly, you're going to work at the Ahnenerbe, Himmler's institute."

"You know more than I do. All I know is that he's invited me to stay at his castle in Wewelsburg for the next few days."

The Master of the Hunt's warm tone disappeared. "Be careful where you place your pretty boots, Frau von Essling. National Socialism is a remarkable thing; it has transformed Germany. It is a revolution in human history, and I am one of its pillars. Like the Führer, I see it as a radiant star, whose light must spread to the rest of the world, burning those who are unworthy. But some people are invested in its even more radical aspect. Himmler, with his damned SS and his fanatic warrior monks, is a perfect example. He professes strange and absurd doctrines. And unfortunately, his empire continues to expand."

The young woman raised a thin eyebrow. "And?"

"If the SS is a galaxy, then the Ahnenerbe is its black sun."

8

As it did every morning at ten o'clock, an inquisitive eye tried to probe the grimy darkness of cell 108. A dungeon cell at the base of the walls, barely lit by a tiny arrow slit.

"*Madre de Dios*, that place smells! Don't you think we should go in? He might be dying," exclaimed one of the guards as he looked in through a peephole to see a body curled up and still on a pile of dirty straw.

"He's French and they say he killed a priest. Do you really want to go out of your way for that bastard?"

"Judge Tieros said he has plans for a special punishment for this one. I don't want him to die before it's ready."

"He's been rotting down here for three weeks now. Your judge has already forgotten him. Given the number of graves he fills each week, it's not surprising. So, we're going to forget about him, too. Give him some water and soup, and we'll come back tomorrow. That way, if he hasn't touched his food . . ."

"We're covered."

"And good riddance! But we'll have to clean the cell from top to bottom. I've never smelled anything like it. It's like the maggots are already eating his insides."

The peephole closed with a snap and the guards moved down the hall. In cell 108, a hand moved, climbed up and dived under its owner's chest. An unbearable smell filled the cell as a partially decomposed rat flew across the room and into the wall.

Tristan had killed it six days earlier.

That morning, he had left his bowl of soup in the middle of the room and sat in the darkest corner of his cell. A first thin rat appeared, tapping his tail on the floor. A scout. Without nearing the food, he explored the perimeter along the walls, then retreated. Another appeared, then moved discreetly towards the bowl, where it froze as if suddenly paralyzed. *The lookout,* thought Tristan. *He blends into the environment and waits to see if any sort of danger will appear. I just have to be more patient than he is.* After several long minutes, the lookout's tail trembled, then wagged on the floor. Finally, the rat moved. It neared the food but didn't touch it. When his snout had thoroughly imbibed the smell of the contents of the bowl, it turned back and disappeared.

At a leisurely pace, as if visiting a tourist attraction, a surprisingly large rat made his way out of a hole in the straw. *The dominant male.* He had sent his lowly servants to scope things out. Now he could eat to his heart's content, without fear of predators. *But you forgot one thing . . .*

The rodent was gobbling down the thick soup. Too thick, in fact. It was usually mostly water with a crust of stale bread. But today the soup was strangely dense . . . *You forgot a taster.*

The sound of the dominant male devouring the food at a frenzied pace stopped suddenly. Tristan got up. Despite the half-light, he could see the rodent's vacant eyes. His body had just given out. He had always beaten his rivals and bitten his females until they bled, but now he would never be able to terrorize anyone ever again. In just a few seconds, the light would completely leave his dazed eyes. He would never understand that the saltpetre Tristan had scraped off the damp walls and mixed into the soup was deadly for a rat. Even for a dominant male.

Just a few minutes more and the smell of his dead body would have attracted his former lackeys. They were starving and full of hatred, and the dead rat would have been dinner. But Tristan had other plans for him.

In just a few days, the rodent's body had begun to decompose, sending a foul smell wafting through the cell. The Frenchman curled up in the darkest corner of the tiny room. Given the daily intake of prisoners, the guards conducted their rounds at top speed. A suspicious smell, an unmoving body. As exemplary government employees, they applied the universal rule: wait. After their morning visit, Tristan knew he had twenty-four hours ahead of him. They wouldn't open the slit in the door again until the next morning. The smell of death he'd unleashed in the cell ensured his solitude and protection.

Over the course of his stay, he had measured every inch of his cell, studied the structure of the vault, and estimated the thickness of the walls to determine that all chances of escape would quickly be thwarted by the expertise of medieval builders.

Yet one small detail intrigued him. Every day, at around the same time, he heard running water near the edge of the arrow slit. At first, he thought a pipe must run along the wall outside, but there was no sign of water, which would have splashed up onto the thin vertical opening. In the end, he decided that there had to be a conduit, dating back to the castle's original construction, contained within the wall. Probably for evacuating latrines. Such conduits were often quite wide, since they were used to dispose of all sorts of things.

Now the conduit had to be used by the prison kitchens, because he had noticed that the sound of running water lined up with the lunch and dinner services. In other words, the path was clear all night long.

Tristan lodged his heel in the bottom corner of the arrow slit and felt along the stone above. In the darkness, he felt a spongy moss growing along the joints in the wall. It would have weakened them. He jumped back down and rummaged through the straw to find a U-shaped piece of metal.

They had locked him up with his shoes, which had heel irons. He had managed to remove the iron from one of the shoes, bloodying his fingers in the process, and was now using it to dig at the fragile mortar beneath the moss between the blocks of stone.

In two hours, Tristan had freed a brick, which he was now pulling out, inch by inch. Finally, the stone fell. The conduit had to be just behind it, but the darkness left room for doubt. Despite the fetid smell, he picked up the rat by its tail and threw it into the black hole that the fallen block had revealed. Tristan smiled. A series of lessening thuds sounded through the hole: the former dominant male had broken into smaller and smaller pieces in the medieval conduit. He had been right. But the hole was still too small for a man to fit through. He would have to remove a second stone. In less than an hour, he had pulled out a second block and the opening was big enough for him to fit through.

The vertical conduit was wider than he had imagined. Despite the darkness, he could make out rectangles of light at regular intervals above. He decided to use these aeration holes as footholds to make his way up. With his back against one wall, Tristan could hope to reach the floor above. He slipped into the conduit, settled his feet in the holds, and raised his hands in search of something to grip. He found a crumbling joint and used it to pull himself up to the first aeration hole. He placed his right foot in the hole, then continued upward. Tristan felt like he was climbing straight up. His heavy breathing echoed against the walls. He didn't dare look down, afraid he would glimpse the greedy mouth of an endless pit. What he would find up above could hardly be worse than what he imagined below. The fear of falling formed a lump in his throat and sped his ascent.

At last, his bloodied fingers found the edge of something. He pulled himself up to find a pipe coming out of the wall. He felt around the decaying joints and realized the wall was made of bricks. A hurried construction, undoubtedly recent. He slowed his breathing and listened closely for several long minutes. There was nothing but silence on the other side of the wall. This was no time to hesitate. Despite his aching muscles, he pulled himself up further, across from the brick area, and kicked it as hard as he could with his heel. One brick flew into the room, followed by another. In just a few minutes, he managed to open a hole large enough to fit through. As he wriggled out, broken bricks cut at his chest. He found himself in a closet full of pipes, closed off by a simple door, which he carefully opened.

The kitchen was swathed in darkness. Tristan crossed the room silently, heading for one of the windows, which looked out over the central courtyard, about ten meters below. Dangerous and pointless. It would be wiser to slip out the door and find a way out from inside the building. Two frayed aprons were hanging near the entrance. Tristan grabbed one, then leaned over the sink to wash his face. He preferred not to see himself, but in this prison the guards were as grimy as the prisoners, so he might go unnoticed.

To keep people from looking too closely at his face, Tristan faked a limp, dragging the sole of his shoe on the floor. Two guards and a nurse he walked past focused exclusively on his foot before pressing on. He managed to walk down a long corridor without attracting any attention. If his sense of direction was right, he was heading towards the outer wall, with the interior courtyard behind him. The main doors were all guarded, but there had to be service entrances that were less heavily watched.

Tristan was looking for one door in particular.

He let his sense of smell guide him.

Death has three distinct smells.

The first is sour and fleeting but permeates everything in its path. Tristan followed this smell of fresh corpses. He found it at the end of the corridor, wafting onto a landing at the top of some steps.

He needed to access the source.

As he made his way down the stairs lit by a bulb nearing the end of its life, the smell grew more pungent. The acidic notes made way for an acrid fragrance that washed over him in tenacious waves.

The smell of bodies that have lost all semblance of dignity.

The morgue wasn't far now. The smell of death clung to his throat and evoked his worst nightmares. The Frenchman held his breath and opened the door.

The space was divided into two areas: the men who'd been shot by firing squad, awaiting their graves—some for days—on one side, and prisoners who'd died of hunger or disease on the other. The latter's skeletons were shrouded in their translucent skin. Tristan moved deeper into the room. To save space, some bodies had been piled up, and were now melting into one another like forgotten sorbet. The smell had changed again, now kindling images in Tristan's head: putrid, decaying flesh and a flock of black crows in flight. Tristan staggered, then regained his footing. At least no one would come looking for him here. He'd learned during his interrogation with Tieros that the corpses of the men who were shot on site were buried in the prison's dry moat. As for the others, they were thrown into a mass grave outside the walls. This was confirmed by the pile of closed bags lying on the ground near the door.

There were eleven roughly sewn bags made of salvaged burlap. All identical. One of them had clearly been used to transport coffee. Death recycled everything.

Tristan inspected the makeshift shrouds attentively. The seventh seemed suitable: it didn't smell too strongly yet, and no fluids were seeping through the fabric. He grabbed the string and removed it carefully. He would need it. The gaunt yet swollen body was lying on its back. Tristan grabbed it by the ankles and rolled it over to the gelatinous pile of firing-squad victims.

Now he could climb in.

Steps sounded in the room just before noon. Heavy boots that struck the ground in rhythm. "How many are we supposed to move this time?"

Papers ruffled.

"Eleven."

"To the usual place?"

"No, that grave is full. The other day, some locals saw an arm coming up out of the ground. We can't have that. We need a new place. Something nearby and discreet."

"So, we have to break our backs digging like slaves again? I'm fed up! Hey, are the bodies . . . dressed?"

"Take a look and see."

Tristan heard some burlap rip.

"As naked as Adam! Well, on the bright side, they won't leave anything behind this way."

"Where should we get rid of them?"

"At Tibidabo."

"In the hills?"

"Yes, not a single hunter's gone up there since the beginning of the war. It's full of game. Especially boars. And they'll eat anything."

The Frenchman heard another rip. A dead man had stood up. "Please, not the boars, not the boars!"

"Call the judge," shouted one of the guards. "It's a prisoner trying to escape."

In his shroud, Tristan knew it was over. When two prisoners had the same escape plan at the same time, they both failed.

"Open all the bags," ordered the judge, who had rushed in.

The blade that cut through the fabric nicked the Frenchman's ear, causing him to cry out.

"I was looking for you," exclaimed Tieros gleefully. "I have some news."

Tristan got to his feet with difficulty.

The judge smiled. "You're going to die today."

9

When he came out of the underground bunker, the smell of cold ashes blocked his throat. It was foul and suffocating like poison gas. He coughed into his silk handkerchief embroidered with a capital C as he took in the stone skeletons before him. The arrogant, majestic Victorian homes were now just hollow, blackened façades. Behind them, huge shadows danced in the light of the setting sun, devouring the glowing city.

"My God, so this is the apocalypse," he mumbled in a halting voice.

All around him explosions and sirens roared. He raised his head and noticed small metal meteorites were falling to the ground, followed by their bright tails. He wanted to scream with rage, but no sound emerged from his dry mouth. London was now just a pile of ruins, flames and dead bodies.

A muffled sound erupted behind the concrete shelter. Another explosion. Bits of rock emerged from nowhere and landed on the end of his muddy shoes.

"We must go back in, Mr. Prime Minister!" shouted the man next to him, a colonel in a tattered uniform.

Winston Churchill turned to the officer, but he was powerless to reply. He was unable to resist as two guards pulled him back into his warren.

His mind no longer obeyed his bidding—it had become a burden for his body. The drugs his personal doctor made him take day and night had decimated his willpower weeks ago.

After several long minutes walking down a damp tunnel, he reached a meeting room, where a group of exhausted officers waited to brief him.

"We've lost, Mr. Prime Minister," offered a general with a thick moustache. "The Germans hold the City and are about to take Piccadilly."

Churchill shook his head in disbelief.

"Where is Wessex? He and his tanks are supposed to move into Hyde Park. He can still save us!"

The officers glanced nervously at one another.

"General Wessex is dead, and his unit has been routed," answered one of the soldiers. "You have to make arrangements, Mr. Prime Minister. You must go somewhere safe. Before . . ."

Churchill's face clouded over. He waved a trembling hand at the officers. "Never! Do you hear me?" he shouted. "Never! I'd rather die here than run away like a coward. Where is King George?"

"In Cardiff with the royal family. They are about to board a battleship heading for Ireland. The Germans say they won't take them prisoner."

Churchill wearily snuffed out his cigar as he stared at the king's austere expression in the portrait on the wall. "So, I'm the only one left to save the Empire."

The colonel who had accompanied him outside grabbed the Prime Minister by the shoulders. "So, go to Scotland! We still have some time. You can take off from the remaining base at Kensington. A Lancaster is waiting for your signal to take you to Edinburgh, where—"

Churchill punched the wall.

"What if the Germans intercept me? Have you thought of that? They'll drag me through the streets to humiliate me! Hitler will have me hanged. I'll never give him that pleasure. I've made my own arrangements."

He rummaged through the pockets of his trousers and pulled out a small, black metal box. He opened it and picked up a tiny glass capsule filled with an amber liquid. "Cyanide will be my last drink. I—"

Before he could finish, a violent explosion resounded overhead. It was so strong that one of the walls caved in on the officers. A cloud of dust filled the room.

After a few seconds, Churchill pulled himself up out of the rubble despite a coughing fit.

Suddenly, before him, he saw men in combat uniforms and gas masks. They were all wearing German helmets.

The Prime Minister backed up to a concrete wall that was left standing.

One of the soldiers moved closer and took off his mask. He was a blond man with fine, regular features. His face was almost angelic, but his blue eyes were full of anger. He reminded Churchill of Saint George slaying the dragon.

And he was the dragon. He tried to huddle down, though he knew there was no point.

The German moved closer still and explained gravely, "I have come for you. England must die. You shall be the first."

Churchill screamed.

And woke up.

His heart was pounding.

Around him, all was quiet. The humming generator was the only sound that broke the silence of his room. He turned on a bedside lamp and instinctively reached for the Browning 12 sitting at the foot of his bed. Just then, there was a knock at the door.

"Mr. Prime Minister, are you all right?"

"Yes, fine, Andrews," answered Churchill in his usual surly tone. "I'm hungry. Bring me my breakfast."

He glanced at the round clock on the wall across from him. It was only six o'clock. Too late to go back to sleep. He sat up in his bed and lit his first cigar of the day while studying the room around him.

The ceiling was low, and the concrete walls were covered with maps of Europe dotted with swastikas. A Union Jack and a portrait of His Majesty King George V were the only decorations. At the far end of the room, there was a metal table with four matching chairs. The only objects that stood out were the Victorian lamps with mauve shades and a luxurious rug from Woolgore and Brothers. A radio was plugged in, but the power only worked sporadically.

Gloomy.

That was the first word that came to his mind.

He tapped the end of his cigar over the ashtray and made his first reasonable decision of the day. Tonight he would sleep at home, above ground, at 10 Downing Street. He'd much rather risk dying from a Luftwaffe bomb than continue to hide out in this rat hole.

Fifteen minutes later, a man with a brick-red face came into the room carrying a large tray.

"Good morning, Mr. Prime Minister. Did you sleep well?"

"Hardly. I had a terrible nightmare. The Germans had won and had come to rub it in my face. I won't be sleeping here anymore. I'll die of depression if I do."

Churchill moved over to the table as his aide laid out the breakfast. Coffee, scrambled eggs, quince jam, fresh bread, butter, bacon, and beans. Quite a luxury in a country resigned to ration coupons, but he didn't feign shame. Those with great responsibilities deserved a royal breakfast. Along with his cigars and whisky, this was his only pleasure. The aide opened the doors to a closet set into the cement wall.

"Which suit would you like to wear today?"

"The grey tweed one my wife gave me to help me swallow the bitter pill of the Munich Agreement. Ah, and let her know I'll be sleeping at home tonight."

A thirty-something brunette peeked into the room. "The files for the War Council, Sir."

"Thank you, Kate. Put them on the desk," he answered without turning around.

The secretary crossed the room quickly in her long, straight, grey skirt and placed a pile of files at the end of the empty table. A rubber band held together a bundle of index cards.

"The meeting is set to begin in an hour and a half, Mr. Prime Minister."

"Thank you. How are your little girls?"

"They've been sent to a farm in Surrey with the rest of their class."

"Good, at least they won't be hit by Göring's bombs."

The young woman smiled but didn't answer. Her smile broke the Prime Minister's heart. It was the smile of a mother separated from her children, trying to hide her pain. Like tens of thousands of other brave British women.

He watched her close the door and turned to his aide as he finished his coffee. "In my dream, I wanted to kill myself. Are there whisky-flavoured cyanide capsules?"

"Not that I know of. I'll find out. If there are, would you prefer pure malt or blended whiskey?"

Churchill gave him a knowing smile. He enjoyed his aide's impeccable sense of humour. He gobbled down a big piece of toast covered in a thick layer of jam, then sat back in his chair and went over his schedule for the day, a sullen look on his face. He'd be busy until ten o'clock that night.

"For Christ's sake! I'm running a war, I have to make decisions that have incalculable consequences for our country, and I've been assigned a meeting with the representative of the Yorkshire Butchers' Association. Is this a joke?"

"Your secretary must want to restock the shelter's kitchen. It's a highly strategic meeting."

"Please get rid of some of these meetings, Andrews. Or shorten them. Unless the Fritzes land in Dover today, I want to go home to my bed."

The aide frowned in concentration as his pen ran over the paper to the sound of toast crunching in Churchill's mouth.

"We could postpone your five o'clock appointment with the clothing industry representatives. You'll see them next week at the guild's headquarters. You could see Commander Malorley of the SOE just after breakfast. He was scheduled for later this morning.

The Prime Minister's face lit up. The Special Operations Executive, or SOE, was the counter-intelligence service he had founded in the summer of 1940, just after France's defeat. His baby. It was fully independent of the traditional intelligence services like MI6 and reported solely to him. As he liked to say, the SOE's mission was to "set occupied Europe ablaze". Sabotage, assassinations, underhanded moves, and misinformation campaigns were the bread and butter of the "Baker Street Irregulars", as their more closely watched MI6 colleagues disdainfully called them. The Prime Minister scratched his head, a pensive look on his face.

"Malorley, Malorley. Ah, yes, the head of propaganda and psychological warfare. Could you let him know about the change quickly?"

"Yes, he was here inspecting the war room's protections this morning. I think he's somewhere in the west wing."

Just over fifteen minutes later, a tall man in a commander's uniform entered the room. He was in his forties, with short hair, a strong chin, and a penetrating gaze.

"Good Morning, Mr. Prime Minister."

Churchill shook his hand enthusiastically.

"Malorley, I'm so pleased to see you again. We met last year when I attended the grand opening of your offices. You studied at Oxford and served in the Third Cavalry of the Indian Army, if I'm not mistaken?"

Malorley nodded. "At your service," he answered.

Churchill gestured to the seat across from him. "Sit down and get straight to the point, Commander. It's going to be a long day and I'd like to go home to Downing Street tonight."

"Of course, Sir," replied Malorley as he opened his bag and placed it on the table next to the breakfast tray. He took out a stack of papers and slid it over to Churchill. "You'll find the summary you asked for regarding the population's morale. It's not great, I'm afraid. My colleagues also included a detailed report on the movement of German troops in Normandy, which has also been sent to the General Staff. Last but not least, there's a file on the German sabotage efforts at our weapons factories in Coventry and Birmingham. We captured three Nazi spies yesterday."

"Excellent work, Malorley. That's the first good news I've heard today. Anything else?"

The commander pulled out a black file. "I'd like you to have a look at these documents pertaining to Reichsführer Himmler's trip to Spain last autumn."

Churchill wiped the corner of his mouth with his napkin.

"Spain. Our ambassador in Madrid danced a gig last year when he found out Hitler left Hendaye with his tail between his legs following his disastrous meeting with Franco. I hope you're not about to announce that the Caudillo has changed his mind."

"No, rest assured. But one of our agents in Spain has shared some curious information."

"What type of information? I'm intrigued."

"Information regarding archaeological research that seems to be important to Himmler. During his stay in Catalonia, he visited Montserrat Monastery with a close friend, Colonel SS Karl Weistort. And Weistort has recently returned to Barcelona."

Churchill frowned. "Remind me who he is again."

"He's the head of the Ahnenerbe. The institution that financed the SS expedition to Tibet in 1938. I wrote a memo on the topic."

"I've never heard of it."

"The Ahnenerbe is a cultural institute under SS control that conducts archaeological and esoteric research. I'm almost certain that the head of the SS made that trip to Spain for a single reason: to visit that monastery. He is passionate about occult science and, as you know, several Nazi leaders are fascinated by esotericism. In his youth, even Hitler had—"

Churchill raised his hand. "Good for them. Let him invoke Satan and disappear from the face of the earth. Listen, my dear Malorley, don't take this the wrong way, but I don't have time to waste on the Nazis' eccentricities. I have a war to run. Speaking of which, there's a war council starting in fifteen minutes. Do you have anything more pressing to discuss?"

The commander's face was as unmoving as marble. He closed his bag but left the black file on the table.

"No, that's all. I'll leave you the file nonetheless, in case you want to—"

Churchill stood up and took the SOE agent by the arm. "I'll

take a look, but between us, Malorley, don't waste your time on this nonsense. I couldn't care less about Himmler's follies. This is real life, not the adventures of Allan Quatermain.* I have hundreds of more important files to digest. Focus on your more critical missions."

Malorley's car and driver were waiting when he exited the Prime Minister's shelter. He climbed into the vehicle and closed his eyes, since the driver already knew they were heading back to SOE headquarters. The Hillman 14 got underway in the morning fog, leaving the bunker behind. It was so thick, the driver could only see a few meters ahead.

The head of the SOE's psychology department took out a cigarette as he studied the pavements lit by sodium lamps and full of pedestrians who moved like ghosts in the gloom. Since the outbreak of war, business hours had been moved an hour earlier. The puffs of white smoke Malorley blew filled the air inside the car, as thick as the fog on the other side of the window. But his mind remained clear. He hadn't convinced the Prime Minister. Total and utter failure.

He was furious but refused to give up. The stakes were too high. He had sworn to do his best, two years earlier, on that tragic night in Berlin.

"Professor!"

The bookseller was sitting in his armchair, his head hung to one side like a limp puppet's. The ropes tied around his chest were the only thing keeping him upright. His shirt was stained with rust-coloured blood.

"Oh, my . . . my English friend. I waited for you . . ."

Malorley tried to remove the ropes, but they were too tight.

"They took the . . . book. A Nazi, an SS officer, stole it. His name is . . . Weistort."

"I'll take you to the hospital. My car is just outside."

Otto was dying. The words came out in spasms.

---

*A popular fictional character in the UK.

"Take care . . . My wife . . ."

"No!" shouted the Englishman.

"My office . . . I . . . left notebook . . . Borealis."

Malorley finally managed to untie the ropes. The bookseller slumped over in his seat. His eyes stared at the city on fire. His city.

"Otto, hold on!"

"No, my friend. I'm leaving this hell."

Malorley returned his gaze to the crowd of Londoners on their way to work. Fifteen minutes late. Just fifteen minutes could have changed everything. He could have saved Neumann and the *Thule Borealis Kulten*. That damn book. He had gone over those tragic minutes so many times in his head. He had walked past two SS officers on the pavement as he neared the bookstore. They walked along calmly despite the fire and bloodshed that surrounded them. He had locked eyes with one of them, the one with the scar. He would never forget that face—the face of his old German friend's executioner.

Malorley opened the car window for some fresh air.

He had managed to save the professor's notebook on the *Borealis*. Pages blackened with notes and a sketch of a medieval castle.

He massaged his temples and tried to block out the image of his dead friend's face. Churchill was stubborn, but so was he! He still had something up his sleeve. His last trump card. But to play it, he wouldn't be heading to a casino, but to a lodge. England's largest Masonic lodge.

10

The heat hit him as soon as his aide opened the door of the Mercedes. A dry, scorching wind swept down the sierra towards the plains. In his black uniform, Weistort contemplated the arid hills, which rose slowly all the way to the Pyrenees, before dropping steeply into the sea. Stands of cork oaks and stone pines howled in the wind. Only the olive trees, protected by small stone walls, remained silent. A few steps from the head of the Ahnenerbe, a Spanish colonel in dress uniform clicked his heels in salute.

"I hope you had a nice trip from Barcelona, Oberführer?"

Weistort nodded and glanced indifferently at the man. He didn't like to be disturbed in his thoughts. Fifteen centuries earlier, at the time of Barbarian Invasions, Germanic tribes—first the Vandals, then the Visigoths—had conquered Spain to make it their kingdom. A kingdom of tall, pale, blond warriors. Nothing like this tiny, olive-skinned Spaniard with curly hair. Weistort smiled disdainfully. The German army had already conquered Poland and France. Spain's turn would come soon enough. One day, all of Europe would be a vast Germanic empire.

"Let me introduce Don Montalban, who is delighted to welcome us to his arena today," offered the colonel timidly.

The last bit piqued Weistort's interest. After all, bull fighting was the one noble thing the Spanish had invented. It proved a man's worth and showcased the animal's bravery.

"Show me the bulls."

"Well, your Excellency, in your honour, the authorities suggested ..."

Don Montalban didn't know how to finish his sentence. In over forty years, he had never been asked to do such a thing. Colonel Orsana leapt to his rescue.

"Oberführer, we have *slightly* modified the show for you . . . There won't be any bulls."

Weistort did his best to minimize his reaction. Didn't the curly-haired midget know that bull fighting was a time-honoured tradition? That it had been used by Roman legions to showcase warrior virtues? That bull sacrifice had been central to the religion called Mithraism, a rival of early Christianity?

"What do you mean, no bulls?"

"No matadors, either, Oberführer. At least not the usual kind. But if you'd be so kind as to follow me, the arena is just a few steps further."

Despite his irritation, Weistort followed the colonel. They passed a hedge that bent in the wind and a long white wall appeared. Riders on horses whose glossy coats ran with sweat paraded in front of the entrance. Each of them spun a long lance around as they rode.

"They're picadors," explained Don Montalban. "At the beginning of each bull fight, their job is to rile the bull up by jabbing it along its spine."

Inside, the arena was a stark white that contrasted with the dark sand on the ground. It had clearly just been sprayed with water. A wave of cool air climbed up into the stands to where Weistort was sitting.

"If there are no bulls and no matadors . . ."

A door slammed shut and one of the riders appeared. He had changed mounts, trading the spry, nervous stallion for a horse with broad shoulders that made him look like a centaur. He moved to the centre of the arena, saluted arrogantly, then trotted over to a red wooden door.

"The show is about to begin," announced Orsana.

The door creaked on its hinges, revealing a long, dark corridor from which a gaunt, naked man emerged, his eyes wild.

"Victor Abril, an anarchist sentenced to death for raping nuns in a convent in Girona."

The prisoner was suddenly whipped. He collapsed onto the sand.

"Get up, you dog, and fight like a man," shouted the Spanish officer.

"What will he fight with?" asked Weistort.

"With the tools he used to commit his crime: his hands and his . . ."

The picador was impatient. He rode in circles around his victim like a bird of prey, jabbing him on every pass. Before long, blood ran down the prisoner's back.

"Do you know why we water the sand in the arena before a bull fight, Oberführer? It's so the sand won't swallow up the blood too quickly. For our viewing pleasure."

"At least the sand is up to the task," replied Weistort arrogantly.

The colonel's expression darkened. He raised his hand and gave a thumbs-down. The picador stopped turning in circles around his victim and firmly rammed the lance into Abril's body, just under his shoulder, then rolled him onto his back. With his arms outstretched and his body covered in blood, Victor Abril looked like Christ on the cross.

"I'll show you how we treat cowards around here! Picador, a cavalcade for our guest!"

The picador urged his horse to a trot. With each step, a muffled sound rang out, as if the animal wanted to mark the sand with his shoes. Two meters from the bloodied body, the rider slowed the pace.

"Walk!"

The first foot crushed Abril's ankle. A cloud of blood and flesh erupted from the wound like a swarm of insects. The second trampled his testicles.

"We cut the jewels off noble bulls, but not off cowards," commented Orsana.

Despite his suffering, Abril tried to get up. He raised his head, then his torso, but it was the last move he ever made. The horse drove a hoof through his stomach. A geyser of entrails exploded like fireworks, then fell to the sand. Next to Weistort, Don Montalban doubled over. He had seen plenty of bulls tortured in the centre of his arena, but now he was about to vomit.

"The sun," he claimed, breathing deeply.

The colonel wiped his forehead. Weistort alone remained impassive. He stared at the dead man's face. A piece of his innards hung from the side of his mouth. His last cry had been muffled by a piece of intestines falling from above. This degrading image delighted him. That's how all conquered people should die—humiliated. It wasn't enough for them to die; they should die in shame.

"I hope you enjoyed the show, Oberführer."

The head of the Ahnenerbe simply nodded. He was thinking. As soon as he got home to Berlin, he would set up a new working group of historians and anthropologists to study the ways ancient civilizations killed their prisoners of war. Himmler would love it. He couldn't wait to tell the Reichsführer.

"We have another prisoner. A Frenchman. He also attacked a monastery."

Weistort whipped around. "Which monastery?"

"The most sacred of all, Oberführer. Montserrat, Spain's spiritual lantern. Here's the prisoner."

Tristan walked down a dark corridor to a low door. Above him, he could see white stands under a windy sky of nearly translucent clouds. They had taken him from Montjuic yesterday and placed him in a military lorry with other prisoners. They had crisscrossed the Spanish countryside, still scarred by civil war. Burned villages, abandoned fields, burned cars . . . It all smelled of defeat. As the lorry continued down the bumpy roads, it unloaded more and more prisoners, delivered to Guardia Civil officers. One time, the soldiers didn't even wait for the lorry to leave before a volley of shots broke the night-time silence, followed by the muffled sound of a body rolling into a grave.

He was the last one.

In the morning, he had been handed over to soldiers in pristine uniforms, who had led him to the mouth of this tunnel, like a gladiator before a fight.

The arena was deserted. The wind howled between the stands, amplifying his solitude. A whistle made him turn around. Three men were seated just above the entrance. A civilian and two soldiers, one of whom was wearing a foreign uniform.

"Come out to the middle of the arena."

Despite the heat, the sand seemed to be wet. Even more surprisingly, an unidentifiable smell clung to the place. A heady scent, as if someone had just raked a muddy pond.

"Stop there."

The low door slammed shut, as if pushed by an invisible hand. From the middle of the arena, the corridor he had come through looked endless. "The door to hell," mumbled Tristan just before he heard a dull rhythmic sound swelling like a storm. One of the men in the stands stood up. This time Tristan recognized the uniform. He could see two silver lightning bolts on his shoulders.

As if expelled from the underworld, a rider appeared.

In his right hand, he held the lance tightly under his arm as he charged like a medieval knight. Just a few yards from Tristan, he lowered the weapon, aiming for his stomach.

A mistake.

Tristan ran in front of the horse, which bucked in surprise. As Tristan rolled aside to safety, the rider clung tightly to the saddle, but his lance got stuck in the sand, throwing him screaming over the horse's head. When Tristan stood up, he saw the picador's body impaled on his own lance. The wood had split in two and driven right through the rider's chest, leaving his arms dangling uselessly at his sides.

Colonel Orsana was furious. He shouted like a child whose toy has just been broken. Sitting next to him, Don Montalban stared at the impaled body in shock. How could this have happened? He had seen the damn Frenchman jump in front of the horse like a goalie in front of a penalty kick, and then . . .

"He's a sorcerer! A sorcerer," shouted Don Montalban.

He turned to Weistort in search of confirmation. "Picadors' horses always wear blinders, so they can't see anything. The Frenchman can't have spooked him by jumping in front of him. It's impossible."

The head of the Ahnenerbe shrugged with a smile. "The horse wasn't afraid of the prisoner," he explained, gesturing to the light that filled the arena, "he was afraid of the light. When he jumped, the Frenchman pulled off one of the blinders."

Dumbfounded and humiliated by the simplicity of the explanation, the colonel's anger exploded. "He won't get away with this! Don Montalban, go get a bull, I swear—"

"You don't murder a man who has cheated death," Weistort said, cutting him off.

"So how do you kill him?"

"Give him to me."

Orsana was afraid he had understood. He had seen the Germans' handiwork during the civil war. Hitler had sent "volunteers" to help the Francoists. The fanatics were happy to raze a village to the ground without any concern for lost lives. They were allies, true, but allies for whom adversaries' lives meant nothing.

"What for, Oberführer?"

Weistort leaned in. "Believe me, Colonel, it's better for you not to know . . ."

The Spaniard lowered his head. Strange rumours had been going around about what the Nazis did to their enemies. Torture and executions that defied the imagination. And Orsana didn't want to lose any sleep.

"He's yours."

Without so much as a thankyou, Weistort climbed down the stands to the arena. The sand crunched under his boots as he walked over to Tristan. "You may have cheated death, but now you belong to the Devil."

I I

Sticky rain was falling in Covent Garden. Like after every bombing, an irritating smell—a blend of burnt wood and wet stone—filled the air, but the Londoners hardly noticed anymore.

The week before, three buildings had disappeared in the blink of an eye just next to the Freemasons' Hall, the only one left miraculously standing. At first sight, the building looked like a church, but an attentive passer-by would have noticed two unique details that marked it as a non-religious edifice. The first, on the façade, was a heraldry symbol featuring a compass and square. The second was a date engraved on a plaque: 1717. The official founding date of Freemasonry. In England, the brothers didn't hide—they chiselled their power into stone and put it on display for all to see.

At the front of the building, a heavy patinaed bronze door over a century old and thicker than the sides of an armoured ship, blocked the entrance. Not a single sound emerged from within the walls. The building seemed as deserted as the surrounding streets, but inside, the temple was full to the brim.

It was meeting night at the highly respected United Grand Lodge of England.

"My dear brothers, it is time to conclude our meeting. Let us take a moment to think of our brothers who are currently serving in the RAF. Their admirable courage will help win the air battle for England."

The eighth Grand Master of the United Grand Lodge of

England was the Duke of Kent. His voice echoed through the temple, which was half the size of a rugby field and reached as high as a cathedral.

From his honorary chair, which was as majestic as a king's throne, he looked out over the four hundred men sitting before him on ten rows of benches arranged in a half circle. They were all wearing black suits and ties, with the Masonic apron attached to the front of their belts. Most of them were too old to be called to service. The younger brothers were away at the front and unable to attend meetings.

"I don't know how long this war will last, but I know light will triumph over darkness in the end. Nazi Germany will capitulate, and its children will cry rivers." The aristocrat paused for a few seconds, then began again in a thunderous voice. "For God and for our beloved king, I say!"

Sitting in the highest row, just next to one of the doors, Commander Malorley's lips moved in time to the Duke's. He knew the speech by heart. And for good reason—he had written the text two days earlier. The SOE officer was satisfied. The Duke of Kent was doing an admirable job of delivering it. It would have given Malorley goose bumps if he had been able to believe a single word of the conclusion. Propaganda had even made its way into Masonic lodges. Hope was a luxury he couldn't afford, but it was becoming a necessity for the British people, who had already suffered so much.

"Order, my brothers!"

The aristocrat clapped three times. The four hundred men stood up in unison. Straight as arrows with their hands glued to the seams of their trousers. The meeting was over. The double doors that closed the inner sanctum opened as if by magic and the Freemasons filed out row by row.

It took a little over fifteen minutes for the temple to empty out completely. Malorley left with the last stragglers and discreetly followed a corridor that led to the building's south wing, which housed the Grand Lodge's administrative services. It was deserted at this late hour. He hurried along under the disapproving gaze of the order's Grand Masters, whose portraits adorned the wain-scoted walls. All of them noblemen or even royals, including the late King Edward VII. In England, Freemasonry had always been a pillar of the established order and enjoyed the protection of the crown. The Windsors were hardly an exception to the rule. The current monarch, King George VI, regularly attended meetings at his lodge.

Malorley pushed through a door that opened onto a dark stair-case and headed quickly down the steps. A minute later, he was outside on Great Queen Street.

The moon was round and silver like a giant shilling over the deserted street. He let his eyes adjust. London had been plunged into darkness every night since the Blitz, so anyone outside was entirely dependent on moonlight. He looked wearily up at the sky. A dozen barrage balloons moved silently in the night air. Malorley was fascinated by the blimp-like defences attached to the roofs of London buildings by steel cables. They were designed to prevent enemy planes from flying too low, but there was something menacing about them. They were like huge insects waiting to explode over the city.

He hurried over to a double-parked dark-blue Rolls Royce. A liveried driver was standing next to the car and opened the back door as the SOE agent approached. Malorley smiled. The car's owner, Sebastian Moran, must be one of the last bankers to still employ a uniformed chauffeur.

He bent down and elegantly slid onto the white leather seat next to a grey-haired man. Moran was around sixty with intelligent eyes and three deep horizontal wrinkles across his forehead.

"Sebastian, why did you want me to come out alone?"

"Some of the brothers are too curious for my taste," replied the banker. "Real gossips."

His voice featured a gravelly Sussex accent.

The powerful engine started up, though they could barely hear its purr. Malorley refused the cigar the banker offered.

"And the Grand Master's speech at the end of the meeting?"

"Admirable. From all points of view."

Malorley nodded in agreement. "These days few people find us admirable—at least in continental Europe. Adolf and his friends are making life hard for our brothers. I heard that, in France, Marshal Pétain has drafted a law to purge Freemasons from government."

"That's terrible, but it's true that some French Masons were entirely too political. They're paying the price for their anti-fascist stance."

The Rolls made its way down a nearly deserted avenue.

"Are you ready for your presentation to our little committee?" asked Moran.

"Yes. I hope I'll do a better job convincing the attendees than I did the Prime Minister."

"You can't blame Churchill, my friend. And I can't guarantee our members will be any more receptive. That said, they can sometimes be quite open-minded."

The banks of the Thames were a spectral shade of white. The car went around a battery of anti-aircraft guns in the middle of the street, aimed at the sky.

Ten minutes later, the Rolls parked on Craven Street, near the half-demolished Embankment station and right outside the opulent façade of a grey stone building. The two men got out of the car and climbed a handful of steps to a dark wooden door. Malorley raised an eyebrow at the plaque fixed above the bell, which read *Prospero's Mansion*.

"Prospero. Is that a reference to *The Tempest*?"

"Indeed," answered Moran. "Prospero, the Duke of Milan, exiled to a desert island with his daughter Miranda and the monster Caliban. Prospero, who became a sorcerer and the master of evil forces out of necessity. An extraordinary play."

The banker rang the copper bell hanging from the wall. A few seconds later, a slit opened, and a pair of inquisitive eyes appeared.

"We're here for the eleven o'clock show," announced Moran.

The door opened to reveal a servant who bowed respectfully.

"They're expecting you," he said ceremoniously as he took their coats.

The two men walked through a majestic Victorian entryway with scarlet velvet walls. An imposing chandelier covered in clusters of Bohemian garnets filled the room with shimmering light. The valet pushed open a door, handed a silver key to the banker, and stepped aside to let them through. They found themselves in a corridor shaped like a half circle, with a series of doorways to opera boxes closed with curtains, like in a theatre. The intelligence officer listened closely. Shouts and a cracking sound filled the air. He slowed near an empty box with open curtains and noticed a stage set up below.

"Take a look, my friend," whispered the grey-haired man.

Malorley moved closer and stopped short when he could see the show. Two red-headed women, in red leather corsets and thigh-high boots, armed with switches, were whipping a bald man with a full beard wearing nothing but his birthday suit and holding a skull in his hands.

"Where in the world are we?" asked the commander, intrigued.

The banker smiled mischievously. "Might I have caught His Majesty's secret agent off guard?"

"I'm in charge of intelligence, not my compatriots' sexual preferences."

The bearded man attempted to recite something between whimpers. The more robust of the two redheads rammed her heel into his lower back. He collapsed onto the floor as his eager torturers looked on.

"To be or not to be!" exclaimed Moran, clearly amused by the show. "*Hamlet*, of course! Act 3, scene 1. The prince of Denmark is reflecting on his troubled fate."

"More like 'To suffer or not to suffer!'" replied Malorley. "I don't remember the stage direction including sadomasochism."

The banker placed his finger on his lips.

"Some evenings Prospero's Mansion revisits Shakespeare from a more . . . erotic angle. The boxes you see here are occupied by those who appreciate the genius of Stratford-upon-Avon, with a rather noticeable hit of erotomania. You can even participate. This Hamlet is one of my colleagues, a very influential man in the City."

"Am I supposed to make my presentation after this? In the company of those charming women?"

"Don't worry, our meeting will take place in another part of the theatre. For optimal security, our circle changes its meeting place regularly. This venue belongs to one of our members and schedules dictated that the meeting take place here tonight."

Malorley was impatient to meet the members of the Gordon Circle, to which his Masonic brother belonged. It was his last hope. Among the influential groups jostling for position in the capital, the Circle was considered one of the most powerful. Its name had been chosen in tribute to General Charles Gordon, a hero of Victorian England. Nicknamed Gordon Pasha, he died in the Sudan during the war against the Mahdi, a religious fanatic and mystic who led Muslim tribes and was sacrificed by the British government for political gain. The scandal it caused drove a group of businessmen, bankers and high-ranking military officers to found a lobbying group to prevent future governments from making such tragic mistakes. Rumour held that the Gordon Circle had supported the rise of the outsider Churchill to the position of Prime Minister, much to the dismay of the presumed heir to the office, Lord Halifax.

"Has the projector been set up?" asked Malorley.

"Yes, of course. Ah, one more thing—don't take the rudeness of certain members personally. It's all part of the game."

Sebastian Moran took out the key as they reached a closed door adorned with a tragedy mask. He opened it carefully and they entered a dimly lit room with no windows.

The room had a low ceiling supported at regular intervals by Doric columns. Eleven men and one woman were seated around an oval table. Behind them stood a film projector on a tripod with a half-full reel.

The banker made his way into the room with his guest. "My dear friends, may I present Commander Malorley, head of the SOE's psychological welfare department. He has taken time out of his schedule to share some . . . unique information with us. Please give him your full attention."

Malorley greeted the assembly and recognized several faces. On the right side of the table were Sir Alan Lascelles, personal secretary to the king, Clement Atlee, Lord Privy Seal, and General Francis Brooke, Commander in Chief of the Home Forces. On the left side sat a woman around sixty years old with jet-black hair. Lady Beltham, who held England's fourth-largest fortune. Next to her was Admiral Cunningham. He didn't know the six other members.

King George VI was also in attendance, or rather his portrait was, hanging from one of the walls. The sovereign watched peacefully over the guests.

Malorley moved towards the white screen which had been placed along a wall in front of the audience, as Sebastian Moran turned on the projector. The lights overhead dimmed as if by magic. A subtle purring sound filled the room. A ray of white light struck the screen and the commander moved aside to avoid being blinded.

His deep voice echoed through the semi-darkness. "The information I'm going to share with you tonight may undermine your certainties about this war. What you're about to hear has not been included in any report to the General Staff and will never be documented in writing. This information must not be shared with the general population. I will deny having said any of this if one of you ever accidentally alludes to tonight's events."

He could barely see the participants' faces in the darkness. He continued, even louder: "Two years ago, Reichsführer Himmler sent an expedition to Tibet. A scientific expedition led by ethnographer and SS officer Ernst Schäfer. They found ... ."

12

The door was locked, but he could open the window. The distance to the ground outside dashed any hope of escape. After spending months in a dirty dungeon at Montjuic, Tristan couldn't believe he was being held in a room with varnished wood floors, where his sheets were changed daily. A Spanish maid came in every morning to make the bed as if he were a special guest. She always kept her eyes lowered and her lips tightly closed. After a few days, Tristan had put together that he was being held in a hotel that overlooked the city. One of the establishments designed around the turn of the century, which must have welcomed high society from all over Europe before the war. In an ironic twist of fate, the hotel was now home to the SS, whose huge swastika flag floated over the steps to the entrance. Where there had once been an army of porters and lift operators, there were now guards in black uniforms, all standing as tall and still as statues.

He had been left alone and forgotten in this room for five days now. Long enough to memorize the wallpaper, the wavering rays of sunlight reflected onto the mouldings, and the blue line of the horizon. In fact, Tristan knew all too well that he hadn't been forgotten. No, they were just letting him stew, leaving him to alternate between hope and despair until he was perfectly cooked for the first interrogation. The Nazis seemed to be wasting time to save time. To keep his mind from running in circles every time he felt anxious, Tristan would lie down on the bed and remember the museums he had visited. It took him two days to walk through the Louvre's main galleries in his mind and a day for the Prado in Madrid—he'd indulged in a rushed visit one day in the middle of the civil war. Since yesterday, he'd been working his way through the Uffizi Gallery in Florence.

He was contemplating a single detail—the radiant black of an armoured breastplate—from *The Battle of San Romano* by Paolo Uccello when the door opened, and a guard clicked his heels. Seconds later, Tristan found himself in the corridor, then on his way down the grand staircase which led to the sitting rooms.

The plush sofas and games tables had been replaced with a swarm of secretaries, all of them as blonde as Valkyries, typing frantically on typewriters or screeching into telephones. It seemed the former luxury hotel had become the hub of the German presence in Barcelona. No one seemed to notice as Tristan walked across the vast room: the Nazi war machine was underway, and nothing could be allowed to distract even a single gear.

"Don't move!"

The Frenchman stopped in front of a large bay window that looked out over a topiary garden of boxwoods. The sun was setting, and the sky was tinted with a delicate orange hue. Its unexpected beauty contrasted with the buzzing of the colony at work behind him. He went back to the Uccello painting his memory had resurrected. In the foreground, knights fought to the death in an indescribable melee, but behind them in the bucolic fields, rabbits and hares ran free. Tristan had never been able to understand why or how the painter had placed the images of war and natural harmony side by side. Now he knew. Evil could coexist with beauty.

A shadow appeared between him and the sky. Tristan emerged from his thoughts. The officer who had taken him from the arena was standing just a few feet away. He wasn't wearing the terrible black uniform anymore, but an elegant travel suit, as if he'd just booked a room at the hotel. Despite his civilian garb, the guard recognized his rank.

"Here is the prisoner, Oberführer."

Weistort sent him away without a word, then moved towards the garden. Tristan followed him to a table, where the SS officer sat down. The estate surrounding the hotel extended all the way down the hill to a winding road that led to the city and the ocean. From far away, Barcelona looked mostly intact—a few dark holes between buildings evoked the intensity of the fighting in the streets. Weistort was looking in the other direction, towards the forest of green oaks that circled the hill.

"Forests inspire me. I enjoy contemplating them, savouring their scent, listening to their sounds. In Germany, forests are the realm of darkness. The light can't pierce the canopy of tall pines to reach the forest floor, where the old gods hide."

He gestured towards a worm-eaten calvary at the far end of the garden.

"How can anyone believe in a God so stupid he ended up on a cross? But it's a new era, and soon a new symbol will dominate the world, bringing with it a reign of order and power."

"I'm not sure the inhabitants of Guernica, who sampled your power in the shape of the bombs that razed their village, share your love of order."

"A historical detail no one will remember," replied Weistort. "Just like you, if I so choose."

The Oberführer had just opened a tattered red file on the table. The typewritten pages inside featured handwritten annotations in the margins.

"The judge who interrogated you at Montjuic did a good job. Surprising for a Spaniard. I see you speak several languages, including German. You studied in Paris?"

"Art history."

"Yes, with a speciality in the early Renaissance. I see you worked on Paolo Uccello. Did you know his masterpiece, *The Battle of San Romano*, was cut into three pieces?"

"Yes, one is in Paris, one in London, and the last one is in Italy."

"The Reich will soon be opening the biggest museum in the world in Berlin—Albert Speer is working on it. I have no doubt this famous painting will be on display there in its entirety. After all, we have already occupied Paris. London is next."

Tristan interrupted him calmly. "Maybe, but I doubt your friend Mussolini will hand over the piece that's in Florence."

"The Duce! He couldn't even defeat the Greeks without our help. I'm certain his gratitude to us for sparing him such humiliation will motivate him to give Germany any treasures we desire."

"A tribute of sorts."

"A tribute paid in blood. Though that must be beyond you, given that you spend your days hunting down works of art like mere game animals and selling them at high prices to rich collectors—Jews, I'm sure."

"I don't ask my clients whether they're circumcised or baptized. If they like art, that's enough for me."

"Provided they can pay, since in your eyes, everything is for sale, and everything can be bought. You're a bounty hunter, an art mercenary."

"A mercenary working to *protect* art," specified Tristan.

Weistort closed the file. The time for this verbal jousting had come to an end. On to hand-to-hand combat.

"But all mercenaries have a price. That's why you're here. And I have a proposal for you."

Though he was surprised, Tristan continued to contemplate the far end of the garden. Every now and again, grey helmets emerged from the perfectly trimmed boxwoods, followed by the muffled sound of a pair of boots. Despite the beauty of his surroundings, it was hard to forget it was a prison.

"A few days ago, Heinrich Himmler made an official visit to Spain. He took advantage of the occasion to visit Montserrat Monastery."

"I didn't know the head of the SS was interested in spiritual matters."

Weistort continued, impassive: "He had the unfortunate surprise of learning that what he sought was no longer there. It seems that before the Reichsführer arrived, you also experienced an irrepressible desire to visit the abbey."

Tristan decided to reply in the same register: "Like the Reichsführer, I hate to miss any occasion to learn something new."

"I suppose you learn better at night, accompanied by armed friends, then?"

"Spain is a dangerous place these days."

"And the caretaker, you must have crucified him because he was such a bad tour guide?"

When both sides are pulling punches, the loser is the one who doesn't know when to quit. Tristan decided not to offer another sarcastic retort.

"If you're alluding to the monastery's treasure, you already know it was handed over to the Republican authorities just before their defeat. There's nothing left of it."

Weistort calmly dusted off one sleeve of his suit, then the other. Then he continued, "You see, the Reichsführer doesn't fancy chalices or crucifixes or even reliquaries. However, he is passionate about paintings."

The Nazis had an ambiguous relationship with art. Hitler, who had failed to get into the Vienna Academy of Fine Arts as a young man, decreed that everything that had been painted, drawn, or sculpted since his birth was perverted art. Monet and Picasso, for example, were degenerate painters, unworthy of museums. Notwithstanding his furious condemnation, certain high-ranking Nazis continued to collect Impressionist and Cubist paintings.

"Like Marshal Göring, the great collector of others' works of art?"

Weistort smiled. The head of the Luftwaffe was known for ravenously pillaging museums in conquered territories. His greed dishonoured him in the SS officer's eyes.

"Unlike Göring, the Reichsführer is very selective in his aesthetic choices. Right now, he's interested in a painting that was among the treasures of Montserrat. But look at that sunset. It's like the forest is on fire. Such beauty! It could be a medieval illumination. I wouldn't be surprised to see the Knights of the Round Table suddenly appear."

Tristan nodded politely. There was no point explaining to Weistort that before the quest for the Holy Grail became a universal myth, it was a French novel. The SS officer would have immediately alluded to a German legend he believed to be the one and only true source of all Arthurian tales.

"Personally," said Weistort, "when it comes to painting, I'm more interested in medieval miniatures. I like their naiveté, their innocence, the young women with braided hair and their knights in golden armour."

"Though I studied that period as well, I find the works of the Renaissance more inspiring. Maybe because, in them, man is the measure of all things," Tristan replied.

"There are men and *men*. They don't all have the same value. Moreover, I'm convinced that all of Italy's great artists are Aryans. Indeed, we should do genealogical research on the great painters. The Ahnenerbe could work on it."

Weistort could already imagine the face the Duce would make, with his wrinkled little scalp, when he heard that Leonardo da Vinci and Michelangelo were German!

"The Reichsführer has a passion for the Stations of the Cross and hoped to see those from Montserrat. You can imagine how disappointed he was when he learned they were no longer there."

"We only took objects of value—gold, gemstones and ivory. As for the paintings from the Stations of the Cross, we didn't touch them because they weren't worth a cent. An anonymous work by an even more anonymous artist. If the monks say we took it, they're wrong."

"To be precise, the abbot doesn't say someone took it. He says *you* took it."

Tristan didn't protest. Like in chess, when you're in a jam, it's often best to wait for the next move.

"In fact, the abbot of Montserrat is quite clear. You took *one* painting. Just one. You must have loved it at first sight, or maybe it was just your take of the treasure?"

"You know as well as I do that the painting is worthless."

"Worthless in artistic terms, yes. So why did you take it, then?"

"Let's call it aesthetic intuition."

Weistort flashed a strange smile.

"So, in Montserrat, surrounded by all that beauty accumulated over the centuries, you just couldn't resist? And you chose just one—randomly—out of all those dusty paintings?"

Tristan shook his head. "No, not randomly. The Stations of the Cross contained twelve paintings. I chose the one of Montserrat mountain. A souvenir, if you will."

The head of the Ahnenerbe clapped his hands and a soldier appeared. "Tell the guards we're coming down."

Weistort stood up and headed towards the lower gardens. Tristan followed.

"When this hotel was built, it used to host huge Belle Epoque parties. All of Europe came here to show off and have fun. Rich industrialists mingled with ruined nobles, experienced courtesans, and practised gamblers. But what really made the reputation of this luxury hotel wasn't its beds as plush as clouds or its gaming tables. It was the wine cellar."

They had just arrived in front of a vaulted door guarded by two uniformed soldiers.

"They say the hotel was built on a hill so they could dig the cellar deep into the best rock. Come, you'll see."

One of the guards pushed the door on its hinges and grabbed a torch. The smell of resin filled the air.

"The last manager had electric lighting put in. An anachronism, no, worse—heresy! We got rid of it, of course. Darkness is much more suitable for our activities."

The light from the flame made the thousands of pieces of quartz dotting the archway shimmer. Tristan understood why Weistort liked the place so much: it looked like an underground room in a medieval castle—a cavalcade of suits of armour and lances might spring from the walls at any moment.

"If you're looking for bottles," announced the Oberführer as he gestured towards the empty shelves along the walls, "you'll be disappointed. The hotel served as a military hospital and a prolonged stay in the cellar was part of the soldiers' self-prescribed treatment programme."

They walked ahead, a thin layer of sand crunching under their feet.

"As for the sand, it has nothing to do with preserving vintages. I had it spread out here. Every step, every sole leaves its mark. After each visit, I have it smoothed—several times a day if need be. So if anyone breaks in . . ."

Surprised, Tristan looked up at the tall, empty metal shelves. Why take such precautions if there was nothing left to steal?

"For optimal wine conservation, the cellar needed to be at a cool, constant temperature, so the hotel owners dug a well."

Weistort pointed. At the far end of the cellar, there was a tall circular rim with gargoyles sculpted into the stone.

"Did you know that in the Middle Ages the well-diggers' guild was suspected of sorcery? You don't come out from the depths of the earth unscathed. Wells were often thought to be the doors to hell."

The guard had put down his torch and was now using a winch to hoist the heavy slab off the top of the well.

"Men have always feared wells and the eye from the depths that watches them."

"Not anymore."

"You think? Look, then!"

Tristan leaned over the ledge, then stepped back, terrified. The walls of the well were dotted with men clinging to any stone they could grasp, dangling into the abyss like flies in a spider's web.

"They don't even scream anymore," announced Weistort. "They're afraid of using up too much energy and falling into the darkness."

"Who are they?"

"Germans, traitors who joined the Republicans. Most of them are communists who came to train in Spain. The information and contacts they have are important pieces of information we need to dismantle their clandestine networks in Germany."

One of the prisoners was having an increasingly difficult time holding on. Tristan noticed he had a number tattooed on his shaved skull.

"28," read Weistort. "He's already been interrogated twice. He has nothing else to tell us."

The guard walked over to the winch to close the opening.

"Drop the slab hard," instructed the Oberführer.

The soldier did as he was told. A loud boom rang out.

Followed by a scream.

The man had just let go.

Weistort took hold of Tristan's arm. "So, why don't you tell me where I can find this painting?"

13

A thick silence reigned in the meeting room. The members of the Gordon Circle focused their attention on the images that flashed across the screen.

Smiling blond Europeans sitting on the ground around a low table with Tibetan monks. Another German measured the head circumference of a laughing farm woman. These images appeared alongside footage of snow-covered mountains and a caravan moving up a steep, winding road.

"Oh, yes," exclaimed the Lord Privy Seal. "The Schäfer expedition. If I remember correctly, we suspected the Germans were developing political ties with the Tibetan government to attack the Indian border."

"That is all true, but only part of the bigger picture," replied Malorley. "After Schäfer left, the nation's leader, the Rinpoche, contacted our agent posted in Lhasa. He was hysterical. He claimed the Nazis had betrayed him and stolen a priceless talisman from his people."

A new image appeared on the screen. A sculpture of a tall man with pronounced Asian features holding a swastika in his hands.

"The Kangyur swastika," continued Malorley. "It is said to ensure stability in the world and contain knowledge of all things. The Germans stole it, murdered the monks guarding it, and sent it to Berlin. With some unexpected consequences . . ."

New images materialized.

"That's horrific!" gasped Lady Beltham.

They depicted two men lying in hospital beds, their faces

mangled as if they'd been burned by acid. The skin had peeled off in strips and their hair was gone, leaving behind bald heads with gaping wounds. Their eyes were shapeless craters and their noses had literally melted.

"One of our agents got his hands on this photo, taken in a military hospital in Berlin. The five SS soldiers who came back with the sacred swastika were all afflicted with a mysterious illness. According to the medical reports, their bodies were ravaged from the inside out. The unfortunate patients were euthanized, and their bodies were immediately incinerated. But this isn't the most troubling aspect of all this. One of the files indicates that these men were exposed to radiation that probably came from the swastika."

"A radioactive material?" asked the Head of the Home Forces.

"No, General Brooke," replied Malorley. "Please listen closely. On the report, the German doctors wrote only, 'Energy of unknown nature, a thousand times more powerful than all sources of radioactivity.'"

Whispers coursed through the room. Malorley quieted them and continued. "They moved the swastika to Himmler's private residence, Wewelsburg Castle. An impenetrable fortress. They have had the swastika since March 1939, six months before they invaded Poland and began the war."

Lady Beltham broke the silence. She seemed enthralled by the commander's words.

"There's something I don't understand about all this. How did the Germans ever learn about this talisman?"

Malorley's face darkened as painful memories surfaced. He gestured to Sebastian to change slides. The image of a bearded medieval king with a fierce expression appeared.

"They managed to steal a book thought to be a legend—the *Thule Borealis Kulten*—from a bookseller in Berlin. It was written in the Middle Ages and is said to have belonged to Emperor Frederick Barbarossa before it disappeared. It tells a curious tale from a time long ago, before Ancient Greece, even before the pyramids. A mythical continent, Hyperborea, cradle of the so-called Aryan race, was faced with the onset of an ice age. Its inhabitants fled to the four corners of the earth, while their four lords hid the symbols of their power. Four swastikas symbolizing water, air, earth, and fire. The talisman revered by the Tibetans and taken by the Nazis in 1939, is thought to be one of them."

The screen went dark as the projector's hum went silent.

"The *Thule Borealis Kulten* should contain clear directions to the places where the other relics are hidden," continued Malorley.

The admiral spoke up. "Is this a joke, Commander? It sounds like you think this Tibetan swastika has . . . magical powers. And that it convinced Hitler to go to war!"

"I wouldn't go so far as to use the word 'magic'," Malorley replied dryly. "I haven't believed in magic since I learned to dress myself. But my profession requires me to take all possibilities seriously. Even the most outlandish. I am convinced that the Germans have a potentially dangerous object, one that has had a clear impact on the outbreak of war. And the problem is that there are three more of them out there somewhere."

Admiral Cunningham raised his eyebrows and replied with a hint of disdain, "Before the war, I was invited to Germany twice by our ambassador, for the Olympic Games in Berlin and then for bilateral talks. I met my counterparts from the Kriegsmarine and chatted with the Wehrmacht generals. They seemed to have their feet properly anchored to the ground of their bloody Reich. They talked about tanks, bombers, and steel, not sorcery and charms."

"With all due respect, you didn't meet the right people."

"What do you mean?"

Malorley looked for support from the banker, who offered an encouraging smile. The SOE officer continued: "I apologize for not being clear enough. When I spoke of the Germans, I wasn't talking about the regular army or even about most of the Nazi officers. I was referring to a few high-ranking officials who are pragmatic and nevertheless firm believers in these stories from another era."

"You've either said too much or not enough. Explain yourself more clearly," said Lady Beltham.

Malorley had expected disbelief. He gestured to the banker to turn the projector back on.

"To make things clearer, I'm going to talk to you about the mystical school of thought in which the Nazi party has been steeped since its founding. Watch the drawing on the screen carefully.

"This is the coat of arms of the Thule Gesellschaft," continued Malorley. "A German secret society founded in 1919, one year after Germany's capitulation in the First World War. Take note of the symbol at the top of the dagger: it's a gammadion, or more precisely, a swastika, with rounded lines. The Thule was made up of aristocrats, wealthy businessmen, philosophers, and soldiers who were disgusted by Germany's defeat, which they blamed on communists, Jews, and Freemasons rather than their incompetent generals. There was nothing original about this way of thinking, which was very common in the nationalist movement of the time, known as the Germanorden. But what set the Thule apart from other *völkisch* organizations was its extreme interest in esotericism. All of its members were passionate about the occult and mysticism, and they all engaged in pagan rituals."

A hand was raised.

"What does *völkisch* mean?"

"They were xenophobic nationalist groups that flourished all over Germany during the second half of the 19th century. They believed national unity could only be achieved by raising awareness about what it meant to be 'German'. Race was a crucial factor for them."

On the screen, a new image replaced the Thule coat of arms. A blond warrior faced off with a polar bear, axe in hand.

"But let's get back to the Thule. They believed that over a hundred thousand years ago, a white, superior race lived on a mythical continent located at the North Pole: Hyperborea. The boreal race. The Thule ideologues were also certain that other, inferior races—non-white, black, Jewish—had tried to exterminate them. In this worldview, thousands of years of human history are reduced to a ruthless battle of the races. And of course, they felt

Aryans must reign again as masters, even if that meant exterminating all the inferior men. Sound familiar?"

"The legend from your book, the *Borealis* whatsit," replied General Brooke attentively.

"The leaders of the Thule decided they needed a populist vehicle to spread their venom, so they created a puppet political party: the German Workers' Party. Which we now know under another name."

He heard murmuring throughout the room.

"National Socialist?" suggested one of the participants.

"Correct. Enter a man you're fairly familiar with: Adolf Hitler. At the time, he was just a lonely demobilized corporal without any claim to fame. Like millions of Germans, he spent his time nursing his frustrations over defeat and brooding in a country devastated by war. The penniless failed artist agreed to work for what was left of the army intelligence services. In 1919, his superiors sent him to spy on a group of agitators."

A male voice Malorley didn't recognize rose up from the right side of the table. "So, Hitler didn't found the Nazi party?"

"No. However, he did gain recognition for his talents as a public speaker. In less than six months, he went from being a lowly informant to a charismatic leader under the protection of the Thule, which filled his head to the brim with its toxic beliefs. The swastika, the Sieg Heil salute, the belief in an Aryan race and its pure, sacred blood, and more."

"And over the next fourteen years, he underwent a total metamorphosis. The amateur painter became a professional dictator," added Sebastian Moran. "Quite the career change."

Approving whispers could be heard in the audience. Malorley knew he had scored some points. But it wasn't over yet.

"What about the Führer's ridiculous moustache? Is it an occult symbol too?" asked the admiral in a biting tone.

Chuckles rang out here and there.

"Commander, if I've understood correctly, you're telling us that the Nazis took their inspiration from a kind of perverted mysticism and that Hitler was hardly more than a puppet in the hands of a group of nutcases. I don't find that to be a very convincing argument for his rise to power. If you weren't a director at the SOE, I would have walked out quite some time ago."

"Let me be clearer. Hitler rose to power thanks to a combination of terribly rational factors. The country was humiliated by the defeat of 1918, ravaged by economic crisis, and influenced by pernicious propaganda. He benefited from support from the military and industrialists, and knew how to work the democratic system to ensure he was properly elected. But what I'm trying to help you understand is the dual nature of Nazism. It's a political party, but also a religion. And like all religions, it is underpinned by beliefs, and its leaders incorporate these irrational tenets into their mindset. Hitler may be the prophet of the Nazi party, but his sacred book was written by others before him. I—"

"I don't see how any of this can help us win the war. What do you suggest? That we send a commando unit to assassinate the leaders of this Thule cult?"

Malorley shook his head. "No. During Hitler's rise to power, he distanced himself from the secret society, though several of his closest advisers, including the party leader Rudolf Hess, were still members for some time. When he finally reached the top in 1933, he dissolved the Thule once and for all. This is the key to my presentation. And it focuses on a new and disturbing character, whom you all already know."

The screen came to life again with a Nazi parade featuring long rows of men in black uniforms marching in step in the dark. Torches lit their faces. A man in an SS dress uniform with small, round glasses and a cunning face waved to them with a satisfied expression. The footage paused on him.

"Himmler, the second most powerful and most dangerous man in Germany after Hitler. What you may not know is that the head of the SS and the police is also a student of the occult, magic, and pagan mysticism. He was never a member of the Thule, but he went even further by creating the SS in the image of a chivalric order. With rites, ranks, and a belief in the magical powers of pure

Aryan blood, which must be preserved at all costs. He despises both Jews and Christians and wants to reinstitute pagan religions in Germany. Like Hitler and a few other party officials, Himmler is no normal man. He is the very embodiment of Nazism's unique duality. He can build Dachau while at the same time founding the Ahnenerbe Forschungs- und Lehrgemeinschaft, an institute responsible for exploring his occult vision of the world, with the help of leading scientists. Whilst by day he dallies with new methods of torture using electricity, by night he sends expeditions to places like the Canary Islands to look for Atlantis."

"What are you suggesting?" asked Lady Beltham. "That we finance a commando operation to take back this swastika?"

The admiral shook his head.

"It would be impossible," answered Sebastian Moran before Malorley could. "The talisman is as protected as a gold bar in the cellars of the Bank of England."

Malorley placed his palms on the table and answered calmly. "New information tells us that there's a second talisman, with the same powers. It cannot fall into the hands of the Nazis. That would be catastrophic."

"Where is it? In Tibet?" asked General Brooke.

"No. Last year Himmler went to Spain, to Montserrat Monastery in Catalonia, to get it. It wasn't there, but clues led his men to the other side of the Pyrenees where they're currently conducting excavations in a castle in the south of France. We must intercept them, whatever the cost. If the Nazis take it, I believe we can bid the free world a final farewell."

"That still doesn't tell us anything about the talisman stolen from Tibet," replied the admiral gruffly.

"That's a job for the scientists. Mine is to get my hands on this relic before the Germans. And to do that, I need the Prime Minister to send a commando unit as soon as possible. That's why I'm here before you tonight."

"Absolutely ridiculous. Comical," muttered the admiral.

"You all know me," intervened Moran. "There's no one more rational than I, but I never leave anything to chance. That's how

I built my fortune. We must help the commander and influence the Prime Minister. A commando unit isn't much in the grand scheme of things."

A man who had been silent to this point raised his hand to speak. It was the personal secretary of King George VI.

"I propose we vote."

14

The dark shadow of the cathedral fell on the walls like a black cloud before a storm. The house of God crushed everything with the weight of its stones. The buildings around it seemed to be on their knees, frozen in a position of prayer. Behind their shutters, closed against the heat, their residents must have been sleeping, their nightmares filled with crypts and gargoyles. In any case, no one was out in the street. The tank, which led the convoy, moved ahead slowly. The black muzzle of its canon seemed to be sniffing each street, each façade, on the hunt for prey. Though General Franco was celebrating victory over his people in Madrid, parts of the country remained outside his control. Partisan groups still held areas in the Pyrenees, bases from which they launched attacks on the plains. Oberführer Weistort had taken no risks. Since they'd left Barcelona, they'd travelled the dusty roads with protection close by. The tank had just parked on the central square. Its gun turret spun around, investigating every last inch of the area before the cars were authorized to park near the cathedral. Doors slammed as soldiers jumped out into the deserted square and blocked all roads in or out.

"The perimeter is secure, Oberführer!"

Still in civilian clothes, Weistort unfolded his tall body as if he'd been locked in a suitcase for the trip. Despite the lack of space in the car, his suit was barely wrinkled. He studied it closely, searching for a fold or pull in the fabric. Once his inspection was finished, he looked around the square until he laid eyes on a typically medieval building next to the town hall.

Museo Gótico.

Tristan got out of the second car, with a guard on either side of him. They let him take a few steps, but he could feel their gaze on the back of his neck. Right where a bullet would be instantly fatal.

"So, this is the museum where you hid out after Barcelona fell?" asked Weistort, though he knew the answer.

The Frenchman walked over and pointed to one of the barred windows that looked out over the square. "That was my office," he said.

"But how did the people here welcome you?" asked Weistort, puzzled.

"On the morning I arrived, I explained that I was a curator at the history museum in Barcelona and that I'd had to flee when the city fell. The authorities had already left, and the locals were afraid of pillagers. Since I was willing to work for room and board alone . . ."

"But after three months they gave you a real salary, and after six, they doubled it."

"Since I didn't have many visitors, I drafted a comprehensive catalogue of the museum's collections."

The Oberführer was sceptical.

"I can understand paying you for that, but why give you a raise?"

"I claimed the museum's rarest pieces had been donated by the town's most prominent families. You can make archives tell any story you like, you know. I named the different galleries after them. They were very pleased to receive such an honour."

The German smiled. Vanity was truly the Spaniards' worst vice.

They were standing in front of the entrance to the museum, where a terrified municipal employee abandoned his post without a word. The smell of saltpetre wafted up from the disjointed floorboards. The scent was dark and foreboding, as if the cellars were about to swallow the old building whole. Without wasting any time on the Roman or medieval relics in their display cases, Weistort hurried into the painting gallery. Two Madonnas feeding

Jesuses from pale breasts hung alongside portraits of obscure celebrities of centuries past, with bald heads and waxy moustaches. Under the blackened varnish, their names—written in faded gold letters—had almost completely disappeared. One display contained a random selection of haphazardly arranged paintings, as if forgotten in a corner. Portraits of ecstatic saints and rapturous Christs with hearts that shone brightly. A religious bric-a-brac no one would ever want.

With his surprisingly white hand, the head of the Ahnenerbe pointed to a small, faded painting which could easily have gone unnoticed. It depicted a mountain shaped like a cone with its top cut off. Several walls and a tower perched at the top. The oversized, five-pointed white star that shone in the sky clashed with the rest of the composition.

"Item AF 133, 'presumed view of Montserrat, unknown artist and date'," announced Tristan.

At the word *presumed*, Weistort looked questioningly at the Frenchman. The latter walked over to a wall and removed another painting by its rickety frame.

"This is a view of Montserrat. As you can see, the abbey isn't on the peak, but set into the flank of the mountain. Moreover, the monastery doesn't have any outer walls."

"What are you getting at?"

"Your painting isn't of Montserrat, but of another location. It's not even an abbey—it's a castle. Look closely at the tower that rises over the top of the walls. It's crenellated. It's not a steeple, it's a fortress tower."

"Could you date the castle?"

Tristan examined the details. "I'm not a medieval history specialist, but the outer wall ramparts don't have any machicolations. There are no flanking towers and it doesn't even have a barbican. No sophisticated defence features. I'd say the painting is of a *castrum*—a castle from the 12th or 13th century."

"Which would suggest the artist saw it with his own eyes, to depict it like this?"

The Frenchman shook his head. "Not necessarily. Though I

was unable to date the painting with precision, given the style and use of colour, it must have been done after 1500."

Weistort liked puzzles. He felt that even if they wore military uniforms, academics should remain researchers at heart. He examined the painting closely to verify his prisoner's affirmations before returning to the interrogation.

"What is your hypothesis?"

"It's a copy of a much older painting or drawing. Most likely medieval. Maybe the original was damaged from the passage of time, so someone made a copy. And then slipped it into the Stations of the Cross. Perhaps to avoid drawing attention."

Cautious, the Oberführer looked over his shoulder, but the guards had stayed near the entrance to the room, where they could hear nothing. He turned back to the painting. This Frenchman was turning out to be quite competent. Almost too competent.

"So, sometime after 1500, someone made a copy of a painting representing a castle from the Middle Ages, to hide it in a nondescript series of stations-of-the-cross paintings?"

Tristan nodded. It seemed Weistort felt the need to reformulate the information he provided to better absorb it.

"Can you identify the castle?"

"If I saw it, maybe. But the painter didn't want people to identify it so easily. Quite the contrary, in fact. There are no visible details on the mountain, outer walls, or tower."

"So why hide it in the Stations of the Cross?"

"Maybe we need to examine it more closely."

Weistort carefully slid open the glass case and picked up the painting, making sure to only touch the back, to avoid damaging the cracked varnish. Up close, they could see that the star was located directly above the tower, and that the walls featured thin black lines, which must have been arrow slits. At the base of the ramparts, the mountain seemed to be fortified with a series of stone walls protecting the only road in. Nevertheless, aside from these architectural details, there were no other clues in the painting. The sky was a homogenous blue and the mountain a faded grey.

One small detail intrigued Tristan. Just below the top edge of the frame, there was a Roman numeral. He showed it to Weistort.

"XI," read the Oberführer. "The number in the Stations of the Cross that generally evokes the crucifixion."

"But there is no cross here, no Christ. The only aspect that fits is the mountain, since the Bible says Christ was crucified on Golgotha, Calvary hill."

"So, we should focus on the mountain?"

"The place or the word," Tristan suggested. "But that's not enough. If this painting has something to tell us, there must be another clue."

Weistort noticed an old Spanish armchair made of worn leather in a corner. A forgotten relic from the Golden Age, he suspected. He pushed it over to the display case and sat down like a lord from another era. He firmly believed one could only think properly sitting down.

"Let's be methodical about this," he proposed. "If we think there's some sort of sign or clue hidden here somewhere that could help us find the castle, where could it be? In the frame?"

Tristan smiled ironically. When he had worked at the museum, he had obviously removed the frame to see if it hid a signature. Rather basic for an art hunter.

"I see from your smirk that we can cross that off the list. I imagine you also checked the back of the painting?"

"The canvas is mounted on a wooden structure to keep it taut. There are no visible marks, inscriptions, stamps, hallmarks, or anything else. But the fact that it's mounted on such a simple wooden structure is already a clue. It means the painting could be quickly and easily removed, rolled up and carried."

"And hidden."

"So, if there's a message, it's somewhere in the painting."

Weistort uncrossed his legs and placed his palms flat on his thighs. He needed to concentrate. Since he remained silent, Tristan continued:

"There are only two possibilities, as I see it. The clue is either in the work itself, hidden under a layer of paint or varnish, or is in its components."

"Speak more plainly."

Despite the danger, Tristan could feel the enthusiasm washing over him. Like every time he found himself in front of an unknown work of art, he felt an irrepressible need to discover its meaning, which time and men might have hidden away. It was like a quest. Each painting was an enigma he had to solve. He had loved puzzles and riddles since he was a child. This insatiable interest in all things mysterious was what guaranteed his reputation in the art world. For him, a piece wasn't only beautiful to look at, it was also a story to uncover, a tale in need of telling.

"During the Renaissance, when this work was painted, intellectuals and artists were particularly interested in double meanings. This was when people began inventing codes. To find it, we need to look for anything that seems illogical or inconsistent. We need to look at it in a new light."

"It can't be the castle, wall, or tower. It all fits perfectly with the usual depiction of a fortress."

"The same goes for the star. It is oversized, but its five points are in line with the usual representation from the time."

"The mountain, then. Does anything stand out?"

Tristan had examined the painting closely and seen nothing. The painting was painfully banal. The artist, who was clearly in a hurry, didn't even take the time to detail a boulder or a stand of trees. It was like he had focused all his efforts on painting the access road, with its multiple twists and turns up to the summit. *Strange,* thought Tristan. *He didn't need to go into such detail. And all the turns are so misshapen. It would take hours to climb this path. It's completely—*

Tristan didn't finish his thought. He pivoted the painting left, then right.

"I've got it!"

Weistort jumped up from his chair. From a certain angle, the path disappeared, making way for a collection of interwoven curves, much like a signature.

"It's a hidden word!" exclaimed the Frenchman. "Start at the bottom, the first letter."

"An 's' followed by an 'é'."

The Frenchman turned the painting around. From the front, the accent on the "e" looked like a section of wall along the path. The Oberführer took hold of the work to better decipher it.

"The third letter is a 'g'."

"And then a 'u'."

"Ségu . . ."

"Ségur," said the intrigued Tristan as he leaned closer to the painting.

"What are you looking for?" asked Weistort suspiciously.

"There's an accent on the 'e'. That's strange, since Spanish doesn't have accented 'e's."

The Oberführer examined the work in turn. There was no doubt, the "e" was definitely accented.

Tristan quickly came to a conclusion. "French is the only language that commonly uses 'é'. If the name—'Ségur'—is written with one, it must refer to somewhere in France."

"Somewhere with a medieval castle," added Weistort, "on a cone-shaped mountain."

Tristan clapped his hands together. A guard near the door turned around, his gun at the ready.

"Montségur! It's a castle in the south of France, in the Pyrenees. It sits on a lone peak and is famous because—"

He didn't have time to finish his sentence.

"Guards!" shouted the Oberführer, his voice echoing through the walls of the old museum. The soldiers ran over. "Seize the prisoner."

In seconds, Tristan's wrists were clamped in palms as strong as a vice.

"Lock him up!"

As soon as the Frenchman had left the museum, Weistort called his logistics officer. "Transmit a priority request to the Reichsführer in person. He must send an SS detachment and an excavation team to Montségur Castle, in France, in the Free Zone."

15

The hammering grew louder every time the roar of the chainsaw quietened. Fine dust fell from the dirty ceiling, leaving a thin layer on the file he was consulting.

Here we go again.

Malorley rubbed his tired eyes and brushed away the grey debris with the back of his hand. How could he possibly concentrate in these conditions? Not only had the Propaganda and Psychological Warfare department been given offices in the dampest part of the building, but they'd also had to put up with the racket from the work for two weeks now.

He shouted in the general direction of the open door, which led to his secretary's tiny office. "Penny! For God's sake, tell them to stop that blasted construction while I'm working."

The jovial face of a red-headed woman appeared in the doorway. "Impossible, Commander. The builders are finishing the floor above us. That said, I do have some cotton-wool balls for your ears. Though I'm not sure that would be befitting for an officer of your rank."

Malorley smiled on the inside. His secretary—whom he shamelessly exploited—had a real gift for defusing tension. An invaluable quality when working at SOE headquarters. He got up stiffly and rested his elbows on the worn windowsill. A sea of umbrellas bustled past on Baker Street below. Rumour held that Churchill himself had chosen the address because of his unbridled love for all things Sherlock Holmes. From the outside, nothing about the elegant façade stood out from the neighbouring buildings. An understated plaque at the entrance simply said

Inter-Services Research Bureau, an unremarkable made-up name. But behind the opulent-looking walls, the formidable Special Operations Executive was hard at work. A hundred men and women toiled day and night with a single goal: to sow chaos in Nazi Europe.

Here, they plotted sabotage missions and organized the airdrops of agents, guns, and grenades. They even planned assassinations. While the leadership was British to the core, the hallways were always full of colourful foreign accents. Their hatred of conquering Germany left many people eager to come aboard. They all hoped to wash away the humiliations suffered by their occupied countries. Cavalry officers from the defunct Polish army rubbed elbows with French soldiers who had escaped Dunkirk and Czech police officers, who had just returned from commando training, where they had worked with former thieves from the Netherlands, Belgian royalists, and Norwegian socialists. They were all on their way to somewhere in this subversive Tower of Babel, all waiting to return home to rain fire on the Nazis.

Malorley was one of the organization's first officers. Shortly after war broke out, he had refused a position with MI6, Britain's official counter-intelligence service, to join the SOE's Propaganda and Psychological Warfare division. It was a perfect fit. Even within the SOE—where he was the third highest-ranking officer—his department was regarded as the shrewdest. Misinformation operations, fake radio stations, manipulation of diplomats, and research on all the Nazi leaders' vices. The Psychology division had become legendary within the SOE.

His secretary caught his eye. "Don't worry, Commander. Section F will be moving out of its offices to Orchard Court. We're at the top of the list for them."

"Speaking of Section F, could you return those files to them, please," asked Malorley, gesturing towards a pile of yellow files on his desk. "Tell Colonel Buckmaster that I have finally selected two of his people."

"Knowing F, he must have been absolutely thrilled to loan them out. His agents are like his own children."

"Sometimes you have to cut the cord," replied Malorley calmly. "I'll pay him a visit in about fifteen minutes."

"No need. He won't stop calling. I'd wager he'll be bursting in here any second."

When the secretary had closed his office door, he lit a Morland given to him by a friend in the admiralty he'd met at the *Times*. Morlands were his one vice—a delightful blend of contraband tobacco from Turkey and the Balkans. He exhaled a deliciously caramelized puff of smoke, then went back to studying the photos of the two agents chosen to accompany him on the commando operation.

A man and a woman. The first was in his thirties. He wore his dark-brown hair slicked back. His tired, anonymous face featured dull eyes showcased by dark circles. The kind of guy no one would think twice about, thought Malorley. His file said his name was Charles Grandel. A captain in the French army, second infantry regiment. He had reached London in August 1940 and volunteered for the SOE shortly thereafter. He had parachuted into the Loire-Atlantique region and was currently building a resistance network from scratch. His cover name was simply Charles.

Malorley passed the second photo in front of the first. Jane Colson, twenty-seven. Franco-British, born in Besançon. She was the daughter of a colonel in the British Indian Army and a French nurse. The family had moved to England two years before the war broke out. Malorley looked closely at the black-and-white picture. In it, the young blonde woman flashed a pouty, mocking expression. Only a handful of female agents had been recruited for active duty since the SOE's creation. Most of the women volunteers worked on administrative and logistical tasks.

Malorley still wasn't entirely sure about this second choice. He was uncomfortable sending a woman to France. Knowing the girl could be subjected to the Gestapo's most gruesome torture methods made him feel uneasy. But F had insisted he travel through the southwest of France with a woman. A couple was less noticeable, and not a single female agent had been stopped by the Germans to date.

Malorley wasn't fooled by F's thoughtfulness—the latter had protested against the operation loudly and clearly, particularly because of Malorley's personal involvement. If a high-ranking SOE officer were made prisoner, it would be a disaster for the service.

He put the photograph down and took a long, deep drag on the cigarette. Outside, the London sky was tinged with jet black. There was no way out now. It was one thing to plan a mission, quite another to participate in it. In less than two days, he would be parachuted into occupied France, near Bordeaux. This was enemy territory, where he would be treated like a spy if the Germans caught him. If such a thing occurred, his life expectancy wouldn't exceed that of a cow in a slaughterhouse—and his death would be far more painful.

He opened a drawer and took out a bottle of seventeen-year-old Oban, a birthday gift from his colleagues. He poured himself half a glass and silently toasted Otto Neumann, his German friend who had died a martyr. Then he raised his glass to the photo of Churchill that occupied the wall over a filing cabinet. Everything had been decided yesterday, when he'd been urgently summoned to Downing Street.

The Prime Minister's office reeked of cigars. Churchill was carefully studying a map of Europe pinned to the wall and hadn't even turned around to welcome the commander.

"So Malorley, you've gone over my head to gain leverage for your ridiculous hunch?"

Malorley stood as straight as a cricket stump. "I don't know what you mean, Mr. Prime Minister."

Churchill turned towards him, his expression furious.

"Don't play dumb! I got a call from His Majesty's secretary, urging me to read your preposterous report on . . . Oh blast, what's it called again?"

"The Ahnenerbe."

"Yes. Let me be clear, Malorley. If it were up to me, I would have sacked you on the spot. I don't believe in any of this magical, esoteric nonsense from another era for a single second. A talisman found in

Tibet, somehow helping Hitler win the war—it's pure hogwash! I refuse to put stock in such foolishness!"

"I didn't—"

"Let me finish. It's clear to me that you have somehow persuaded the Gordon Circle to back you. Which says a lot about the mental state of certain members of our society. So, get to the point. What exactly do you want?"

Malorley stared unblinkingly at Churchill. "The green light to put together a commando operation in southern France to find the other relic our enemies are after. We could parachute in six SOE agents and rely on local resistance fighters for the rest."

"Six agents, is that all? You say you really believe in this nonsense, but how far you are willing to go? You mean to risk the lives of valuable agents, who would be much more useful on other strategic missions."

Malorley continued to look the Prime Minister in the eye, despite his ironic expression. "I don't understand, Sir."

"Then let me be clearer. Are you willing to lead this mission, to venture into the wolf's den?"

Malorley's heart raced. He hadn't expected this suggestion. A few seconds ticked past.

"It would be an honour, Sir."

Churchill seemed disappointed.

"My God, you are just as crazy as the bloody Nazis. I just wanted to test your determination."

"I'll go."

Churchill shook his head. "It's too dangerous. You know too much about the SOE."

Malorley placed his hands on the desk. "We have new cyanide capsules that can be set into fillings. The department's dentist is a genius."

The Prime Minister had started pacing the room in irritation, his head bowed. He stopped suddenly and stared straight at Malorley, a look of determination in his eyes. "All right. You can send your team over. But make sure to use a convincing-enough fake goal in all your reports. I don't want anyone finding out, once I'm gone, that I authorized the quest for King Arthur in the middle of a war. When you get

*back, you'll fill me in on all your discoveries in person. Nothing in
writing. That is, if you discover anything at all, and actually make it
back. Are we clear?"*

"Yes, Sir."

*"And you can only have two SOE agents. You'll have to make do
with the French resistance fighters for the rest. I can already imagine
their faces when you tell them what you're after. Consult with F on
the details. And . . ." He waited a few seconds before concluding, "Enjoy
your trip to hell."*

*Malorley saluted and headed quickly for the door. Just as he was
about to leave, Churchill's voice echoed through the room.*

*"Commander, I hate being forced into things, even if it is by the
King himself. Don't ever do anything like that again or I'll have your
head dangling from the top of the Tower of London."*

The hammering had stopped, but the strident spinning of a drill
wasn't much better. Just as he was about to put the cotton-wool
balls in his ears, the door to his office burst open. A tall man with
thinning blond hair and a long, pale face stopped right in front
of his desk. F's expression was rather unfriendly.

"Have you chosen?"

Malorley pushed the two photos towards F. Colonel Buckmaster's
face darkened.

"Not Charles! He hasn't finished putting together his network.
There are ten other men with the same profile."

Malorley shook his head. "He's the only one who spent his
entire childhood in the Ariège region. In Lavelanet in fact, which
is just six miles from our target. He knows the area like the back
of his hand. Would you not agree that first-hand knowledge of the
terrain is an invaluable asset, Colonel?"

"Enough on that, let's talk about your target. I'm the head of
the France section and I still don't understand why the Prime
Minister's office is keeping everything under wraps for this mission.
I mean, for Christ's sake, are you after my job, Malorley?"

The commander's eyes widened in surprise. "Where are you
going with this?"

F pushed the files aside and sat down on the desk. "Don't play the fool. This is the first time since the France division was founded that I haven't been read in on a mission requiring help from my agents. It must be a big deal, since you're going as well. We both know that if all goes well, you'll be hailed as a hero."

Malorley smiled. "The results of this mission—whether positive or negative—will never be revealed to anyone at the SOE. So rest assured, I have neither the desire nor the required skills to take your job. I'd be happy to sign something to that effect, if you like."

F stared at him for a minute, then fished a cigarette out of his pack. "You're a strange man, Malorley. Truly strange. No wonder you're in charge of the Psychology division. So, how do you plan to proceed?"

Malorley unfolded a map of southern France and placed books over the edges. "Two days from now, Jane and I will be in the air, weather permitting. We'll parachute into Pessac, where the head of the Gironde network will welcome us. Charles will be waiting there."

There were two yellow lines on the map between Pessac and Toulouse.

"Jane and I will take the train from Bordeaux and pass into Free France on our way to Toulouse. A second contact will be waiting for us there. Grandel will take a lorry in order to minimize the risk of any of us getting caught."

Malorley's finger followed a red line along a twisting road to a small town. Buckmaster put on his reading glasses and leaned in towards the map. "Montségur. I've never heard of it before. I'm surprised there's anything of importance in a one-horse town like that." Buckmaster was true to his reputation—he never gave up.

Malorley continued calmly: "Once we've accomplished our mission, we will make for a small Mediterranean port, Collioure, where we'll wait for a submarine just off the coast."

"A submarine. Is that all? My agents usually come home through Spain and Portugal, or manage to get on a plane. Are you sure you still don't want to tell me more about this business?"

"I'm sorry, Colonel. On the bright side, if I don't make it back, you can help choose my successor. Somebody less strange . . ."

F took off his glasses and rubbed the bridge of his nose. "Contrary to popular belief, I like you, Malorley. I sincerely hope you'll succeed. And that you'll bring my agents home safely."

"I'll do my best."

"In our line of work, doing your best is only the first step. Good luck to you!"

Malorley stared pensively at the door F had just closed. As farewells go, it was a step up from Churchill's last words.

He pulled a new file out of the drawer, opened it and took out a photograph. The face featured an icy smile. The man wore a black-brimmed hat with a skull symbol. A thin scar travelled the length of his cheek. Though he was smiling, his expression was arrogant. A rectangular sticker on the bottom of the photo read *Oberführer Karl Weistort* in thin, precise handwriting.

He'd only seen him once, in Berlin, on *Kristallnacht.* There had been a corpse between them: the man he hadn't been able to save. Professor Neumann.

Malorley ran his finger over the blurry picture.

This time, Weistort, we'll do more than cross paths on the street.

16

Three days later
Castello d'Empuries
May 1941

Tristan came stumbling out of the museum's cellar, pushed by two soldiers shouting like men possessed. One of the cars parked in front of the cathedral took off quickly, its tyres squealing on the square's cobblestones. Frightened residents watched the scene from behind their shutters. Who was the man they were dragging? And who were these soldiers in jet-black uniforms? Their guttural shouts echoed against the façades. Suddenly, they picked up the prisoner and threw him into a car as its motor revved. Behind the windows, women crossed themselves while the men uttered prayers for the dead, their fists clenched in frustration at their powerlessness.

The car got underway. Its long silhouette projected a predatory shadow onto the walls, as if it were on the hunt for game. Once silence had returned, Weistort stepped out of the museum. Wearing a straw hat, he looked every bit the tourist, a sight which only added to the townspeople's confusion. But they'd got used to so much during the civil war that they were hardly surprised by such terrifying scenes. Weistort held the painting in his hand. It would be sent to Berlin, by diplomatic purse, then on to the Ahnenerbe laboratories, where it would be studied down to the tiniest detail. They would restore its varnish and examine every single brush-stroke. They would investigate every aspect, but they would find nothing. Of that the Oberführer was certain. Tristan had already found the message. The message from the past that would catapult the Reich to the zenith of its glory.

Weistort crossed the square. Behind him, the tank's engine had just roared to life. Soon they would disappear, as mysteriously as they had arrived. And no one would ever know that the outcome of the war was determined at Castello d'Empuries.

But first, he had to do something about Tristan, whom he'd held prisoner while waiting for the research team to arrive in Montségur.

In the lower part of the city, a stretch of the defensive outer wall had survived the invasions and destruction. Built of heavy ochre stones, the ruin rose up over a former ditch, which was never fully dry. The soldiers hadn't chosen the place randomly—it was perfect for a firing squad. The bullets that went straight through the body would end up in the wall, and as for the bodies, the bottom of the ditch—damp and easy to dig—made a perfect final resting place. Weistort watched attentively as they carried out the rituals that preceded the execution. It was his first time, and rituals—particularly those related to death—fascinated him.

A sergeant lined up the soldiers and selected a few shooters. Five in all. The men stepped out of line and held out their rifles. The sergeant collected their guns and distanced himself from the group to load them. When he'd put in the cartridges and checked the breeches, he came back and placed the rifles on the ground. When their names were called, the soldiers each selected a gun from the pile. They all knew that one of the guns wasn't loaded, so every man could hope he hadn't fired the fatal shot.

Weistort shrugged. This ritual was ridiculous, unworthy of soldiers of the Reich. The new man Nazi Germany was building was supposed to know neither fear nor remorse. He had only to follow his will, his strength, and his absolute faith in his superiority. Soon consciences and humanity would be but a vague memory, a vestige of times past, like the charred walls of synagogues in Berlin and Warsaw.

Tristan was still in the car. A guard kept his face pushed into the back of the driver's seat. He could hardly breathe. His heart was pounding in a bid to escape his chest, to flee far from his ill-fated body. There was a shout outside, and the guard got him up. The sun was blinding. He was thirsty. The sergeant roughly removed Tristan's jacket to check he wasn't wearing a chain or medallion that could withstand a bullet, then tied his hands together and walked him over to the wall.

Tristan realized what was happening when he felt the uneven stones push into his back. The firing squad was already in place, rifles at their feet. He thought of Goya's *El Tres de Mayo*, which he had admired one spring day in Madrid. He could see the contorted bodies riddled with bullets. The dead in the painting were Spanish and the bullets French, but the firing squad was the same—silent and impassive. He looked over at the ash-coloured ditch. He'd never imagined he might be buried face-down. The sergeant clicked his heels and readied a black blindfold. Tristan refused. They could take his life, but he would own his death. The officer turned as if in a parade and joined the squad.

The first order rang out.

The soldiers levelled their guns.

Then, there was a second order, but Tristan didn't hear it.

His body bounced off the wall and rolled into the ditch.

He awoke with a scream when they removed his shirt. The wadding from the bullets had charred the material and burned it into his skin.

"Risen, like Christ," said Weistort ironically.

Tristan instinctively ran his hands over his chest, but a shovelful of dirt landed in his face. He coughed and opened his eyes. A soldier was digging a hole next to him.

"Don't worry, we won't bury you alive."

Men came for his shoes next. Tristan recognized the sergeant who had led the firing squad.

"What are you doing?" he mumbled.

"We're finishing you off," replied the Oberführer calmly. "For the moment, everyone thinks you're dead. The soldiers who fired on you and the townspeople who heard the shots. But that's not enough. Take off your trousers."

Tristan complied without understanding. Pain shot through his upper body. He had four round holes in his chest.

"Non-lethal rounds. The sergeant loaded them into the guns. They burn, you bleed and sometimes the wounds get infected, but they won't kill you."

Tristan felt sick. A vile smell wafted through the air. One of the bullets must have pierced his body anyway. He was rotting from the inside out.

"It's true, he's starting to smell," agreed Weistort. "Not surprising, given the fact that he's been in the boot for at least two hours."

The Frenchman thought he was going mad.

"Look up."

An unmoving hand hung lifelessly over the edge of the ditch, surrounded by a buzzing swarm of flies.

"We picked him up on the way. Most likely a hastily executed prisoner. Around your age and height, same hair colour. Two bullets to the heart. We'll just add two more."

The sergeant was already dressing the corpse in Tristan's clothes.

"Don't forget to tie the shoelaces."

Tristan stood up, his back against the side of the ditch. He was dizzy as he watched the SS soldiers continue their work unflaggingly. The hole was the shape of a grave now and the body looked like Tristan. The Oberführer handed the Frenchman's forged papers to the sergeant, with dried blood covering the picture.

"Slip them into his back pocket and finish up."

The sergeant backed away, aimed and fired two shots into the chest.

"Now you're dead," announced Weistort.

Tristan staggered in shock.

"Let me explain what will happen next. In an hour or two, the people will come. They'll dig up the body and empty his pockets. When they see he was a foreigner, they'll be terrified and alert the Guardia Civil."

Tristan figured out the rest. Once the execution had been recorded by the local authorities, the information would be sent to the French embassy in Madrid. In a month, he would be dead. Officially. For good.

"You no longer exist," continued Weistort. "You'll have to get used to that."

The soldier who had just hastily filled the grave opened a rucksack and took out a light-green uniform for Tristan. Still stunned, Tristan put on the fatigues. He had risen from the dead, but now found himself in hell.

A car was parked in the shade, beneath a stand of grey trees. The sergeant opened the doors. He was wearing his service pistol just below his belt buckle, the handle turned to the right, ready for him to grab it at a second's notice. Weistort gestured to the Frenchman to get in the car.

"We're leaving. It's still a long way to the border."

Two little swastika flags adorned the bonnet of the car, just above the headlights. Tristan was sitting in the back seat next to the sergeant, who didn't take his eyes off him. All the road-blocks they encountered let them pass without question when they saw the Nazi flags—it was like magic. Some of the Spanish officers even went so far in their admiration as to execute the Nazi salute, which Weistort answered half-heartedly. As they entered Girona, someone even handed him a photo of Hitler, cut out of a propaganda newspaper. Its former owner must have cherished it like a relic.

"The Catholic church has too much influence in this country. It's condemned the Spaniards to superstition and the fanaticism of the ignorant. Do you believe, Tristan?"

"Not at the moment."

Weistort burst into laughter.

"You should, though. You've risen from the dead. And now you've been reincarnated as a German soldier. You're moving up in the world."

"Why didn't you just kill me?"

"Because I respect intelligence, and yours could serve Great Germany's cause."

Tristan didn't push it. They had just stopped in a village of alleyways so narrow that the buildings on either side seemed to touch. The heat was stifling, even in the shade. The driver popped the bonnet to cool the motor, then went in search of water. A door slammed and a young woman appeared with a wicker basket in her arms. She was headed for the wash house. Her espadrilles tapped the cobblestones at a relaxed pace. Neither the soldiers nor the heat seemed to bother her. She was like the beating heart of the city. As she walked along the side of the car, Tristan listened to the silky swish of her dress against the metal. He closed his eyes to fully appreciate the sensual music. How long had it been since he'd dreamed of a woman? The sound of her footfalls was fading, but not the hope she'd kindled in him. He had forgotten there was still a world beyond dead bodies on the side of the road and prisons filled with screams of suffering. He suddenly felt as if a bright future full of promise stretched out before him, delicate flowers that would soon yield fruit. The bonnet slammed shut. A thin cloud of steam rose up from the motor. Tristan wondered if the girl had been a vision. In myths and legends goddesses always disappeared in a cloud of fog.

"Can we go?" Weistort asked the driver impatiently.

"Right away, Sir," he replied with a click of his heels.

The car got underway. As soon as they left the village, the blue silhouette of the Pyrenees appeared in the distance. The last olive fields now climbed terraced hills, which grew increasingly steep and rocky. Pine forests rose alongside the grey flanks of the mountains. The French border was near.

"How long until we reach immigration?"

The sergeant unfolded a map and followed a road that twisted and turned amid areas of green until his finger reached a red dotted line.

"Two hours, Oberführer."

Weistort turned to Tristan. From the side, the SS officer bore a striking resemblance to a bird of prey.

"Just before we reach the border, we'll give you German military papers. You'll have a name and a rank. If they ask any questions, I'll answer for you, but after that you can fend for yourself, since you speak German. Montségur, here we come!"

PART TWO

I remember the Knipperdolling Anabaptist cult in Münster. Like the Third Reich, they combined romantic ideals of salvation with cruelty, and religious altruism with absurd oddities. Devotion was intertwined with brutality, and intense obedience with enthusiastic dilettantism. This approach to community nearly ruined a Westphalian village in the 16th century and threw the entire world into chaos in the 20th.

Albert Speer, Adolf Hitler's architect and Minister of Production. (From "On Nazism" in *L'Empire SS*, Robert Laffont, Paris, 1981.)

17

The castle's outline was barely visible in the darkness that had washed over the countryside. Approaching from the north, only the round, crenellated tower, which seemed to fade into the sky, was visible. In the cold night air, the stars had disappeared behind clouds fleeing eastward, towards solitude. If it weren't for the heady purr of the car's engine and the wan rays from its headlights, it could have been another era, the age of wandering knights and hungry wolves. The car swerved suddenly, stopping at the edge of a ditch. A group of men had appeared before them. In nothing but their shirtsleeves despite the spring chill, they walked along silently, escorted by guards on horseback.

The officer sitting next to the driver turned around. "Prisoners from Niederhagen. They're restoring the castle on the Reichsführer's orders, to speed things along."

With her legs crossed and her hands on her knee, Erika von Essling remained silent. She watched the men with their vacant eyes as they passed by, as if sleep walking.

"This way," explained the officer enthusiastically, "even political and racial deviants can be a part of the collective effort to build our Great Reich."

As he spoke, he gazed intently at the young woman, trying to imagine the body under her tailored grey skirt suit. He smoothed his collar so she would be sure to see the two silver "S"s, but it was no use. She had barely spoken since the beginning of the journey.

"How long until we arrive?"

"Less than five minutes."

He searched for the castle entrance at the end of the road. At least once there, he'd be able to be himself again, with his SS comrades. Since he'd picked up this . . . What was she again? Oh yes, this archaeologist, he'd felt rather helpless. He, who had fought on the front lines in Poland and France! Her indifference made him feel worthless. He didn't even exist for her. He was just like his farmer ancestors, anonymous for generations, good for nothing but tending nobles' land. She, however, was clearly a member of the elite. Her family's name had resounded over every battlefield in Europe for the past millennium and was now a leader in German manufacturing.

"Here we are."

Erika leaned towards the window. A row of torches framed the bridge that led to the castle's main courtyard. The car slowed as it entered.

"Stop, please. I'd like to walk the rest of the way."

The driver complied and the officer hurried around to open her door. The young woman noticed that he took advantage of the occasion to glance furtively at her legs. These SS officers, who fancied themselves the country's new elite, lacked refinement. Their pristine black uniforms and boots as shiny as mirrors could do nothing to change her mind.

"May I ask why you chose to become, um, an archaeologist? Is that right?"

She smiled disdainfully. How many times had she been asked this question? Excavating sites, drawing up maps, and publishing reports seemed unthinkable for a woman. Especially at a time when masculinity was on parade in every street and glorified in every shouted speech.

At the age where she should have been choosing a husband, she'd decided to take up studying history. Probably in part due to her uncle's influence. He was a traveller of the world, who had told her amazing bedtime stories when she was little. The discovery of Troy, the tombs and pyramids of Egypt, the Mayan ruins . . . Magical tales that marked her for life.

At the university in Cologne, she had been the only woman to study archaeology. And, to add insult to injury, she finished first in her class.

"Aren't you going to answer me?" asked the SS officer.

They had just entered the large, cobblestone courtyard. Light from several of the windows revealed medieval sculptures on the walls.

"Do you really want to know what archaeologists do? Then look up. You see that sculpture in the corner there?"

"Yes, it's a hunting scene. A hunter with a bow and arrow chasing a boar."

"But, as the shape of the windows reveals, this castle is from the 17th century, when hunting was most often accomplished with guns."

"I don't understand."

"Didn't you say this castle was being restored? I'm guessing your leader, Himmler, who is incredibly passionate about the Middle Ages, decided to age it a little, even if that means stretching the truth."

"The Reichsführer is a very cultivated man. He would never—"

"Look at the bow."

The stunned officer looked up again.

"The string is much too tight to shoot an arrow with any sort of precision. It would be impossible to land a fatal shot on the boar. They wouldn't have made that mistake in the Middle Ages. It's a fake."

They had just reached the grand staircase, which led to the rooms upstairs.

"But how can you know that?"

"I killed my first buck at fifteen. With a single arrow."

Built by a bishop, who distrusted both the surrounding farmers and the neighbouring nobles, the castle had been designed to inspire fear. Outside, its three threatening grey towers did the trick. Inside, it was the endless hallways, freezing rooms, and dark, narrow staircases. The only part of the castle that had been restored now housed classrooms for the SS officers. Its halls were filled with blond heads, black uniforms, and boots marching in time. The activities of the busy and disciplined ant colony made the confined locale feel even more oppressive.

"This is where we train Germany's future elite. Racially pure and committed to our ideology. The best of the Order come here to learn the basic truths of German superiority."

"The Order?" asked Erika, surprised.

"Of course! We're a true chivalric order, like the Teutonic Knights and the Knights of the Round Table before us."

The archaeologist shook her head. "You do know that King Arthur and his knights never existed, don't you? It's just a story made up by a French monk. There is no historical evidence to support it."

The young officer showed her a classroom where students took notes under a portrait of Adolf Hitler. "Here you'll find the leading specialists in literature and history. I'm sure they'll prove that King Arthur existed—and that he had German ancestry, of course."

Erika didn't reply. She wanted the visit to end as quickly as possible.

"I was summoned by the Reichsführer. We've been touring this . . . boarding school for half an hour now. I wouldn't want to keep him waiting."

The officer consulted his watch. "Himmler himself drew up the schedule for your visit. He wanted you to see the young people who are the future of the SS for yourself. These men—"

A door to the corridor opened suddenly. Held tight by two soldiers, a prisoner mumbled in a foreign language, his mouth full of blood. From his clothing, Erika recognized him as one of the forced labourers from the road outside.

"Some of them are mad enough to try to escape," said the officer, "but don't worry. The SS knows how to handle problems like this. Take him to the crypt."

He turned to Erika with a smile. "I'm sure the Reichsführer will be delighted to have you attend this man's execution."

18

With planters full of geraniums hanging from every window and its freshly painted green shutters, the border post looked like a holiday home. A customs officer was smoking a cigarette near the front door, enjoying the shaded porch, while his colleague disinterestedly inspected a cart piled high with wood. Neither the tragic defeat of June 1940 nor the thousands of Republican refugees who had crossed the border at the end of the Spanish civil war seemed to have had an impact here. The unflappable French administration still moved about as fast as a cat stretching in the sun. After all, from the Loire to the Mediterranean, southern France had escaped the Occupation—a privilege, when so many European countries had been cowed by the Nazis' bloodied boots.

Annoyed by the time the inspection was taking, the driver honked, but got no reaction. It seemed like the customs officers might be feigning indifference to exasperate the Germans and make them wait. Tristan smiled to himself. Resistance begins in the details.

"This is unbelievable, Oberführer!" exclaimed the driver. "They don't seem to have a care in the world."

The government employee, who had just finished his cigarette, came over, his pace slow and deliberate. He silently held out his hand for their papers. The driver could barely hide his impatience.

"Not a single word! Infuriating!" he raged to his passengers.

His annoyance turned to disbelief when the customs officer took a magnifying glass from his pocket and began analysing each page of the documents. Tristan lowered his head so no one could see his smile. Only Weistort remained impassive, as if none of this concerned him.

"We're on an official mission!" shouted the driver. "It's urgent. We're in a hurry, you know. Do you understand?"

The employee raised his hand to his ear in a gesture of power-lessness. It wasn't his fault—he couldn't understand them. And he flipped back two pages, as if to check a detail that had escaped him. Then, without warning, he handed the papers back, moved away from the car, and had the barricade lifted. The car took off at full throttle, heading for Montségur.

"I've been wondering something. How did you first pick up the trail of the Montserrat painting?" asked Tristan.

Weistort ran his finger along his scar, then replied, "Since you're already dead, I suppose I can tell you. Before the war, we got our hands on an incredible book, the *Thule Borealis Kulten*. Tradition tells us it was written by Emperor Frederick Barbarossa. Inside, there was a drawing of the painting you stole. And a geographical clue: *Montser*."

"If I had known the painting would cause so much trouble," joked Tristan, "I would have stolen a wafer box or some other old reliquary!"

"You'd do better to thank your intuition. Without it, I never would have saved you from the fight to the death in the arena."

The countryside had changed since they'd crossed the border. The car drove through hills covered in a thick coat of green oaks and high, grey peaks that reached the thin clouds.

"We're in Cathar country now," announced Weistort. "So, what do you know of Montségur?"

"That the castle was at the centre of Catharism, the heretical medieval belief system that took hold in this region, and that it was besieged and conquered by crusaders from the north. Their religion disappeared through a series of massacres and executions at the stake. Like so many others during that time. Nothing exceptional."

"You're wrong," replied the Oberführer. "The Cathar leaders were a terrible threat to the Catholic church."

"Why?"

"Because they believed they were closer to God than the uneducated priests and bishops of the time, who were more devoted to counting their coins than to the spiritual realm. The Cathars did not recognize the authority of the clergy and refused to pay the tithe, attend mass, confess, or take communion. In their eyes, the church was an obstacle between man and God. An obstacle that needed to disappear."

"They must not have made many friends."

"No. Particularly given that their movement spread like oil on water from Montpellier to Bayonne, from the Pyrenees to the Dordogne region. It caught on with farmers starved by the high church taxes, and with nobles, who were constantly battling with the ignorant, greedy clergy. In the 12th century, southern France was full of heretics."

"How did the Catholic church react?"

"First by sending 'symbolic figures', like Saint Bernard and Saint Dominique, to try and win back the love and faith of the people. But it was a resounding failure. And to let Catholics know they were no longer welcome, Cathar knights murdered the Pope's legate in 1242. A few months later, Montségur was under siege."

"But why this castle in particular? It must not have been the only one belonging to the heretics?"

"No, there were many. Bigger castles, like Peyrepertuse, and better protected ones, like Queribus. But for whatever reason, the Cathar leaders decided to take refuge at Montségur. There must have been a reason—one that has remained secret ever since."

"Did the siege last long?"

"Ten months, which is exceptionally long. But the castle's location at nearly four thousand feet above sea level made it nearly impregnable. It took more than six thousand men—a remarkable number at the time—to finally take Montségur. Speaking of which . . ."

The car had just reached a hilly plateau, home to the ochre roofs of a village hidden in a valley. But what was most striking for Tristan was the shadow. The huge shadow that fell across the short grass in the fields and the rocky paths. He looked up. A mountain rose before him, like a lance pointing skyward. At the top, among the clouds, he could see a damaged circular wall.

"Montségur!" exclaimed Weistort.

19

The prisoner had disappeared, carried off by the guards, leaving only a winding trail of blood on the wooden floor. The officer seemed unconcerned. "A maid will clean it up. Now, please follow me."

They walked down a corridor in hostile silence. There were no classrooms here, but vast sitting rooms decorated in the medieval style. Through the doorways, Erika caught glimpses of gothic fireplaces, waxed wooden choir stalls, and shining suits of armour, but what she noticed most was the omnipresence of skulls, the SS's favourite symbol.

"The Museum of our Origins was created at the Reichsführer's behest. He wanted to bring together in Wewelsburg the most remarkable pieces from our long history and proof of our superiority throughout the ages."

Erika kept herself from alluding to the time when Rome built forums, temples and baths, while Germanic tribes still lived in wooden huts in the forest. With a serious expression, the officer stepped aside to let her through. She entered what must have once been the castle's chapel, though all traces of religion had been removed. Tall display cases with bright lights had replaced the fonts and the altar. Their contents quickly attracted the archaeologist.

"All the objects here are from excavations conducted by the Ahnenerbe, the SS's historical research arm. They're from all over the world, from Tibet to Iraq and Scandinavia to the Canary Islands."

"Ah, Frau von Essling, the Canary Islands," said a surprisingly metallic voice. "Did you know we found some incredible things there?"

Erika turned towards the entrance to the room. A thin silhouette was visible in the doorway. Heinrich Himmler had just made his grand entrance. His shoulders were so narrow and his legs so skinny, he looked like a hanger for his uniform.

"In 1939," continued the Reichsführer, taking Erika's arm, "an Ahnenerbe team was sent to the Canaries, where it met with remarkable success. We found runic writing in the very heart of the island—proof of the presence of a Viking civilization."

"What an unexpected discovery," commented Erika, who knew she needed to be careful.

"Not a discovery, but a confirmation, Frau von Essling. I knew the people of the Canary Islands were pure Aryans."

"How could you have *known*?"

Himmler smiled from behind his round silver-rimmed glasses. "Have you ever noticed that the Canaries are just mountains that spring up from the bed of the Atlantic Ocean?"

"Of course—"

"Well, those steep mountains were a refuge for survivors from the greatest tidal wave in history."

"Which one is that?"

"The one that sank Atlantis and . . ."

The cry of a hunted animal rang out. The prisoner, thought Erika.

Himmler continued, unfazed, ". . . another legendary continent located further north: Hyperborea. The motherland of the Aryan race. An unequalled civilization, which we will bring back to life. In the meantime, please come with me to the north tower."

This was the first time Erika had met the Reichsführer, though her parents had spent some time with him. Her father had noticed him early on among the coterie of men circling Hitler. Flattered to receive an invitation from members of the aristocracy, Himmler had consistently worked to protect the von Essling family's interests since then. A favour that Erika feared the Reichsführer was about to ask her to return.

"You are an esteemed archaeologist, Frau von Essling. I've read some of your excavation reports. They testify to the impressive breadth of your knowledge, even if the results don't always fit with our ideology."

"Archaeology is apolitical."

"In history, any time you interpret something, it becomes political. But let's not argue. I have a surprise for you. Come in."

Erika walked into a circular room adorned with massive columns like those of a church's ambulatory. Lit only by torches, which cast tortured shadows on the vaulted ceiling, the place felt like a secret grotto readied for a dark ritual.

"You're a medievalist. Have you ever seen such architecture?"

"Yes," replied the archaeologist with a nod. "Certain chapels, particularly the oldest among them, feature this type of circular arcade around the altar. It's a way to separate the most sacred space from the rest of the church."

Himmler's eyes sparkled behind his lenses. "I see you have mastered the subject, but do you know where the tradition comes from?"

Erika shivered. She was cold and couldn't shake the prisoner's scream from her mind.

"From an archaeological perspective, there are several hypotheses. This type of sacred circle has also been found in prehistoric caves."

Himmler shook his head and interrupted. "For the Ahnenerbe, there is only one possible origin: they are Celtic cromlechs, like Stonehenge, where pagans worshipped the energy of life, born of the marriage of earth and sky."

Erika preferred not to say that when the first Celts appeared in England, Stonehenge had already been around for centuries.

"Now, look at the floor."

At the centre of the room, a strange pattern appeared in green marble. Erika had never seen anything like it. Lightning seemed to emanate from a nebulous centre, irradiating everything in its path. Or maybe they were roots growing out of a dark earth. In any case, the symbol exuded a strangely intense energy.

"Symbols cannot exist unless we give them power," said the head of the SS. "For example, for our swastika to reign over Europe, we had to wash it in the blood of our enemies. You'll see."

Himmler crossed the room towards a door in the wall, which led to a spiral staircase. Erika followed the Reichsführer into a room with a high ceiling, lit by a fire.

"This fire never goes out. It is the symbol of the SS's power: the flame that must purify the world."

His face reddened by the unbridled dance of the flames, Himmler looked like a monster, escaped from the depths of hell. Suddenly Erika realized how this man could scare even Göring.

"But to live, fire must constantly consume. So, we have to feed it."

Two guards, who had been still and silent in an alcove, stepped out with their prisoner, his eyes wide with fear.

"A Pole," stated Himmler. "Useless. But his death will serve a purpose. Go ahead."

With her eyes closed tightly, Erika heard a revolting crackling as the vile smell of burnt fat filled the room. Every fibre of her being was disgusted by the horrific show she'd been invited to attend, but she was careful not to reveal her distaste.

"We can go back up now," announced the Reichsführer. "The fire will redeem him."

Once upstairs, Himmler took Erika's arm and walked her to the centre of the room. "Now, listen closely. To seize power, some things are even better than death. There are objects that have fed off humanity's pain for centuries."

The archaeologist stared at him in confusion. She felt like she was listening to a medieval monk telling her about the power of relics, of the bones of martyred saints, or of splinters from the Crucifixion cross.

"Believe me, in a few sacred places, fervour and suffering have created objects of pure power."

Himmler looked down at the symbol beneath them.

"This is the black sun of the SS, which catalyzes telluric forces and magnetic energy. But to feed it, I need a relic forged from fire and blood."

Erika contemplated the symbol, unable to take her eyes off its intertwined green veins, which now looked like a writhing nest of snakes.

"And you're going to find it for me."

20

The sun grew less dazzling as it dipped towards the horizon. Its light no longer reached certain corners of the valley, which exhaled thick banks of fog. Now and again, a cold, damp breeze took hold of their ankles, like a hand rising out of the ground. Tristan shivered in his uniform jacket. He'd never liked the mountains. Depressing grey boulders and soaked prairies always felt foreign to him. They had just stepped out of the car, which was parked on a recently levelled area on the side of the road. A path maintained by passing herds climbed through a field of short grass.

"The *prat des cremats*," announced Weistort, who had had time to do his research while Tristan was locked up in Castello. "On March 16, 1244, Catholic troops took control of the castle. All those who renounced Catharism were allowed to live, but only a handful chose that option. Mostly soldiers who were exhausted by the siege and desperate to escape the hellish conditions."

"And the others?"

"They refused to renounce their faith. Two hundred and twenty people, whom the church decided to burn, all together. Here, in this very field. The Catholics built an enclosure of spiked logs, filled it with kindling, locked the prisoners inside, and set it alight. People said the smell was unbearable."

They had just reached the edge of the field. Tall box trees climbed along the hillside in tight lines. The trail became a narrow path as it snaked through the boulders. With every step they risked slipping on the mud or tripping on a rocky outcropping.

"Can you imagine the pope's crusaders sweating in their chainmail, their vision impaired by their helmets as they climbed this rocky rampart? A single arrow would be enough to bring a man to the ground for good."

Tristan looked up, short of breath. They still couldn't see the castle. The climb was difficult, and the box trees scratched their bodies and faces. They had to grab onto whatever was available to avoid tumbling down. His hands were bloodied from holding on to rough branches and sharp brambles.

"If the castle is impregnable, then how did it fall in the end?"

"Turn around."

The countryside extended for miles, right up to the foothills of the Pyrenees. A maze of shaded valleys, dense woods, and vast plateaus.

"After their first attempts to take the castle, the crusaders decided to surround it to prevent the Cathars from receiving food or support. But the siege line was far from secure. It had many holes, and the besieged never went hungry or thirsty. It could have gone on like that for years."

They had just made their way out of the brush. The rest of the path up to the castle was bare and rocky. The Frenchman stopped in surprise. It looked nothing like the painting.

"If you're looking for a first line of defence, there's nothing. Not a single machicolation, nor a barbican."

"Or maybe nothing's left of them," suggested Tristan. "Given the steep hill and the passage of seven hundred years, the defences could have collapsed and fallen down into the valley. We'll have to look more closely through the boxwood forest to see if there are any piles of carved stones with mortar left. It's the only way to confirm that the castle matches the painting."

"I'm delighted to see you working with us."

"Do I really have a choice?"

"No, not at all."

"You still haven't said how Montségur fell."

Weistort stopped for a moment to catch his breath. He pointed to a steep bluff to the right of the castle.

"The Cathars hadn't placed defences on that outcropping, because of the steep cliffs on three sides—they were certain no one could ever climb up. But the crusaders hired a group of Basque mercenaries. Men who knew no fear, especially not of heights. They climbed the cliffs during the night, took possession of the outcropping, and held it until they could put together a trebuchet."

Tristan imagined the castle, pelted with huge stones until its walls were ravaged and its tower collapsed.

"The heretics held on for several months, then surrendered."

The base of the castle was getting closer. In the middle of the south-facing wall, there was a wide opening that led out onto a wooden platform, where two German soldiers stood surveying the countryside with binoculars.

"This is the Free Zone," protested the Frenchman. "What are soldiers doing here?"

"We came to an agreement with the Vichy government. We cooperate on scientific and archaeological projects. German researchers have also been authorized to conduct studies at Carnac and Les Eyzies."

What could the Germans be looking for in the prehistoric caves of the Périgord and among the megaliths of Brittany?

"Montségur has been designated a special research site. A discreet military unit protects the area. And a team of archaeologists will be arriving tomorrow."

The last few meters of their climb were the most difficult. Tristan, weakened by months of captivity, felt his legs begin to shake as his mind grew anxious. He hadn't been in control of his own life since Montserrat. He was beholden to a fate determined by others. Next to him, Weistort climbed eagerly, a smile on his lips. The German was full of life—unlike Tristan, who was now but a fallen shadow in the power of a demon.

They had just entered the castle's courtyard, which was dotted with fallen stones from the walls and brambles. It felt like a grave to Tristan. It wasn't noticeable from the outside, but from here, he could see how the outer wall was shaped like a coffin. An open tomb. A few stones still stuck out of the walls where a proper staircase must once have stood. To escape the feeling of being buried alive, the Frenchman clambered up the wobbly steps. Ahead, at the end of the courtyard, he saw the ruins of the dungeon keep. The square structure featured a number of arrow slits and was totally flat at the top. No crenellations, no machicolations, and no vestiges of a roof. Moreover, it was located at one end of the castle—nothing like in the painting, where the tower was in the centre.

"It's strange. This castle doesn't look anything like the *castrum* in the painting," said Tristan.

Weistort crossed his arms over his chest. "True, but castles are often destroyed and rebuilt a number of times. Nothing proves the building we're in now is the one that withstood the siege of 1244."

A group of soldiers entered the courtyard carrying crates filled with tools. Tristan hurried back down the stairs. Though fatigue still tugged at his aching muscles, his anxiety had abated, making way for his survival instinct. He'd already died once. The next time it would be definitive. He had no choice, he had to cooperate. To the best of his ability . . .

The soldiers had cleared a relatively flat area and set up tents. Tristan came over. Some of them housed excavated artefacts while others were home to cots and workspaces. A smaller tent had been erected against a wall, a few steps from the others. Inside, a folding table was already covered in maps and reports. A sentinel guarded the entrance. The Frenchman could feel Weistort's gaze on the back of his neck. But being watched didn't mean he couldn't think for himself. He had counted eleven beds, plus the one in the little tent, which must be meant for the group's leader. So, twelve people for a dilapidated castle tucked away in the Pyrenees. And most of the soldiers bore the insignia of military engineers on their sleeves. They were specialists who could build roads, bridges, and more. These dozen men would know how to reach every nook and cranny of Montségur. All this because of an insignificant painting.

"Come with me to the rocky platform to the east, where Montségur's fate was sealed."

Weistort held a map of the castle in his hand. On the left, there was the rectangular shape of the dungeon keep with its lateral arrow slits, the circle of its spiral staircase and a room at the far end that must have housed a cistern. Since there were no wells nor visible springs in Montségur, the besieged Cathars must have relied entirely on rainwater. The outer wall looked like a flattened trapezoid. The architect must have done his best, given the narrow space available, which was still covered in boulders. But on the blueprint, the shape of the castle evoked a medieval sarcophagus awaiting its corpse, with the head on its side in the dungeon and the body in a foetal position occupying the rest. Tristan's first, macabre intuition was confirmed: this castle reeked of death.

They exited by the south door, turned left through some boulders, which seemed to be growing against the outer wall. A few meters on, the wall suddenly veered left, following the narrowing edge of the plateau. It became increasingly difficult to move forward. They had to come back and walk right along the castle's eastern wall.

"This is the castle's Achilles heel, because it opens out onto a plateau," explained Weistort as he pointed at the map. "That's why the wall has been reinforced with a second line here."

Now they were walking through fallen stones. Despite the brush, they could see the traces of the original foundation on the ground, but Tristan couldn't see the big picture. This rocky overhang, which extended out towards the rising sun, must have once been home to some sort of structure. But what? Housing? Defences?

"Here we are."

A seemingly deserted space emerged from the shadows of what looked like the walls of a tower. Weistort moved closer.

"This is where the Basque mercenaries managed to hold their ground. They took over this tower first, killing its defenders, then moved to the safety of a ditch protected by a wall, which must have been—"

A woman's voice cut him off. "Behind you."

The young woman stood in the light of the setting sun. With her brown coat and her hair tucked up in a side-cocked beret, she looked like a poacher on the hunt. But her steady, grey gaze was fearless.

"The defensive line was between these rows of brush. You can still see what's left of it, though the walls have been demolished."

Weistort removed his hat, bowed, and clicked his heels. "Oberführer Weistort, at your service. You speak beautiful German, Mademoiselle. Might I ask where you learned it?"

Her grey eyes grew stormy. "I'll be asking the questions, here, thank you! And I only have one: What are you doing on my land?"

21

Malorley had just finished his last set of push-ups in the farm
courtyard. He was drenched in sweat when he stood up. The cool
morning air tickled his lungs and irritated his throat.

The Englishman contemplated the fields and woods around him.
Everything was white. It wasn't snow, but a thin layer of frost,
which covered the ground as far as he could see, like in the farthest
reaches of Surrey and Wales. He realized he'd never thought of
France as a cold place. Before the war, he'd only ever crossed the
Channel to go to Paris or the Riviera, so unlike this forgotten corner
of the Gironde region. France usually brought images of joy,
sunshine and luxuriant greenery to his mind. But as far as he could
see here, it was grey and khaki, colours of despair. And the country
was cut in half, from Lake Geneva to the Pyrenean foothills.

He was finally in France. All his efforts had paid off. Even his
lies. To convince the Gordon Circle to support his cause and
persuade Churchill, he had resorted to a small forgery. The photographs of the irradiated SS officers in their hospital beds had come
straight from the SOE propaganda office. Magnificent work. The
men in the images were really soldiers burned during the Battle
of Belgium, cared for in a rural hospital. The SOE forgers had
added a flourish here and there to give the men an irradiated look.
Malorley wasn't proud of his trickery, but the images had led the
committee to decide in his favour. He pushed his negative thoughts
out of his mind. The mission was all that mattered, and he fully
believed in the evil power of the relics. That was enough. He blew

into his hands to warm them. The sun was about to rise—it was time to go.

Malorley watched the road that ran along the side of the farm again, unable to quash his fear that the Germans would be coming after him soon, a fear which had plagued him since his arrival. But all was quiet. Maybe too quiet.

He turned around and pushed his way through the heavy oak door to the dining room. The smell of a dwindling wood fire clung to the low ceiling and thick walls. The two SOE agents were enjoying a hearty breakfast. The farm's owner—a huge man with a jovial face—served them bowls of a strange, thick, steaming, dark liquid. Jean Vercors was a simple man, but a man of principles. He hated the Germans, whom he'd fought in the Great War. The former adjutant had been decorated at Verdun but had retired two years before war broke out again in 1939. Much to his disgust, his reserve unit was never called up during the invasion. He'd only been part of a small, nascent resistance network for three months now, but his farm had provided refuge for a dozen agents who had parachuted in on their way to the four corners of France. His younger brother, Blaise, who worked the farm with him, also served as a people smuggler.

"Liquorice, chicory, and a capful of cognac," explained the resistance fighter cheerfully. "There's no better replacement for coffee. It greases your arteries nicely. It could wake a corpse!"

Malorley sat down in the middle of the group and managed to gulp down a little of the liquid. He successfully hid his disgust and discreetly pushed the bowl to the side. A map of France was unfolded in the middle of the table. He tapped it with a spoon.

"So, let's go over the plan again. Our aim, as you know, is to reach Toulouse."

"We've been over this ten times," Charles complained wearily. He was the oldest of the agents and wore his black hair slicked back.

"Well, then this will be the eleventh," Malorley replied coldly. "It may just save you from having to repeat it for the Gestapo."

Since they'd met, just a day earlier, the two men hadn't got on. Malorley could feel Charles's latent hostility and was already regretting his choice. He turned to the young woman, a blonde around thirty years old, with an oval face and gentle eyes framed by charmless glasses.

"Jane?"

"I am Madame Henri Darcourt, your doting wife. We will head to the Saint-Jean train station in Bordeaux together, where we'll get a train to Toulouse. There will be two inspections on the way. The first at the station, the second in the train at the Demarcation Line."

The former adjutant came and sat down. "You should know the Germans have asked the French gendarmes to help them at Saint-Jean. And don't forget to keep an eye out for the plainclothes Gestapo officers—the place is crawling with more of them than ticks on a stray dog."

Malorley nodded and turned his attention to Charles. With a sigh, the latter recited his text monotonously. "I'm a tinned-food salesman. I'll take a lorry to Libourne, with Blaise, the pig farmer. Speaking of which, thanks for making me travel with such charming animals. Once we cross into Free France, he'll drop me at the Mirande train station, where I'll take the express train to Toulouse."

Malorley kept the questions coming as he folded up the map. "Meeting point in the Pink City? Meeting time? Password?"

"The Cochon Jovial restaurant, rue Bouquières," replied Charles dryly. "Between eight and nine o'clock in the evening. There will be a man at the back of the restaurant, his black hat with a grey felt band sitting on the table. The password is, 'A good hat is priceless.'"

"The contact must reply, 'Even in the spring.' If he doesn't, flee the restaurant and pray to God almighty."

Charles smiled for the first time. Malorley remained impassive.

"There's nothing funny about any of this. If it happens, it means you're sitting across from a German agent or a member of Vichy's anti-communist police, in which case his colleagues will be waiting for you at the exit to bring you in. And send you back to occupied France."

Charles ran his hand through his hair. "With all due respect, Commander, I was building an important network of resistance fighters when I was asked to join you. Could I at least know the goal of our mission?"

"No," replied Malorley frostily. "If you're arrested by the Gestapo, I don't want you to be able to compromise the operation. Once we've all reached Toulouse, I'll give you new instructions regarding our goal. Anything else?"

At his words, everyone's faces fell. The commander's definitive tone had left a chill in the air.

Vercors stood up and announced, "Come, friends. It's time to go. Monsieur and Madame Darcourt, I'll take you to Saint-Jean station myself. Blaise will take care of our tinned-goods salesman."

The lorry was driving slowly down a winding road on its way to Langon. In the back, the dozen pigs in the cramped space between the delivery crates wouldn't stop squealing. A vile smell wafted through the air, even inside the cab. Charles shot dirty looks at Blaise, the smuggler who wore a cap to hide his bald head.

"Your lorry stinks. It's disgusting," said Charles, holding his nose.

The farmer smirked. "Yes, that's exactly what the Germans say when they inspect it. It keeps them from finding the hiding places where I have all the guns for the network."

Despite the danger, the former adjutant's brother seemed totally relaxed.

The agent pulled out a pack of Gauloises and held it out to the driver.

"No thanks. I don't smoke," answered Blaise. "We'll reach the Demarcation Line in half an hour."

"Are there many smugglers around here?" asked Charles.

The farmer chuckled. "Well, that depends what you mean exactly. I do it on principle. Others do it for the cash. They can make twenty thousand francs per run. And an extra ten thousand if they betray their clients to the Germans."

"What?"

"Not all of them, but still. We had a real weasel in our village. Amédée, the blacksmith. He pocketed the savings of two Jewish families and then dropped them at the Kommandantur in Pessac. I doubt he took it with him to heaven, though. He bumped his head on his anvil two days later. Such a silly death."

"An accident?"

"That's what they say . . ."

The SOE agent lit a cigarette and contemplated the vineyards dotted with dense shrubs. "I tasted a Saint-Emilion once, before the war. A 1927, in a restaurant in Caen. I can still remember it. It was incredible."

Blaise smiled softly. "You're lucky. I've never been able to afford it. Nowadays the Germans requisition all the good bottles. Seems they have good taste in wine."

"We'll get them back soon. Once we do, I'll buy you a case."

The driver's hands tightened on the wheel. "I wouldn't be so sure, pal. The Germans crushed us. The army is gone, and on the other side of the Line, the old Marshal could die any day."

"But what about England? And de Gaulle? The Appeal of the 18th of June!"

The lorry slowed at a hairpin turn, then accelerated down a hill. The pigs expressed their discontent yet again. The driver shot his passenger a friendly look. "As for the Brits, maybe. They've held out. But de Gaulle, what a joke! Last year he wanted to take Dakar from the Vichy troops. What a disaster!" laughed the smuggler. "The General is better on the radio than on the ground. I doubt he has much of a future."

"But why help the Resistance, then?"

"I hate the Krauts. That's enough for me. I—"

He didn't finish his sentence. A deer had just bounded out of a thicket and was standing stock still in the middle of the road with head held high, eyes wide open and nostrils flared.

"Oh Christ!"

Blaise stomped on the brakes and turned the wheel. The left side of the lorry barrelled into the animal and the squeals from the back started up again in earnest. Charles gripped the door handle tightly to keep from falling forward. Oak branches scraped the windows and ripped the tarpaulin over the back of the lorry as it slid down into a ditch.

It took the men a few minutes to collect themselves. The smuggler got out of the cab first, to inspect the extent of the damage. The lorry looked like a hippo lying listlessly in a pond. The back wheels were half submerged in a muddy puddle. He heard squeals behind him and turned around to see three pigs making a break for the vineyards. The SOE agent did his best to close the hole in the tarpaulin through which the rest of the animals were noisily trying to escape.

"Oh hell," exclaimed Blaise. "Your mission's not off to a great start."

22

The door to the manor house slammed as if a gust of the May wind had just rushed in. But from the sound of rapid footsteps echoing through the tiled entryway, Jean d'Estillac knew his daughter was home. She had gone up to the castle despite the cold and the setting sun, and now she was back, just as furious as when she'd left. Jean was comfortably seated in the deep black-leather armchair he'd purchased in England the year he'd taught there. It had been an excellent investment—one that helped him remain calm when faced with the brunt of his beloved daughter's strong personality. He listened as she crossed the vast living room, stomping across the herringbone-patterned wooden floor like a charging cavalry unit. Sometimes he wondered how the walls held up to her temper.

Laure was livid. That German officer, with his cold politeness and triumphant arrogance, might as well have laughed in her face. In three sentences, he explained that the castle was now a special research area, requisitioned by the Reich, with approval from the Vichy government. The official papers were at her disposal should she desire a copy. She had turned and left without a word, enraged by her powerlessness. "With approval from the Vichy government." What would they do next? It wasn't enough to have toppled the Republic, now the old man who ruled from the city of springs felt the need to do the Germans the favour of handing over France's national heritage? A monument her family had owned and protected for centuries? As she walked down the corridor to the library, she noticed a portrait of Pétain that her father had hung on the wall. She couldn't understand how her countrymen had agreed to follow this ghost . . . It was beyond her. She grabbed the frame and knocked it off-kilter. The old marshal found himself dipping dangerously low. His cap threatened to slide off his head. Bad things happened to those who stood in the way of Laure d'Estillac.

"Papa!"

Her shout made even the oldest books in the library tremble. The layers of dust accumulated over the centuries fell from their bindings and the invisible insects that had been sleeping between their pages for decades shot up as if from a nightmare. Seated comfortably in his chair, Jean waited calmly for the hurricane to strike. His daughter stood tall, like Justice wronged, her eyes dark, her hair wild, and her lips red with anger.

"The Germans are at the castle. They've just moved in and there are already tents in the courtyard. Soldiers are guarding the entrance. Worse still, I ran into two officers on the plateau," she announced with disgust. "SS officers. The one who spoke to me was named Weistort."

Her father decided it would be best to reassure her.

"They must have told you they're here to conduct archaeological excavations as part of a mutual agreement between France and Germany, then."

"Only one of them spoke. But how did you know that—"

"The Préfet told me."

"Why didn't you say anything?"

"It would only have riled you up."

"I hate the Germans!"

"My dear, let me remind you that we lost the war and that we are now beholden to them. It would be wise for you to express your hostility more discreetly."

"Soldiers wearing uniforms adorned with skulls have taken over the castle where I played as a child, and I must remain silent?"

"Don't go back up there. They'll only be here for a few weeks or months at the most. If they want to excavate the castle ruins, let them."

Desperately, Laure gestured to the books that filled the shelves of all four walls, from floor to ceiling. "How can a man who taught the history of heresy throughout Europe, a man who devoted his life to studying the Cathars, simply accept that the Germans are desecrating their final refuge, their last sacred place?"

"It's just four stone walls, at the top of the mountain. It's a building, not a symbol."

"Especially since Vichy approved it, right? You're just falling in line. You're a sheep like the rest of them."

"Maybe because, when the flock knows a wolf is on the prowl, they need a shepherd to guide them."

"And you've chosen that old simpleton, whose portrait you hung in the corridor, to be your guide?"

Jean nearly jumped up. He couldn't stand it when people insulted the marshal, the hero who had saved France in Verdun and averted the worst in June 1940.

"This is my house and I forbid you to use that tone when speaking of the man who has made so many sacrifices to protect us."

"Now you sound like Radio Vichy."

"It's the voice of reason, patience, and hard work—the only path left open to us."

"There are others . . ."

Laure took off her coat, which was covered in tiny water droplets, and walked over to the fireplace.

"If you're talking about that colonel who fled to London, the deserter who appeals to the people to disobey and revolt—"

"His name is de Gaulle, Papa."

"I don't want to hear his name in my house."

The fire crackled softly. The sun had just set. It occurred to Laure that Montségur was full of soldiers again for the first time in centuries. She shuddered in disgust. But she wondered what sort of dreams the men would have up there, suspended between the earth and the sky. She had never slept at the castle—she regretted that now. It felt like the soldiers up there might steal a secret from her.

"How long has the castle belonged to our family?"

"For nearly two centuries."

"So why are you the only one in the family who was ever interested in the Cathars?"

"Because almost everyone else had forgotten." Nobody remembered the crusade, the heretics, the siege, or the men burned at the stake anymore. At the end of the 19th century, academics brought Montségur back into the spotlight. They scoured the archives, wrote articles, and published books. The past entered the present."

Laure thought back to the Nazi officer looking for the place where the crusaders had set up their trebuchet on the plateau. "Papa, why are the Germans interested in Montségur?"

The academic shrugged. "It's nothing new. In the early 1930s a young researcher named Otto Rahn conducted excavations at Montségur, convinced the Holy Grail was hidden there."

"But there's surely nothing to excavate. The castle sits on bedrock. There are neither cellars nor wells. They wouldn't dare demolish the walls, would they?"

Her father smiled. His daughter was impulsive and sometimes spoke without thinking, like an acrobat without a net.

"You still have much to learn about Montségur. Precisely where you were standing this afternoon, on the overhang where the crusaders installed the trebuchet, there's a chasm in the rock, hidden by the brush. And it's not the only such crevice—there are many more on the mountain."

"Have they been excavated or explored?"

"Only by bats," joked Jean. "But there's another mystery which has never been explained. The Cathars moved into the castle around the year 1200 and stayed for over forty years. Two generations, hundreds of men and women . . ."

"Yes, so?"

"Many of them died. Where are their graves? Where are they buried? No remains have ever been found."

"So, you think there's a necropolis somewhere?"

"It's likely, yes. Especially since there's another clue. When the besieged surrendered in 1244, they asked for a two-week truce before giving up the castle."

"And the crusaders accepted?"

"Yes. They didn't want to have to fight their way in—it would have cost them too many lives."

"But why did they ask for those two weeks? What did the Cathars do during that time?"

"No one knows, but there must have been many dead to bury, following the bombardments and the most recent fighting. At least several dozen. So, what happened to the bodies?"

Laure had moved away from the delightful warmth of the fire to sit next to her father. She felt like a little girl again, like when he used to tell her stories in the evening. She had always wanted to hear one more. "So, you think the Cathars spent the two weeks burying their dead?"

"Maybe in one of the underground chasms. They could have used debris to hide the entrance. There was plenty of it, given the damage caused by the trebuchet."

Laure was captivated as she listened to her father. How could someone so wise when it came to history be so blind in politics? Worse, how could a man who had devoted his life to denouncing the violence brought against the heretics by those in power, support a repressive political regime like Vichy?

"If the necropolis exists, do you think the Germans might find it?"

"Maybe, although it will take significant means and talented specialists. But it's been hidden for seven hundred years . . ."

Laure yawned. "Sorry Papa, I'm tired. The climb to the castle has worn me out. Besides, all these stories . . . They put me to sleep after a while. I'm going up to my room to rest."

Her father watched her as she climbed the stairs, then headed to the library, where the leather bindings reflected the light. He took hold of the brackets under a shelf, which opened a panel out into a narrow desk. A telegraph sat on the oak panel, which was usually hidden from view. Jean immediately started sending a message in Morse code: WEISTORT HAS ARRIVED AT MONTSEGUR.

23

The grey lorry stopped on a side street that ran past the station's freight warehouse. A thin fog still clung to the cracked walls.

"May God be with you," offered Jean Vercors as he shook Malorley's hand through the window.

"I'm not sure God keeps track of our affairs," replied Malorley. "Thank you for your help."

The Frenchman seemed to hesitate. "Could I ask you for a favour?"

"If I can help, I will."

"You know the little capsules you're given, for if you're captured? One of your colleagues told me about them."

"Yes, what about them?"

"Might you have any for my brother and me?"

Malorley looked at him compassionately.

"I'm not saying you'd betray us if the Germans caught you, but they'd torture you and . . ."

"I'm sorry, but we're only given one per person. I can't risk them discovering the goal of my mission. But I will have some sent for you in the next drop."

The former adjutant smiled sadly. "I don't really mind either way, but my brother Blaise is still young. I don't want him to suffer in the hands of those brutes. You hear terrible things."

Jane, who had overheard the entire conversation, stepped in front of Malorley and held a small metal box out to the Frenchman. "Here. You can have mine."

The Englishman remained impassive as the resistance fighter opened the box and pulled out a small amber-hued glass capsule.

"You just break it between your teeth," explained Jane. "It works instantly."

The man shook her hand warmly. "It's strange. You've just given me . . . death."

"In this war, life itself has become stranger than death," she replied thoughtfully. "Thank you and your brother for your bravery."

They waved goodbye one final time before the Citroën disappeared into the fog.

Malorley turned to the young woman. "You never should have given him your cyanide. It's against regulations."

She picked up her suitcase and defied him with her kind eyes. "I've spent the entire war disobeying orders. I disobeyed my French mother to join the SOE instead of becoming a hospital nurse. I disobeyed my English father when I refused to marry my aviator boyfriend, and now I'm disobeying you. At least I'm consistent. Shall we go?"

She took off without waiting for his reply. Malorley contained a smile—he'd been warned that SOE agents had strong personalities. Hers was tough as steel. He hurried to catch up with her and they soon found themselves in front of the main entrance to the station, which was built of grey stone with a slate roof. A prime example of the train stations built at the end of the last century in big provincial cities. The central clock read ten forty. They had nearly an hour before their train left.

There was a crowd waiting to get in. It occurred to Malorley that people didn't stop travelling in wartime. The only difference was the presence of inspection points at the entrances and exits. French gendarmes and German soldiers were positioned on either side of the long line of travellers. The two agents fell in alongside them. Malorley pulled two ID cards out of his jacket pocket.

"Let's pray the Orchard Street forgers have outdone themselves."

The young woman had turned towards the wall and was holding her head in her hands. When she looked back at him, her eyes were red, as if she'd spent the whole night crying.

"A less common use for pepper," she explained.

It took a full fifteen minutes to reach the inspection post, which was run by two French gendarmes, their kepis worn high on their foreheads. Just behind them stood two men in beige trench coats, their hands in their pockets and their faces sullen as they observed the travellers. Behind the two men, Malorley saw a couple and their two young children sitting against the wall, surrounded by German police. The woman held her daughter tightly and shot frightened glances in every direction.

Malorley couldn't ignore them. They must have been Jews attempting to flee occupied France. In London, diplomatic reports had told of Jews being massacred all over Europe. But mostly in Poland and Romania. He had a hard time imagining France could ever do such a thing.

"We're next," whispered Jane.

"Sorry," offered Malorley as he refocused on the task at hand.

They finally reached the gendarmes. The Englishman could feel the men in trench coats—Gestapo agents, he surmised—staring at him. He tried not to look directly at them, but his stomach was roiling, trying to digest itself. A blinding wave of fear crashed into him. Gnawing and relentless. He knew what the Gestapo did to spies.

The gendarme took the couple's ID cards and inspected them carefully. The SOE agent felt his heart beating hard in his chest. No type of training could ever recreate the real dangers encountered in the field. Jane wiped tears from her eyes. She was playing her role with gusto. Malorley was ashamed of his fear.

The gendarme went over their identity papers. "Monsieur and Madame Darcourt, of Toulouse."

He glanced at Jane, then Malorley. "Your wife doesn't seem well, Sir."

The Englishman pulled a piece of paper from his pocket and

explained in perfect French. "We've just attended her mother's funeral in Lacanau."

SOE forgers had drafted a counterfeit death certificate.

The gendarme nodded, but didn't give back their papers. He had noticed Malorley looking at the family along the wall again. The Englishman wanted to know for sure.

"Who are those people?"

"Jews trying to flee to Free France. They were swindled by their forger. Their ID cards wouldn't even have fooled my twelve-year-old son."

"What will you do with them?"

The gendarme shrugged. "Me? Nothing. But the Germans want to take them to a work camp."

"Even the children?"

"Why, you looking to adopt? I bet the yids would give you a good discount," he laughed. "Next!"

Still chuckling heartily with his colleague, the gendarme handed back their ID cards.

Malorley had to force himself not to punch the man. He was ashamed of his own complicit smile, but took the papers and walked past the two men in trench coats, who appeared totally emotionless. Much to his relief, they were focused on the next passengers.

"We've made it past the first obstacle," he whispered to Jane. "We have time for a drink while we wait for the train."

They entered the station, which was half full of a strange mix of defeated-looking French travellers and happy Wehrmacht soldiers. German signage repeated the French everywhere. The huge skylights shone a pale light on the platforms, where a half dozen trains sat waiting.

The couple walked along a wall covered in posters for a movie starring Fernandel and Raimu, who smiled knowingly at one another in the advertisements.

"Oh," exclaimed Jane. "*La Fille du Puisatier*. Maybe we could go to the movies when we reach Toulouse."

"You had better be joking," mumbled Malorley as he hurried

to put as much space between them and the gendarmes as he could.

"Yes, too bad you didn't laugh. I really do like Marcel Pagnol, though."

They reached the departures sign and looked up. Train 1432 for Toulouse was scheduled to leave from platform 2. They still had over half an hour to wait and Malorley needed a drink. They made their way to the counter at the station's only bistro. The Englishman ordered a glass of cheap Bordeaux to calm his nerves. Jane asked for warm milk.

"A glass of red before eleven o'clock. That's not very professional," teased the young woman.

"I need it. Is that terribly shocking?"

She smiled. "No, it makes you seem almost human, dear husband."

He drank the wine in one big gulp.

"Am I too tense?"

"No more than a tightrope. No offence."

A heavy hand landed suddenly on Malorley's shoulder. "Police. Come with us, please," said a voice in French.

The Englishman turned around and found himself face to face with one of the men in beige trench coats.

24

With his black-and-purple gloved hands, the blond knight in shining armour raised the golden chalice above his head. Behind him were the ruins of a castle set against a dusk too orange to be real. In the foreground, knights in white capes and damsels in blue dresses knelt, their exalted faces uplifted. The voices of the majestic choir filled the huge space, which was full to the last folding chair.

Then Parsifal solemnly placed the Grail on a circular black stone table. The sound of string and brass instruments rose up from the orchestra pit as the conductor, the great Wilhelm Furtwängler, waved his baton wildly, guiding his musicians through the last movement of the final act. It was the zenith, the culmination, symbolized—according to Richard Wagner's explicit instructions—by the appearance of a white dove. The Holy Spirit flying above the sacred cup.

But this performance was different: no white bird appeared in the sky. Instead, it was a swastika. Heavy and glowing like an incandescent ember. The fiery swastika came down from the ceiling above the stage, then hung motionlessly over the Grail.

Inside the large centre box, the head of the Nazi party, Rudolf Hess, seemed to be hypnotized in his brown jacket. His face was blank, and his eyes seemed to sag under the weight of his prominent brow. Seated next to the Führer—a remarkable honour—he couldn't take his eyes off the symbol that had enchanted all of Germany. The power of that symbol! For it was just a symbol, but it was their most important asset, the one that had secured their power.

Overwhelmed by Wagner's music, he closed his eyes and another swastika appeared. The one the SS had brought to Germany from Tibet, which had helped them conquer Europe. If Himmler managed to get his hands on the second, the world would be theirs. Nevertheless, Hess was plagued with doubt. The Reichsführer was more powerful than ever. But so much power could be unwieldy— he could lose all control.

A surge of applause filled the opera house, where the lights were slowly coming back on. It was a torrent that carried away everything in its path—souls, hearts, and the ability to reason of all the men and women sitting in perfect rows.

Then there was a second departure from the usual presentation established by the champion of Bayreuth. The conductor quieted the applause and turned towards a box located above the stage which was still dark. He straightened his arm and shouted enthusiastically, *"Sieg Heil!"*

Arms shot up in unison throughout the audience. It looked like a field of wheat ready for harvest, swaying in the wind.

Sieg Heil!

Above, a brown shadow emerged from the darkness. His familiar face shone in the light of the imposing Bohemian crystal chandeliers. The imperious man unfolded and raised his arm nonchalantly. Adolf Hitler put on a debonair smile as the shouts grew louder still.

He stood for a full minute, then sat back down. The voices quieted below until they reached the usual post-concert level. A crowd of tuxedos, military dress uniforms and sumptuous evening gowns bustled between the seats.

The Führer smirked. His light-blue eyes studied the room. "Look at them, my dear Rudolf. All these handsome men and women in elegant clothing. Arrogant aristocrats, overweight manufacturers, and self-important officers as far as the eye can see. They cheer for me now that I've delivered them Europe, but none of them would have wagered a single mark on me when I wandered the streets without a cent to my name. How many of them supported us fifteen years ago, when you and I were imprisoned at Landsberg in Munich, after our putsch failed?"

"A few, mein Führer," replied Hess. "It has certainly taken much time and energy to get them to accept our vision for Germany."

The Reich's leader answered with a throaty burp. The scent of cooked cabbage wafted through the box.

"I despise these rich frauds," he said. His face fell and he massaged his temples as if to ease a headache, then hammered a frenzied fist into his knee. "But the people, Rudolf, the real German people. I have devoted my life to *them*. *They* will never betray me."

Hess decided not to mention the fact that the industrialists had contributed generously to financing the party during his rise to power. He nodded carefully and adopted a serious tone.

"I've always known that you and our race are but one. The ties are unbreakable. No one will betray you. No one . . . But now is a time to rejoice, mein Führer. What did you think of this *Parsifal*, conducted by our friend Wilhelm?"

Hitler's face brightened immediately. He stood up and put on a pair of white gloves. "Admirable! Spectacular! Moving! Replacing the dove with the symbol of our glorious movement was a stroke of genius. I nearly teared up. Was it your idea?"

Hess stood up in turn and climbed the stairs behind his master. He puffed up his chest. "Yes, my modest contribution to Wagner's magnificent work. I've never liked seeing that pathetic Christian dove flying over the Holy Grail. As if it might defecate in it! The swastika is better suited. It reveals the true meaning of the pure, Aryan Grail."

"Ah, the Grail. If only it existed."

"It does exist, mein Führer."

The Chancellor smiled. Rudolf Hess held a special place in his heart. He had been a loyal friend from the beginning. Though he espoused strange beliefs, Rudolf had always been there in times of doubt and had never abandoned him. His loyalty had earned him his position as head of the National Socialist Party. A position that was more political than strategic.

The Führer leaned over and whispered in Hess's ear. "Oh, Rudolf, you never change."

"I never give up on my convictions, whether political or spiritual."

When the two men reached the exit, Hitler placed a hand on Rudolf's shoulder. "I envy you," he explained. "Since I've been running this country, I have been mired in the material world. It's even worse in wartime. I need to get back to my salutary reading, like in Munich. I should attend more operas like this one. Thank you for urging me to come and see *Parsifal*."

The man with the bushy eyebrows bowed his head respectfully. "I also have a few extraordinary books to recommend, including one by an American historian who has shone new light on the Ku Klux Klan. He has some wonderful passages on the symbolism of the burning cross. I truly believe we should build bridges with the representatives of the Aryans in the United States. And in England, too. We still have friends there."

Germany's master's expression soured immediately. "England? Are you trying to ruin my evening, Rudolf?"

Hess bit his lip, regretting his misstep. Hitler couldn't bear to hear anyone speak of the British. In the spring of 1941, the United Kingdom continued to defy Germany. The insolent Churchill had even become a hero to his people.

"No, mein Führer, but it saddens me to see that our Aryan English cousins don't understand that you're not their enemy."

"Himmler shared your point of view, but he now thinks we should turn on Stalin. He's right. We need to be ready to face our most threatening enemy."

"An invasion of Russia?" Hess asked worriedly. He'd never supported the idea.

Hitler smiled, his expression charming once more. "Ah, Rudolf. Let's stop talking about war. It feels like I haven't read anything but military reports, diplomatic notes, and the production statistics for tanks and planes Himmler sends me, for months."

"Let's hope the Reichsführer hasn't overstepped with this one," warned Hess.

The two men stepped through the door and found themselves in the corridor that led to the boxes, all of which were empty for safety reasons. Two warrant officers in black SS uniforms stood at attention on either side of a portrait of Wagner placed on an easel. They executed a perfect salute. Hitler stopped short.

"Rudolf, give me a few minutes. I need to think alone. Find a more discreet way out of here. I don't want to have to mingle with all the puppets waiting for me downstairs."

"Yes, mein Führer," answered Hess as he hurried down a stairwell.

With his hands joined behind his back, the new master of Europe contemplated the portrait of the composer of *Parsifal* and *Lohengrin*. The musician's face was deformed by a proud yet tormented expression. Hitler had admired Wagner since his youth, when he'd attended the opera for the first time to see *Rienzi* in Vienna, in the peanut gallery, with the poor. The indigent student who'd been rejected by the Academy of Fine Arts had been deeply moved by the opera. It was no coincidence when he became friends with the composer's granddaughter, Cosima, years later.

The two SS officers remained silent and unblinking, eyes straight ahead. Hitler broke the silence by turning to the one on the right. "Do you know what makes Wagner such a genius?"

"No."

The dictator raised an eyebrow. "I can explain it with a single word: *Gesamtkunstwerk*. Comprehensive art! Have you ever heard of it?"

The guard shook his head.

"That's a shame," replied Hitler gently. "I will have to ask my dear Heinrich to improve the artistic education of our country's elite. In the meantime, let me fill in the gaps for you. Wagner practised comprehensive art or total artwork, a romantic concept from the 19th century. In other words, he exploited all available resources in the service of his masterpieces: music, décor, the Bayreuth Opera House itself, as well as legends and Aryan philosophy. Nothing—nothing at all—was left to chance. He wanted the musicians to be totally immersed in the work, enchanted. Wagner himself lived his art as if his life depended on it. Like the great emperor Frederick Barbarossa, he embodied the soul of an entire people."

The guard didn't reply. He continued to stare straight ahead.

Hitler continued gravely, "*Gesamtkunstwerk* . . . National Socialism is also total artwork, and the world will soon witness the scope of my genius."

25

Montségur
May 1941

The densely forested mountains that surrounded Montségur were now a sparkling green hue. Every morning, millions of leaves bathed in dew shone brightly in the light of the rising sun while the damp, grey fog loitered in the valley below. Sitting atop the outer wall, feet dangling, Tristan took a moment to enjoy the sunshine before his new life caught up with him. It was still early, and the soldiers slept in their tents. He had the whole castle to himself as it prepared to set sail on an endless sea of fog. Joyous birdsong rose from the thickets gathered at the feet of the old fortress, reminding Tristan of children at play.

The war that raged in Europe seemed so far away that Tristan sometimes forgot even the most terrible events he had experienced. Montjuic prison, the ditch in Castello, all the unhappy memories seemed distant, like the swallows darting back and forth across the Pyrenean sky. In the gentle morning warmth, Tristan took advantage of the last moments of calm and solitude before the camp came to life. He hadn't seen the young woman who'd raged about them occupying her castle again. She was intriguing. He occasionally glanced over at the brush, hoping to catch a glimpse of her beret making its way up the hill. He had been truly impressed by her bravery during the exchange with Weistort, who had dubbed her the Lady of Montségur. And those grey eyes . . .

A muffled sound brought him back to the harsh reality. The bell had just rung. A new day of servitude was about to begin.

Since Weistort and his SS team had requisitioned the castle, a strict schedule had been put in place. Every morning, the first group, made up of surveyors, took possession of the site. As he came down from the wall, Tristan saw them head out. Carrying pitons, ropes and measuring tape, they had already measured the castle's outer wall, the keep, and the height of the defensive walls. Now they were exploring the plateau, inch by inch, on the lookout for any signs of past constructions. The Frenchman watched them make their way to the northernmost section, a narrow outcropping, which had already revealed a certain number of artefacts. Tristan headed for the mess tent, where the cook filled bowls with warm milk. Coffee and sugar had become so rare that they were reserved for officers and scientists.

In the middle of the courtyard, on a long wooden table, an architect had just unfolded a huge blueprint of the castle as well as a map of the peak beneath it. His assistants used pencils to fill in the measurements taken by the surveyors.

To make the map as accurate as possible, another team was tasked with clearing the vegetation from the plateau, cutting back the boxwood and brambles to reveal old paths and collapsed walls. Each discovery was recorded on the map, like a position on a battlefield.

The outcropping where Weistort had taken Tristan on the first day had been the first area to be cleared. Now it shone smooth and naked in the sun. There were piles of rubble, sections of walls in ruins, and ditches everywhere. The archaeologist in charge of mapping and studying the terrain was a frail, pale young man, who hobbled around the site. His rather uncharitable colleagues had nicknamed him 'Goebbels', because of the resemblance he bore the Reich's Minister of Propaganda. Unfortunately, he lacked the latter's charisma. This morning, Tristan was helping him with his work. For the past two days, they had been studying the tower that barred access to the outcropping. It was where the Basque mercenaries had appeared one spring night to massacre the guards and take control of the area. When Tristan had told 'Goebbels' the story of the attack, the archaeologist had laughed.

"Look at the foundations of the tower. Its base was small because of the uneven ground, so to remain stable, it couldn't have been more than two stories high. In other words, it housed a few watchmen at most. Not much of a massacre," he explained.

Tristan didn't answer. It occurred to him that archaeology was the opposite of his job as an art hunter. Archaeologists put legends to rest by confronting them with the realities of a given site, whereas Tristan found a painting and then aimed to tell its story, to find where it came from and bring people back to life.

"But even more importantly, there's this," announced 'Goebbels'.

He had just removed a fragment of light-yellow mortar from between two fallen stones, and was examining it enthusiastically, like an art lover would contemplate a Michelangelo sculpture. The Frenchman's sceptical look prompted an explanation. "Mortar is unique every time it's mixed. The proportions of sand and lime always differ, making it easy to identify."

"And?" asked Tristan.

"We know this tower is part of the original structure. However, we don't know if the current castle is the one from the siege of 1244, or if it was rebuilt later. To find out, all we have to do is compare the mortars from here and from the castle. If they're the same, it's original. If not—"

"If not, the castle must have been rebuilt after the siege, right?"

'Goebbels' rubbed the back of his neck. The spring sun was stronger in the Pyrenees than in Berlin. "Yes, it would mean the crusaders destroyed the original castle to build a new one. But why?"

Tristan picked up the two pieces of mortar. "I'll take them to the architect myself," offered Tristan.

With sweat beading on his brow, 'Goebbels' glanced towards the deserted outcropping. "Down in the village, they tell strange tales about the history of the fortress. The soldiers who go into town for supplies come back with the stories and—"

"What stories?"

"About the heretics burned at the stake at the foot of the mountain. Over two hundred people burned alive. They say that

. . . that their souls have never left," explained the archaeologist, lowering his voice. "Some even say that maybe the crusaders built a new castle not to protect themselves from invaders, but to keep the tortured souls from escaping."

The Frenchman smiled. He'd always found superstitions charming. "The Castle of Wandering Souls . . ." That would make a good title for a novel.

Back within the castle walls with the mortar fragments, Tristan stopped for a moment to study the map of the site, which was constantly changing. To the east, the fortress now featured a watchtower, a dry moat, and a barbican. To the south, beneath the entrance to Montségur, defensive walls stood halfway up the side of the mountain. It no longer looked isolated at the top of the mountain; instead it was placed at the centre of a remarkable network of defences.

The most surprising discovery was to the north. There had been nothing but brush and thickets when they arrived, but now they had found a series of terraces, with remnants of past constructions.

"The surveyors are doing great work. I think we've found the Cathar village," announced Weistort. "This must have been where they had their homes, workshops, stores, and cisterns."

"Workshops?" asked Tristan, surprised.

"Of course, the heretics lived here for several decades. They must have had potters, blacksmiths, weavers, cobblers, and more. We've already found artefacts from their work: rusted nails, worn leather . . . Look."

Two soldiers had just come through the door carrying an open wooden chest full of pieces of ceramic. They headed for the warehouse—the largest tent, where all objects found were stored and classified.

"You should take them the mortar while they're over there."

The Frenchman walked into the tent, where a civilian in a tie, with scarlet cheeks and a damp forehead, took note of the place, date, and person responsible for each discovery. A soldier standing next to him photographed the pieces of mortar from several different angles, then placed them in a cardboard box that he labelled and sealed. German efficiency, thought Tristan.

The man in the tie called to him. "Hey, you, don't forget to take the form back to the map team."

The Frenchman grabbed the form which the civilian had just filled out, then made his way to the centre of the courtyard, where the architect was recording the day's discoveries on the map.

"What do you have for me?"

"We found some mortar at the base of a tower on the far-east edge of the outcropping."

"Ah, yes, 'Goebbels' is excavating over there. He's good at his job. Come closer. You mean this tower here, on the last rock, facing east?"

Tristan checked the position and topographic contour lines and confirmed. The architect drew a striped red triangle, followed by the ID number of the mortar fragments in the warehouse.

"The triangle symbolizes a construction artefact. In a few more days, we'll know everything about this site."

The Frenchman took his leave and went to sit at the base of the keep. The castle courtyard teemed with activity, like an anthill. Soldiers came in and out, constantly taking things to the excavation areas and bringing others back.

Outside he could hear the blows of an axe. A pillar of white smoke rose over the top of the walls. Soldiers were clearing a new site and burning the freshly cut trunks and branches. Montségur had changed dramatically over the past few days, and Tristan still didn't understand why. How could academics and scientists invest so much time and effort, based solely on an anonymous painting and the phonetic similarities between the names Montserrat and Montségur? The only plausible explanation was that Tristan didn't know the whole truth.

Weistort was keeping the darker aspects to himself.

26

The office reeked of damp cigarettes and acrid sweat. The faded green walls were decorated with propaganda posters celebrating the glorious alliance between the new France and Germany. A framed photograph of Maréchal Pétain hung alongside one of the Führer in his Commander-in-Chief uniform.

One of the Gestapo agents was rifling thoroughly through the couple's suitcases, which were open on the desk, while the other examined their papers. Malorley and Jane watched from a white bench against the wall. On the other side of the glass door, an armed guard paced to and fro. The Englishman tried to remain calm. There was nothing even remotely suspicious in the suitcases. SOE specialists had prepared the contents down to their underwear. The clothes were French or had been copied to perfection by a Jewish tailor who worked exclusively for the Service. The cut of a jacket, the style of a dress, the length of a pair of trousers— nothing was left to chance, right down to the half-used booklet of ration coupons. Nothing inside would betray them. But fear had returned, and his brain was paralyzed.

"So?" one of the Gestapo agents asked his colleague.

"Nothing."

He turned towards the couple, their papers in hand. "I'm from Toulouse, too. I went to university there. Such a beautiful city. Ruined by the arrival of Spanish riffraff in 1939, but that will soon change with the Maréchal. I see that you reside in Avenue Jules-Julien."

"Yes, at number 18," answered Jane.

The agent stared straight at her. "I know the neighbourhood well. Les Minimes is a nice place to live. Do you like it?"

Malorley wanted to answer, but the agent stopped him.

"I'm asking your wife."

The Englishman felt his heart pounding in his chest again. He'd been through interrogations during training at Orchard Street and knew the city map of Toulouse by heart. But Jane . . .

She pulled out a handkerchief, delicately wiped at her nose, sniffed, and replied bitterly, "I wouldn't know. We're on the road to Narbonne. Are you sure you lived in Toulouse, Officer?"

The agent smiled but continued the interrogation. "Do you have family there?"

Malorley shook his head. "No," he said.

"No kids? A couple like you should produce children for France."

The way the collaborator smirked when he said "children" sent shivers down their spines.

"Is there a problem?" asked Malorley hoarsely.

"Just a routine inspection."

"Because . . . our train leaves in ten minutes."

The agent shrugged. "There's another in six hours."

The telephone rang and the man answered, his eyes still focused on the couple.

"Yes, of course. Thank you for letting me know."

He gestured to his colleague, who quickly closed the suitcases.

"You can go," he told the couple. "Sorry for the delay. We'd heard about a couple who were running a black-market network between Bordeaux and Toulouse, but my colleagues have just caught them at the entrance to the station. You can go and get on your train."

"What if we miss it?"

"The Gestapo doesn't provide reimbursements. We're more the type to bring money in—right, Marcel?" The two men laughed crassly.

They rushed down the stairs and sprinted across the platform. The stationmaster was just about to blow his whistle. They climbed onto the train as its wheels began to turn and walked down a nearly deserted corridor.

"Those Frenchmen were worse than Germans," said Jane. "What do you suppose pushes men to betray their country like that?"

"Ideology, power, money . . . My bet is on the latter for those two jerks. The Gestapo has recruited thugs to do their dirty work in occupied France."

He checked his watch.

"And it's not over yet. We cross into Free France in less than half an hour."

"Will we have to leave the train?"

"No, on the contrary. We'll stay calmly seated. The Germans will come and inspect everyone's papers in the compartments."

"I envy your confidence. I was terrified."

"Everything will go to plan, you'll see."

He was lying. The unexpected Gestapo inspection had petrified him. He felt like he had a rock in his stomach and his heart was racing. He was scared. He'd never been this scared before.

Countryside near Libourne

The truck's back wheels sent mud flying again. Charles gestured wildly at Blaise. "Stop! There's no point. We need to put planks under the tyres."

He placed his foot on the back bumper, which creaked dangerously.

"Don't touch that! It's fragile," the farmer shouted worriedly.

The two men had been trying to get the lorry out of the rut for over fifteen minutes. In vain. No one had driven past.

The agent checked his watch. He could still make up the lost time if they found someone to help get the lorry out of the mud.

"I know a winemaker not far from here," said Blaise. "About thirty minutes away. He has a tractor and—"

A rumbling sound came up the road. An armoured car was rushing towards them, followed by a military lorry. German. Easily recognizable thanks to the black cross painted on the tarpaulin.

Charles tensed. He didn't have a single weapon to defend himself. "Oh shit, the Fritzes! What do we do?"

"Collaborate. It's all the rage at the moment," offered the smuggler. "People say the Krauts around here aren't so bad."

He moved towards the middle of the puddles, waving his cap in the air.

"You're crazy," shouted Charles as he looked around. Except for the woody area on the side of the road, where he could hide, there was nothing but vineyards as far as he could see. Perfect for getting shot if he ran.

Blaise caught the anxious man's eye. "Don't worry. You're in safe hands with me."

The German convoy reached them and braked hard. Two soldiers jumped out of the car and levelled their guns at the smuggler, who already had his hands in the air. They wore *Geheimpolizei* identification tags around their necks.

Blaise raised his voice. "I'm stuck in the mud. Could you please help me?"

A portly officer wriggled out of the Mercedes and walked over to the smuggler, breathing heavily. His cheeks were pink as a baby's and his neck hung in folds over his shirt collar.

"Officer, you're my saviour," said Blaise. "My lorry is stuck in the mud because of a goddamn deer."

The lieutenant sized up the farmer warily. The pigs started squealing again and the German's face lit up. He pointed accusingly at the lorry. "Black market! *Verboten*," he yelped angrily.

"Not at all," replied Blaise. "I have all the necessary papers. I'm delivering these pigs and tinned goods to the other side of the Demarcation Line."

Blaise took the papers from his pocket. The lieutenant examined them carefully, then handed them back to the smuggler, his expression more relaxed.

"Everything seems to be in order. We'll help you. We're not

here to trouble the French people. But first, my men will check inside to make sure there's nothing suspicious."

Despite a thick German accent, his French was understandable.

"Of course. Thank you so much," replied Blaise.

The officer crossed his arms over his chest while three soldiers climbed into the lorry. They came out a few minutes later, their faces contorted into expressions of disgust from the smell. Charles caught a reassuring glance from Blaise.

"Sir," continued the lieutenant, "help from the German army isn't free."

"What do you mean?"

"I'll have to write up a report. Using military personnel for civilian matters is against the rules," he explained. After a long silence, he smiled warmly. "But, if you donated one of your pigs in the name of Franco-German friendship, I could forget about the report."

"I would be delighted," replied Blaise.

The officer barked at his men and pointed at the lorry.

Charles came over and held his pack of cigarettes out to the lieutenant, who looked him over suspiciously. "Your papers, please. You don't look like a farmer."

The Frenchman smiled. "I'm a tinned-goods salesman. The strawberry and raspberry farmers in Marmande, in Free France, don't have a production factory. So, I'm going to suggest different jar models. You know, for compotes and jams. They're very good."

"Ah, I adore French jams!"

The officer enjoyed a cigarette while his men got the lorry out of the ditch.

"This whole Demarcation Line business makes things difficult," said Charles. "You were hard on us."

"I understand. I wouldn't like my country to be cut in two either. But . . . you shouldn't have lost the war." The officer burst into laughter, pleased with his joke.

"Couldn't you tell them to stop blocking people crossing the line?" asked Blaise. "It's not very conducive to business."

The officer smiled. "That's the goal. You know what one of my superiors likes to say?"

"What?"

"That the Demarcation Line is a bit placed in France's mouth. If the country bucks, we pull on the reins. It ensures your Maréchal listens to what we have to say."

The lorry was almost out of the mud. Blaise put his cap back on.

"That should do it," said the lieutenant, looking longingly at one of the pigs.

As soon as the lorry was back on the road, the back bumper fell to the ground. Charles watched Blaise freeze. The German officer laughed heartily.

"Ach, French material. Not as solid as our Mercedes. We'll put it back on for you."

"No, there's no need. We can handle it. Thanks very much. We're running late," said the farmer as he walked over to the bumper. But one of the soldiers had beaten him to it and grabbed the piece of metal. When he picked it up, he stopped short and shouted, "Lieutenant!"

The soldier showed him the hidden ammunition boxes inside the bumper.

The plump officer's expression changed in an instant as he unholstered his Luger. "You'll be coming with me to the Kommandantur now. I'm sure the Gestapo will want to continue this conversation."

27

The keep bell rang, halting all activity. Archaeologists, technicians, and soldiers made their way to the far end of the castle. Benches had been set up in rows in front of a large board, where the map of Montségur they were working on was on display. Once everyone was seated, Weistort began his speech.

"We've been studying this site for several days now, with a first group of surveyors and archaeologists from Berlin, as well as a team of military engineers. As you know, this work is a priority for the Ahnenerbe. Indeed, it is laying the groundwork for an extensive excavation campaign which will be underway shortly. It was thus critical to establish where the original buildings were, to find all remnants of them, and to identify and map them for analysis. This mission will soon be over. To ensure that we complete our task effectively, I have asked one of you to provide a draft summary of the discoveries made."

'Goebbels' blushed as he stood. The papers in his hands shook. Public speaking must have been torture for him, but you didn't disobey an order from the head of the Ahnenerbe. He reached the board, took a deep breath, and began.

"Thanks to our excavations, our understanding of Montségur has changed drastically. We have learned that the castle used to be surrounded by an impressive defence network. First, to the east, where we found remnants of a watchtower, a moat, and a barbican. Next, to the south," he continued as he picked up a ruler and pointed at the slope beneath the fortress, which was demarcated by several hatched lines, "where we exposed the base of several walls, which once protected the entrance to the castle."

Just like in the painting, thought Tristan.

"It is interesting to note that all of these defensive elements, to the east and south, were deliberately destroyed," explained the archaeologist, moving the end of the ruler towards the top of the map. He glanced at his papers, then continued: "On the exposed northern side, a series of terraces have been found, with cisterns, warehouses, and the foundations of many homes. This area was, beyond the shadow of a doubt, the Cathar village, where the people stayed during the 1244 siege."

A line appeared across the archaeologist's face. "However, although we found ceramic and metal artefacts, we haven't found anything made of wood."

Weistort's face curled into a smile. "Remind me when the Cathars were burned alive, will you?"

"In March. The 16th."

"At the end of winter, then. It's hard to find dry wood at that time of year. Especially given the quantity required. Imagine, over two hundred people to be burned . . ."

"You don't think that—" choked 'Goebbels'.

"That they used the beams, roofs, and floorboards to burn the heretics? Of course I do! But don't let that bother you. Go on with your presentation."

The archaeologist continued hesitantly. "We . . . we now have two original structures—the village and the defence network—so we can analyse how they were built, how the stones were carved, what mortar was used, and so forth. And then we can compare the results to the current castle."

The Oberführer's shadow, cast by the sun, fell on the attendees in the front row like a falcon diving to catch its prey.

"And without the results of this precise technical study, if you compare the two groups—the castle and the original structures— what do you think?" asked Weistort.

"We must remain cautious," explained 'Goebbels', "but it's

almost certain that the castle we are standing in now was built after the fall of the Cathar fortress."

"And what do you think became of the old fortress?"

"Demolished, like the rest."

Weistort looked at Tristan, who nodded discreetly. Now they knew why there was no central tower, like in the Montserrat painting. It had been demolished, destroyed, removed from the rock down to its foundations.

The presentation was over. The map of Montségur had been turned over on the architect's table, where the assistants were recording new data, which was arriving constantly. A new section of wall, the remnants of a forge. 'Goebbels' had returned to the outcropping. He preferred the company of stones to that of people. Their silence spoke to him and reassured him.

As for Weistort, he remained inside the walls. From time to time, he stomped hard on the ground with the heel of his boot, eliciting a dull sound, for which he listened carefully. Tristan, whom everyone took for the Oberführer's secretary, stood beside him.

"There's a layer of fallen rocks above the bedrock. If we want to find the foundations of the original tower, we'll have to strip it back throughout the castle."

"Why are you so interested in the tower?"

"I think that as soon as the crusaders entered the castle, they destroyed the homes in the village—easy enough, given that the walls were made of cob and the roofs of lightweight tiles. Then they evened out the crenellated parapets to 'demilitarize' it, but they didn't have time to demolish the tower, not before the fire."

"I don't follow," replied the Frenchman.

"Come with me, then."

The colonel's tent was set up against the north wall. An SS guard stood at the entrance. Inside there was a folding table covered in administrative papers, a narrow cot, and hanging from the fabric wall, a portrait of Hitler in Nazi regalia. The only thing that stood out in the ascetic setting was a suitcase on its end against the chateau's stone wall, where it served as a mobile library.

"Right after the two hundred people were burned at the stake, the remaining Cathars were interrogated by the Inquisition. Monks specially trained to hunt down heretics. Men of God determined to rid the earth of the Cathars by any means necessary. And for them, the fall of Montségur was a necessary part of the process. Bring me the book with the black binding. The thickest one."

Tristan did as he was told and placed the volume on the table, which Weistort had just cleared. He opened a marked page. On the left, there were tight waves of tiny writing, and on the right, this transcription:

> *This volume contains records from all the interrogations—hundreds—conducted by the inquisitors. Each defender of Montségur was asked the same questions. The meetings took place without torture, but with a certain degree of persuasion, given that the ashes from the fire were still hot.*

The Frenchman turned the pages. Names appeared, making their way from past to present. It had been seven hundred years since the quill had squeaked against the parchment, seven hundred years since the scribes had copied each word—whether true or false—and the words were still fascinating.

"The inquisitors wanted one thing," explained the head of the Ahnenerbe. "A comprehensive list of all those who had stayed at the castle during the siege. So they meticulously compared each answer, each name mentioned."

"And they realized that some of them hadn't fled? Is that it?"

"Yes, and three men went missing. Their names were Hugo, Amiel, and Aicard. They disappeared the very day the Cathars gave up the castle."

"But why didn't they escape during the truce? That would have been easier, with a limited watch."

"Not at all! The crusaders set up camp at the foot of the castle walls. There was no way to get through such a tight circle. However, on the day of the fire, it's likely the guards assumed the castle was empty and hurried down to watch the show."

"And the three men fled easily."

"Four, to be precise. The last one is mentioned, but not named. So the question is: where did they hide between when the soldiers entered the castle and the beginning of the fire?"

"Not in the village," replied the Frenchman, "since it was searched thoroughly."

Weistort stomped again. "There's only one place left, then: the tower. Most likely in an underground room. We need to find the foundations of the original dungeon's keep."

Tristan thought silently. Four men. Why so many?

"A new team will be arriving tomorrow, to take charge of all further excavations. The best the Ahnenerbe has to offer, led by a remarkable archaeologist."

The Frenchman buttoned his jacket. Despite the spring sun, there was a cool wind from the north. It was time to join 'Goebbels' on the outcropping.

"Oh, I almost forgot," added Weistort. "The leader is a woman."

28

The powerful Mikado TA 141 locomotive cheerfully puffed fluffy clouds of white steam into the sky near Toulouse. Its compact black shell shone brightly in the last rays of light from the setting sun, which would soon dip behind the Pyrenees.

Alone in the compartment with Jane, Malorley contemplated the peaceful countryside on the other side of the window. Pale, flat fields had disappeared in favour of gentle, green hills. Spring had already sprung in this part of France. The regular jolts of the wheel trucks on the rails had nearly rocked him to sleep. It was hard to believe Europe was at war, thought the SOE agent as he stretched his legs. They had made it across the Demarcation Line without any trouble, though the train had been stopped for over an hour so the Germans could meticulously inspect each of the compartments in all ten carriages. They had forced a dozen passengers off the train. All men, their hands behind their heads.

Malorley turned to Jane, who was absorbed by the book she had been reading since they left. He frowned as he read the title.

"Céline. *Les Beaux Draps*. You read antisemitic French authors who support collaboration with the Nazis?"

She looked up at him in surprise. "I didn't know English military men liked French books. Yes, it's his most recent work. The SOE teams packed it among my things. Speaking of which, they could have skipped the wool stockings and wood-soled shoes. They're awful. As for what I'm wearing, it would work just fine as a parachute."

Malorley smiled. He thought she looked lovely in her tailored gingham dress. The black scarf that held up her hair gave her a mischievous look. She had to look like the average French woman: eager to preserve her discreet elegance despite the hardships of the Occupation. Or so said the SOE experts. The Englishman refrained from proffering compliments—he didn't want there to be any ambiguity between them during the mission.

"I really enjoyed *Journey to the End of the Night*, before the war. How is this one?"

"Stylistically, it's extraordinary, but the content is a load of trash. I knew he hated Jews, but this is over the top. And now he's apparently against Freemasons as well. There's only one worthwhile idea in the entire book, in my opinion: he suggests lowering the number of hours worked per week to thirty-five."

Malorley smiled. "Thirty-five hours. Very funny, what a French idea. It would be great if he could convince Hitler to apply it in his ammunition factories. It could help us win the war."

Jane put the book away in her bag, stood up, and stuck her head out into the corridor. It was empty. Satisfied, she closed the sliding door.

"I have a question. If Charles doesn't reach us as planned, what will we do?"

Malorley looked at his watch. "Our contact is under orders to come back at the same time for two days. After that, Charles will be considered lost."

"Why two days?"

"It's the maximum length of time someone can resist torture."

She nodded. "What if he's just late?"

"He'll have to get back to his network in Nantes, or find a way to cross into Spain, and then on to Gibraltar or Lisbon."

"And you still don't want to tell me our final destination?"

He smiled. "I was planning to tell you in Toulouse, when we've met up with the rest of the commando unit. But since we're in Free France . . ." He unfolded his map of southern France and placed his finger on a spot. "Our target is here. In a tiny village in the Ariège region. Montségur."

The young woman opened her eyes wide. "Are there military operations there? It looks like the middle of nowhere. Do we have a production plant to sabotage?"

"No. We are to retrieve an object. A very important object, with a direct impact on the outcome of the war. And we're not the only ones after it. An SS unit has set up camp there to find it."

"An object. That's quite vague . . . What exactly are we talking about?"

Malorley folded up the map and placed it back in his bag. "I can't tell you that."

"And the three of us are supposed to take on an SS unit? Without any weapons?"

"Backup is waiting for us there . . ."

Pessac Kommandantur

Charles didn't have a single tear left in his body. His eyes had dried up. Lying naked on a battered mattress, he didn't even have the strength to jump in surprise. It had only been a few hours since the German officer had handed them over to the Gestapo, but a few hours in hell was a long time. His body was a broken heap of bloody flesh. Only his legs remained intact. He and Blaise had been methodically beaten for three hours in a row, without being asked a single question. The Gestapo was readying them for interrogation. The SOE trainers had explained the technique. The butcher's method. That's what they called it. To tenderize the meat. They had paid a lot of attention to his face. Though he couldn't see it, he could feel the bumps, cuts, and bruises deforming his skin.

He felt along the mattress to gently ease himself into a seated position. As his fingers rubbed against the metal bar of the frame, every neuron in his brain registered excruciating pain. Just before bringing him to his cell, they'd inflicted a second form of torture, called the manicure, where they'd ripped the nails off his left hand, one by one, at a slow and deliberate pace. And still, there were no questions.

He had screamed. Much more than while he was being beaten. He wouldn't have believed such a small area of the body could be the source of such intense suffering. And this was just the beginning. The real interrogation would be underway shortly. Despite the pain, he wasn't surprised—the SOE experts had briefed him on the Gestapo's methods.

Footsteps sounded at the end of the corridor.

He knew he would crack. The goal was to hold out for as long as possible before giving up everything he knew. He'd been trained for this. He ran his tongue over his hollow tooth. The ultimate solution, the only way out of this hell. All he had to do was place something hard in his mouth, over the tooth, and bite down. The filling would pop, and the cyanide would set him free.

That was the theory anyway. Deciding to take his life, to be his own executioner, wasn't an easy choice to make. Obviously, none of the officers at the training centre had any real-life experience of it.

The lock turned, causing the metal door to vibrate. A ray of light filled the cell. Two imposing silhouettes loomed above him. His remaining eye identified his torturers. Charles curled up into a ball and picked up a small rock, which he placed in his mouth.

A strong German accent announced, "I'm sorry to inform you that your friend the pig farmer didn't survive our . . . questions. He died of a heart attack at the beginning of the interrogation. A regrettable mistake made by my colleagues."

A small, dark-haired man with a sickly complexion stepped into the room, wearing a white coat. He sat down on the bed next to Charles and placed a stethoscope on his chest. He nodded and whispered something in his boss's ear, causing his face to light up.

"What wonderful news. Your heart is in perfect condition. We can get back to our discussion."

Charles let himself be dragged by the shoulders on the cold, tiled floor of the corridor. As they entered the torture chamber, he bit down hard. He felt the bitter liquid flow down his throat and closed his eyes. He prayed silently. He was fighting for the good guys. This half-baked operation was for a good cause. Absurdly, however, he would die without knowing what it was.

29

Montségur
May 1941

The façade of the d'Estillac manor house seemed to have been slumbering for centuries. Nothing looked like it had changed since the beginning of the Hundred Years War. Not the tall windows with transoms and diamond-shaped panes overlooking the garden, nor the barred basement window of the old dungeon, which was now a wine cellar, nor the pepperbox turret. Only the front door, which opened out onto a sunlit courtyard, seemed to welcome visitors with a shy smile. An orange tabby cat came out of the house and inspected the feet of the rosebushes before rolling around on the battered slabs of the old threshing floor. Laure watched him for a moment, from the arched window on the second storey, then looked back to the mountain. She could see the trees they'd felled and the brush they'd cleared. Without the underbrush, the base of the castle shone like a new suit of armour. Further to the right, the naked outcropping was like a mirror reflecting the sun.

"Mademoiselle . . ." said a farmer standing at the door, beret in hand, as he gestured for her to come down.

"I'm coming, Bastien!"

Laure charged down the spiral staircase in seconds, ran through the entryway, and hurtled into the courtyard. Bastien was wiping sweat from his forehead.

"I can't stay. I'm expected at the farm. I just wanted you to know that the mountain has been cordoned off by the Germans. They're not letting anyone through."

Laure felt a wave of anger wash over her. She hadn't been back to Montségur since her stormy exchange with the SS colonel. And now, they'd not only taken over the castle, they were also keeping everyone else out.

"I hear they're conducting major excavations on the northern side. We wonder what on earth they can be looking for. There's nothing but brush and wildfowl out there."

Laure thanked him with a glance before silently giving in to her rage. How could she be barred from her own castle? If those SS goons thought they could keep her out, they were sorely mistaken. And her resigned old father wouldn't be making her decisions either. He hadn't even left the library since their last discussion anyway. As if his books could save him from this enemy invasion! Laure stared at the mountain again. If the main entrance was blocked, how could she get in? Via the outcropping? The Germans were already swarming there. The north side? Surveyors were everywhere. She turned to the west, behind the dungeon keep. There was a ledge the Germans hadn't cleared yet. Probably because it didn't interest them for excavations. Too narrow and rocky. If Laure wanted to get into the castle, that was the way she'd have to climb. Up the steepest side of the mountain.

She'd been climbing for an hour, slipping between trees, avoiding the slap of their branches, and crawling under thickets. Her face was dotted with sweat. She cursed her heavy, oversized coat, which kept getting caught in the brambles. Her boots were covered in scratches from slipping on rocks. Just before the ledge, she'd got a whiff of the heady odour of a group of boars. The hairy black pigs had just come through and she could still see their tracks on the ground. Laure took a deep breath. The ridge was just ahead, not more than three or four meters from where she stood. She had to find a way up, somewhere with protruding rocks for her to grasp. She slipped between two rock walls, scratching her cheek, and managed to stand up on the ledge. A lichen-covered boulder sat against the keep. Laure climbed up it until she reached the tower wall and an arrow slit shaped like a stirrup. She looked through it. The dungeon floor had been cleared of debris and carefully levelled. There were holes in the ground at regular intervals. Probe holes, she thought. They had built a small lean-to with a roof of leaves and branches against one wall.

As Laure turned her head for a better view of what was inside, the door to the castle courtyard swung open. A man in uniform—she recognized Weistort—entered, then stepped aside to let a woman in. They made their way to the lean-to. Afraid of being spotted, Laure backed away from the arrow slit. She only caught a glimpse of the unknown woman. With tanned skin and incredible blue eyes, she wore her blonde hair in a crown of braids. Laure was about to try to take another look when the woman's voice echoed off the old walls.

"Oberführer, I've looked closely at the preliminary report you sent me in Berlin. Your team has exposed the foundation of the outer fortifications and found vestiges of the original village, but since I'm here now, you must not have found what you were looking for."

Intrigued, Laure leaned in again. The young woman was already inspecting the floor of the keep.

"I see you've used probe holes everywhere," she said as she looked up at Weistort.

"Every two meters, but we've found nothing but bedrock under the top layer of dirt."

"So, no traces of past excavations or crevices in the rock? That's what you're looking for, isn't it?"

Laure thought of what her father had said. He was sure there must be an underground necropolis under the castle. Apparently this Weistort was also looking for a hidden breach in the rock.

"Among the documents we sent you was a collection of interrogations conducted by the Inquisitors. So you will know that, while hundreds of Cathars were burned at the stake at the foot of the mountain, four heretics escaped. Despite the fact that the castle was occupied and had been searched by the crusaders, no one ever found them. That's why I'm certain there must be a hidden chamber somewhere."

A mocking laugh bounced off the walls of the keep. "And you want me to find where they hid? Seven hundred years after the fact, in a castle that, according to you, was demolished and rebuilt?"

The woman's ironic tone made Laure smile despite herself. Part of her enjoyed watching the colonel squirm.

"You're a recognized specialist, Frau von Essling. Your publications on medieval archaeology have become reference volumes. And your family friend, Reichsführer Himmler, recommended you himself."

"Yes, but as you know, I don't work for the Ahnenerbe."

"Not yet," replied Weistort. "But I can find you a position worthy of your talents . . . and our expectations."

"Except that, and please correct me if I'm wrong, we're talking about an organization run by the SS, whose expeditions, like those in Tibet, use archaeological research as a cover story?"

"I see you're well informed, but the Führer has given us a priority mission: to find the roots of the German nation and prove its superiority."

"And in your opinion, this superiority is based on lost mystical knowledge?"

"Yes, knowledge which I will find, you can be sure of that."

"Do you really think the Cathars held this secret?"

Weistort's voice deepened. "The Cathars, as their adversaries called them, were dualists who believed that the world we live in was created by the Devil, that it was the embodiment of Evil, but that we could climb up to reach God. A spiritual climb that required secret powers."

Laure noticed when the archaeologist shrugged discreetly. "Not many historians share your view. They see the Cathars as rebels resisting the stifling authority of the Catholic church, who wanted to get back to Christianity as it was in the beginning, with neither priests nor sacraments."

"So why did those men flee?"

"You know as well as I do that the church prevented people from accessing the holy books—the Old and New Testaments—which it aimed to keep for its own knowledge and use. If the

Cathars had Bibles—God's true words, in their eyes—maybe they wanted to save them from the flames?"

"But four men to carry books?"

"We know the Cathars held material possessions, and particularly money, in great contempt. Nevertheless, when you live a clandestine life, you need money. The men who fled may have taken treasure with them to continue the fight elsewhere. As you know, the Cathars didn't fully disappear for another century."

"Since you haven't read all the interrogations conducted by the Inquisitors, Frau von Essling, let me tell you something. At Christmas 1243, two months before the fall of Montségur, two men escaped from the castle, carrying 'large quantities of gold and silver', according to several witnesses. They delivered the treasure to northern Italy, where large Cathar communities were still free to practise their religion. So, yes, the money got out, but months before the fortress fell."

"So, you think that since the money was pre-emptively evacuated to keep it out of the Church's greedy hands, there must have been another treasure carried off on the day when the two hundred heretics burned at the stake?" Weistort didn't answer, so she continued: "If they took it, as you imagine, there's no reason to look for where it once was."

"Haven't you ever been interrogated by the police, Frau von Essling?"

"Of course not!"

"I have. In Munich, in 1923."

Laure glued her ear to the arrow slit.

"In November, the Nazi party had attempted a coup. The police shot into a crowd of protestors, and twenty people died. Hitler was imprisoned and I was interrogated. What the investigators really wanted was to identify the people behind the failed putsch, assess the extent of their participation, and determine their whereabouts. Every hour, they alluded to my friends and colleagues . . . So, I talked."

"And none of it was true?"

"The details were real. Like the nails you hang a painting on.

Enough to get the investigators to believe my story and send them on a wild goose chase."

"So, you think the Cathars interrogated by the Inquisitors lied voluntarily, that they gave fake names and invented an escape that never happened?"

"No, I think they gave real names—precisely so the Inquisitors would follow them. As for the escape, I believe it really happened as well. Bait set for the Inquisitors to follow."

Fascinated by what she was hearing, Laure placed her eye against the arrow slit once more. The archaeologist stared at the colonel.

"So, this secret you're desperate to find?"

"Is still here," affirmed Weistort as he gestured around the courtyard. With a firm hand, he grabbed the young woman by the arm. "And you're going to find it. Whatever the cost."

30

I keep promises—even those made by others!

The slogan in bold black letters stood out on the small propaganda poster glued to the lamp post. The Maréchal's smooth, serious face seemed to be staring severely at Jane from beneath his kepi adorned with gold leaves. His posture fitted perfectly with the boastful slogan. Beneath the image, a short text taken from one of his speeches praised the benefits of collaboration.

"Such a shame," mumbled Jane, who had placed her suitcase on the ground and was sadly contemplating the decorated old man.

Right next to it, another poster featured a knife cutting a loaf of bread. *Cut it into thin slices and use the heels as croutons for your soup.*

"A stale old crouton for a leader and stale bread on the table. Poor France," said the young woman with disgust.

"Are you coming?" asked Malorley from the pavement on the other side of the street. "Our meeting isn't with Pétain."

Jane crossed the narrow Rue Bouquières as they made their way to the little restaurant tucked away on the ground floor of an old red-brick building. She had already fallen in love with the Occitan capital as they travelled from Matabiau station through the streets of the city centre. Dusk cast a gentle, blushing glow on the façades, creating the perfect atmosphere for a romantic walk. For a few precious moments, as they strolled the calm alleys in the cool evening air, she had forgotten about the war. Reality was suspended for a moment.

As for Malorley, he'd marched ahead without paying the slightest attention to the charms of the Pink City.

"I really don't understand why Pétain has agreed to be Hitler's lap dog," Jane announced when she reached Malorley. "He taught the Fritzes quite a lesson at Verdun."

The Englishman nodded as he pushed open the door of Le Cochon Jovial. "Deplorable, it's true. Thank goodness there's still de Gaulle to save France's honour."

The thick smell of stale smoke and old barrels filled the restaurant. Behind the counter, just past the entrance, an older woman in a candy-pink dress sat on a stool like Cerberus. She looked like an old baby with chubby cheeks, except for the pile of wild grey hair on the top of her head. She stared distrustfully at the couple, then barked, "If you're here for dinner, the kitchen's closing in half an hour," in a voice just as limp as her face. Her sing-song accent contrasted with her surly expression.

"Bonjour Madame, yes, we're here for dinner," replied Jane with the biggest smile she could muster.

"Do you have ration coupons?"

"Yes, more than enough."

"All right, then," crooned the owner in a gentler tone. "The dinner tables are at the back."

The SOE officer glanced quickly around the room. The walls were decorated with advertisements of laughing pigs, feasting away. An army of big hams and thick sausages hung from the ceiling. His mouth watered. His contact had chosen an excellent location for their meeting.

The restaurant was half-empty. A middle-aged couple was sitting next to a table where three men were playing dominos. Two men sat silently at separate tables. One read the newspaper as he waited for his dinner; the other was bent intently over his plate. Only the three domino players looked up at them as they crossed the room.

"Charming welcome," Jane joked. "I'll be sure to come back to Toulouse for the hospitality."

"And no one here has a black hat with a grey band," muttered Malorley, tensely. "Our contact must be late."

A skinny, white-haired waiter with a growing bald spot came over to their table, a towel thrown over his forearm. He chewed intently on a toothpick. "Good evening, Sir, Madam." His dark eyes were partially hidden by thick lids, which seemed to weigh a ton.

"Good evening to you. We're starving!" replied Malorley.

The waiter offered a small smile. "Like almost everyone in the country, Sir . . . Tonight we're serving pork-skin stew with turnips. To help it all go down, we also have lard, for an additional price, of course."

Jane opened her eyes wide and pointed towards the ceiling. "How about you take down one of those sausages for us?" asked the young woman, blinking sweetly.

The waiter made a weary gesture and explained. "I would advise against it, Mademoiselle, for your lovely teeth. They're only decorations, reminders of a time not so long ago when we had the originals in the cellar. Before we all began the Vichy diet. However, I do have some sauerkraut with bacon, but at your own risk."

"I guess the pig's not so jovial anymore. We'll stick with the special," replied Jane. "Do you have any wine?"

"Of course, like all restaurants worthy of the name, we have a house pitcher. But we can only offer one glass per customer. That's the law. It's a Minervois, however, and it won't give you an ulcer."

"That will do," said the SOE officer as he watched the old waiter walk away, dragging his feet.

"Strange," added Jane. "I was sure that there were fewer restrictions in the Free Zone."

"It would seem not, or perhaps he's saving his best dishes for his loyal customers," said Malorley with a glance at his watch. "Our contact is already ten minutes late. And so is Charles."

The young woman raised an eyebrow and looked him over with sincere curiosity. "You're too uptight. I hope you're not like this with Mrs. Malorley."

"There is no Mrs. Malorley. We divorced last year."

She unfolded her napkin and placed it on her lap, then took a gentler tone. "Would it be indiscreet to ask why you separated?"

"Yes," he replied bitterly. "I don't ask about your private life."

"I'm happy to tell you about it," she offered in a mischievous tone. "It might help you relax a little."

"We're on a mission. I'll relax when we're back in London."

"Since you keep mentioning the mission, let me remind you that we are supposed to be husband and wife," she insisted as she rubbed up against his shoulder. "You could be more affectionate. I wouldn't turn down a kiss."

The Englishman was dumbfounded. She kissed him before he could answer. Then she sat up straight again, as if nothing had happened, an impish look in her eyes.

Despite his surprise, Malorley wasn't entirely displeased. He hadn't kissed a woman in over a year. Since the beginning of the war, his love life had been about as exciting as a Scottish heath in winter.

"Are you always like this with men?" he asked as he unfolded his napkin.

"Don't misunderstand. It's purely professional. Between hand-to-hand combat and sabotage classes, we learn a few other things during our training at Arisaig House. At least the women do."

"Lucky instructors," he added laconically.

The waiter returned with two steaming plates, which he placed in front of them. Shapeless shreds of meat were drowned in a lumpy yellowish broth.

"Fit for a king's feast," joked Jane. "We should expect indigestion."

For the first time, Malorley smiled.

The waiter pulled out an advertising brochure and placed it on the table next to the piglet-shaped saltshaker.

"What's this?" asked the Englishman.

The waiter gestured his head towards a thin man sitting at a nearby table. "That guy over there is a sales representative. He's distributing brochures for a well-known tailor."

Malorley handed the brochure back to the waiter and shook his head. "We're not interested. You can give it back to him."

The waiter's small eyes narrowed. He kept his arm by his side.

"You should open it. There's an accessory that would suit you well," suggested the waiter as he turned his heels.

Malorley opened the brochure to find a collection of canes and hats, including a black model with a grey band.

The Englishman looked over at the representative. The man caught his eye, dabbed at his lips with his napkin, and stood up to join them. Beneath his ruddy complexion was a mask of small pockmarks. His bushy moustache hid his upper lip, compensating for a lack of hair. He looked good for his age of around sixty, with just a hint of portliness. He leaned in towards them and pointed at the hat.

"It's magnificent, isn't it?"

"A good hat is priceless," said Malorley.

"Even in the spring," replied the stranger.

"We're Mr. and Mrs. Darcourt. Please sit down."

"Pleased to meet you. I'm Georges. Or Jo, as my friends call me."

Just as the representative was about to sit down, the door to the restaurant swung open and a young boy in a cap ran straight to their table. The child whispered in Georges's ear. The moustached man nodded and handed the boy a piece of paper from his pocket, then turned to the couple.

"New plan. Come with me."

Malorley and Jane looked at him, speechless for a moment.

"We've just started eating," protested the young woman.

"There's no time for discussion. There's a group of plainclothes cops at the end of the street. And they're not regulars at the restaurant. Hurry up."

The two agents stood up suddenly, grabbed their suitcases and followed their contact, who moved with surprising agility, given his corpulence.

"Don't worry, everyone here is on our side."

The waiter cleared their table at the speed of light, without any reaction from the owner or the other patrons.

"Do the police know who we are?" asked Malorley.

"I don't know. Sometimes they do a raid just to check papers.

They're a bit overzealous. With the war, the Pink City has become the new Tower of Babel. There are two hundred thousand refugees in and around the city, and just fifty cops or so. Tens of thousands of escaped Spanish Republicans, French Jews who understandably prefer not to return to the Occupied Zone, Poles on their way to somewhere, antifascist Italians, and more. Not really the ideal French city, according to the Maréchal's standards."

They entered a storeroom full of crates and rubbish bins. They found a huge wooden cask up against a brick wall. Georges felt around the side of it with his fingers. There was a click and the base of the barrel opened as if by magic, revealing a stone staircase that descended into the darkness. The man stepped aside to let them through.

"*In vino veritas,*" he whispered glumly. "Hurry up." He closed the door to the cask behind him. The steps were totally dark, except for the rays of light that shone through the gaps in the barrel.

"It's a tight fit with these suitcases," complained Jane.

"There's no light," added Malorley.

"Hold onto my jacket. There are about twenty stairs, then we'll follow a straight tunnel. It doesn't take long."

The smell of saltpetre filled the air around them. Jane wished she had a handkerchief to filter out some of the foul smell. They walked for three or four minutes, then stopped in the dark. Georges knocked five times on a surface that sounded metallic, pausing between blows. They could hear someone fiddling with a lock and then a sliver of light appeared as the door creaked open. A man in his late fifties with a high forehead, thin lips, and jet-black hair slicked back from his face stood in the doorway. He studied the new arrivals for a while. His enigmatic expression made them feel like he was judging their souls.

Finally, his upbeat voice and Italian accent broke the silence. "Welcome to hell!" he said.

31

"Wake up! Something's happening."

Someone was frantically shaking his forearm. It was 'Goebbels', his glasses all steamed up. Tristan bolted upright on his cot. The sun was barely shining in the castle's courtyard, but he could hear hurried footsteps and shouts of alarm.

"An attack?" asked the Frenchman as he lunged towards the lamp.

For the past few days, a rumour had been circulating that there was an armed group operating along the border with Spain. Some said it was Spanish Republicans who had regrouped and were ready to fight again, others said it was an underground French Resistance network. The gossip came up from the valley with the villagers who supplied the castle's food.

"I haven't heard any gunfire," said 'Goebbels', "but they say the woods are full of rebels."

Despite the sudden awakening, Tristan smiled. Only an archaeologist specialized in the Middle Ages would call them that. *Rebels.* Where were the hermits and sorcerers?

"You know what?" 'Goebbels' went on. "Yesterday, some surveyors working in the northern sector heard strange noises coming from a thicket."

"Maybe it was elves," Tristan joked as he dressed. "They say they're rampant in these parts."

"Don't make light of such things. Rebels may have been watching us for weeks."

"And this morning they're attacking with rope ladders and grappling irons, like in the good old days? Listen, I'll tell you what your surveyor friends heard in the brush: boars. That's all there is to it. Now let's go and see what's happening outside."

In the courtyard, soldiers were standing at the ready at the entrance, whilst snipers lay on their stomachs across the ramparts, watching the sleeping countryside. Weistort was shouting orders so quickly that Tristan couldn't understand what he was saying. As for 'Goebbels', he remained safely behind the Frenchman, glancing worriedly at the roof of the keep as if attackers might suddenly appear at any moment.

"It's a sentry," announced Weistort. "We've just found his body."

A young woman came out of a tent barefoot in a khaki shirt she was trying to button over the top of her uniform trousers. The SS colonel clicked his heels.

"I'm sorry, Frau von Essling, but we have a problem."

He didn't have to explain. Four soldiers came through the main doors dragging a taut, heavy sheet on the ground. A sergeant hurried over with a torch. A corpse lay on the off-white fabric. His entire body seemed to be dislocated—his arms were positioned in a braided crown around his head and his legs formed right angles, each one going in its own direction.

"Suicide," whispered 'Goebbels'. "He must have thrown himself off a cliff."

Tristan didn't answer. He looked at the man's face. Or rather, his lack thereof. His head was turned completely around. All that was visible was the back of his broken neck, with vertebrae jutting through the skin, and a mop of bloody hair.

"Do you have a doctor?" asked Frau von Essling.

Weistort shook his head.

"Bring him into my tent, then. I'll examine the body. The dead fall into my area of expertise."

The colonel made a vague gesture of assent. Tristan watched the young woman leave, followed by the funeral parade. She must be the archaeologist from Berlin. She had elegant hands. He had noticed them when she'd buttoned her shirt. Hands like a pianist.

He couldn't imagine them digging in the dirt on a hunt for ruins or a tomb.

"Soldiers!" shouted Weistort in a deep voice that reached the farthest corners of the courtyard. "I don't want anyone going out without my authorization. For the time being, this castle is a fortress."

D'Estillac Manor

Laure's father was an early riser. He usually had his breakfast alone in the kitchen, where he listened to the ticking of the clock and watched the sun rise through the window. He was surprised to find his daughter there this morning, with one bright-red cheek and circles under her eyes.

"I went up to the castle yesterday, from the west."

"Brambles?" d'Estillac asked calmly, pointing to his daughter's cheek.

"No, I scraped it against a boulder while I was climbing. Then I spent quite some time with my face glued to the wall of the keep, so that didn't help either."

"You didn't take the easiest way up."

"It was the only one they weren't watching."

The cat came into the kitchen, meowing for his milk. D'Estillac picked up the bottle and poured some into the animal's bowl. The interruption gave him a minute to think. His daughter clearly wanted to talk, but she didn't seem to know how to go about it any better than he did.

"From where you went up, you must not have seen much of the occupants' excavations." He had chosen the word "occupant" carefully since he knew his daughter viewed the requisition of the castle as an injustice.

"I didn't see anything, but I heard a lot," said Laure. "A new archaeologist has arrived, straight from Berlin. A woman, sent by Himmler himself."

"A woman?" repeated d'Estillac, surprised. "Did you get her name?"

"Von Essling. She seemed sceptical about the excavations. Not

Weistort, though. You mentioned an underground room. The SS teams are looking for it, too. It's their priority. But I don't understand why the Nazis are willing to invest so much in a seven-hundred-year-old cemetery. It doesn't make any sense."

Her father remained silent. He'd always been enigmatic. Unlike Laure, who took after her mother and always expressed her feelings, whatever the circumstances.

Once again, she'd have to figure things out for herself.

Montségur

Now the castle resembled a front line. Soldiers monitored all entrances and the archaeologists were under protection. The thumping of boots and the clicking of weapons could be heard all around, as if an invisible enemy were in the courtyard. Other noises further heightened the ambient anxiety. The situation could easily get out of hand.

Weistort listened carefully to the young archaeologist's report on the dead soldier's tormented body.

"I'm not a coroner, but I took an anatomy course to be able to work on medieval tombs. The way bodies are placed in graves, their position, the way their arms and legs are arranged, are all important clues for dating and interpreting findings."

She pointed at the body on the table. "In this case, there's a clear anomaly: the dislocations. The joints of both the upper and lower limbs have been compromised."

"Could a fall do that?"

"It would have had to be an extremely violent fall, during which the body encountered a series of obstacles."

"There are plenty of boulders between the place where he stood watch and where he was found," commented Weistort. "He rolled several dozen meters."

"That doesn't explain how it all started. Did he jump or was he pushed? In the first case, it's a suicide. Otherwise, it's murder."

"It's a suicide, regardless," decided the SS officer. "The men need to be reassured immediately."

He turned to a subordinate. "Write up a report that concludes he took his own life. And start a rumour that we found a letter from his girlfriend among his effects. A letter ending things between them. I'll have to go to Foix immediately to keep the Reichsführer up to date on the progress of our research via a secure line. This *incident* cannot be allowed to slow our work."

"There's still the problem of the head," added the archaeologist.

The tent went silent. Everyone tried to avoid looking at his gaping neck.

"No matter how hard he fell, there's no way it could have twisted his head around like this."

"Meaning . . . ?" Weistort enquired coldly to ward off growing feelings of unease.

"The cervical vertebrae have been broken and dislocated, and the skull has been severed from the spine."

"So, it's a murder?"

"He was attacked from behind. He would have died quickly, no suffering."

Tristan was watching Weistort. It wasn't alarm or anger on his face. No, it was something else. Something more intense, more secret: a slight fold at the corner of his lips, a sudden redness in his cheeks, a fire kindled in his eyes. Excitement, thought Tristan. The excitement of the hunt. Weistort had found an adversary to fell. And he wouldn't stop until it was done.

"The man who killed this soldier cannot even imagine how he will suffer. I want that man. I'm going to kill him."

32

"*Buonasera* Georges," offered the man with the jet-black hair and a tangy voice.

"*Buonasera* Silvio. I see you're still putting on that theatrical entrance of yours. These are friends from London."

"English! Welcome to my humble shop."

The couple politely said hello.

The man brought them into a storeroom packed full of half-opened boxes of books, stacked from floor to ceiling. The smell of old paper replaced the stench from the tunnel.

"Come, follow me, please," urged Silvio as he closed the metal door with a steady hand and gestured towards a new stairwell, going up this time. "Watch your heads; the ceiling is low."

Malorley noticed an engraved acacia branch hanging over the lintel and followed the head of the network behind the Italian. He climbed the steps four by four, acutely aware of his surroundings.

"Where are we?" Malorley whispered to Georges.

"This is Silvio Trentin's place. He's an Italian friend. One of the first antifascists. He arrived in Toulouse in 1935 and set up this incredible bookstore. It's been home to our clandestine meetings for several months now."

They found themselves in a room featuring the pink Toulouse brick walls and floor-to-ceiling bookcases, which were all overflowing. Two apple-green fabric couches sat across from one another in the centre of the room, with a coffee table in the middle, piled high with books.

The Italian bookseller held out his arms. "Welcome to the hell of banned books. These shelves are covered in half a thousand works censored by the Duce, the Führer, the Maréchal, and the Caudillo."

"You're forgetting the erotic books banned by the popes," added Georges.

"Amen," said the Italian, crossing himself ironically. "Please, put down your suitcases and take a seat. Have you eaten?"

"Not really. Your friend extracted us just as our food arrived," replied Jane as she settled into one of the sofas.

Trentin laughed cheerfully.

"He did you a favour! That pig is hardly jovial anymore. I'll bring you some Bigorre ham, and I must still have some Mauzac goat cheese, and a good Fronton wine. I rarely have guests from London."

As the Italian left the room, Malorley sat down facing the sales representative.

"Aren't you being watched by the police?"

"Those idiots have never suspected there might be a secret passage between the restaurant and the bookstore. Vichy cultivates obedience, not imagination. But it won't last forever . . ."

"And they've never raided?" asked Jane.

"They have, twice. But this room is well hidden. You have to take another passage to reach the library. We're in the Saint-Etienne neighbourhood, where the Cathars developed an extensive network of underground sanctuaries to hide from the crusaders. It's how they escaped the Inquisitors. Silvio set up this hiding place on the day France signed the capitulation, in preparation for the dark days ahead. I can't even tell you how much work it was to install the aeration and heating system down here to protect his precious books."

Trentin arrived with a tray and set it down on the table.

"How is Mr. Churchill?" asked the bookseller as he uncorked the bottle of dark-red wine.

"Very well. He's in remarkable health despite all the cigars he smokes and the undisclosed quantity of whisky he drinks."

Trentin served his guests. "Admirable, admirable. And the United States, will they declare war?"

"They say President Roosevelt is for intervening," declared Jane, "but most of the country doesn't even want to talk about it."

The Italian brandished a glass overhead. "Cheers! May that *pezzo di merda* Hitler betray Stalin, break the non-aggression pact, and attack Russia," toasted Trentin with a fiery glow in his eyes. "That's the only way we can change the outcome of this war. Open a new front to the east, where Hitler will die in the icy steppe, like Napoleon. Otherwise England is doomed, and so are we."

The three guests raised their glasses in turn.

"England always finds a way," added Malorley. "Always. From noon to midnight."

The bookseller drank half of his glass, then answered. "How did you know?"

"The stylized acacia branch carved above the door to the stairs. Unless it's from your predecessors."

Trentin shook his head. "Good eye. Grand Orient, or at least what's left of it. I had it carved before the war and haven't been able to bring myself to erase it since."

"United Grand Lodge of England."

"I suspected as much. But you require your brothers to believe in God . . . Well, no one is perfect. Cheers, my brother!"

"Could you explain what you're talking about?" asked the young woman, wide-eyed with confusion.

The two men remained silent. Georges smiled and lit a cigarette.

"They've just realized they're both Freemasons. 'From noon to midnight' is one of their passwords."

"Freemasons . . . So you hold black masses and such?" she asked awkwardly.

Trentin smiled and answered. "Of course, and we sacrifice young virgins in the next room. It's best not to believe all the nonsense spread by our adversaries. Now it's my turn to ask a question. You're quite young to be taking such great risks. As Ronsard wrote, 'Youth takes flight and never returns.'"

The young woman finished her glass and placed it back on the table.

"'Better to waste one's youth than to do nothing at all.' Courteline."

Trentin's face lit up. "The young lady is quick-witted."

Georges stood up and took his friend's shoulder. "We're running out of time, Silvio. I must ask you to leave us, for your own safety."

The bookseller nodded. "I know. Call me when you're finished. I'll be working on translating Steinbeck into French. I have a long night ahead."

Georges waited for him to close the door, then spread a map of southwest France out on the table. "So, you'll sleep here tonight. At noon tomorrow, a colleague will take you directly to Montségur in his company car. He works for Supply Services and conducts health inspections at farms in the Ariège and Haute-Garonne regions. You'll arrive in the late afternoon."

Malorley's face displayed an embarrassed expression. "Another agent was supposed to join us at the restaurant tonight. He must have been held up. I would like to wait for him until tomorrow night."

The sales representative tensed. "That's impossible. The driver has to attend his scheduled meetings. Any change would be suspicious. You could wait to go until next week, though, once he's back from his trip."

"What about the train?"

"I wouldn't recommend it. There are more and more inspections on the Foix line."

Malorley hesitated. Time wasn't on his side—he couldn't wait another week. On the other hand, he would be down one agent in the field. "Okay," he finally agreed, serving himself a second glass of wine. "But if he doesn't arrive tomorrow night, he must have been intercepted."

"I won't be going back. The restaurant will be closed indefinitely, beginning tonight. We'll intercept your man when he enters the street. If he comes . . .

"In Montségur, you'll be met by Trencavel—that's the code

name for the head of the regional network. He'll welcome you personally. I don't know what you're planning to do there, but he warned me the area is swarming with Germans. And not just any Germans—SS officers. They're the worst scumbags to traipse the earth since the Huns. And honestly, I think Attila must have been more fun."

Unlike Jane, Malorley didn't react.

"But we're in Free France," she said.

The Frenchman laughed darkly. "The only thing 'free' about it is in the name. The Germans are everywhere, like syphilis in a rural brothel. It's not like our old Pétain could stop them."

"Do you know what they're doing there?" Malorley inquired calmly.

"Trencavel told me they're conducting archaeological excavations. I don't believe it for a second, though. They must be looking for a treasure. That's why you're here, isn't it?"

Malorley smiled but remained silent.

"Keep quiet if you like," said the resistance fighter with a shrug. "But to be clear, in exchange for our help, London will parachute in a hundred thousand francs, as agreed?"

"Of course, don't worry about that."

The young woman looked at Malorley in shock. "Money? I thought you were resistance fighters!"

"We are, but the government authorities we bribe aren't. The prefecture employees who provide us with papers, the prison guards who pass on messages . . . None of them do it for free. And the money will allow us to rent a new, safer space, on the outskirts of the city. Silvio's bookstore is too exposed."

"How many men can you provide in Montségur?"

"Five, maybe six. Spaniards, former members of the Republican army. They organized a small network in the Ariège after escaping from a Vichy detention camp."

Malorley grimaced. "That's not many men to take on the SS."

"Our friends are seasoned soldiers. They'll be delighted to slice and dice a few Nazis."

"What about weapons?"

"That's not a problem. The Spaniards brought their guns with them when they crossed the border in 1939."

Georges took out a pistol with a dark grip and put it down on the table in front of Malorley. "9mm, CZ model, made in Czechoslovakia, 1927 version. Reliable and effective. The pride and joy of Republican army officers. You'll need it."

"Don't I get one?" asked Jane in an innocent tone.

"With all due respect, it's not a toy for young women," replied the resistance man.

Jane picked up the CZ with an agile hand and brandished it level with her eyes. Then she pulled out the clip and the breech. In less than a minute, the gun was sitting in pieces under the surprised gaze of the moustached man.

"I prefer the Polish VIS, anyway. 1935 version," said Jane as she twirled the clip between her fingers. "It's more precise and jams less, but we'll make do with the Czech 'toy'."

Malorley smiled at Georges's surprise.

"All our agents receive extensive weapons training. Including women."

"What strange times we're living in," mumbled the resistance fighter. "Soon they'll be asking for the right to vote."

33

The pale Berlin sun filled the vast space, currently used as a smoking
room, with a gentle light. The mauve velvet wallpaper that had
once adorned the room had been replaced by austere filing cabinets
and swastika banners hanging from the ceiling. The only deviation
from the bureaucratic aesthetic was the portrait of Adolf Hitler—
instead of the official portrait of the Führer in his party uniform,
the room featured a copy of the portrait painted by Hubert
Lanzinger. In it, Hitler wore a medieval knight's suit of silver armour
and brandished a combat banner. His fierce expression, focused
on the quest for the Grail, was supposed to inspire the employees.

A carefully aligned row of grey metal desks—the administration's
standard model—had replaced the opulent green Chesterfield
armchairs that belonged to the office's former owners. Behind their
desks, ten men and two women worked doggedly, their heads
down, focused on the task at hand. The sounds of pencils scratching
paper as they followed the edge of a ruler were constant.

Standing in the door frame with his hands on his hips, Rudolf
Hess watched his devoted team. He had chosen only the best
candidates via a gruelling series of tests and interviews conducted
throughout the Greater Reich, in all of the occupied countries.
From the farthest corners of Brittany to the shores of the Baltic,
to the plains of Bohemia, and the fogs of Bruges, he had been
ruthless in the selection process. Most of the candidates chosen
were German, but there were also two Poles, a Czech woman, and
a French woman.

All of these experts had enjoyed flattering reputations before the war. It hadn't taken Hess long to find them as the Wehrmacht advanced. Convincing them wasn't difficult either. Except for the Reich subjects, the others had been forced to choose between collaboration and the firing squad. They had all enthusiastically offered to use their expertise to support the new European order. The Polish Jew had even turned out to be one of the most talented. The accuracy and relevance of his work amazed Hess, to the point where he was considering providing him with an Honorary Aryan certificate.

Hess observed his remarkable team with satisfaction. These men and women, who looked like any other government employees, all spent their days doing the same thing. They listened to the stars and spoke to the planets. They were astrologers.

Officially, the service was known to the rest of the party administration as the Forecasting and Special Calculations Office. A name suggested politely to Hess by one of his enemies, Hjalmar Schacht, the Minister of Finance. Though the Führer himself had authorized its creation, it was impossible to earmark funds in the budget for an astrology department. The Forecasting and Special Calculations Office . . . Hess hated the name, which reeked of technocracy, so he had put up his own sign at the entrance to the offices. Its silver letters read: *Skuld.* She was one of the three Norns of Norse mythology, who wove the cosmic tapestry of men's fates. Urd was responsible for the past, Verdandi for the present, and Skuld for the future.

The FSCO, or rather Skuld, was overseen directly by Hess, and no one was allowed in but him.

A trio of German astrologers focused their efforts on studying the star charts for the Reich's main enemies: Stalin, Franklin D. Roosevelt, and Winston Churchill. The latter received particular attention from Hess, who was an amateur astrologer in his own right. He knew the obstinate bulldog's birth chart by heart: born November 30, 1874, at 1:30 a.m., at Blenheim Palace in Oxfordshire. Sagittarius, Virgo rising. Moon sign Scorpion. His weaknesses included capriciousness, unpredictability, and depressive tendencies.

Hess liked to place Churchill's birth chart side by side with the Führer's. Hitler had a truly astounding star chart. Taurus, Capricorn rising. Strength and energy underpinned by ambition and tenacity. Even more incredibly, he was born under a perfect Venus–Mars conjunction. A rare astrological occurrence, which resulted in a person enjoying a perfect balance between masculine and feminine traits. The chart was so extraordinary that Hess had framed it and hung it as a curio in his living room.

The head of the Nazi party walked over to the astrologer in charge of Churchill. Hess hated the British Prime Minister as much as he loved the English people. He had several high-ranking friends among them, mostly secret Nazi sympathizers, like the former king, Edward VIII, and Sir Oswald Mosley, head of the English fascist party, who had been rotting in prison since the beginning of the war.

Because of Churchill, Göring kept bombing the country day and night, and Hess couldn't bear it. The English didn't deserve such brutality.

"Tell me that bastard Churchill is going to contract syphilis!"

The astrologer, whose eyes were red with fatigue, looked up at his protector. "I'm calculating the passage of Mercury in the third house. If it's confirmed, we could expect a sudden period of depression."

"Good, good. And what about my special project?"

The astrologer glanced fearfully towards his colleagues, then whispered, "I'm wrapping up the charts. Everything should be ready tonight."

He showed Hess the piece of white paper where he was drawing the star chart. Outside and all around the edge of the black circle were the positions of the planets within the constellations of the zodiac and the astrological houses. Inside there were geometrical shapes—triangles and squares—drawn in red or blue pen, created by the relative positions of the planets.

Hess leaned over the table to inspect his work. Though he was only an amateur, he knew how to read a chart. "Wonderful, Yaros! Your work will help save millions of lives."

The astrologer thought he must have misheard. Hess had never been concerned with the welfare of the human race before.

"Aryan lives, of course," Hess quickly added with a chuckle.

The star specialist bowed and smiled weakly. He often found himself shaking with fear at the idea that his master might one day become dissatisfied with his work and send him to a concentration camp.

Hess left the astrologer to his charts and headed over to a private office, which belonged to the only astrologer with his own space: The Great Woltan. That had been his stage name when he had spent his days telling fortunes in Munich. Now he focused on the charts of the highest-ranking Nazi officials, from the Führer's personal guards to party and army executives. Hess sent each of them a horoscope chart for their birthday every year. Most of them threw them out immediately. The man with the bushy eyebrows knew as much, but didn't care, because the charts helped him predict their behaviour. Skuld was his "office of astrological intelligence", as he called it when with his wife.

He entered without knocking and shut the door behind himself. The Great Woltan was an older man with a narrow face and a carefully groomed beard. He looked up and started to stand.

"It's an honour, Herr Hess."

"Don't get up. I just need to confirm an intuition."

"What is it?"

The head of the party sat down on the mage's desk. "I have a problem with Heinrich Himmler. As you know, I like him, but I can feel negative energy around him at the moment."

"What kind?"

"I wonder if he's making bad decisions. Can you show me his chart for the year?"

"Yes, of course."

Woltan unrolled the chart and studied it attentively. The name of the SS leader was inscribed in thin letters at the top of the document. "You're right! You are so astute. The Reichsführer is under the influence of a square. Jupiter, which governs pure reason, is in dissonance with Pluto and Saturn—the two most evil planets."

"I knew it! That's why he keeps pushing our Führer to make bad decisions."

"Yes," agreed Woltan. "You should be careful. He grows more powerful every day with his SS army."

Hess gave him a dirty look.

"Well, ahem, not as powerful as you, of course," mumbled the bearded fortune teller, realizing his faux pas.

"I don't have the Führer's ear—I have his brain! You focus on reading the stars and leave politics to those of us who know a thing or two about them," Hess replied dryly as he jumped up and left without a goodbye.

The head of the party made his way to his own office, his expression clearly betraying his irritation.

The stars never lie. Woltan had confirmed his fears about Himmler. He needed to meet with the Reichsführer as soon as possible to be sure.

The sound of his boots echoed in the silence. He had always liked the sharp, virile sound. When it came to men's shoes, he had chosen his camp long ago: real men wore shoes with stiff soles. The only time he ever deviated from the rule was at home, where his wife demanded that he wear slippers when they were alone.

When he reached the end of the corridor, he pushed open the two swinging bronze doors to his personal sanctum. The room featured a vaulted ceiling and looked like the nave of a church.

He loved this magical sanctuary, which was calmer and more private than the chancellery on the other side of Berlin, where he spent most of his time, to his great displeasure. People were always shouting, rushing around, scolding, and gossiping. Whenever he could, he took refuge here to think.

He had got rid of the original Masonic lodge décor, except for the painted ceiling—a vault of starry skies—and the symbols on two sacred lamps secured to the marble wall at the far end of the room: a golden sun and a silver moon. He'd burned the rest of it, beginning with the cursed delta triangle with the eye inside. It had been almost six years, day for day, since he had taken possession of the building at the head of a party squad. Before a frenzied crowd of Berliners, they had thrown everything from the lodge out of the windows: furniture, sculptures, books, keepsakes, paintings. The two old guards, who had unfortunately bumped their heads against a club, remained inside. The Nazis waited for nightfall, then lit a magnificent fire on the charming Kortenberg Platz. The date of the fire hadn't been chosen at random. June 21, Saint John's solstice. On that day, four planets form a perfect square in the Scorpio constellation.

The flames had kindled such joy that they had to prevent the most enthusiastic radicals from spreading the fire to the lodge itself. They even had to get out their clubs again—this time to disperse the most determined activists. It would have been a shame to destroy this magnificent 18th-century building when he planned to use it for himself. The next day, the building changed hands legally. The Supreme Master of the Grand Lodge—a frightened bank manager—had spontaneously gifted the title to Hess. The Nazi had made sure to add to the sale contract that it was "a gift to make up for the harmful influence Freemasonry has had on the German people for the past two hundred years."

Hess entered his quiet retreat and closed the doors.

Across from him, on either side of the central aisle, stood two rows of huge statues. He had commissioned them from Arno Brecker, the regime's official sculptor. On the right were half-naked men in a combat position, with determined chins and defined muscles. On the right, women whose outstretched arms were laden with offerings of wheat, cornucopias, and babies. On the right, the virile virtues of courage, perseverance, strength, and bravery; on the left, maternity, gentleness, humility, and grace. His taste in art was as inflexible as his taste in fashion. Hess liked the combination of beauty and simplicity. Simple ideas that any Aryan would understand from looking at a statue. Far from the degenerate art he had helped to destroy. Behind the statues, enormous wall lamps shed a warm, almost fiery glow on the room.

He liked to walk up and down the aisle, between his marble guards, to reach his desk, perched on the platform at the far end of the former Masonic lodge.

Facing east, as was the Masonic tradition. How ironic. A sign. Hess had been born in the east, in Egypt. In the country of pharaohs, the very same people who had reduced the Jews to slavery.

Pain snaked its way through his feverish brain. He staggered and reached out to steady himself on one of the Valkyrie statues.

The headaches were becoming more and more frequent.

Suddenly, a voice appeared out of nowhere.

"Big day for you."

His face brightened. He recognized the deep voice. It was coming from one of the statues, the one nearest his desk. Baldr. The god of light. His protector, who had guided him for years.

Hess had heard him speak for the first time about a year earlier, not long after the statue had been placed. He had asked Woltan and his personal secretary to join him, to see if they could also hear the god speak. In vain. But for good reason—Baldr had chosen him, and no one else. The god didn't speak to him every day, of course, just on special occasions.

He stopped in front of the statue. *"Make sure to cover your ears this winter. It will be cold."*

Hess didn't know how to interpret the advice. For some time now, the god's messages had become obscure, but he thought he knew why. The only rational hypothesis was that Baldr knew Rudolf's enemies were listening to their telepathic conversations and didn't want them to hear his advice. So, he spoke in code.

"Make sure to cover your ears this winter. It will be cold."

He copied the message down in the notebook he always had with him, to decode the hidden meaning later.

"We'll discuss this later."

The pain eased and the voice disappeared.

He walked to the end of the central aisle and climbed the stairs as if nothing had happened. He slumped down into a comfortable armchair placed in front of his desk—a rectangle so perfect it could have been a ledger stone.

He picked up his phone and dialled his personal secretary. "Call Reichsführer Himmler and tell him I must speak to him urgently."

"Yes, Sir."

Since he'd been at the head of the party, he'd made many enemies, who all strove tirelessly to discredit him in the eyes of the Führer. All opportunists and bootlickers, who had joined in the glory without taking a single risk. They spread rumours about his so-called insanity and his esoteric whims. Even his brief stay in a psychiatric hospital got Göring and Goebbels going. The idiots knew nothing of the occult forces that governed the world, using men as their puppets. They had bribed his cook, his valet, his driver, and maybe even his wife. He wasn't sure. He needed more proof.

Himmler picked up the phone before the end of the first ring.

"Rudolf, how are you?" asked Himmler's staticky voice. The poor quality made it seem like he was calling from the farthest reaches of the country, although his office was only a few blocks away.

"Have you found the Montségur relic?"

"I've just heard from Weistort. My hopes are high. And once we have it, we'll be able to begin the final battle."

Hess furrowed his bushy brow. "I need to meet with you briefly."

After an awkward moment of silence, the head of the SS answered annoyedly: "I'm very busy at the moment. Too busy. The invasion of Russia—"

"No!" Hess interrupted. "We cannot open a second front while still fighting England."

"My dear Rudolf, you didn't call me to discuss military strategy, did you?"

"We must discuss this face to face."

After a few frigid seconds, Himmler replied, "I have to visit an important construction site tomorrow. I'm meeting with the architect and his team. Let's meet there."

"Very well. Is it one of the new buildings designed for Germania? I saw the model at the chancellery. It's magnificent."

"No, not at all. It's a camp," Himmler answered smoothly. "A new concentration camp. Birkenau."

34

The castle looked like a military fortress again. Before leaving for Foix, Weistort had strengthened its defences. He didn't want to risk delaying or stopping the excavations because of a potential threat. He had added patrols and increased the number of men per group. As for the guards, they had been ordered to shoot anything suspicious on sight. They were following their orders to the letter—rustling in a thicket or the sound of a falling stone elicited shots that rang out over the mountain. Their easy trigger fingers worried Tristan. Not for him, but for the young woman in the beret, whom he feared would come back up to the castle, with no knowledge of the new security measures in place. Since he hadn't been given a specific mission, Tristan decided to accompany the group of soldiers who went down to the village for the week's supplies. In theory, he should have told von Essling, but she was busy readying the next wave of excavations. 'Goebbels' and the other scientists paced the courtyard in boredom, discreetly glancing now and again at the tent where the archaeologist had been busying herself all morning. Her way of establishing her authority over a group of men, thought Tristan.

At the entrance to the fortress, a coffin lay on the ground. The Frenchman walked over. The SS runes were engraved in black under the dead soldier's name. Tristan wondered if his face had been placed back in its normal position.

"We're taking him down to the village," announced the Rottenführer, the head of the section. "The logistics team will take care of him."

Given the men's reluctance to approach the coffin, Tristan could tell the rumours were spreading like wildfire. He kept quiet and joined the back of the group. As soon as his colleagues—after all, he wore their uniform now—went down for supplies, he'd try to find the castle's owner. It took half an hour to reach the valley because the rocky path was so steep and slippery. Little by little, the procession made its way down the path, fighting back box branches coated in dew. The warrant officer led the group, followed by the jolting coffin carried by four men trying their best not to stumble on the wet rocks.

"If we're attacked, we'll be easy pickings," said one of the soldiers, nervously clutching the butt of his rifle.

"I'm more afraid of what's inside there," said a young recruit, gesturing towards the coffin.

"Did you see his body? He saw the Devil's face before he died." Tristan got closer, to listen in.

"The quicker we get down this hill, the sooner we'll be rid of him. So, don't slow down. I heard they're going to burn him, like they did the heretics from the castle."

"Do you really think demons are afraid of fire?"

The precautions Weistort had taken had been useless. Fear was spreading through the ranks. Irrational fear—the hardest kind to combat. To see how bad things were, the Frenchman tried to offer a simple explanation.

"Maybe he really did just fall, right? The rocks could have broken his bones."

"And turned his face all the way around? No, that was the Devil."

Tristan didn't get a chance to answer. They'd just reached the outpost guarding access to the castle road. Relieved, the men put down the coffin. They quickly uncorked their canteens and the smell of schnapps wafted through the fog rising off the valley. The Frenchman didn't linger. He made his way discreetly towards the village.

At this time of day, most of the residents were already in the fields or tending to animals in the stables. A lonely dog barked from the far end of an alley. Since the Germans had arrived, the village had become withdrawn. Many of the shutters remained closed, and the people went out as little as possible. In the main street, the grocery store was the only place open. Most of the shelves in the small shop were empty because of rationing. However, there was tobacco. Tristan went in and said hello to the hunched silhouette behind the counter. It was a woman of indistinguishable age, with a black shawl covering her hair and shoulders. A widow, most likely.

"A pack of shag, please. And a bit of information: where do the owners of the castle live?"

A skinny finger came out from under the shawl and pointed to the end of the street. "Go straight to the cemetery, then turn left. The dirt road. When you reach the gate, you're there."

Tristan thanked her and left. The street was still deserted. A cold wind accompanied the fog, which was as thick as ever. It occurred to him that he was wearing the enemy uniform and didn't have a weapon. He was an easy target. But he didn't turn back. French to the Germans, German to the French—this war had turned him into Janus, the two-faced god. Maybe he even had a third that no one else knew about. His heels tapped loudly against the dirt path, hardened by the cold. He'd just passed the cemetery. On the left, a grassy path led into the fog. He turned up the collar on his jacket and started whistling.

The gate was open, so he crossed the courtyard and rang the bell. The door opened to reveal the woman he had been hoping to see, though this time she was without her beret, and her eyes were even more full of anger than the first time they'd crossed paths.

"We met at the castle a few—"

"I know where we met. What do you want?"

"I'm Tristan."

"I'm not interested in knowing your name. The uniform you're wearing tells me enough. And you didn't answer my question. What do you want?"

A wary cat pushed his head past the half-open door. He must not have liked the uniform either, because he immediately started hissing.

"I know you're Laure d'Estillac and that your family owns the castle."

"Or used to own the castle, since you've taken it from us."

"The situation is only temporary."

"So, you're just tourists, then?"

Tristan almost burst into laughter. She had plenty of nerve and wasn't short of bravery either.

"We're conducting important archaeological excavations, which require additional security. The mountain's entire perimeter is off limits to any unauthorized visitors."

"*Roda que rodaras, mai dins ton pais tornaras,*" she replied in a gravelly voice.

"I'm sorry, I don't understand."

"It's an Occitan proverb: 'Travel if you must, but you'll always return home.' You won't be here forever!"

"Thank you for the language lesson. I'll do my best to remember it. In the meantime, I just wanted to warn you that the guards have been ordered to shoot trespassers on sight."

Laure took a step towards him. "Did Colonel Weistort send you?"

"The Oberführer has other priorities at the moment."

She frowned in surprise. "So, you decided to come on your own?"

He was about to reply when a deep voice echoed from inside the manor.

"Laure, do you have a visitor?"

"It's my father. I'd rather he not see me talking to a—"

"I won't inconvenience you further."

He waved goodbye and turned to go. As he passed through the gate, he heard two words. Just two.

"Thank you."

'Goebbels' was waiting for him at the entrance to the castle. His usual aloof demeanour had vanished—he could hardly contain himself.

"Hurry up, Frau von Essling is about to make an announcement. Everyone's gathered in the courtyard."

That woman really knew how to kindle enthusiasm, thought the Frenchman. Tristan didn't hurry, though. Part of him was still down in the valley. His visit with Laure was an unexpected ray of light in this dark time as a prisoner in the stifling fortress. He was still wondering what the young woman must have thought of his impromptu visit, until von Essling's voice put a sudden end to his musings.

"Oberführer Weistort has placed me in charge of the excavations in his absence, and we are about to take a new direction. The surveying phase has been completed," she said, turning towards the architect and his assistants. "We have a detailed map of the area and will now focus our efforts inside the castle walls."

Most of the archaeologists did their best not to gawp in confusion. There wasn't anything to be found in the castle. Nothing but boulders and rocks.

"As we now know, the fortress that surrounds us is not the fortress that withstood the siege of 1244. At the time, it was a *castrum*, with a defensive tower."

"You mean the dungeon keep?"

"No, not at all. The original tower was located right around there," she said as she gestured towards the centre of the courtyard. "We will now turn our attention to finding an underground chamber that was beneath the original tower."

"But we'd have to excavate the entire castle and courtyard," objected the architect. "That's a huge amount of dirt to dispose of. It would take months."

"Unless we know where the original tower stood."

A shocked 'Goebbels' turned towards Tristan. Was *this* really the elite archaeologist Himmler had chosen?

"Have you looked closely at the arrow slits on the current keep? There are five of them, identical in every way. A thin vertical slit with a rectangular base. This type of opening at the bottom widened the archer's range, allowing them to reach enemies at the foot of the walls. It's a technical innovation from northern France and characteristic of the 14th century. You did a great job excavating the whole plateau for weeks, but this simple detail should have immediately told you that the current castle was built by the crusaders."

In one fell swoop, she'd established her authority over everyone in the courtyard.

"I hear her name's Erika," whispered 'Goebbels', now captivated by her genius.

"However, if you inspect the south wall closely, you'll find four filled-in, but still visible, arrow slits with triangular bases, which date back to the original castle. And since, at that time, arrow slits were only used on defensive towers . . .

"We'll remove the fill from the slits this afternoon. Once we've opened them from the inside, they will help us trace the perimeter of the tower inside the courtyard. Then, we'll start digging."

The archaeologist was about to applaud, when a soldier entered the courtyard. "Oberführer Weistort is back!"

35

The three crows perched on the roof of the old dovecot had been cawing in unison since the car had arrived. It was parked next to a barricade on the side of the road that led to the village of Montségur. The driver had left over half an hour ago to find the group of resistance fighters. He'd told Jane and Malorley to wait for him at the car, but he was taking his time and the sun would be setting soon.

Malorley stood in front of the car, studying the castle with a pair of binoculars. The mountain stood out in the dusky sky, with the foothills of the Pyrenees in the background. The stone structure reflected the ochre light of the setting sun. The Englishman couldn't take his eyes off it. He knew its history and tragedy by heart.

The battles, blood, and finally ashes, of the unfortunate Cathars burned by the Inquisitors and crusaders from the north—precursors of the Nazi hordes. In the great book of human cruelty, written in the blood of men and dictated by a blind god, there is no final chapter.

The SOE agent felt the hairs on the back of his neck rise as he took in the incredible view.

Déjà vu . . . He felt like he'd been here before, long ago. Before leaving London, he'd studied the Cathars' beliefs. He knew that some of them believed in reincarnation. Could he be one of those souls that had travelled the river of time and was only now in the body of an Englishman from Devonshire?

He chased the silly theory from his mind. Since he'd been studying the esoteric beliefs of his adversaries, his view of the world had changed somewhat. He had strange ideas. He needed to focus on the commando mission. He was here to attack the fortress. That was his mission.

He was about to risk lives, including his own, for what might be little more than a pipe dream—a talisman that may or may not be hidden somewhere in the bowels of a fortress in ruins.

A relic that some believed could change the course of history.

He couldn't tell Jane—she'd think he was crazy. But hadn't the entire world descended into folly and immorality since the beginning of the war?

Hitler and his goddamn Nazis. An army of fiends, an entire people turned into monsters. Including Colonel Karl Weistort, who was just inside the castle walls. Almost within reach.

They were finally about to meet. Malorley would be able to keep the promise he had made to himself in Berlin, on that tragic November night in 1938.

One of the crows flew off suddenly, breaking his train of thought. The bird brushed past him as it made its way to a branch above the car.

Jane got out and brandished her shiny pistol at the bird. "Damn bird! Shut it or I'll shoot. I don't even care if it alerts the Krauts!" she grumbled.

"Are you superstitious?" he asked, walking towards her.

"Not at all. When I was little, my parents had a house near Bourges, right next to a farm. The countryside was beautiful, but full of crows. I had to walk past them every morning on my way to school. It was so gloomy. I threw rocks at them, but still couldn't make them go away. They sat there and teased me every day. In the end, I took care of the problem, though."

"How?"

"Bang! Bang!" she said, aiming at the crow. "That's how my dad taught me to shoot, on my twelfth birthday. I went on to become one of the few women in shooting competitions. And I—"

"Shh!" he cut her off.

Malorley listened carefully. He thought he'd heard a noise coming from the path into the forest. The scraping sound of soles on stones grew louder.

He grabbed the binoculars and recognized the driver coming out of the brush, followed by a small group of armed men walking in a single-file line. They all wore tattered clothes and most of them were skinny and bearded with unkempt hair tucked haphazardly into woollen hats.

"They look more like bandits than soldiers," he said, handing the binoculars to the young woman. "I hope they're not anarchists."

Jane laughed. "What were you expecting? The Royal Horse Guards?"

Malorley frowned. "I know a fair bit about Spain and its people," he explained. "I went on two missions there during the civil war, in Teruel and Barcelona. Some of the Republican battalions were so disciplined, they'd make His Majesty's troops look bad. Especially the communists. And God knows they held a special place in my heart. But the anarchists . . . They were unruly beyond reason. Real jackasses."

"If I were you, Englishman, I'd hold my tongue. I've cut throats for far less."

The hoarse voice with a Spanish accent had come from behind them. The couple turned around to find two men armed with automatic Erma-Vollmer pistols—easily recognizable by their wooden grips. The first one was about forty, with dark-brown hair, a chunky pair of glasses, and a sideways cap. He was chewing on a toothpick. The second had a halo of white hair and a serious face.

"Good thing we aren't Germans," added the older man. "Hasn't anyone ever taught you to watch your back?"

"Who are you?"

The older man bowed slightly and spoke. "Jean d'Estillac, also known as Trencavel. And this is my friend, Captain Enrique Bujaraloz, aka La Cebolla."

The man in the hat remained impassive and continued to observe the SOE agents warily. Clearly dissatisfied by what he saw, he ran his hand over his wiry beard and spat on the ground as the group of resistance fighters reached the car.

"It's not your lucky day, Englishman. In Spain, I was part of the Durruti Column, 26th division, *centuria negra*. You'd be hard-pressed to find anyone more anarchist than me and my friends in the area, maybe even in all of France. We jackasses might just piss in your shoes."

Malorley sized up the captain. He had to establish his authority now if he wanted to maintain his control over the operation. He approached the two men, until he was only a yard away. "I hoped your defeat by Franco's troops would have taught you a lesson about the virtues of obedience and discipline. But given the look of you and your friends, I fear that nothing has changed."

Tensions soared. And the new arrivals' faces soured. Jane gripped her pistol tightly in her pocket.

"I'm not sure this is the right approach with these people, Commander," she whispered in Malorley's ear. "You should be more . . . positive."

"I don't need your advice, Jane. Stay out of this."

The Spaniard got in the SOE agent's face. "Englishman, do you know why I'm called La Cebolla?"

"If memory serves, that means 'onion'," replied Malorley without flinching. "With those glasses, you obviously couldn't have been much of a sharpshooter. Maybe you were a cook?"

The Spaniard turned to his friends. "The Englishman thinks I was a *cocinero* during the war!"

His men broke out in merry laughter. The Spaniard turned back to the SOE agent. "Onions make people cry. That's what I do. I liked to watch the tears stream down the fascists' faces before I finished them with my knife. Maybe you'd like a demonstration?"

D'Estillac tapped the anarchist's shoulder. "Enrique, now that you've been introduced, let's get to the heart of the matter. This is no time for a pissing contest." Then he turned to Malorley. "These people will be shot at for you, so apologize. Right now. Or they'll leave immediately."

"He's right. You should do what he says," encouraged Jane in a whisper.

Malorley remained silent for a few seconds, then bowed his head half an inch. "Gentlemen, please excuse me," he said, his face about as warm as a thermometer in Siberia.

La Cebolla smirked. Laure's father had a coughing fit, then wiped his brow with a handkerchief.

"We'll have to attack the castle sooner than expected," he announced in a hoarse voice. "The Germans are about to begin excavations inside the castle."

"Don't take this the wrong way," Malorley interrupted, "but aren't you a bit old to be on a commando mission?"

"Don't you worry about my health. La Cebolla will lead the attack. He and his men know the ground well. They already murdered one of the SS guards at the castle."

"I threw him over the boulders myself," added La Cebolla. "The superhuman flopped around like a cheap ragdoll."

"Okay, but the attack will be on my orders!" hissed the SOE agent. "To be perfectly clear, as agreed with your boss in Toulouse, this operation is mine to manage. Otherwise, you can forget the money and materials promised to your network."

The Spaniard's eyes narrowed. *"No problema, amigo,"* chuckled La Cebolla. "You can take us sightseeing on the area's hiking trails."

"I studied the terrain before leaving, but don't worry, I'll leave you in charge of the operational aspects of the attack. Get us inside the castle and neutralize the guards, that's all I need from you."

"Is that all? Maybe you'd also like a good paella for dinner?" La Cebolla replied sarcastically. Then he turned to Jane. "And you, Miss, will you be coming along?"

"No, I'll be mending your socks and waiting for you by the fire. I can also do dishes and clean the house."

D'Estillac smiled for the first time. The young woman's eyes shone with the same defiance he saw in Laure's.

"Trencavel, we need to do it tonight." La Cebolla's voice brought him back to the present. The Spaniard had laid out a drawing of the castle walls on the bonnet of the car. "The Germans are mostly inside the castle. They've set up a guard post halfway up the path. Here's what I suggest. We'll . . ."

36

In honour of the occasion, the prisoners had built a varnished wooden stage that overlooked the construction site of the future camp. A red carpet ran from the official car over to the steps to protect the Reichsführer's polished boots from the mud, which had turned the countryside into a marsh over the past week. The architect in charge of the project nervously watched Himmler walk forward, terrified that a speck of dirt might sully the SS leader's uniform. Hess, who wore a Bavarian jacket buttoned up to the collar, remained silent at the Reichsführer's side. The architect wondered which of the two men he feared more. In any case, an official visit from two high-ranking dignitaries was not a good sign. And the rain just wouldn't stop. The mud was everywhere. As for the construction site . . . The architect shook his head discreetly. They were getting nowhere. They'd barely managed to clear the trees and outline a vague quadrilateral, which now contained the materials for building the future prisoner lodgings. If things continued at this rate, everything would rot before anything got built.

Himmler had climbed up onto the stage, followed by Hess. The workers went about completing their tasks, clearly suffering the effects of hunger and exhaustion. The architect had given up on the idea of having them line up for the Reichsführer. They were too skinny and dirty—an army of wretches.

"So, what do you think, Rudolf?" asked Himmler, gesturing at the site.

Hess unbuttoned his jacket. The humidity was stifling. He took his time before answering. All he could see was a huge field of mud with a few piles of wood and some waiflike workers wandering here and there. "How many prisoners will this new camp hold?" he asked.

"A hundred thousand."

His long experience with Hitler had taught Hess never to display a visible reaction to absurd statements or outrageous projects. He'd learned long ago that nothing was unthinkable for the Nazis. He asked another question instead. "When is it scheduled to open?"

Himmler looked inquisitively towards the architect, who stood at attention, his feet in the mud.

"October, Reichsführer. As you requested."

Hess studied a group of prisoners, shivering in their oversized pyjamas as they pushed wheelbarrows full of rocks. Himmler leaned towards his friend. "They're Polish soldiers we captured. Rather than feed them to sit around, we use them as workers. The problem is that they're not very sturdy. I'll have to authorize a new wave of recruitments."

Rudolf nodded slowly. One of the detainees had just fallen to the ground and was already covered in a thick coat of mud. Neither the guards nor the other prisoners reacted.

"This will be the camp of the future. Four hundred acres, over three hundred detention units, ten miles of barbed-wire fences. A model to look to."

As he listened to Himmler speak, the architect was seized with panic. Six months, only six months to finish this hell on earth, or he'd end his career in the camp next door. Auschwitz—terrible things happened there.

"Here," continued the Reichsführer, "we will re-educate entire populations through work. Tens of thousands of men and women will help build our Great Reich. This is where our Führer's dream will truly take flight."

"A project in line with the noblest of goals," agreed Hess. "But there's one thing I don't understand. Where will the prisoners come from to fill the camp? They won't be Poles, given how fast you go through them. French? Too risky, that would jeopardize our collaboration with Pétain."

"Think harder," said Himmler with a smile.

"Political prisoners? We've imprisoned or killed them all. Jews?"

"Not yet, but that will come," announced the Reichsführer. "Rudolf, you are short on imagination this morning!"

With a wave of his hand, Hess sent the architect away. He hated to have an audience when he felt unwell, and his headache was coming back stronger than ever. He could hear Baldr's voice again.

"Ask about Russia or your ears will freeze!"

Hess's face brightened. So that's what Baldr's warning referred to.

"Yes, Baldr. I understand."

"And don't let him push you around. You already know what you must do."

"Are you okay, Rudolf?" asked Himmler. The Reichsführer's voice brought Hess out of his daydream.

"Yes, just feeling a little dizzy. Go on, Heinrich, don't keep me guessing."

"The Russians! We'll defeat the Russians once and for all."

Hess looked at him worriedly. "You plan to attack the Soviet Union? But you know we aren't ready. Remember what happened to Napoleon. Invading the east is like jumping headfirst into the darkness, like diving into a well. It's suicide. We must negotiate an agreement with England first. It's the only solution if we want to defeat Stalin."

"There's no more time for negotiation, Rudolf. Only for total war. We will wipe the Slavs off the map. That's why I'm building this camp. As soon as we begin our lightning attack, we'll have entire herds of Russian prisoners, without forgetting the Jewish parasites of Ukraine. Birkenau will be the solution."

Hess shook his head in disbelief. "Invading Russia would be pure folly," he repeated.

"For normal men, yes. But not for us."

Hess took a step back.

"We're about to get our hands on the second relic at Montségur."

A gunshot rang out. One of the guards had just fired a shot into the air to try to get a group of weakened Poles, which the mud threatened to swallow whole, to move faster.

"When?" asked Hess impatiently. Himmler mistook his tone for enthusiasm.

"In just a few days the swastika will be in Wewelsburg. Now you understand why we're going to attack the Soviet Union, and win."

The Reichsführer stared silently at the muddy clearing, the felled trees, the haggard prisoners, but he didn't see any of them. He contemplated his kingdom, which would soon become a reality. His empire with roots of blood, which would make him the most powerful man in the Reich.

Baldr was right.

Unlike Himmler and Göring, who reigned over the SS and the air force respectively, Hess owed his position entirely to his friendship with Hitler.

Since Germany had declared war, the Führer had needed generals, engineers, tacticians, and technicians. Power had been seized, and now the world was being divvied up, and Hess didn't have a share.

But it wouldn't remain that way for long.

Then and there, he made a decision: it would be him, not Himmler, who would change the course of history.

37

They had set up a perimeter in the castle courtyard. Inside, a group of archaeologists cleared away debris, placing it carefully, piece by piece, in wheelbarrows that the soldiers ferried to another team, sitting at long tables at the foot of the keep. They examined the pieces meticulously and sorted them according to size and shape. The tedious process left Weistort feeling impatient. He'd told the Reichsführer that the discovery of the hidden treasure in Montségur was imminent and he had every intention of keeping his word. With Tristan by his side, he paced the dig site at a gallop, his mind full of questions.

"The archaeological layer we're currently excavating includes parts of the demolished walls of the original tower, but when they fell, they spread over a very large area. Too large," explained Erika.

"So, let's get more people in here to clear away this pile of ruins more quickly," urged the Oberführer. "We'll save time. Berlin is eager to have the object in hand."

"Saving time is exactly what I'm trying to do by keeping the dig site small."

"But how?" baulked Weistort. "By sifting through each little pile of debris?"

"By finding the cornerstones, for example, which would tell us exactly where the foundations of the tower stood."

Weistort almost shrugged but stopped himself. The archaeologist had been the only one to guess where the underground room might be. Beginning a confrontation with her was not in his best interests. It was better to make her feel supported, but to keep an eye on her. He was sure this woman, from a wealthy, aristocratic family, only paid lip service to Nazism because she had little choice. He'd also learned that she'd been invited to Göring's most recent hunt at Carinhall. A privilege for a woman. The Ogre never invited anyone without good reason.

"I trust you to successfully complete this mission, Frau von Essling, but you know how important it is," he explained. "I'll leave my assistant with you, to keep me up to date," he said, gesturing towards Tristan.

Spending two years in prison had taught the Frenchman to contain his reactions. He turned to the archaeologist and clicked his heels, but skipped the "Heil Hitler" salute, which any SS officer would have performed. Erika raised an eyebrow, studied Tristan as if this were the first time she'd laid eyes on him, then invited him to sit down next to her. On a scale of one to ten, she had just given him a two, thought Tristan as he watched her confidently sort the debris brought to her.

"Are you always so quick to judge men?"

"Usually faster."

She wore her hair up in a ponytail, but several blonde strands had fallen out along the back of her neck. Each time she tossed a rock aside, a gleam of light reflected off her locks, illuminating the Frenchman's face. The archaeologist's hand suddenly stopped on a piece of debris that was smoother than the rest, with a preserved right angle.

"The outer edge was chiselled. I can see the marks. We've just found part of a cornerstone. Now we must find the other pieces. Come with me."

Von Essling headed towards the dig, where 'Goebbels' and his colleagues were hard at work.

"The zone is divided into four sectors, each with its own team of archaeologists. They record a number on each excavated piece, so we know exactly where it came from. And this one came from . . ."

She turned around towards the northeast sector and passed the fragment around. One of the archaeologists, whose face was already dripping with sweat, raised his hand. "I found it."

"Where exactly?"

"Here."

The piece of the cornerstone had been found near the very centre of the sector.

"From now on, only excavate a strip two meters wide down the central line. Two groups, working towards each other from the far ends. Move inch by inch and don't miss a thing. Got it?"

She turned to Tristan. "Go tell your boss that I'll come see him in two hours. And there's no point in you coming back before. I prefer to work without any pets under foot."

She was about to turn and leave when the Frenchman replied, "Pets sometimes have a good nose. Did you notice the direction of the chisel marks on the surface of the stone?"

"Why would it matter?"

"The chisel marks all go from left to right. That means the worker who carved it was left-handed. A unique signature. That detail could come in handy for finding a single stone in a big pile, don't you think?"

"Are you an archaeologist?"

"No, but I loved getting puzzles for Christmas as a child."

Von Essling took several steps back, as if she wanted to take his picture.

"I didn't know insolence was among the qualities required of members of the SS."

"Indeed, it's not the organization's most prominent quality."

"You don't use the word 'order' like your colleagues?"

Tristan could tell he was on a slippery slope. He'd better not go any further. "Have you excavated underground rooms in the past?" he asked, changing the subject.

"Yes, but most of the time they're just cisterns or storerooms for food. The architecture and uses are very basic . . . Not especially interesting."

"Frau von Essling," shouted a voice. "The other fragments, we've found them."

She hurried over, with Tristan right behind her. 'Goebbels' was expertly gathering the pieces. The chisel marks all went from left to right.

"The stone must have broken when the tower collapsed."

Erika drew a mental line between the place where the pieces had been found and the base of the outer wall. "Perfect, we can cut the excavation area in half." She turned to the Frenchman. "Ask Weistort to send us some soldiers. Now we'll clear everything down to the bedrock."

Despite the spring heat, the soldiers had kept their jackets on. Probably because Weistort hadn't taken his eyes off them. They had exposed the bedrock along the full length of the wall. It was perfectly smooth and shone like a mirror. It was too smooth though—they couldn't see a trap door or stairs down. Tristan was starting to have his doubts. He walked over to von Essling, who was supervising the men as they cleared the area. She was staring at the original arrow slits, from which a soldier was carefully removing the fill. A ray of light shone through one of them and struck the ground. After seven hundred years, light had once again reached the inside of the *castrum*.

"Half the surface area has been cleared," noted the Frenchman. "So, our chances of finding the entrance to the underground room have been cut in half."

"Back to serving as your master's puppet, I see?" replied Erika with a discreet glance at Weistort.

"Perhaps—" he began, but didn't finish.

"Look!" A thick stone wall had been uncovered. Erika was triumphant until the colonel rained on her parade.

"Given the length of the wall, it'll take hours to reach the foundations."

"It's the only way," replied Erika dryly. "Do you think they reached Tutankhamun's tomb in half a day?"

Tristan was still studying the freshly restored arrow slits.

"Haven't you noticed anything about them?" he asked. "They're all different sizes."

"The middle one! It's shorter than the others," exclaimed 'Goebbels'.

"Why would that be?" the Frenchman wondered aloud.

Von Essling shook her head. "No idea."

The midday sun fell directly on the castle, brightening the usually dark walls where the besieged had pushed back attack after attack mounted from the valley. Suddenly, Weistort turned to a warrant officer. "Quick, a Bible."

While the soldier ran to the tents, everyone turned to the Oberführer.

"The Cathars had a favourite Gospel, if I'm not mistaken."

With a click of his heels, the soldier handed him a black leather-bound volume. For a few seconds, the only sound was the rustling of pages turned by a gloved hand. Then Weistort's arrogant voice broke the silence.

"The light shines in the darkness . . ."

Everyone turned towards the central arrow slit, where a ray of light filtered onto the floor like an unmoving snake.

" . . . and the darkness has not overcome it."

Tristan turned around to face the dark portion of the wall, then pointed to a spot perpendicular to the place where the light turned to darkness. "That's where you need to dig."

To reduce the risk of a leak, Weistort had sent the archaeologists away to the outcropping until the evening. Only 'Goebbels' and Tristan remained to take apart the wall fragment they suspected contained the entrance to the underground room under von Essling's orders. Armed with chisels, they chipped away at the mortar, then removed the stones one by one while Weistort paced the site like a wild animal circling its prey.

"This is it," said Erika.

They had just uncovered a layer of stones forming a vault. The rounded shape blended into the foundations. The mortar seemed less sturdy. Chisel in hand, 'Goebbels' turned his steamed-up glasses to Erika, who nodded enthusiastically. His tool attacked the joints. Tristan had stood up to avoid being pelted with fragments. All their faces expressed an excitement they could barely contain.

Tristan moved away to sit down on a pile of stones. He thought of the nocturnal attack on Montserrat, of Lucia—what had happened to her?—of the months he spent in Montjuic, of his fake death at the foot of the Castello ramparts. So many seemingly unrelated events that all led to this moment.

"Stop!" Erika shouted suddenly.

One of the stones had just fallen in, bouncing off what sounded like stone walls.

"What if it's just a well?" asked 'Goebbels' pessimistically.

"We'll know soon enough," replied Weistort. "Take out all the stones to open a way through."

Erika baulked. "If we destroy the entrance, we risk losing precious information that could help us understand the site."

"The only precious thing here is inside, Frau von Essling."

A cold draft blew through the entrance 'Goebbels' was clearing.

"Whoever said hell was hot?" joked Tristan as he came closer.

Erika grabbed a lantern, which revealed an unstable vaulted stone roof.

"The original entrance was bigger," realized 'Goebbels'. "Several people could go in at once. They must have built this vault to hide it during the siege."

"Demolish it, then," ordered Weistort.

"It won't be hard to do," replied 'Goebbels'. "It's already cracked. I can probably remove just one stone if I choose wisely."

He leaned in and struck the mortar around a loose stone hard with his chisel. He barely had time to back out before the vault collapsed, creating a large opening. Erika leaned over the edge. They no longer needed lamps since the sun now filtered into the chamber.

"There are stairs!"

Tristan walked over. The last steps, which were covered in debris, led to a wide tunnel under the courtyard. A wave of emotion washed over him, like when he found a new painting.

"I can't believe it's been seven centuries since the last people stood here."

Weistort placed a vicelike hand on his shoulder. "Yes. And now you are going to follow in their footsteps."

38

Weistort posted two guards at the entrance to the chamber, then barked his orders. "No one goes through without my permission!"

He had a Kreistel torch that was bigger than the standard-issue version used by the German army. The ray of yellow light swept back and forth, slicing through the darkness.

An ecstatic Weistort turned to Erika and Tristan. "Can you feel the magic? We're about to enter a room that has been deserted for centuries. Like Lord Carnarvon and Howard Carter at King Tut's tomb."

He moved carefully down the first steps. The heels of his boots clicked on the stones below. Tristan and Erika followed him at the same pace. The Frenchman reached out to touch the wall and found it to be damp, almost slippery under his fingers.

"Archaeologists feel that kind of excitement before any major discovery," explained Erika, "not just for Tutankhamun." Her voice echoed around the enclosed space.

"It's more than that. So much more, my dear," said the colonel. "We're not about to find gold treasure or some ancient ruins. No, we're about to unearth a mystery. What we're doing is indescribable. At least, if it's anything like what I saw in Tibet."

Tristan kept quiet. He knew exactly how Weistort felt. There was something unreal in the air around them. Something lay hidden in the bowels of the castle, something from the depths of time that awaited their arrival to awake.

Seconds ticked past as they climbed down the stairs. At the

bottom, the halo of light revealed a wide corridor. At the end, not more than twenty meters from them, there was another arched opening.

Weistort proceeded cautiously down the corridor. He knew from experience that underground spaces were easy to set traps in: snares, pitfalls, spike strips, and more. Despite his excitement, he didn't let his guard down. He would be the one to bring the sacred relic to the Reichsführer, and he'd rather be all in one piece to do it. Erika didn't share his fears. She was just steps behind the SS officer, eager to reach the sanctuary whose entrance she had uncovered. The three of them arrived at a new passageway.

Their eyes filled with wonder as they stepped into a dripping cave. Its ceiling of stalactites sparkled in the light. Weistort couldn't help but cast the rays from the torch here and there on the rock formations. An infinite number of water droplets ran down the walls and fell from above, reflecting the light like diamonds.

They stepped further into the room, captivated by its fantastical beauty.

"Magnificent," echoed Weistort's voice in the natural cathedral. "The water must have been dripping through here for millions of years."

"Your name will go down in the history of speleology," joked Tristan.

"There, on the right, against the wall!" Erika said excitedly.

Weistort directed the torchlight towards the area indicated by the German archaeologist. Two skeletons sat on either side of a rectangular entrance carved into the rock. Their skulls were frozen in a sinister expression.

Weistort seemed satisfied as he contemplated the chilling scene. "We're not far from our goal. Skeletons also marked the path to the sanctuary in Tibet. They must be sacrifices. A common practice in ancient civilizations. The souls of the dead are meant to ward off any attempts at intrusion by the living."

The light shone on the new opening.

"Another tunnel," said Erika.

"No," corrected Tristan. "It looks like a closed room. The ceiling is timbered. Wait, do you hear that rumbling sound?"

They looked down. The sound of falling water was coming up through a rusted vent in the floor.

"An underground river, just beneath us," exclaimed the archaeologist.

But Tristan wasn't listening anymore. He'd stopped suddenly.

At the far end of the room, less than ten meters from them, stood a statue, revealed by the torchlight. It rose straight up in front of them, like a stone ghost.

"It's identical to the one in Tibet," affirmed Weistort.

The man with crudely carved features shot out of the rock as if he'd been trapped in the wall below the waist. His face was distorted with pain as he contemplated them in silence. Both his arms were outstretched, as if in supplication. Each of his open palms, turned upward, held a swastika.

They inched closer.

The two relics gave off a phosphorescent ruby-red light.

Tristan couldn't help but feel strangely unsettled as he gazed at the statue's deformed face. It seemed like it was offering poisoned gifts to its visitors. Weistort broke the sepulchral silence.

"This statue dates from long before the Cathars. It's probably thousands of years old. The same civilization sculpted this one and the one in Tibet."

"That would explain why the Cathars later chose Montségur, which was considered sacred," added Erika.

The head of the Ahnenerbe moved closer still to the ancient statue, touching the stone as if to confirm it was real. Then his gaze settled on the swastikas.

"Two red swastikas," he said, perplexed. "Strange. The *Thule Borealis Kulten* only mentioned one."

"Do you have it with you?" asked Tristan.

"No, it's still in Germany at the Ahnenerbe headquarters." Weistort caught the Frenchman's inquisitive glance and continued. "And you would do well to mind your own business anyway," he said, irritated.

"This is just incredible," whispered von Essling, her eyes still fixed on the statue.

Tristan glanced furtively at Erika. She had left behind her haughty demeanour. Her face expressed pure fascination. The Frenchman contemplated the wall behind the statue, then frowned and moved closer.

"Colonel, could you shine the light over here?"

The beam moved towards Tristan and revealed an inscription in the rock, as well as etchings of a scorpion and an ornate swastika.

Croiz rog

Crotz rog

Salut cap sinistra

He ran his finger over the letters, which looked like they could have been written just the day before.

"It's not Latin. It's Old French," remarked Erika, who had joined Tristan.

"Probably Occitan," he added. "That's what they spoke around here before French."

"Don't waste your time on linguistic musings," barked Weistort. "We're in a hurry."

The colonel opened his bag and took out a pair of gloves like those used by glassblowers to protect themselves from the flames.

"For the greater glory of the Reich."

Just as he was about to seize the first swastika, Tristan shouted, "No!"

Weistort turned angrily towards the Frenchman. "Have you lost your mind?"

Tristan pointed at the inscription. "It feels too much like a trap."

"Don't be stupid, there wasn't one in Tibet."

Erika turned to Weistort. "He's right. We should think for a minute before taking them."

"Shine your light behind the statue," urged Tristan.

It revealed two iron chains that hung down from the ceiling and were fastened to the base of the statue, where it jutted out of the rock.

"Now shine it on the front."

Tristan knelt down and placed his index finger on the upper arm.

"That's it. There must be a mechanism inside the statue. The arms are mobile. I think they must be operated by these chains."

He looked up and scanned the ceiling. Crisscrossed wooden beams covered the entire surface. He came back to the inscription and ran his fingers over it once more. "I'm willing to bet that if we choose the wrong swastika, we'll be buried alive under tons of rock."

"We need to decipher the message, then," said Weistort.

"So perceptive," said Tristan sarcastically. "The problem is that the inscription is undoubtedly in medieval Occitan. A forgotten language that almost no one understands anymore. We need help."

"Who?"

"The daughter of the castle owner. Laure d'Estillac."

D'Estillac Manor

Laure sighed as she caught sight of the pile of boards stacked against the door to the attic in the south wing. The manor was falling apart and André, their last servant, had too much joint pain to help. She'd been telling herself for weeks that she was going to get out her mother's sewing machine to make herself a dress worthy of the name.

She'd exchanged two sturdy laying hens at the haberdashery in Pamiers for four meters of printed fabric that was "all the rage in Paris". Given the birds were worth one hundred twelve francs apiece, the shop owner had struck a great deal, but Laure had been unable to put it off any longer. Every time she walked past the shop's window, the dress popped into her mind, as if by magic. She had inherited capable fingers from her mother.

After the trade, which she'd concluded three days earlier, she had felt guilty, but the manor's chicken coop was still quite full. No one, not even the Germans, had dared requisition anything from the d'Estillacs. She doubted her father or André kept an exact record of the coop's occupants.

She moved the boards one by one, eager to get her hands on her coveted treasure. She had turned the manor upside down looking for it, and this was the only room left. She rested the tips of her fingers on the windowsill and looked instinctively towards the mountain. Knowing that the Germans were digging up the defenceless old fortress made her hair stand on end.

But she was even more annoyed with herself. The face of the mysterious Frenchman who had come to warn her—Tristan, he was called—came to mind all too often. He exuded a kind of poisonous charm, both dangerous and ironic. She hadn't ever met a man like him since she'd been old enough to be interested in the opposite sex.

Don't be a ninny.

This questionable character was the type of guy who'd run off at the first lingering glance. Plus, he worked for the Germans.

Laure tore her gaze from the rocky outcropping and focused on the closed door. She pulled the skeleton key from her pocket and inserted it into the lock. Much to her surprise, the hinges had been oiled and the door opened with a discreet creak. The smell of polish and wax filled the air. She flicked the switch and a light bulb chased away the shadows.

The attic was strangely tidy. A large 19th-century wardrobe dominated the room, next to a buffet shrouded in a beige wool blanket. In the middle of the space stood a pile of books, small broken pieces of furniture, porcelain and pots, lamps without shades, stools, and empty pots of paint. She walked slowly, closing her eyes as the scent of wax and turpentine found its way to her nose. She felt instantly nostalgic for her happy childhood. She could see her mother renovating old pieces of furniture she found at the local markets.

She opened her eyes and glanced quickly around the room.

Her gaze stopped on the part of the gabled roof to her left. Her face lit up.

The old Singer was there, just under a blacked-out old skylight, wedged between two old desks with broken feet. At last she'd found the precious machine with its side wheel, golden-walnut stand, and belt-driven pedal. A familiar shadow stood in a corner—her mother's fabric mannequin, which she used to tailor her creations.

Laure sat down at the machine and ran her finger under the needle. Everything seemed to be in order. She unlocked the pedal and pressed down.

Nothing happened. Disappointed, she tried again, but the mechanism wouldn't budge. She tried to turn the wheel with her hands, but the Singer was stubborn.

"Oh no! You can't leave me with a pile of useless fabric," she exclaimed annoyedly.

She leaned over and removed the outer covering. She felt around impatiently and after a long minute she managed to unlock the gear box. The case opened as the tension in the spring eased.

She froze. Where the gears should be, she instead found a small wooden box. Intrigued, she opened it eagerly. Inside there was a collection of electrical wires and spools, as well as a small set of headphones. She pulled it all out to study it.

"I'm afraid you won't be able to use your sewing machine for quite some time."

She jumped and turned around all at once.

The familiar male voice had come from the door. She recognized her father's hunched silhouette. He walked over slowly. When he was just a few meters away, he crossed his arms across his chest. Like he had done when scolding her as a child. "You've always been too curious for your own good."

The young woman held up the device. "Is this what I think it is?"

"I don't have to explain myself to you, Laure. Get out of this room."

The young woman shook her head. "I will not. A radio

transmission device in my mother's sewing machine demands an explanation."

"You never should have found it. It's all too dangerous for you."

"What do you use it for?"

The old man's wrinkles were even deeper in the light from overhead.

"It's a spare, in case the first one, which is hidden in the library, stops working."

Laure's eyes widened in surprise. "But I thought you were a supporter of—"

"Vichy? At first, yes. I really thought Pétain was the only one who could protect France from the Nazis. But I realized the error of my ways last autumn."

She stood up and walked over to him, her expression grave. "What are you talking about, Papa?"

"The treatment of the Jews, cutting our country in half . . . Pétain betrayed France. So, I reached out to certain contacts."

"What kind of contacts?"

He took his daughter's hand and left the attic with her. Once they were in the corridor, he closed and locked the door, then put the key in his pocket.

"You forget that your old father was once a colonel in the French army," he replied. "I lead a network for the southern half of the region. Now forget everything you've seen and heard tonight. Some dangerous things will be happening soon, and I don't need you mixed up in them."

"Are you talking about the excavations at the castle?"

"Yes. You must pack your things and go to your aunt's house in Carcassonne until things blow over. The gardener will take you to the Foix train station."

She shook her head. "No, Papa. I'm proud of you. How can I help?"

The Count took hold of her shoulders. "Leave, like I said. You're young, you have your whole life ahead of you."

She shook free. "My life is my business."

As he was about to counter her affirmation, a lorry motor

revved outside. He looked out the window and his face went white. "The Germans are here!"

They heard knocking at the front door. The father and daughter exchanged fearful glances.

"I'll go down and see what they want. Go back to your room."

"I don't think so."

He gave her a stern look. She was just like her mother, just as beautiful and just as stubborn. Maybe more.

"Sir!"

They turned towards the stairs, where the rattling voice of their old butler floated up. D'Estillac leaned over the railing and saw the servant's sweaty face two floors below.

"The soldiers want to see Mademoiselle Laure. Immediately."

39

The North Sea
May 10, 1941

The dull sound of the propeller blades reverberated along the wings and the fuselage until it reached the cockpit and rang in the ears of Rudolf Hess. The repetitive noise didn't bother him though—quite the contrary. Like all enthusiastic aviators, he found the aggressive purring of the motors reassuring—soothing, even. He was in his element, alone above the sea, like one of the half-gods from Norse mythology who parted the clouds to soar high into the sky.

If he succeeded in the mission he'd assigned himself, he would become one of Germany's immortal heroes, a new champion of the Reich, whose fame would equal that of the Knights of the Round Table. He smiled at the thought. Hess was about to do something big, something that would restore the Führer's faith in him. His smile turned to laughter. Yes, they would all recognize his superiority very soon. As Baldr had promised. The voice in his head guided him down the path of life.

Hess glanced at the fuel gauge: the levels were in line with his expectations. Just to be safe, he'd had two additional tanks mounted under the wings of the Messerschmitt 110 to make sure he would reach his destination.

Since he'd taken off from Bavaria, his flight plan hadn't encountered a single obstacle. He'd flown in the wake of the bombers on their way to rain down death on London, following the Heinkels and Stukas at a safe distance. They were just reaching the English coast. He increased speed to join their formation and avoid radar detection. A lone plane in enemy airspace was tempting prey for the British fighter pilots in their Spitfires. They were always eager to add another downed plane to their list of achievements.

He wouldn't give them the satisfaction.

The North Sea disappeared, making way for rolling hills, which extended all the way to the suburbs of London. The moon cast an icy glow over the countryside. Unlike Himmler, who saw the sun as the ultimate Aryan symbol, Hess believed the moon to be the patron deity of the Germanic tribes. He'd spoken to Hitler about it once, but the Führer remained indifferent. He certainly had a flair for which symbols would strike the people's hearts and imaginations, but he didn't like to theorize about it. In any case, Hess had been the one to suggest the swastika as the Nazi party's symbol. He had been right about that.

The bright white light of the moon made it difficult to clearly identify the constellations. He turned a light on above a piece of paper on which his astrologer had drawn a map of the sky.

The night of May 10–11, an alignment of planets in the Taurus sign, the symbol of power and victory. This rare conjunction was precisely why he had chosen the date. The astrologers were certain—he couldn't fail. He changed headings to move away from the bombers and towards the northwestern part of the country. English radar would be able to see him now.

To escape it, he would have to fly very low. The throttle vibrated in his hands and the altimeter was going crazy. He'd always loved this feeling of diving out of the sky towards the ground like a bird of prey. The English countryside was getting closer. He could distinguish the checkerboard of fields, the dark forests, and even villages hiding in the darkness. He stabilized his altitude, verified his position, and took a deep breath. Tonight was the biggest night of his career: the one that would change the course of the war.

The moon began its descent towards the sea. The wan light shone diagonally across the land in a shower of silver rain. Hess almost expected to see a knight in shining armour appear from behind a hedge or charge out of the woods. Rudolf was flying as low as possible, occasionally brushing the tops of trees. This was the best way to escape the radar, but the Messerschmitt was far from silent. Its nocturnal hum would panic the people below. He decided to pull up a little, to avoid anti-aircraft defences. To his left, a floodlight flashed on and began scanning the sky. He must be near a town. He headed west: this was no time to be shot down like a common crow. The first explosion rang out, shaking the fuselage. A cluster of black flakes burst in the sky. An anti-aircraft defence unit had caught sight of him. He needed to get higher and out of range. A new volley of detonations flashed in the night. He felt the rearing motors glue him to his seat. A few minutes later, he was invisible again.

Hess had always dreamed of flying. The first time he'd climbed into a plane, it had been a revelation. He had signed up for the army in 1914, convinced he would become a hero. Instead, he became a mud-covered ghost in the trenches at Verdun. A shell exploded, seriously wounding his legs and back, but it saved him from a slow death devoid of glory. As soon as he had recovered, he headed back to the front, but a bullet in the lungs put a stop to his ambitions. Having had his dose of land warfare, he volunteered again, but this time as a pilot. Misfortune struck once more, and his plane crashed during training. Only a week after he got back up in the air again, the armistice had been signed. It was like he'd been cursed. Hess never really got over it, especially when he saw Göring in parades, decorated for having brought down twenty-two enemy planes. But he could be patient, and today he would get his revenge.

Sunlight was slowly replacing the moon. Hess could see better now. On the ground, the landscape had just changed. Fields bordered with hedges and thick woods had given way to a series of steep hills and heaths. Scotland was in view. Hess leaned towards the windshield, his eyes burning from lack of sleep. This ancient Celtic land, dotted with castles and myths, had always fascinated him and he fully intended to bring a new legend to the unique region.

White light reflected off a large body of water on the horizon: the Irish Sea. Rudolf had unfolded a map on his knees, which he now consulted in the grey pre-dawn light. After bypassing London to the east—to put them off his scent—he had turned sharply to the west, crossing England in a diagonal line. Despite a few shots from anti-aircraft defences, he must not have been seen. Now he followed the coast to keep his bearings. According to his calculations, he was less than two hours from his destination. He tapped the fuel gauge. He still had one full tank. More than enough to reach his target, known to him alone: the village of Eaglesham. If Hess succeeded, the name would go down in history.

"You'll be welcomed like a king! And your ears won't freeze."

His mind raced and his vision blurred. Baldr had made a bad habit of speaking to him without warning.

"You're a messenger of peace. Glory will follow your name for centuries!"

"Thank you, Baldr, but I need to concentrate to fly the plane. We'll talk once I've arrived."

The sound of the propellers filled the cabin once more. Baldr had disappeared.

To stave off the excitement that was beginning to wash over him, Hess concentrated on the information he had. For several weeks, the Reich's intelligence services had been filing alarming reports on Churchill's political missteps. The endless bombings were turning London into a living hell and were breaking the British people's spirit of resistance. In Parliament, more and more MPs were losing hope. And though Buckingham Palace remained silent, everyone knew the monarchy hoped for a rapid truce. The Bulldog, as his adversaries called him, might soon lose the majority. The man rumoured to replace him was Lord Halifax.

Hess had immediately consulted his astrologers, who unanimously agreed that the planets announced an exceptional political fate for this fervent pacifist, who was champing at the bit in Washington, where Churchill had sent him as ambassador. Halifax was a pragmatist and an isolationist. He would put an end to the war and offer the Germans a deal: Europe for the Reich, Africa and the Far East for England.

Halifax's probable rise to power had determined Hess to begin his current undertaking. He still had to figure out how to contact the future Prime Minister. It hadn't taken long to find him. For years, the German Minister of Foreign Affairs had kept detailed files on all British subjects inclined to support the Nazi cause. There was a thick dossier on the former King Edward VII, and even a film of the royal children performing the Nazi salute. There were many more names as well: notable anti-communists, conservative members of Parliament, and well-known aristocrats. One particularly prestigious name had immediately kindled Hess's interest: Lord Hamilton. He'd met the man at the 1936 Olympic Games. The English gentleman had been particularly friendly and had made no secret of his admiration for Hitler's Germany. Thanks to the file, which was regularly updated by German diplomats, Hess had learned that Hamilton was also a close friend of Lord Halifax.

The Irish Sea was covered in a grey blanket of fog, which was trying to climb to coastal cliffs. He was an hour or less from his destination: Hamilton's manor, which just happened to have a landing strip. Hess neared the ground. He was no longer afraid of being spotted. He needed to turn east. The Scottish countryside raced by below. Hess looked at the compass. If he maintained his heading, he should soon see the two landmarks he'd circled in red on the map. He came even closer to the ground to avoid the fog banks. Dew sparkled on the slate roofs of the farms. Suddenly he saw them: two green lakes on either side of a straight road, the road that led to Eaglesham. To lighten his load, he dropped his two extra fuel tanks. At the last minute, he turned sharply, steering clear of the village. At this altitude, the two black swastikas on either side of the plane were visible to the naked eye. It would be best to land out of sight. The landing strip appeared. All of a sudden, Hess realized he'd made a mistake. The Messerschmitt couldn't land here: the band of asphalt below was much too short, barely long enough for a small tourist plane. He climbed again to make a decision. There was really only one choice: he'd have to jump.

In a barn at Floors Farm, Dave McLean rested his pitchfork against the wall. His back and arms called for a rest. He'd been moving hay since dawn. He dropped down onto a chopping block covered in sawdust and took out his tobacco pouch. That was sure to help him forget his aching muscles. Once he'd rolled his cigarette, he stepped out of the barn. There was no way he'd smoke next to a pile of hay that nearly reached the rafters. He'd burn the place down in seconds! As he was about to flick his lighter on, an explosion sent a pile of roof tiles flying past his head. He got down onto the ground to protect himself, then stood up again, still trembling. Just behind the barn, the sky was lit by incandescent flames. As metal debris fell to the ground, the bitter smell of burnt fuel filled the yard.

"Jesus Christ," mumbled Dave in disbelief.

In the sky overhead, a white mushroom had just opened up. Dave hurried into the barn and came back out with a pitchfork in hand. The parachute was already on the floor of the yard and the man was undoing his harness. He limped closer.

"I am—"

The sharp tines of the pitchfork stopped him from saying more.

40

Laure d'Estillac glanced disdainfully at the SS soldier who had accompanied her to the cave entrance. Tristan walked over quickly and gestured to the guard. "Go back to the entrance. Colonel's orders. I'll take care of her."

The man didn't move.

"Go see your superior officer if you don't believe me," Tristan urged annoyedly.

The German mumbled an insult and turned to go. Tristan watched him leave, then spoke to the young woman.

"Very kind of you to come. You won't regret it."

"Did I have a choice?" asked Laure, eyeing him with hostility. "As for you, it seems you enjoy betraying your country."

"It's just a quest," he replied dryly. "I'm neither a soldier nor a cop, and I don't share their ideology in the slightest. Believe me. As for my patriotism, it's been dead for quite some time."

"Are you trying to convince me of something?"

He shrugged and gestured towards the inside of the cave. "Not at all, but I would suggest you hurry. The Colonel doesn't like waiting for his guests."

She followed him in, and her surly mood instantly dissipated. She never could have imagined that such splendour existed underneath the castle she had extensively explored since childhood.

"Unbelievable," she whispered. "How did you find this place?"

"Would you believe it if I told you that it's part of a treasure hunt which I began two years ago in a Spanish monastery called Montserrat?"

She didn't answer. She was too busy looking all around, amazed by the beauty of the underground world.

"And it's not over yet," added Tristan as he pointed to the alcove where the statue stood.

Just before entering the sanctuary, she jumped. She'd stepped on the grate in the ground. She bent over. A muffled roar rose up from the darkness.

"An underground river," explained Tristan. "It runs underneath the entire cave."

When Laure looked up, she could see the silhouettes of two Germans in the glow from a torch.

"Ah, at last!" said Weistort eagerly. "We need your help. Hurry up now."

Laure walked into the sanctuary, devoured by curiosity despite herself. Erika observed her coldly, as if she were out of place.

"Did the Cathars sculpt this statue?" asked Laure.

"No, it was probably sculpted thousands of years ago," answered Weistort. "But your heretics seem to have added a mechanism. A trap of sorts, to keep people from taking the relic. At least that's what Tristan here believes."

She moved closer to the statue's hands and saw the two swastikas.

"Swastikas? Don't tell me there were Nazi Cathars! How appalling! I'd always admired them and their cause."

"The swastikas are also from before the Cathars," Tristan explained kindly. The Germans' faces had all hardened.

Weistort grabbed her by the arm and placed her next to the two inscriptions. "I don't care what you think. Translate this, since I hear you know the language."

"I don't *know* the language, I embody it. My family is one of the oldest in the region. I had Cathar ancestors burned at the foot of the castle."

The Nazi smiled. "My condolences. Now translate."

"You're hurting me!" said Laure as she tried to get away. "I'm not going to help you with anything."

The colonel let her go, then pulled a Luger out of its holster on his belt. "I'm going to count to five."

Tristan wanted to intervene, but Weistort aimed his gun at the Frenchman. "Stay where you are!"

The SS colonel spun around and glued the barrel of the Luger to Laure's temple. Her face conveyed her panic.

"I'm listening," said the head of the Ahnenerbe in a suddenly sweet voice.

Laure looked at the inscriptions carefully, but seemed to hesitate.

"If we ignore the two different symbols—the swastika and the scorpion—both messages say the same thing. It's about a cross: *Croiz* in Old French and *Crotz* in Occitan. The swastika was seen as a variation on the cross at the time. As for the word *Rog*, it means red. And the third line, *salut cap sinistra*, could be translated as: 'the salvation of the left head'."

"Perfect," said Weistort. "The swastika symbol must refer to the true relic. The first one."

Tristan shook his head. "I don't understand why they would have taken so much time to hide the relic and create such an easy riddle. One of the swastikas is referred to with an Occitan—so Cathar—term, while the other is referred to in the enemy's language."

For the second time since they'd located the foundation of the original tower within the castle, Erika looked approvingly at Tristan.

"He's right, Colonel. The scorpion must be the key. Why choose that symbol?"

"We're wasting valuable time!" said Weistort, losing his patience.

Tristan had crossed his arms across his chest, his thoughts churning.

"The scorpion is an astrological symbol, but the Cathars didn't believe in that. It's also a symbol of danger, death, poison, evil . . ."

"Like Nazism," joked Laure. "You're on the right track."

Infuriated, Weistort pushed her hard into the statue. "One more comment like that and I'll shoot you right here."

Erika studied the rock wall. "The scorpion . . . The scorpion . . . Let's think back to the context of the time. The Cathars were fighting crusaders from the north and the Catholic church."

Tristan suddenly banged his fist into the wall. "That's it! The Orient! From its inception, Christianity had to fight heresy. In Judea, in Syria, in Egypt . . ."

"I'm not sure I follow," said Erika.

"The early Christians called heretics scorpions: the deadly animals from the desert. Heretics hide under the stones of the church and their beliefs are poison for the faithful. In the end, all those who were persecuted by the new faith used the scorpion as a call sign between them."

He walked over to the statue, then continued. "If that logic holds, the true relic is the one with the scorpion."

"Not necessarily," said Erika. "It could also be a way to trick intruders. The swastika wasn't a symbol used by the church either."

"What about the third line? What's the story behind that?" asked Laure. "*Salut cap sinistra*, the salvation of the left head."

Erika stood next to the statue and ran her hand over the stone. Her hands moved up the bust towards the shoulders, then stopped at the base of the neck.

"There's a very thin gap between the neck and the body," she exclaimed.

Without waiting for a reaction, she seized the statue's head and turned it to the left with a creak. One of the chains that ran along the wall grew taut.

"Salvation . . . The head turned to the left is salvation. Very smart. The mechanism must have two trips," said von Essling. "I assume that if we choose the right swastika, the second chain will be blocked as well."

"We still have to figure out which one is the right one."

"The one with the heretics' scorpion," said Tristan.

"I'm not convinced," replied the archaeologist. "The other

choice makes just as much sense. The Cathars, who developed the riddle, knew what they were doing. They wanted to drive anyone trying to solve it mad."

Weistort broke the ensuing silence. "There's only one way to know for sure. Our French friends will decide. Erika, come back over here. The two of you stay next to the statue."

The Germans moved out of the sanctuary, leaving Tristan and Laure side by side.

"Go ahead, Tristan, if you're so sure."

"But what if I'm wrong?"

"We lose the relic and you die. Hurry up!"

Tristan studied Laure's anxious face for a few seconds, then spoke. "If you free her, I'll do what you ask."

Weistort laughed heartily. "So now you're a knight in shining armour? So romantic. How very French."

"Your choice, but as you said, we're wasting time."

The German hesitated for a few seconds, then gestured with his head for her to move. "Okay, back up."

Laure turned to Tristan. "Thank you . . . You're not such a bastard after all."

"Get out of here before I change my mind."

The young woman joined the colonel and Erika as Tristan moved closer to the statue.

The two relics seemed to tease him. The one with the scorpion or the one with the swastika?

Tristan could almost feel the sweat dripping from his pores. The quest was almost over. His life might be as well.

He closed his eyes.

The people behind this terrible trap were Cathars. They didn't think like their enemies.

Think like them.

Everything was opposites. They believed the world was run by the Devil, not God. Reality was but an illusion, and dying was deliverance. They weren't afraid to die. Unlike their adversaries from Rome.

Fear . . . Fear is but an illusion.

He had a realization. If he was scared, it meant he was thinking like a crusader.

I shouldn't be scared. I'm a Cathar, pure and perfect. The trap is an illusion. Yes!

The trap was too obvious. The chains and the roof above, with tons of rock ready to pour down on his head. And the abyss beneath the grate under his feet. Hell.

The entire décor was designed to scare away intruders, to prevent them from using reason. The Cathars had exploited the religious fears of the crusaders. The Catholics knew that with one poor choice, they'd go to hell. And if they made the right choice, nothing would happen: they'd leave victorious to conquer the world with the power of the relic. Revelling in the legitimacy of their triumph.

Like the Nazis.

Tristan opened his eyes.

Exactly!

The Cathars were exploiting their enemies' fears.

It was so obvious. He understood the trap now—there wasn't one.

Without any hesitation, he moved his hand over the swastika with the scorpion. He closed his eyes again, then quickly removed it from the statue's hand. They heard a new click in the statue, and the second chain went taut with a sinister creak. Then silence.

Tristan weighed the relic in his hand. It was heavy, like lead. He turned it over and saw an engraved cross, about the size of a coin. A cross, the symbol of Christ. He smiled silently. He had succeeded.

"Congratulations, Tristan! Hurry now, bring the swastika to me," said Weistort, his voice echoing through the cave.

Erika and Laure seemed relieved.

Tristan turned around, the relic in hand. He walked slowly, afraid another mechanism might be tripped. But nothing happened.

Weistort held out his greedy hand at the entrance to the

sanctuary. "I might have to offer you a job at the Ahnenerbe. I'll tell the Reichsführer that—"

He never finished his sentence.

A burst of machine-gun fire sounded at the entrance to the cave.

41

A muffled rumbling sound came from the far end of the corridor. They could hear shouting and explosions. The head of the Ahnenerbe took out his Luger and fired at random towards the entrance.

"Don't shoot!" said a German voice from the corridor. "It's Werner."

Weistort lowered his weapon. One of the SS soldiers came in screaming, his jacket covered in blood.

"We're under attack. A whole commando unit. They came out of nowhere."

"Where's the other guard?"

"I don't know," said the soldier as he shook his head, his eyes wild. "It all happened so fast."

Weistort grabbed the guard's machine gun and looked at the clip. "We have almost no rounds left. They'll take us down like rats."

Tristan came over, the sacred swastika still in hand.

"The relic, quick!" shouted Weistort.

Without a word, the Frenchman complied.

Laure was huddled against one of the cave walls, her heart pounding. It was her father coming to get her, she was sure of it. She had to help him. But how?

The wounded guard rested on a boulder. He could barely breathe. He was desperately trying to keep the life from leaving his body by holding his hands over his wound, but the blood spurted between his fingers.

"There's still one . . . chance. The alarm has been triggered. Hans at the entrance . . . He won't . . . ' surrender. Reinforcements . . ." mumbled the soldier before passing out.

"We won't be able to hold out long with the ammunition we've got," exclaimed Weistort.

Erika grabbed the guard's blood-covered pistol and took aim at the entrance. Her lips curled into a strange smile.

"Do you think this is funny?" asked the colonel.

"It's just the irony of the situation . . . Dying at the bottom of a deep hole in the middle of nowhere in France. All to get our hands on a swastika, when there are millions of them in Germany . . ."

Another round of machine-gun fire rang out, followed by a scream. Steps echoed in the tunnel. Weistort fired.

"Cease fire. We've got a deal to offer," shouted an unfamiliar voice.

"What deal?" asked Weistort. "You won't make it out of here alive! My men will be here any second." He fired several more times to emphasize his seriousness.

"Maybe, but not in time to save you. All I have to do is throw a grenade and you'll all be ripped to shreds. Let me come in, unarmed."

Tristan turned to the colonel. "It's worth a try, Weistort. It'll buy us some time."

"He's right," said Erika.

The head of the Ahnenerbe nodded. "Okay, come over! Hands up."

A few seconds passed before a silhouette appeared in the torch-light. Malorley moved to the centre of the room, arms raised. He stared at the SS colonel for some time, then spoke. "Give me the relic and I'll let you live. Even though I'd be delighted to kill you. I've been on your tracks for so long . . ."

Weistort froze. "Who are you? Do I know you?"

Malorley turned a gaze full of hate on the head of the Ahnenerbe. "We bumped into each other in November 1938, in Berlin. You were coming out of a bookstore as I went in. You might not remember me. I'm not surprised. You were drunk on your own power at the time."

"1938 . . ."

"Let me refresh your memory for you. On Kristallnacht you killed one of my friends. Professor Neumann, a man of impressive learning. He ran a bookstore not far from the synagogue. Is it coming back to you now?"

"A Jew!" Weistort replied. "They're not people. Why should I remember?"

"Really? Well, at the time this particular Jew was of great value to you, if I remember correctly. You stole a book from him. The *Thule Borealis Kulten.*"

"You . . . you know about that?"

"I got there too late. I wasn't able to save him, but he was still able to speak."

The SS colonel took a step back. He didn't like being confronted by ghosts from his past.

"Once you've given me the relic, you'll also hand over the book," added Malorley. "And your friends will be safe."

"I don't have it, you idiot! The *Borealis* is safe and sound in Germany. You'll never get it back, unless you invade the Reich. And you could never do that!"

Malorley's lips formed a seductive smile. "I could if I get the relic, however . . ."

Hurried steps sounded and d'Estillac appeared, short of breath. Behind him stood La Cebolla and two of his men, machine guns in hand.

"Where is my daughter, Laure?"

"I'm here, Papa."

Before she could step forward, Erika glued her gun to Laure's left side.

"Ah, it seems we have a bargaining piece," said Weistort triumphantly.

The seconds ticked past in silence. Then there was a strange whistling sound followed by a strident hiss.

"Smoke bombs! Down, *amigos*!" shouted La Cebolla, who'd

just thrown grenades into the cave. Columns of grey smoke rose from the floor. Gunfire rang out immediately. Tristan raced to the sanctuary. D'Estillac hurried towards his daughter, but Weistort shot him before he could reach her.

"No!" shouted Laure, escaping Erika's grip.

Malorley fired on Weistort several times, but he kept disappearing behind the smoke. The German fell backwards to the ground and dropped the swastika. Erika threw down her weapon to grab the relic, then crawled to a safe corner.

On the ground, indifferent to the chaos around her, Laure held her father's head in her hands, running her fingers through his hair as if she were trying to wake a child. Malorley joined her.

"There's nothing you can do. Come."

More gunshots sounded, towards the entrance.

"*Los Alemanes*, they're coming," shouted La Cebolla. "We have to go now."

Malorley pulled Laure away from her father's body, taking her to the Spaniards.

"If I'm not back in five minutes, get out of here! I have to find the relic."

He returned to the sanctuary. The smoke was thinning into something more akin to fog. He heard the sound of rushing water beneath him, roaring like a wild animal fighting for its life in the tunnels below. Hell couldn't be worse than this. He stumbled over Weistort's body, eliciting a groan. So, he wasn't dead after all. The Englishman resisted the urge to put a bullet in the SS colonel's brain. Neumann's ghost danced before his eyes for a few seconds, but he didn't have enough ammunition left in his clip. He took a step forward, carefully scanning the smoke-filled room. He'd seen a woman take the relic and hide. She'd crawled . . . He crouched down. There she was, huddled against the rock like a venomous snake.

Erika saw a man stand and aim his gun at her. She held the relic tight to her chest. A stupid reflex, she thought, but she didn't have time to think. Tristan had just appeared in front of the Englishman. His body blocked Malorley's shot. She wanted to get up and flee, but the smoke suddenly thickened in the sanctuary, swallowing up both Tristan and his adversary.

La Cebolla held Laure by the shoulders. He looked worriedly towards the entrance to the cave, where the explosions were growing louder.

"My men outside won't be able to hold them off much longer. We have to go."

Laure tried to escape. "We can't let him—"

Malorley appeared suddenly, as if emerging from the depths of hell. La Cebolla met him.

"Let's get out of here. Now."

The dazed Englishman didn't answer. He just followed along. He had completed his mission.

42

They ran breathlessly down the slope, doing their best to avoid the spots of yellow light that danced around them. The castle's alarm screeched in the night. Bullets from German machine guns ripped through the bushes around them. One of the Spaniards screamed and fell to the ground, shot in the back. Only three of the original commando members remained: Malorley, Jane, and the Spanish leader, with Laure now in tow. One of the resistance fighters who'd remained behind to watch their backs and keep the SS soldiers from charging them had died, too. The Englishman limped on, having twisted his ankle as he left the castle courtyard.

"Take cover behind the wall!" shouted La Cebolla, who was about ten meters ahead of them. Malorley and the two young women threw themselves against a pile of dry rocks. Below, the path was exposed, no more rocks or bushes, just a grazing field full of searchlights.

Laure stayed huddled in a ball, shaking like a leaf. Jane hugged her tightly, then took her face in her hands. "We're going to make it out of this alive. I promise."

Laure's tears sparkled in the moonlight. "I . . . I can't move. Go on without me."

"I don't think so," said Jane. Then she turned to Malorley. "We can't stay here. They'll find us."

"Do you really think *I* want to spend the night on this goddamn hill?" asked Malorley as he massaged his ankle. He turned to the Spaniard. "Hey, Onion! What options do we have left?"

"We're surrounded. As long as they have that damn spotlight, we're toast. It's the only path to my comrades below."

La Cebolla picked up his binoculars and studied the road below the field. There was barely enough light to make out the black outline of a lorry. Suddenly, as he glanced towards Montferrier, he caught sight of three pairs of headlights winding down the road towards his men.

"*Caliente. Muy caliente.* That must be French gendarmes they called in as reinforcements. I told my men to cut down some trees to block the road, but it won't hold them for long."

"And we're pinned down by the Germans above," said Malorley. "We're screwed."

"One of us will have to climb up onto the outcropping and take out the searchlights at the watchtower. That would buy us enough time to cross the field and reach the lorry. Given the state of your ankle, I'll take care of it."

Jane jumped up and grabbed the Spaniard's rifle. "I'll do it."

"Out of the question," exclaimed Malorley. "I—"

La Cebolla shook his head. "No, *señorita*. It's too dangerous. There are still Germans up there, and it's a difficult shot."

The waves of machine-gun fire picked up again. The bullets hurtled into rocks less than a yard from the group.

"I was a sharpshooting champion before the war," Jane countered confidently. What about you, *señor*? Given those thick glasses, I doubt you're the best shot."

Malorley raised his voice. "I forbid it. Do not disobey my order!"

"We both know I'm not afraid of you. I'm the only one who can reach them. And I can run fast, very fast. I'll reach the lorry long before any of you lot do."

The Spaniard sized her up, a sad look in his eyes. "You won't have time to reach us."

She loaded the rifle and placed the strap across her chest. "You've never seen me run. I'm a lightning bolt."

"All right, if you're sure . . . If we leave before you get there, two of my men will wait for you. They know the land around here like the backs of their hands and may be able to escape with you through the woods."

"Great, I love camping," she joked.

The machine guns had gone quiet. Yellow haloes danced across the field again, as if of their own volition. One of them was getting closer and closer.

Laure started screaming. Malorley forced her to the ground, so she wouldn't be seen.

"The Germans don't want to waste their bullets," noted the Spaniard. "They're waiting for reinforcements. They know we're stuck here."

Jane waited for the spotlight to change direction, then hurried onto the dark path.

"Jane, no!" yelled Malorley, standing to catch her, but the pain in his ankle brought him right back down.

The young woman turned around and quickly made her way back to the group. She took his face in her hands. "This time, it's not professional," she said coyly as she pressed her lips to his. The kiss seemed to last an eternity for Malorley. Then, before he even realized what had happened, she was standing over him, a mischievous look in her eyes. "You'll have to take me to dinner to get any further," she added. "To the best restaurant in London."

"You're crazy, I—"

And she was gone.

La Cebolla watched her climb the path and disappear into the darkness. "*¡Que valiente!* I knew a few women like that during the civil war. Soldiers in the Republican army. Your agent is made of the same stuff." Then he gestured towards Laure, who was still sobbing. "As for her . . ."

Malorley sat next to Trencavel's daughter and placed his hand on her forearm. "Don't worry, Jane will—"

"Don't touch me!" she exploded, ripping her arm away as if his hand had burned her skin. "Leave me alone! Go away! All of you!"

"She's in shock. Let's give her a few minutes to get her strength back," whispered the Englishman to La Cebolla.

The Spaniard shook his head in annoyance. He crouched down next to her and grabbed her shoulders. "Your father would be ashamed of you, *señorita!*"

"Shut up, you idiot! You barely knew him!" she shouted, full of rage.

La Cebolla slapped her without warning. "Only two people have ever called me an idiot. *Mi madre*, may she rest in peace, and a short communist colonel. He ended up in a ditch, a bullet between the eyes. You should look to the other *señorita* as an example. She's risking her life to save yours."

The purring of lorry motors echoed through the night air. La Cebolla picked up his binoculars again and searched the road. "The lorries are about to reach the barricade. If Jane doesn't succeed, we'll have to split up. With your ankle, I doubt you'll get far."

Laure, who was finally able to hold back her tears, stared at the field before them. *"Le prats dels cremats . . ."*

"What?" asked Malorley.

The young woman seemed to have gathered her wits. She explained slowly, enunciating carefully. "This is where over two hundred Cathars who had survived the siege—including women, children, and the elderly—were burned alive. The chronicles say it took a whole day and a whole night to burn them all. And now we may die here too, when—"

Two gunshots rang out, one after the other.

The spotlights disappeared from the field, as if by magic. The machine-gun fire began again.

La Cebolla jumped up. "She did it! *¡Estupendo!*"

Malorley stood up and passed the strap of his satchel over his head with a grimace. The pain was stubborn. Finally, Laure got to her feet and grabbed his arm without a word.

"Thank you, but I'll try to do it on my own," said the Englishman.

She shook her head and sniffled. "I might as well be useful. Let me help steady you."

Malorley looked back at the path up to the mountain. He squinted, looking for Jane. In vain.

"She'll make it. I know she will," Laure reassured him.

"We have to go!" shouted the Spaniard.

They emerged from the bushes and rushed down the sloping field as bullets whizzed past. "We're going to make it! They're firing blind."

With Laure's help, Malorley managed to hobble along faster than he'd expected. When they'd reached the middle of the field, an ominous sound filled the air above them.

"Mortar! Get down!"

The three runners hit the ground as an explosion rang out behind them. The shell sent a pile of dirt and scorched grass flying in their direction.

"Up! Let's go!"

Covered in mud, Malorley and Laure barely managed to stand. Not far off, at the edge of the woods, two men waved wildly at them.

Another shell hurtled through the night, but they'd already reached the woods. The explosion missed them once again.

The two resistance fighters helped the three escapees into the back of the lorry.

"Jefe! We placed charges at the feet of a few big trees just after the next turn, on the road to Fougax," said one of them, a short man with deep wrinkles. "As soon as we're past, we'll blow them so the gendarmes can't follow us. That will hold them for a while."

"If we aren't torn to bits by their damn mortars first," grumbled La Cebolla.

Yet another explosion felled a tree a few meters away. They felt the blast even inside the vehicle.

"We have to go," shouted one of the two fighters who'd been waiting. "They won't miss again. And if *una bomba* doesn't get us, the gendarmes will pick us off like ripe fruit."

"Wait a little longer," ordered the Englishman, who had pushed back the tarpaulin on the back of the lorry so he could search the field with his binoculars.

"I'm sorry, *señor*, it's too dangerous," replied La Cebolla.

Then he turned to one of his men. "Paco, go wait for the girl.

If she makes it, take her to the Monts d'Olme refuge. The Germans won't find you there."

The resistance fighter nodded and hurried back to the field, his automatic pistol in hand.

The other man turned the key in the ignition. The engine came to life, shaking the whole lorry. The wheels turned in the mud for a few seconds, then caught, and the vehicle headed down the road away from the improvised barricade.

"No, stop!" shouted Malorley as he was jostled around the lorry, his fingers curled tightly around the binoculars. "Look— there, in the field. It's Jane! She did it!"

Laure stood up next to him on the railing, holding fast to the tarpaulin. La Cebolla banged his fist on the metal between the bed of the lorry and the cabin. "Stop, Pedro!"

The lorry's brakes squealed.

Jane's silhouette became clear through the binoculars. She was running down the hill without a gun. The Englishman's heart jumped into his throat. "She's going to make it!"

Jane was running at top speed, but two more silhouettes emerged behind her. Armed silhouettes.

"Germans!"

"Come on, dammit!" shouted Malorley, still holding onto the railing.

She was more than three-quarters of the way there when a new explosion rang out. The blast sent the young woman flying forward, as if she'd stumbled on something.

"No!" shouted the Englishman.

He watched as Jane tried to get up, reaching an arm towards the black sky, but she fell back to the earth.

Malorley held his binoculars so tightly he could have crushed them. His position as a helpless spectator left him full of rage.

"She's wounded. We have to go get her!"

The Spaniard placed his hand on Malorley's shoulder. "There's nothing we can do. Paco's the only one who can save her now. If she's still alive . . ."

"I'm not leaving her," shouted the Englishman as he prepared to climb out. "If you're too much of a coward, I'll go. It's my responsibility. I'm in command of this mission."

The SOE man suddenly felt a hard object ram into the back of his skull.

"No, *señor*. I'll take it from here," said La Cebolla, his palm wrapped tightly around the butt of his pistol.

Malorley collapsed onto the bed of the lorry. As his eyes fluttered shut, he saw La Cebolla bang on the wall of the cabin again. "*Vaya*, Pedro!"

Not far off in the field, Jane lay on the ground, her arms outstretched. She couldn't stand and her eardrums had been ruptured by the blast. Everything was so quiet, silent.

She lay there, the back of her neck on the cool grass, in the exact place where two hundred people had been burned alive in the night seven centuries before. She felt no pain as her thoughts slowed to a trickle under the vaulted, star-dotted sky.

PART THREE

The ancient Barbarossa,
Friedrich, the Kaiser great,
Within the castle-cavern
Sits in enchanted state.

He did not die; but ever
Waits in the chamber deep,
Where hidden under the castle
He sat himself to sleep.

The splendour of the Empire
He took with him away,
And back to earth will bring it
When dawns the promised day.

"Der alte Barbarossa" by Friedrich Rückert (poem taught
in all schools under the Third Reich).

43

On the outskirts of Salzburg, after coming through the Salzach Valley, the government Mercedes slowed as it made its way up into the Bavarian Alps. In the back seat, Joseph Goebbels closed his eyes. He'd always hated the mountains. Their bare plateaus and snowy peaks inspired nothing but disgust in the adoptive Berliner, who now preferred the capital's constant bustle. Unfortunately, the Führer's tastes were diametrically opposed: he swore by the purity of the mountains and revelled in the blueness of the sky at high altitudes. This passion led him to have an Alpine retreat built—the Berghof. He spent most of his time there in the warmer months. He enjoyed long walks and passionate discussions under the stars.

Goebbels shook his head. Hitler's endless outdoor monologues were the bane of his existence. He fidgeted any time he wasn't speaking, so he truly hated having to quietly listen to the German leader's lyrical speeches glorifying the vegetarian diet or Wagner's operas for hours on end.

"We're coming into Berchtesgaden, Sir."

Joseph nodded. Never confide in the staff. That was the rule. Especially since he suspected Himmler had planted spies in his entourage. That was hardly surprising—the head of the SS and the Gestapo was totally paranoid. He spent all his time spying on the regime's high-ranking officials. Just last week, a strange rumour had rippled through Berlin. Göring, who was known for his collections of paintings and statues, had now found a new passion:

brassieres. He was filling entire display cases. A picture was even going around. For Goebbels, there was no doubt—Himmler was behind the rumours. It was his attempt to weaken the head of the Luftwaffe in order to replace him at Hitler's side.

The tyres made a crunching sound on the gravel road up to the Führer's estate. Joseph squinted as the huge white façade came into view, reflecting the sunlight. The glass doors were open. Hitler had to be mulling over his anger on the patio. This time Himmler and Göring were likely in for a rough ride. The Dwarf, as the others called him, shrugged disdainfully. How could the head of the Luftwaffe let Hess get away in a plane? How could the head of the SS, who was always watching everyone, have seen nothing? Was he criminally negligent or an accomplice? There was also the fact that Himmler and Hess shared a passion for the ridiculous occult, of which Goebbels felt it was high time to cleanse Nazism.

The car stopped at the guard post. A warrant officer came out to inspect the vehicle. When he saw the Minister of Propaganda, he clicked his heels. Joseph smiled. With Göring mired in his erotic fantasies, Himmler in his esoteric musings, and Hess on the run in enemy territory, Goebbels was beginning to think this stay at the Berghof might make him like the mountains after all.

Hitler sat in a wicker chair, his face shaded by a Tyrolean hat, contemplating Obersalzberg and the surrounding peaks in the setting sun. He never tired of the view. Not only because of its wild beauty, but also because of its fascinating legend. Emperor Frederick Barbarossa was said to slumber still in a secret chamber beneath the mountain. The prophecy held that when crows fell from the sky, he would awake and re-establish his empire for a thousand years to come. Hitler couldn't help but identify with the legendary emperor. The first time he'd visited this region, in the early 1920s, he'd been little more than an anonymous political agitator and the Nazi party had been a powerless extremist group. His mentor, Dietrich Eckhart, had suggested he rest and gather his strength in the fresh air of the mountains, far from the conspiracies of Munich.

"I'm taking you to see the old emperor's mountain. The magic mountain."

He'd instantly fallen under its spell. A sign. Fate. One day he too would turn legend into reality. Years later, he'd had his eagle's nest and refuge—the Berghof—built here. Of all the Führer's official residences, this one was his favourite. He had made all his major decisions for the future of Germany at the Berghof. And for Europe . . . He liked to think that across the way, in the Obersalzberg mountain, the old emperor silently guided his choices. And soothed him.

But this time, he was unable to find his peace. Anger was eating away at him. His oldest friend had betrayed him.

"They're here, mein Führer."

The voice of his secretary, Martin Bormann, brought him back to reality.

Hitler turned to Bormann. As always when the Führer was angry, his right-hand man was jumpy. No one dared mention it.

"Are they all here?"

"Field Marshal Göring and Reichsführer Himmler are waiting outside, mein Führer. Since it's a small council meeting, I didn't summon Chief of High Command Keitel or Albert Speer."

"What about Goebbels?"

"He's just arrived."

Hitler stood up and headed to the spacious living room. Despite the full sunlight on the windows, a fire crackled in the red marble fireplace. A gift from Mussolini. The Führer climbed the three steps that separated the room into two spaces and got comfortable in the left-hand corner, far from his desk, piled high with maps of Eastern Europe. It was his favourite part of the living room: a sofa, two old armchairs, and an old coffee table. Functional and understated. He took off his hat with a feather in its brim—a Bavarian symbol he despised, but there was something to be said for local colour—and began contemplating the coffered ceiling. The beams were perfectly symmetrical. Exactly what he needed to think. In his Berghof hideaway, nothing could distract him from his inner thoughts. He had chosen pure, airy lines, big

windows to let in as much natural light as possible, and understated furniture. Behind him, Bormann stood silently. He wouldn't
interrupt the Führer's daydreams for anything in the world.
Besides, he thoroughly enjoyed making Goebbels, Himmler, and
Göring wait. The Reich's three wild beasts had to learn to behave
like pets at the Berghof. Fearful and obedient.

Hitler was still deep in his daydream. With his back to the fire,
his hands resting on the armrests and eyes half-closed, he looked
like a sleeping feline, but Bormann knew he was getting ready to
devour his prey.

"Bring Göring in. Alone."

The Field Marshal's heavy boots struck the marble like a blacksmith's hammer. The Ogre had grown even fatter, thought the
leader of the Reich as he listened to Göring's laboured breath on
the steps.

"Mein Führer!"

"Sit down, Hermann."

That was one of Hitler's secrets. Despite the rage building up
inside him, his voice was perfectly calm. But it never lasted.

Göring was wearing his Luftwaffe uniform. It was covered in
medals that clinked with the slightest movement. Drops of sweat
beaded on his forehead and his red eyes kept blinking. Fear was
even more apparent on his face than his habit of overindulgence.

Hitler crossed his arms over his chest and began his interroga-
tion. "So, a plane can cross Germany, from Bavaria to the North
Sea, then fly over the Channel and all of England, then land in
Scotland without you knowing about it?"

"Mein Führer, let me be clear. Hess used an unregistered plane.
A prototype which he'd been training on for weeks."

"Are you sure of that?"

"Absolutely. Luftwaffe security interrogated the mechanics
responsible for the plane's maintenance. Their stories all line up."

"Weeks," repeated the Führer. "So, you mean he deliberately
prepared his escape?"

"That's what the facts lead us to believe," replied Göring. "But
I'm not the one responsible for keeping him under surveillance."

Hitler's narrowed eyes turned towards Bormann. "Send Himmler and Goebbels in."

Once again, the sound of boots on the floor, but quicker this time. Himmler clicked his heels before bowing. Goebbels was still coming up the stairs, slowed considerably by his leg.

"Heinrich, how is it you didn't notice Hess's criminal actions?"

"Mein Führer, he's one of the highest-ranking officials in the country," replied the head of the SS. "The police don't monitor him."

Göring chuckled. "Come now, Heinrich, we all have a file with our name on it in your offices! A file you regularly update. Every rumour and piece of gossip is recorded. I should know! There's no way you could have missed Hess's escape preparations."

"Let me remind you, Hermann, that he took off from a Luftwaffe airport. It's hard to believe you weren't made aware."

Following a quick glance at Goebbels, Hitler barked, "Bormann, the report!"

The secretary took a memo from his pocket and read: *"According to our information, Hess took off from a Bavarian airport yesterday, claiming he was conducting a training flight. Since he had been testing the plane regularly with the approval of the production factory, his request, though surprising, did not raise the technicians' suspicions."*

Hitler nearly bounded out of his seat. "I cannot bear the thought that those responsible for German armament efforts may be mixed up with . . ." He continued in an inaudible mumble, his hand slamming angrily into the table. His anger had overwhelmed him, keeping him from finishing his sentence.

"Mein Führer, we're arresting them now, claiming their attendance is required at a workers' meeting in Berlin," explained Himmler.

"And I imagine they'll have an accident on their way, won't they?" laughed the Ogre.

"Bormann, continue."

"The plane crossed all of Germany until it reached the North Sea, where it joined a formation of bombers headed for London. That's where our radar lost track of it."

"Hess was well informed," noted Himmler as he cleaned his round glasses. "But I won't point any fingers."

The furious Göring shot him an angry glance, his eyes as dark as a stormy sky.

"This morning," continued Bormann, *"our network of informants in England notified us that Hess's plane crashed in southwest Scotland, just a few miles from Glasgow, near a village called Eaglesham."*

"An accident?" asked Goebbels.

"We don't know. We don't even know why he was flying over Scotland. However, we do know he successfully deployed his parachute and survived."

"Unfortunately," concluded Himmler.

Hitler started shouting. "He has been with us through it all. He shared my cell, ran the party, had my trust. Why? Why would he betray me like this?"

"I can tell you why," replied Göring. "Hess is a madman with delusions of grandeur, thanks to his horoscopes and the voices in his head. He runs an army of astrologers who spend their time making all sorts of crazy plans. Remember when he told us Churchill would fall from power, that it was written in the stars . . . ? A real nutcase. His passion for the occult has destroyed his mind. He's not the only one, either."

"It's entirely possible," suggested Goebbels, "that spending all his time with his visionaries has cost him his ability to reason. That would explain things. Maybe he felt he was carrying out a divine mission by establishing peace between our country and England."

"Do you think so?" asked Hitler, surprised.

"Of course. I'm sure a celebrated psychiatrist would be happy to say as much publicly. The devoted Hess succumbed to the weight of his responsibilities. A victim, not a criminal."

"If Hess is declared mentally incompetent," continued Göring, "his actions are no longer political, but pathological. It changes everything."

"Especially if the diagnosis was made several months ago," suggested Goebbels. "If we're all in agreement, I'll send a press release to the German and European newspapers." He was silent for a moment, then continued: "All we need is some good prop-aganda! And it's high time we tidied amongst our ranks. We don't need people who think we can win the war with horoscopes, rituals, and who knows what else. It's a departure from the German way—one we can no longer tolerate!"

Göring turned towards Himmler. A limp smile slowly appeared on his flabby chin. "I agree with Joseph. Give us your orders, mein Führer, and we'll put an end to these ridiculous perversions."

Himmler's calm voice surprised everyone. "It's already been done. SS soldiers have arrested the group of astrologers who worked for Hess. They'll talk. Very soon."

Hitler, who had grown frantic from the tension, suddenly relaxed. "Thank goodness I have you, Heinrich."

Just as the faces of the Dwarf and the Ogre fell in displeasure to see Himmler come out on top, an assistant opened the door to the living room, slipped in, and silently made his way to the table. "I have someone on the line asking urgently for the Reichsführer."

Göring hissed like a snake. "Go ahead, Heinrich. I'm sure the astrologers have much to tell you. Do you think they already know how they'll die? What do the stars have to say about that? Hanging or firing squad?"

Himmler shook his head. "Neither. We're opening a new concentration camp in Birkenau. They can be the first inmates."

The assistant held out the phone.

"Reichsführer?"

Himmler recognized Erika von Essling's eager voice.

"We have it!"

44

Tristan looked out the window. They were still there. Parked next to one another in the street, watching the hotel entrance. Every hour the Frenchman saw them get out and pace the pavement. Two heavyweights with jawlines as square as their shoulders. They were worse than guard dogs. Irritated, Tristan moved away from the window and sat down on the bed. He'd slept poorly, his night interrupted by violent images of swastikas, Weistort lying on the ground in a puddle of his own blood, and the metallic sound of bullets echoing through the cave. He couldn't shake them.

After they'd found the swastika and been attacked by the commando unit, it had all happened so fast. A Luftwaffe Heinkel plane had picked him and Erika up from a military airstrip in Pamiers. Weistort had been taken to Foix hospital in critical condition.

Their plane had made a stopover in Châlons-sur-Saône to refuel, but they hadn't been allowed off. Then they flew straight to Berlin. They'd been separated immediately after disembarking at Tempelhof. Erika and the relic in one car, Tristan in the other, driven by two Gestapo agents.

They were still downstairs.

Probably waiting for a decision regarding his fate.

Weistort was in no condition to testify, so only Erika could save him now. But she'd left him without a word.

He walked over to the mirror to study his face for a moment. His growing beard made him look even more tired than he was.

He barely recognized himself. His eyes were hard, his body thin and wiry. It looked like he'd just escaped from hell. He wondered what had happened to Laure. She'd disappeared during the battle in the cave. Even if she was still alive, he'd never see her again. The day he'd met her on the outcropping in Montségur, with her quick retorts and deep-grey eyes, seemed like a lifetime ago. He looked at himself in the mirror again, then raised his head. He had to live in the present now.

He'd done what he had to do.

There was a knock on the door. Tristan backed away instinctively. It was unlikely someone was bringing up his breakfast. He grabbed his shirt and quickly threw it on. Another knock. If the Gestapo guys came for him, they wouldn't bother with such niceties. Tristan took a deep breath and turned the knob.

Erika was standing in front of him.

He almost didn't recognize her. The archaeologist had disappeared. No more grey canvas trousers and mud-stained jacket. Instead, she wore a fitted skirt and a button-up top that highlighted a figure he hadn't known she had. Dumbfounded, Tristan stood still in the doorway.

"Are you going to let me in?"

Her familiar tone was new too. The Frenchman moved aside, and Erika von Essling made her way to the mirror, where she adjusted her hair. The braids had also vanished. She wore her blonde hair down around her shoulders.

"My stay in Berlin has been rather dreary so far," began Tristan, trying to regain his wits.

But Erika wasn't listening. She looked out the window. One of the Gestapo thugs had just left the car for a café on the corner.

"He's going to make a call. We don't have long."

"For what?"

Her expression had changed. Her almond-shaped eyes stared intently at him, as if she saw something in him that even he didn't know was there.

"Why did you save me in the cave?" she asked.

Tristan thought back to the moment when he'd prevented death.

Why had he done it? There was only one possible explanation, but it wasn't time to explain yet. Von Essling came closer.

"Weistort was down. If I had died, you would have been free. Your local girlfriend would have helped you escape."

Tristan crossed his arms and looked at her jadedly. "Free to do what? Hide like a rat in the Ariège mountains alongside bedraggled resistance fighters? Be hunted by the French gendarmes and a regiment of SS soldiers dying to take their revenge? Thanks, but I went down that road in Spain. I aspire to a more . . . rewarding life."

She came even closer, her eyes bright.

"Even if that means a life under National Socialism?"

"I'm sure this room is full of bugs placed by your Gestapo friends. But I don't care. I reject all ideologies, Erika. They all promise paradise and deliver nothing but hell. Nazism, communism, liberalism, socialism, anarchism, patriotism . . . Just the sound of a word ending in *-ism* makes me sick."

"The Nazis want to build a new world. A great Europe is coming, and they'll need everyone."

"Tell that to the Jews. I doubt they will much enjoy the bright future promised by your Führer."

They were only inches away. Tristan moved his lips towards her ear and continued in a whisper: "I couldn't care less about your great Europe, Hitler, Pétain, Stalin, or any of the guys on the other side. I just want to make it out alive. I helped you find your goddamn relic. I hope to be rewarded in consequence."

"At least you're honest," she said with an ironic smile.

She raised her hand and ran her fingers over Tristan's cheek. "I can think of one reward . . ."

She gazed at him intently, then undid the first button on his shirt. A little pearl button which shone in the light like a nod from destiny.

"Maybe this will convince you to tell me why you saved me?" she suggested playfully.

Tristan's hands rested delicately on her waist. The flesh under her skirt was like a warm promise full of life. He thought he'd forgotten the sensation.

Her décolleté was more revealing now. He moved his lips forward. The skin on her chest was of an effervescent beauty that reminded him of sea foam on summer waves. Tristan felt Erika's fingers in his hair as their breath quickened. The room was no longer there. Space, time, everything seemed distant. Like in the old fairy tales, a magical fog must have descended to hide them from view. Tristan's lips climbed towards Erika's mouth, lingering along her neck, then kissing her suddenly feverish cheeks. She popped the rest of the buttons off his shirt, sliding the palms of her hands along his rough skin.

She felt his body warm under her fingers, as if her affections had brought him back to life. She moved lower.

Her eyes took on a mischievous glint Tristan had never seen there before.

"I think I have my answer."

Tristan drew her close and kissed her passionately. His hands grew bolder and more insistent. He burned with desire. It had been over a year since he'd touched a woman and the one against him now was surprisingly sensual.

Erika sighed at length, driving him wild.

She trembled under his touch, and just seconds later they were entangled on the bed. Their clothes were thrown aside to make room for two feverishly impatient bodies.

When he woke in the morning, it was already late. His mind still foggy, Tristan rolled over in the sheets, his hands searching for his lover.

The bed was empty.

Erika had disappeared. Vanished.

For a few seconds, he wondered if he'd imagined their magical night together. He sat up on the side of the bed, his muscles sore, and contemplated the room he was in. His prison.

The hair on the back of his neck stood on end and he wondered if Erika's reward for him had been the gift given to a prisoner before his execution.

The door swung open forcefully. The beginnings of an answer.

Two men in black leather trench coats stormed into the room. They stood there in front of him, their hands in their pockets, faces hard. One of them threw Tristan his trousers. "You, Frenchman, you're coming with us."

45

Despite the blindfold over his eyes and the handcuffs on his wrists, it didn't take Hess long to figure out he was being smuggled out. It was time. The purring motor, the fine fabric seats . . . It was clearly a luxury car. Nothing like the damp seat of the lorry that had delivered him to the nearest prison following his crash. For three days, he'd been left to rot in a tiny cell like a common thief. A doctor had come by to wrap his sprained ankle. They had then given him oversized clothes and a pair of shoes with no laces, and begun interrogating him. Hess had found the whole thing unbelievable. A poorly shaven warrant officer had placed a typewriter on a table, lit a cigarette, and loudly asked him to state his name.

"Rudolf Hess."

Without any hint of recognition, the soldier had typed his name and asked a few routine questions. Then he had stubbed out his cigarette without another word. For two days, Hess saw nobody but the guard who brought his meals. Then suddenly, the situation had taken a turn. A barber had shown up—under the watchful eye of armed men—and they had brought him a tweed suit and a pair of shiny shoes. He'd barely had time to tie them before he found himself blindfolded and handcuffed in a car driving hurriedly through the night.

Beneath the opaque fabric, Hess felt sure of himself. Now his real mission was underway. In a few hours or minutes, he would be officially welcomed and then . . . He almost burst into laughter as he recalled the warrant officer who had recorded his name without realizing who he was. He must regret it now. In Germany, he would have been executed. He imagined how shocked the members of the English government must have been. What, Hess? The Führer's closest adviser? Here, in our country? Panic must have washed over them. They must have been petrified—that was why it took them so long to react. Who would they send to negotiate with him? Churchill? He was about to lose power. His successor, then? Yes, Lord Halifax. Hess would eat him alive. He would bring peace: all of England would adore him. Maybe he'd even be invited to Buckingham Palace. His astrologers hadn't predicted that, but everything was possible now. He couldn't wait to see Goebbels's and Göring's faces when they saw him sitting next to the king!

The car stopped. A door slammed. A gloved hand guided him out of the vehicle.

"Take off his blindfold and handcuffs."

The sun had just begun to rise. Hess rubbed his eyes. He was standing on the steps of an old church with a grey tower overlooking a cemetery. The lichen-covered crosses seemed to have been forgotten for centuries. A current thundered somewhere below. The English have a gift for setting the stage, thought Hess. An officer gestured to him to walk. He waited a few seconds, to avoid appearing too obedient, then headed towards the door. For a second, he wondered if it was a trap. What if the British authorities had kept his landing top secret? What if Churchill's government had decided to eliminate him, to maintain its reputation and its hold on power? What better place than a forgotten rural church? Maybe there was a crypt? Maybe he'd end up under a nameless slab . . .

"Someone's waiting for you."

A table stood in the middle of the nave. Two chairs faced each other. Hess coughed. There must be candles burning somewhere. He hated the rancid scent of religion. A door creaked. Rudolf turned around. A massive silhouette appeared, followed by a heavy hand, which stubbed out a cigar in the nearest holy font. The Führer's confidant realized who it was even before his voice echoed through the vaulted room.

"Do you believe in God, Mr. Hess?"

Churchill had just taken his place on the stage.

A new cigar appeared on the Bulldog's lips, followed by the ephemeral flame of a match. Hess, like Hitler, neither smoked nor drank, and he consumed very little meat. Discipline and respect for the body were essential to founding a new civilization destined to last a thousand years. If the British Empire was anything like its leader, it didn't have much time left. In addition to destroying his lungs with every puff on a Havana, the broken capillaries in his eyes and bright-red cheeks indicated the Prime Minister was also torturing his liver. An alcoholic, thought Hess.

"You haven't answered my question," said Churchill.

"I don't believe in God, no. However, I believe in fate. And today, fate is German."

The Bulldog had sat down. Hess could hear his fast, heavy breathing.

"Was it *fate* that made you jump out of your plane with a parachute over Scotland?"

"Of course."

"That's not what your leader thinks."

Churchill summoned the officer to the table. He placed a pile of German newspapers in front of the two men. "Since your spectacular escape from Germany, you've been all over the front pages. Look."

Rudolf skimmed them, then shrugged. He'd expected as much. Of course, neither the party nor Hitler himself could publicly admit what his mission was really about.

"'Is Hess crazy?'" read Churchill. "'Hess: psychotic break?' Your friend Goebbels is fashioning public opinion as we speak. Today they think you're crazy. Tomorrow there will be proof. The Dwarf won't miss his chance to get rid of you."

"Of course, we're manipulating public opinion, but for something else entirely. We're much better at it than you are."

"If you're talking about your friends, like Göring and Himmler, they're much stronger than you are. They're taking the warm place you left at the Führer's side. It's over for you, Mr. Hess."

"You're the one who's finished, Herr Churchill."

The two men looked at one another like poker players, trying to figure out who was bluffing. Winston put his cards down on the table first.

"Here's the front page of tomorrow's *Times*. I must admit, I really like the headline: 'Rudolf Hess requests political asylum in United Kingdom'. Hitler's friend fleeing dictatorship, seeking refuge in the world's leading democracy. The entire globe will rejoice."

"Especially when they realize I came in the Führer's name, to bring peace."

Winston raised a weary eyebrow. "You? Peace?"

"Yes, a peace that could save your Empire. From Canada to the Indies, by way of Africa."

"And Europe is yours? Is that right?"

"Supremacy on the seas for England, power on land for the Reich."

"Never!" the Bulldog suddenly barked.

Hess laughed. "Don't tell me you care about Europe. You despise the French. You know nothing of the Czechs or Poles. The only reason you're refusing peace is to keep your power."

"We English might love to speak ill of our friends, but they are still our friends. I was elected by the people to win this war."

"And what will the people say when they realize their children will die in the bombings just so an old alcoholic can continue to enjoy his whisky at 10 Downing Street?"

Churchill stood up, relit his cigar, and called the officer at the door.

"You can take Mr. Hess back to his usual lodgings."

Rudolf stood up in turn. "Are you refusing my offer?"

"What offer?"

"Then you'll lose the war. England is alone."

Churchill smirked. "Unless your great Führer decides to attack Russia, like Napoleon before him. Then there will be two fronts . . ."

Hess's face darkened, but he didn't reply. Even if he wanted to, he couldn't betray the Führer. Churchill would call Stalin seconds later to talk about it. He tried to reach Baldr telepathically, but the god was strangely silent.

"Maybe you have something to share with me on the topic?" pushed the British Prime Minister.

Hess shook his head. "Our leader and Stalin signed a pact of non-aggression. The Führer always keeps his promises."

"Of course!" laughed Churchill. "Like in Munich, when he promised peace after invading Czechoslovakia. Chamberlain used to wake up in a cold sweat over how that one panned out." The Bulldog coughed, then continued mercilessly. "Well, I've wasted enough time. We'll transfer you to a prison more worthy of your rank soon. Probably the Tower of London. With any luck, one of your friend Göring's bombs will take care of you for us."

"London won't be destroyed by Luftwaffe bombings," shouted the sickened German.

"I already knew that," said Churchill with a shrug as he headed for the door.

Hess shook with anger. "No, it will be destroyed by another weapon! A much more powerful weapon!" he shrieked. "One we've awoken from the distant past. An invincible weapon that will bring England and the rest of the world to their knees!"

Churchill stopped short. He felt the hairs on the back of his neck stand on end. A signal he knew all too well. He felt it every time he was on the brink of disaster.

"You're bluffing, Mr. Hess. There is no such weapon."

"You're right, Herr Churchill. It doesn't exist . . . Not yet. But we are working on it. Or rather, bringing it back to life."

"For the first time in years I'm going to have to believe German newspapers: you really are a lunatic."

"The weapon is made up of four elements. We already have one and the second will soon be in our possession."

"Where did you get it?"

"In Tibet, in 1939."

Winston froze. The feeling in his neck spread to his brain and a name came to the surface. Malorley.

"And since then, we've defeated Poland, France, Norway, Greece—"

"That's enough!"

Hess's grey eyes met Churchill's unsteady gaze.

"You're the lunatic if you refuse this peace."

The Prime Minister's unmarked car bolted through the countryside towards the closest military airport. A civilian plane with no official flight plan was waiting to take him back to London as discreetly as possible. The fog was slowly lifting. With his stubby fingers, Winston wiped the condensation from the window and pressed his burning forehead to the cool glass. He'd felt like his head was in a vice since leaving Hess. Everything was a jumble in his mind. Malorley, Tibet, the dilapidated castle in southern France. What was it called again?

Amid the thick heath appeared a dark runway. The car parked in front of a hangar filled with the sound of spinning blades.

"The plane is ready, Mr. Prime Minister. We'll be in London in—"

"Find me a phone. Immediately!"

They took him to a camouflaged hangar. At the far end, in an office panelled with unvarnished wood, a surprised technician saluted.

"Give me a moment."

A secretary answered on the third ring. "SOE, Section F. How can I help you?"

"This is the Prime Minister. Get me Buck!"

Churchill didn't have to wait long.

"Buckmaster, Sir. At your service."

"Do you have news from Malorley?"

"Yes, Sir, but . . ."

"Spit it out then."

"I'm sorry, but the network of French resistance fighters responsible for his logistics was discovered. All its members have been arrested."

"Which means?"

"We lost them, Sir."

46

The Reichsführer's living room resembled a ballroom, the likes of which Erika had only ever seen in Italy. She almost expected dancers to appear on the long, wooden floor, moving to the lively beat of a waltz. This was nothing more than a dream, however, since Himmler never played music between these old walls and there were never drinks on the frugal tables. Nevertheless, as Erika looked around at the SS dignitaries invited to the party, she noticed their faces were merry and red. Many of them had indulged before arriving, she thought.

The young woman hated spending her time with this crowd of arrogant men. She wanted to leave immediately for Tristan's room. She'd never experienced such exhilaration before. The Frenchman wasn't as handsome as the few other men she'd been with, but he was infinitely more charming. He was both gentle and passionate. He made her feel like more than a conquest. And she'd enjoyed more than just pleasure in his company. The idea that the Gestapo might torture Tristan troubled her. She needed to speak to Himmler about him again.

She pushed Tristan from her thoughts and moved to a quieter corner of the room. It had become a habit for her at parties of late. But this time, the decorations on the wall were nothing like those at Göring's chalet. A black leather whip on the white wall caught her eye. It looked like a venomous snake slithering upwards. It didn't look like her father's, but it evoked the same feelings. Suffering, pain, humiliation. Her father had used a knout, a braided rope with several large knots, designed to keep the muzhiks in line. It had been his favourite teaching tool with the servants. And others.

She looked away from the despicable object and noticed that one of the guests, a Hauptsturmführer, was staring at her intently. Generous amounts of alcohol had left his cheeks aglow, highlighting the many scars that crisscrossed his face.

"Otto Skorzeny," said Himmler, who'd just arrived with the SS. "He's a member of the Führer's personal guard. One of our most promising officers."

The captain bowed to Erika.

"If you're troubled by his scars," added Himmler, "as women usually are, you should know they're from the many duels he fought with a sabre during his tumultuous youth."

"I've handled skulls ravaged by leprosy, crushed by rocks, or burned alive," replied Erika. "A few cat scratches don't scare me."

Surprised and wounded, Skorzeny simply clicked his heels and disappeared.

"You really know how to talk to men," teased the Reichsführer. "So harsh. You know," he added, "you're the perfect embodiment of an Aryan woman, as I see it. You'd make beautiful children, strong and ruthless soldiers for the SS."

Erika almost choked as the master of the castle spoke, but she remained impassive. White and cold as marble.

"I owe it to my father. He instilled these values in me."

My bastard of a father.

He'd taught her what pain was and how to overcome it. He'd taught her how to kill. She chased him from her mind and continued:

"Speaking of men, I'd like to know what's to become of the Frenchman, Tristan, who helped me identify the thing you wanted most."

"I know you're interested in his fate," said Himmler. "And so are we. We'll do what must be done later. Don't get too sentimental. It's bad for your health."

His frigid tone made von Essling tremble. He knew.

"I haven't yet congratulated you for your remarkable work at Montségur," continued Himmler. Without leaving any time for a reply, he took Erika by the arm. "When I told him of your discovery, the Führer was struck by the similarity of the names Montségur and Montsalvat, the castle of the Grail in Wagner's *Parsifal*."

"I didn't know the Führer was interested in—"

"You don't know much about the Führer," he said, cutting her off. "Follow me."

They took a staircase that led to a landing guarded by SS soldiers in dress uniform. When they saw Himmler, they opened a door to a long, tiled corridor. Erika noticed there were no windows. It was like they were underground.

"There's only one way in," explained Himmler, "for optimal security."

He pointed to a single door at the end of the corridor.

"Any special reason?" asked von Essling.

"Yes, this is Hitler's room."

Himmler pulled out a bronze key and pushed it into the lock.

"When I designed Wewelsburg, the Führer agreed to have a room in the castle, but on one condition: he would only come here after our ultimate victory. A pact of honour between him and the SS. Another way to spur us to triumph over our enemies."

The Reichsführer moved aside to let von Essling in.

"In the meantime, we have arranged it according to his precise orders. It's probably the place on earth that best represents who he is. We call it the Barbarossa room."

"Like the Holy Roman Emperor? Why?"

"He's the Führer's role model." Himmler adopted a confidential tone. "I'm certain he's his reincarnation, in fact."

As she entered, Erika noticed the simplicity of the room. A monastic ambience reigned. A single window covered with thick curtains, an austere cot, and a rustic wooden table with a handwritten score on it.

"A gift from Wagner's family. Did you know Hitler is a friend of theirs? During his prison stay in 1924, they provided the paper he used to write *Mein Kampf*. And the children of the family love him—they call him Onkel Wolf!"

"Uncle Wolf? What a strange nickname!"

The head of the SS ignored her comment.

"As for the cane next to the bed, it belonged to Nietzsche. The philosopher's sister gave it to the Führer in recognition of all he's done for Germany."

Erika was about to remind him that Nietzsche's sister was best known for shamefully twisting her brother's texts to make them conform to Nazi ideology, but she kept quiet. The large bookcase that took up most of the room had caught her attention.

"Out of the sixteen thousand volumes in his private collection, Hitler has chosen his favourite books to keep in here."

Von Essling stepped closer. A series of identical bindings filled a whole shelf. Each spine was engraved with a pair of initials: *A.H.*

"These are the first translations of Shakespeare into German. The greatest playwright of all time, in the Führer's eyes."

"An Englishman?"

"Hitler is a reader above all such prejudices. Look, for example, at the shelf near the window."

Here the books were mismatched, bruised, and yellowed by time.

"They're the volumes the Führer bought in Vienna while he was studying for the entrance exam to the Academy of Fine Arts. At the time, he skipped meals to buy books. They're probably the works he cherishes most."

Despite their worn covers, Erika managed to decipher a few of the titles: *The Prophecies of Nostradamus explained*; *The Dead Are Alive*; *"Parsifal": The Message Revealed*.

"You see, Hitler's interest in the occult aspects of Wagner's work dates back some time."

"But spinning tables and the predictions of a Renaissance astrologer?"

Himmler came closer. "That's one of the Führer's greatest strengths. He is beyond good and evil, beyond truth and lies. He defies all limits. You should aspire to the same."

Erika was suddenly worried. The Reichsführer was very close to her. Was he making a proposition? Or was he just truly amazed by the power and genius of his master, searching to convince her, too?

"Look down."

One by one, the varnished floorboards disappeared to reveal a transparent floor over a circular room with stone walls. A spotlight flicked on, then a second, third, fourth, each showcasing a swastika carved deeply into the stone.

"I had them installed just below the Führer's room. The home of the sacred swastikas."

Himmler pointed to one of the carvings. "To the east, the swastika recovered from Tibet. To the south, the one you found in Montségur."

Fascinated, von Essling contemplated the symbol, which looked like a serpent eating its own body.

"With each new swastika, Germany advances, like an inescapable wave. First Europe, soon Russia . . ."

"Do you really think these objects have the power to win the war?" asked Erika.

"Do you remember the hall of eternal fire, from your first visit to Wewelsburg?"

Erika nodded silently. She preferred not to talk about it. The piercing screams of the prisoner burned alive still echoed in her ears.

"In Tibet, at Montségur . . . everywhere these relics were left, they retained their powers by serving as receptacles of intense human suffering."

Le prats dels cremats, thought the archaeologist. The cursed place where hundreds of victims perished in a fire worthy of hell itself.

"But over time, their power weakened. We need to recharge their energy."

"How do you plan to do that?"

"You seem surprised. But archaeology is how we discovered the tombs of kings who had their servants buried alive with them."

"A barbaric ritual!"

"No, forgotten age-old wisdom. That of the superior race, which can only survive and thrive by annihilating all inferior men. Take a good look at the swastika you brought back from Montségur. It hasn't enjoyed a good sacrifice in seven centuries. It's hungry for pain."

A door opened beneath them. Two guards entered the crypt carrying a naked young man tied to a chair. They put him down next to the central pit, then another guard arrived, pushing a naked woman forward with the barrel of his machine gun.

"Communist activists," explained the Reichsführer. "Fanatics. Incorrigible fanatics."

"Are they lovers?" asked Erika as the woman flung herself around the male prisoner's neck.

"Indeed."

A soldier pulled her away and ordered her to stand a yard from the pit.

"The Ahnenerbe's ethnologists have noted a common fact about human sacrifices in all great civilizations."

The SS officer had just given the woman a dagger, all the while threatening her with his Luger.

"All the victims went willingly. That's why we won't kill this couple. We'll let one of them decide to do it."

"But they have no reason to."

Himmler watched them as if they were lab rats in a new experiment.

"They do—love! That despicable sentiment. The soldier is offering the woman the following choice: either she executes the love of her life herself and she'll be set free, or she refuses and will be raped, then tortured in front of her lover. She has ten seconds to decide."

"That's horrific," mumbled Erika.

"Don't bring emotion into it," replied Himmler. "I'm no sadist. They're not human, not in my eyes at least, so why would I feel anything for them?"

Frozen in place, von Essling watched the woman take the dagger and clutch it to her breast. She was crying and shaking, unable to move. The soldier stepped closer and placed his pistol on her temple.

"The guard is counting down," said Himmler nonchalantly. "Imagine what's going on in that woman's head . . . She's torn between two impossible choices."

The poor woman walked over to her companion and brandished the knife. The man seemed to encourage her.

Erika glanced discreetly at Himmler. The bespectacled head of the SS seemed to be hypnotized by the show. His upper lip trembled.

Suddenly, the woman turned the dagger towards her own body and pierced her chest. She wavered for a few seconds, then collapsed onto the swastika. To Erika's astonishment, the Reichsführer laughed with satisfaction. "She was unable to choose and preferred to commit suicide. Clear proof she was of inferior stock. Such weakness. But at least their deaths will be useful. It's not over just yet."

The guard dragged the woman's body across the floor and threw her into the circular pit. Then, with the help of a newly arrived colleague, they threw the man in as well.

"You see, I'm not a monster. He'll die alongside his beloved. Of hunger and thirst."

The guards placed the slab back over the hole.

Erika couldn't move, petrified by the barbaric nature of what had just happened before her eyes. Himmler hadn't invited her to this atrocity for no reason. He was testing her. Showing the slightest sign of disgust would result in her death. But there was something else that sickened her, something deep within herself. She had been fascinated by the swastika as it soaked up the blood. She didn't see a curled-up snake anymore, but a beast. A beast from the darkness, one that had fascinated all mythologies. The beast who was always hungry for more . . .

"Frau von Essling?"

Himmler's interrogative tone brought her back to reality.

"Please forgive me, Reichsführer, I was distracted for a moment."

"Fascinated, I think. Everyone who has seen the sacred swastikas has felt it. Can you imagine what it will be like when all four are here?"

The archaeologist stared at the two empty places for the remaining relics. She felt dizzy.

"And now that Weistort's gone, it's your job to find them."

47

The rising moon shone softly in the sky above the cove, shedding a gentle light on the surrounding coastline. The waves washed onto the shore one after another with the regularity of a metronome. The tiny beach was covered in foul-smelling black seaweed. Clumps of it gathered along the feet of the battered wooden cabins left behind by the thriving pre-war tourist industry.

Sitting on an abandoned dock carved out of the cliff, Malorley placed his satchel between his legs and nervously checked his watch, then picked up his binoculars to study the dark surface of the sea. Nothing. Not a single light. Nothing but the empty Mediterranean as far as the eye could see. So placid, hopelessly placid. His rage threatened to boil over. It was all too ridiculous. He had successfully completed the mission, only to find himself abandoned on a beach. His journey from Montségur had been harrowing, but relatively short thanks to the shortcuts they'd taken to avoid gendarme inspections. They'd left the Ariège region an hour after being smuggled out of the castle. The lorry had entered the Pyrenees foothills via the road to Prades. The driver had decided it was better to avoid Perpignan, preferring less damaged roads, and drove straight through until they reached a cove near Collioure. Malorley hadn't spoken during the entire trip. He was haunted by the last time he'd seen Jane in the field.

"Still nothing?" asked Laure, her back resting against the door of a dilapidated fisherman's hut.

"Yellow Triton is taking its time," mumbled the SOE man. "Two hours late."

"Yellow Triton. Yet another ridiculous code name invented by Radio London," quipped La Cebolla as he went about his business in a small rowing boat tied to a rusted ring. The Spaniard's cap-wearing comrade placed a pair of oars on the jetty.

"Triton refers to the Navy's submarine model. The colour tells what type of mission it's on. In this case, a rescue."

"It will be dawn in an hour. We won't be able to stay here for long," said the Spaniard. "We need to hide in the backcountry near Montauriol."

Laure d'Estillac moved closer to Malorley. "How's your ankle?"

"Fantastic," he replied in a tone he meant to be cheerful. He'd braced it between two boards from a delivery crate. "I can start training for the next Olympics."

One of the Spanish resistance fighters started singing a woeful song. The lyrics wafted through the moonlit sky.

"*Cállate coño*," scolded La Cebolla. "You'll get us caught!"

"That's Catalan, isn't it?" asked Laure.

"Yes, my man is from Girona."

"What's it about?"

He smiled in the half-darkness. "I don't know if I should translate it in front of a young lady . . ."

"Don't worry, I'm a big girl."

The Spaniard pointed to the lights that shone on a hill to their right. "You see that village over there? It's Collioure. Carles's song is about Collioure, or rather about the castle that overlooks it. The translation would go something like: 'Way up high atop the mountain sits Collioure, where the guards will break your balls.'"

The young woman shook her head. "I don't understand," she said.

"They call it the Château Royal. We spent five months there, right after arriving in France in 1939. And let me tell you, there's nothing royal about it. It's a prison camp, where they crammed us in like animals. Thanks to the forced labour, beatings, and meagre rations, four of my comrades died of exhaustion."

Malorley listened casually as he continued to watch the sea.

"I thought France was your ally at the time."

"A strange ally indeed. France opened its borders so we could escape Franco's wrath, but leaving a defeated army to go about its business with the men's terrified families in tow was out of the question. Instead, they imprisoned us, in inhumane conditions. Our fate depended on the humanity of the commanders in charge of each camp. Unfortunately, in Collioure it was Captain Raulet. A member of the Foreign Legion and an admirer of the Caudillo."

"*Hijo de puta,*" muttered Pedro.

La Cebolla slapped his friend on the back.

"My comrades and I escaped that hell pit and sought refuge in the Ariège region. Coming back here makes me very nervous. Especially since my country is just a few miles away and I—"

"It's here!" interrupted Malorley. "The submarine has arrived!"

Laure and the two Spaniards turned to look in the direction the Englishman was pointing.

Far out to sea a yellow light blinked at regular intervals against the black waves. Malorley picked up his briefcase, aimed his torch and sent a short message in Morse code to let them know the group was there.

"Let's go!" shouted La Cebolla. "The boat's ready!"

The two Spaniards installed the oars as Laure and Malorley sat down in front. They rowed as if their lives depended on it, their muffled grunts the only sound above the waves. It took ten long minutes to reach the rendezvous point.

Before them sat a long, thin, black shape that seemed to tremble in the dark water. From head to tail it had to be nearly a hundred meters long, thought Malorley, impressed. He'd seen a model before, on the docks at Portsmouth before the war. Real predators. In the middle of the structure stood the sail, crowned with antennae. A man in a thick Navy turtleneck jumper stood on the circular walkway and scanned the ocean with binoculars. On the deck below, three sailors huddled beside a 102mm canon bolted to the metal beneath them. They waved encouragingly to the group in the rowing boat.

The small boat, jostled by the waves, bumped into the iron side of the underwater predator. La Cebolla threw a rope to one of the sailors, who pulled it tight to steady the boat.

"We'd started to think you weren't coming!" said Malorley.

"So did we!" answered the warrant officer who tied the rope to a rig. "We picked up two U-boats off the coast of Malta. We had to do some fancy manoeuvring to lose them. Come on up!"

"Just a second, sailor. We have to say goodbye to our friends."

Malorley and Laure turned to La Cebolla. "If you hear from Jane, send me a radio message," said the Englishman, his voice tense.

The Spaniard looked at him sadly. "There's little hope, *señor*. I told you my man wasn't able to get to her in the field."

"You never know. Promise me!"

"I promise. But in exchange, promise me something, too."

"Depends what it is."

"If your country someday manages to beat the Nazis, you must tell Churchill that it's only the beginning of *our* fight. We will head for Spain to rid the country of Franco. We will need England's help."

Malorley shook the soldier's hand. "To put an anarchist in his place? I'm not sure our Prime Minister could get on board with that. But I promise you I will pass on the message."

"Hurry up," shouted the officer atop the conning tower. "I don't want to wait around here. We've got word there's a French patrol ship off the coast of Port-Vendres."

As Malorley climbed up the side of the hull with help from a sailor, the Spaniard took Laure by the shoulders. "*Señorita*, your father was a real bastard!"

"What?" asked the young woman in disbelief.

"An aristocratic asshole, but with *cojones* like this," he said, gesturing as if he were handling a pair of coconuts. "It was an honour to fight by his side. I hope you will be worthy of his memory and continue his work."

She hugged him tightly, then walked over to the submarine,

where two sailors pulled her aboard. They threw back the rope and the small vessel began to drift away.

"I'll do my best," shouted Laure to the Spaniard, who had picked up his oars.

The SOE agent watched the skiff disappear into the night, and a wave of intense compassion washed over him. These men he would probably never see again were returning to France to fight in a hostile country, motivated by a single hope: that they would someday fight in a new war in another country. Their own country. The one that had exiled them.

Malorley and Laure cast a last glance towards the boat's outline, then made their way towards the sail.

Suddenly, a siren wailed in the night.

The bow of a huge black object with a massive searchlight was coming around the outcropping at the edge of the cove.

"Enemy ship!" shouted the lieutenant.

He'd barely sounded the alert when the mysterious ship opened fire. An explosion just hundred meters from the submarine shot a huge fountain of salty water up into the air. It drenched them like a tropical storm.

"French Navy. That was your first warning," blared a loudspeaker in the night. "Cut your engines and prepare to be boarded!"

The searchlight was racing towards them.

"Dive!" ordered the lieutenant into the microphone. Then he turned to Malorley and Laure, who were soaked through. "Hurry up or we'll throw you overboard!"

A strident alarm sounded inside the submarine. The two new arrivals clambered into the opening and down the metal ladder. They found themselves in the command post amid sailors hurrying to and fro. The officer slipped in behind them and quickly locked the water-tight door to the sail. With the door closed, the space reeked of machine oil and sweat.

"Down thirty meters," shouted the officer. "Hold on tight to the leather straps. This is going to be rough," he explained to Laure and Malorley.

The captain had pulled out the periscope and was spinning in all directions, his eye glued to the lens. "Coast guard. We cannot fall into their hands. They'll be wanting to make an example of us, after what happened at Mers el-Kébir. Maximum dive speed, lieutenant!"

His second-in-command pushed a big red button.

A new explosion made the hull tremble and knocked the submarine off-kilter. Malorley and Laure grabbed the leather straps that hung from the metal ceiling just in time. The crew began their perfectly coordinated mechanical ballet. Laure couldn't help but admire them and wonder how they could find anything at all amid the forest of valves, levers, gauges, and displays.

"Full speed ahead," ordered the commanding officer as he moved a compass and square around an ocean map on the wall.

The floor suddenly slanted downward. A wave of nausea hit Malorley and caused him to slip. He grabbed his bag as he fell. The officer in the turtleneck jumper picked him up off the floor, seemingly unbothered by the constant pitching of the ship.

"Where are my manners? I'm Lieutenant Commander Richard Peacock. Welcome aboard the *Tetrarch*. You are now on British soil. At least for the moment, if that damn French ship doesn't throw any underwater grenades."

"You can't possibly know how happy I am to be back home," answered Malorley, moving like a puppet on invisible strings. "What route are we taking?"

"We're heading for Gibraltar, to make sure we avoid the Italians. They have a chokehold on the entire stretch between the Balearics and the Iberian Peninsula."

"How long will it take us to get there?"

"Ten hours, if all goes to plan. Then you'll head to Lisbon, where you'll get a flight to London. With any luck, you'll be crossing Piccadilly Circus in two days."

A new rumbling sound echoed through the steel walls. This time the ship leaned in the other direction. Everything was vibrating from the blast. Water began shooting out of a winding pipe over their heads but the commander was unfazed. A sailor hurried over with a rag and a wrench.

Laure shot a worried glance at Malorley, who managed not to react despite his own fears.

"I'm going to have my work cut out for me over the next few hours," the commander said, his voice preoccupied. "Don't take this the wrong way, but you're not making it any easier standing there. Why don't you go and rest in my cabin? There are two beds."

"Thank you. I think I'll pass out straight away," said Laure, exhausted.

"Sorry about the lack of privacy, Miss," Peacock replied. "This whale is as long as three tennis courts, but its insides are full of motors, batteries, and weapons. People are just temporary guests. Comfort is about as necessary as lipstick for us naval officers and sailors."

He gave a few more instructions to a low-ranking officer who was checking on a pressure gauge the size of a clock. The mechanic left his work and gestured to them to follow him as the *Tetrarch* continued its dive.

They walked through several compartments, their walls and ceilings covered in a jumble of wires and pipes of all different sizes. As they moved further back, the purring of the diesel engines became a muffled but powerful vibration. Like the regular breathing of a huge animal.

They finally reached the commander's tiny cabin, which neighboured the officers' mess. Two bunk-beds sat next to a nightstand and a metal chair. All the furniture was bolted to the floor.

"We'll wake you two hours before we arrive," said the petty officer in a friendly voice. "If we haven't sunk in the meantime, that is."

He disappeared back out into the bowels of the ship with a nod.

A much more powerful explosion than the last one sent them flying into the wall between the cabin and the mess hall. A sinister creaking sounded all around them, as if the ship were twisting back in on itself. Malorley looked worriedly at Laure, hoping she could keep herself together.

"I hope you're not claustrophobic," he said.

"If what you're really asking is: 'Are you going to start sobbing again like at Montségur?', the answer is no. But that doesn't mean I'm calm. The thought of drowning in this . . . this steel coffin terrifies me."

The vessel finally levelled off and Laure climbed up onto the top bunk. Malorley sat down underneath. He carefully placed his briefcase next to the pillow and stretched out. His feet hung over the edge of the bed and he wondered if it had straps to keep him from falling out.

"You know you promised my father you'd take care of me," said Laure from above.

"And that's precisely what I'm doing. You are safe. And with each passing hour, you get further away from the Nazis' reach."

"That's not enough for me. I want to go home as a fighter. I want to avenge my father."

"I don't know if—"

"Jane is gone. I can take her place."

Malorley crossed his arms behind his head. "You would never make it. The training is brutal. Ninety percent of applicants get sent home, and the survival rate for field agents is ridiculously low. However, I'm sure I could find you a job somewhere in the SOE. Your profile could—"

The young woman jumped out of bed and knelt on the floor. "I can't be a secretary or a nurse! I'll go home to France on the first fishing boat that will have me, if that's the case."

He yawned at length to discourage her, but she didn't move. She was determined.

"All right. I'll look into it when we get to London," he finally agreed reluctantly.

"Do I have your word?"

"Yes. I keep my promises—even those made by others, as Pétain likes to say." Satisfied, she climbed back into bed.

Malorley felt exhaustion win out over his body. Jane's face danced before his red eyes. He prayed once again that she'd had time to swallow her cyanide capsule.

In terms of human losses, the mission was a disaster. He'd lost almost the entire commando unit, as well as d'Estillac. If only Churchill had agreed to give him more men. He could have avoided this bloodbath.

"Malorley . . ."

The Englishman was losing his patience. "Aren't you asleep yet?" he asked.

"That Tristan, the collaborator who was working with the Germans . . ."

"Yes. Too bad I didn't manage to take him out in the cave," replied Malorley. "I hate Frenchmen who betray their country."

Laure seemed to hesitate. She could still see his face, from when he'd come to see her at the manor. "In the cave, he let us go, even though it would have been easier for him to hand us over to the Germans."

"Yes, I noticed. But he's the reason the Germans left with the prize."

"But he had such a strange expression on his face, don't you think? As if he was trying to tell us something."

The SOE officer chose not to answer at first. He slipped under the rough wool blanket issued by the Navy. "Who knows? Even the worst people on earth sometimes have a drop of humanity hidden away somewhere. Good night!"

He turned out the light without waiting for Laure to reply. The only glimmer in the cabin was now a small red nightlight on the ceiling.

Another explosion sounded, causing the *Tetrarch*'s body to cry out.

Malorley huddled himself into the foetal position, his back against the metal wall. Knowing that just a few inches of metal separated him from millions of tonnes of freezing water terrified him.

He fell into a dark, deep sleep.

48

The tall and imposing building that housed the headquarters of the Geheime Staatspolizei—the Gestapo—hadn't always been synonymous with fear and cruelty. Before April 1933, it had been home to a magnificent decorative arts museum where Berliners flocked to enjoy a vast collection of works renowned throughout Europe. But since Hitler's climb to power, its exhibition rooms had been turned into torture chambers. Sumptuous 19th-century lace dresses had been replaced by black leather trench coats, and artists' sketchbooks removed to make way for lists of suffering prisoners.

Over the years, the Gestapo had become a fearsome and tentacular bureaucratic organization. Under Himmler's authority, an army of competent and devoted agents—15,800 officers—worked feverishly to annihilate enemies of the Reich: communists, Jews, liberals, democrats, Catholics, and reluctant Protestants. In short, anyone who didn't believe in the victorious National Socialism. Of which there were many. To succeed in its colossal task, the Gestapo was home to a host of different professions: police officers, spies, accountants, interrogators, secretaries, statisticians, drivers, code breakers, and more. There were even doctors and nurses appointed to ensure interrogated prisoners survived in the building's dreadful basements.

Though 8 Prinz-Albrecht-Straße didn't house the full Gestapo army, which was spread throughout Germany and occupied Europe, the site was home to the administrative and repression departments. Pen-pushers and executioners sat side by side in the canteen at lunch.

Held in a cell on the building's fourth floor, Tristan still wondered why he'd been sitting there for over two hours answering a police officer's questions. He was exhausted and on edge. It was a far cry from the welcome he'd expected to receive in Berlin.

"And the young woman?" the police officer sitting across from him asked kindly. "This Laure d'Estillac. I see in the report that her father led a resistance network with a band of dangerous Spanish communists."

The officer's syllables ran together, and he hesitated rather frequently, but his French was still perfectly understandable. His tone was almost polite. Maybe he was embarrassed to be asking the same questions again and again.

"For the umpteenth time," said Tristan, visibly annoyed, "I didn't know her. I didn't know her or any of the members of the commando unit."

He rubbed his temples in a bid to relieve the insidious headache he'd had since he was arrested in his hotel room. He felt himself wasting away, albeit in the height of luxury, compared to the hellish dungeon they'd left him in in Barcelona. Tristan had eighty square feet, a bed and a toilet at his disposal, and they'd even provided two warm meals per day since he'd arrived. He was beginning to wonder if the sinister reputation of Nazi prisons had been exaggerated.

Tristan looked up at the police officer, who kept fiddling with the file on the metal table which they'd brought in specially for the interrogation. He was in his sixties, with many wrinkles and ruddy cheeks. His rough features were a far cry from the Aryan ideal. Detective Drexler had introduced himself politely—too politely, perhaps—and hadn't stopped asking questions for the past three hours.

"Such a shame you let her go," he said, joining his hands as if in prayer. He looked like a fat old monk from some godforsaken rural village.

Tristan slammed his fist down onto the table. "I'm not the Gestapo. I don't kill people who don't deserve to die."

"Who told you I killed people?" asked the officer calmly. "I'm a Kripo detective. I'm not with the Gestapo. My job is to track criminals of all types. I'm just lending a hand with this case."

He pulled a pack of cigarettes out of his pocket and lit one.

"Well, *I'm* not a crook. As I've been trying to tell you, I helped Colonel Weistort with a strategic mission for the Reich. Jesus! How long do I have to stay here?" shouted Tristan as he jumped up.

The officer shrugged. "Sit down. You'll stay for as long as you're needed, my friend. Do you know why they picked me to interrogate you personally? Besides the fact that few of my colleagues speak French?"

"No. Do you have a secret passion for archaeology?"

"Not at all. The Violinist respects me for a very precise reason."

"The Violinist? What, do you play in the Berlin Symphonic Orchestra?" asked Tristan lightly.

The police officer leaned over the table. "The Violinist is one of the nicknames of Obergruppenführer Reynhardt Heydrich, Director of the RSHA and Himmler's right-hand man. A virtuoso with a bow. Just one of his many qualities . . ."

The police officer looked deep into Tristan's eyes and added, in a perfectly neutral tone, "I'm the best lie-detector around."

Tristan didn't react. Seconds ticked by in silence.

The officer picked up again calmly. "Throughout my long career, I've had to put quite a few delinquents through the fire. I regularly help out my colleagues at the Gestapo. They're good at what they do, but they're not particularly interested in psychology. A trip down to the basement levels of this building is proof enough of that."

"I can agree with you on that," replied Tristan. "The past few days have been trying. I would rather spend my time relaxing at a thermal spa. I hear Germany is famous for its fine establishments. And its prison camps, of course . . ."

The detective's eyebrows jumped. "I would advise you not to make jokes. You might get away with it with me, but not with my colleagues. And your record from the war in Spain isn't exactly in your favour. You must admit it's quite a coincidence that the commando unit at Montségur was also made up of former Republican fighters."

"I was just on the wrong side of things, okay? As for those men, I didn't know them. And let's not forget that Colonel Weistort couldn't have cared less about my past."

The officer turned his attention back to the file. "Maybe, but he's not here to testify on your behalf. A real shame."

"Good grief, call Erika von Essling. She'll confirm my story."

Detective Drexler stared at him for a moment in silence, then narrowed his eyes and continued: "You have no real attachment to National Socialism or Germany. Weistort's own annotated report says as much. What's your real motivation?"

"Survival. For the thirtieth time! I want to survive. My country has been beaten, England is on its knees, I hate Stalin and his friends, and Germany has won victory after victory. Do I have to spell it out for you? I picked the winning side. It's in fashion in all the occupied countries at the moment."

"What I like about you is your idealism."

"Let's leave idealism to revolutionaries, patriots, and idiots."

The detective scratched his square chin, then lumbered to a standing position and picked up Tristan's file. "Thank you for your cooperation. I'll be honest with you. You haven't completely convinced me. There are too many vague details. Police officers hate secrets and shadows—we like bright, clear days in the sunshine. The blinding light of truth."

"I'm sorry I didn't dazzle you," muttered the Frenchman. "What will happen next?"

Drexler sighed. "I'll call the Violinist to share my assessment. From there, he'll have two options. Either I come back, and we continue our little discussion until the grey clouds clear and we can see the horizon—the best possible outcome for you—or, he decides to hand you over to the Gestapo and you'll get a nice good look at their underground cells. Or maybe they'll just take you out of the city to execute you in some forgotten woods. I saw a memo about that just recently. Managing corpses has become a real problem."

Tristan felt his throat tighten. Drexler banged on the door, then turned back to the prisoner. "I'm going to get some lunch. Do you want something to eat?"

"I'm not especially hungry after what you've just told me."

The door opened and the detective walked out into the corridor. "They have delicious mushroom schnitzel in the officers' mess. If I were you, I'd accept. It could be your last meal," offered the detective in a tone that was almost friendly.

"You can take your schnitzel and shove it!" shouted Tristan as he threw his chair towards the door.

The seat fell to the floor with a clang just as Drexler slammed the door shut.

Tristan stood at the window to calm his anxiety. Fluffy cumulus clouds danced quickly across the blue sky over the city. The wind hit the bulletproof windows with considerable force. He felt like they could explode at any moment. And so could he.

How long had it been since he'd had a truly peaceful moment? The last time, when he was hiding out in Catalonia, hadn't lasted long. He gazed at the façades of the buildings across the way. There were men, women, and children behind those windows. All perfectly Aryan, of course, obedient subjects of their beloved Führer. In the evening, he imagined they must have dinner together and make jokes. He despised them and was jealous of them all at the same time. He had chosen another path, a solitary one, long ago.

And now his path might come to a sudden stop. The image of Spaniards slitting SS soldiers' throats in the castle popped into his mind. Even those bastards must have had someone to cry at the news of their death.

No one would cry for him.

His luck had run out.

The more he thought about the German cop's threatening last words, the clearer his future became. He hadn't convinced him he was telling the truth. On to the basement . . .

The idea of torture left him petrified. Dying had always been a possibility in the life he'd chosen for himself. But being mutilated, lacerated, skinned, or burned . . .

He sat silently for over ten minutes, his eyes directed skyward. Escape was impossible. There had to be hundreds of policemen in the enormous building. His chances were about as good as those of an earthworm in an aviary.

He looked down towards the private courtyard six stories below. There was a third option. One the police officer hadn't thought of. A running jump. From this height, there was no way he'd survive.

Tristan ran his finger over the cracked putty around the window-pane. It would be easy to remove, but the bars wouldn't budge. He couldn't throw himself to his death in the courtyard after all. He came back to the middle of the cell and started thinking as fast as he could. He didn't have any sharp objects to slit his wrists, and even if he did, it would take hours to die that way.

He looked down at his shoes. No laces. They had taken them away when he'd been incarcerated.

Suddenly, the sound of boots rang out in the corridor.

Kripo or Gestapo?

Guttural exclamations sounded behind the door. It wasn't Drexler's voice.

His mind on fire, he picked up the chair and held it tightly in his hands. A useless weapon, but he wouldn't go without a fight.

The door opened with a sinister groan. Two men appeared in a ray of white light. They were wearing black leather trench coats.

Tristan understood right away.

49

Suburbs of Berlin
May 1941

Suddenly Tristan found himself in the hallways, which had been deserted by the usual guards. He tripped as they passed a gate—they hadn't even given him enough time to put his shoes on properly.

"This way."

They started down a metal staircase that creaked loudly as they walked. It must not have been used for years. An emergency light flickered weakly on each landing.

"Turn right."

Tristan found himself in a narrow courtyard full of rubbish. A sickly-sweet musky smell clung to his nostrils. Rats. Suddenly a torch revealed a wooden door barricaded with a metal bar. One of the men pushed hastily through.

"Quickly."

A pair of headlights was waiting outside. They placed a blindfold over his eyes and threw him into the car. A hand tapped the roof of the car and it started down the drive.

Berlin, Ahnenerbe headquarters

"Not what you were expecting?"

Von Essling hesitated, then walked across the pristine grass that led to the front steps, where five white double columns held up a massive porch, onto which a series of French doors opened. The immaculate white building looked nothing like a research institute.

"Feel free to look around," added Himmler, smiling broadly under his thin moustache.

For a moment, Erika felt like a wife visiting her future home. Nevertheless, she walked along the façade, then passed behind the last two columns and turned down the side of the building. A garage jutted out of the side of the house, along with a greenhouse, which rounded the angle with the rear façade. She noticed that the bushy branches of an oak tree brushed up against the building's pediment.

"We requisitioned it, of course. It belonged to an aristocratic family. A rather decadent one. Now this is where the fate of the German people will be decided. And your own as well."

Suburbs of Berlin

The car had just slowed. A new turn. With his face pushed into the leather seat, Tristan found it difficult to breathe. One of the guards had opened a window. The cold air slipped under his shirt, where it froze his skin, like a sneak peek at death, which was just around the corner. The vehicle picked up speed again. How much time did he have left? An hour? More? He'd already been executed once, but this time he wouldn't walk away. He knew too much. From Montserrat to Montségur, the secret trail he'd followed had to disappear. And him with it. Without a trace, with nothing but images of Lucia and Laure in his head. As for Erika . . . The car slowed again. He heard the wind whistling in the branches of a tree. Woods, thought Tristan. In a few minutes, they'd force him out, make him walk to one of those silent ponds on the outskirts of Berlin.

They wouldn't even need a bullet. A bag and some stones would do the trick.

Ahnenerbe headquarters

As Erika observed, the building and its annexes seemed to be divided into separate research divisions, each working in a specific scientific field. In a wainscoted room with windows that looked out over the back garden, archivists were carefully organizing a private collection of books that had just arrived from Norway.

"We have our own SS commando units specialized in gathering precious documents and works of art," explained the Reichsführer. "This collection fills an order placed by one of our researchers, a specialist in ancient writing. He deciphers runic inscriptions from all around the North and Baltic Seas. His work is a priority: runes are the sacred alphabet of Germanic peoples."

"An order?" asked von Essling, surprised. Throughout her career as an archaeologist she'd had to fill out piles of paperwork just to get an extra shovel or pick.

"He needed these books, so we obtained them," answered Himmler matter-of-factly. "Let's go and see the archaeology department. Do you know anything about Carnac?"

"Of course, the Carnac stones. The megalith formations in Brittany."

"Hundreds of stones standing on end," continued Himmler enthusiastically. "A forest of granite. And we have only found a small part of it. Look!"

They had just walked into a room with corkboard walls covered in photographs. Most of them featured megaliths lying on the ground as archaeologists cleared away bits of lichen and heather.

"Our researchers have found dozens of fallen megaliths hidden beneath the dirt. We're measuring them, establishing where they stood, and mapping them carefully."

Erika leaned in for a good look at the map dotted with red and black Xs.

"Have you found any other artefacts at the site? Carved stone, fragments of pottery?"

"Yes, but nothing significant," answered the Reichsführer. "Carnac is first and foremost an astronomical observatory. The oldest in Europe."

Von Essling had heard people advance this theory, but no studies had ever confirmed it.

Himmler's finger tapped one of the photos. "And we're going

to prove it." He turned towards her with another smile. "Shall we continue the visit?"

Berlin

The car still hadn't stopped. Now it was driving down a cobble-stone road—Tristan had easily recognized the characteristic jostling. One of the guards had placed his hand on Tristan's neck. They had slowed down, and he could hear the engine's purr echoing off walls around them. They must be back in Berlin. The Frenchman listened carefully for any noise, a voice, but someone had rolled up the windows. Maybe they were taking him to a new prison? He ran out of time to wonder when the driver braked suddenly, throwing him into the back of the passenger seat. A door slammed and the same shouting voice he'd heard in the prison commanded, "Get out!"

Ahnenerbe headquarters

They had gone upstairs, to the series of rooms that looked out over the porch. Through one of the open glass doors, Erika saw a bearded man sculpting a face.

"This is Captain Schäfer," announced the Reichsführer. "He ran the expedition to Tibet. He's an SS hero."

The officer pushed a few blond strands of hair off his forehead to reveal his pale, almost white eyes. Himmler gestured towards Erika to introduce her.

"Frau von Essling. The archaeologist who led the dig at Montségur."

Schäfer bowed. "Congratulations on the success of your mission. It's a shame, what happened to Weistort. I was with him in the Yarlung Valley. He was, shall we say . . . particularly efficient."

"Frau von Essling is going to replace Colonel Weistort. She'll be heading up the Ahnenerbe. Temporarily. Until he awakes from his coma."

Erika frowned. She hadn't accepted the Reichsführer's offer

yet. As for Schäfer, he managed to mask any surprise he may have felt at her nomination. He took her by the arm.

"During my travels in Tibet, I took facial measurements of hundreds of Tibetans and I came to the conclusion that they are a dual people. Farmers and nomads on the one hand, inferior beings from the Mongol invasions. But on the other . . ." he continued, placing his hand on the face he was sculpting, "the master race. Those who run Tibet. A long, thin chin, inconspicuous cheekbones, a high forehead and clear eyes. In short, they are Aryans."

"Schäfer's work will allow us to establish anatomical standards of Aryanness so we can meticulously sort people," explained Himmler. He glanced at his watch and continued, "My dear Schäfer, please excuse us. I have to show Erika something very important."

The pair moved towards a corridor that led to a former oratory, its walls decorated with Nordic frescoes and lit by stained-glass windows bearing the SS insignia. In the middle stood an altar. A red leather-bound book sat upon it, protected by glass panels.

They walked over and Himmler placed a hand on the transparent barrier. "The *Thule Borealis Kulten.* This is where it all started . . ."

He stopped speaking while he removed and carefully cleaned his glasses. Nothing seemed more important to him. It was as if the entire world depended on the act.

"You haven't said if you'll accept Weistort's position temporarily."

"Do you have any news?"

"He's been transferred to an SS hospital on the outskirts of Berlin. He's still in a coma. I need you to take over for him. So?"

The young woman knew there was only one possible answer.

"My answer is yes," she said.

Himmler put his glasses back on. "I'm so glad," he said with a smile. "Soon you'll be studying this book. But for the moment, follow me. We're going to attend a little ceremony."

One anonymous hand pulled the blindfold off Tristan while another dug the cold barrel of a pistol into his back. They were in a thicket.

The Frenchman marched mechanically down the sandy path which grated under his feet. A clearing appeared through the leaves—the fine grass of a lawn. As he and the guards continued, Tristan could see the façade of a two-storey building with a long balcony on the second floor. The pediment featured a round window that seemed to watch over the surrounding estate.

"Pick up the pace. You're expected."

A group of SS soldiers in dress uniform appeared in front of the building. Shiny helmets, white gloves, rifles on their shoulders. Tristan slowed instinctively. This was the second time he'd been faced with a firing squad. An officer strode slowly through the gravel, examining the soldiers' weapons and uniforms.

Tristan grimaced. Unlike the Spaniards, the Germans did it in style.

He watched as the soldiers and the officer suddenly straightened. A man in an SS uniform had just come out of the main door to the building at a quick pace.

A unanimous click of their heels sounded to salute his arrival in the courtyard.

Tristan recognized him immediately. He was the only high-ranking Nazi official who wore glasses.

Himmler had come to see his execution in person. Quite an honour.

His heart started racing.

Her!

Erika had just appeared. She would also apparently be attending the show. What kind of woman could sleep with a man one day and watch him be shot to death the next?

He puffed up his chest and straightened his neck. He looked away from the soldiers and focused on giving Erika the most disdainful look he could manage. He wouldn't let her see him frightened.

Himmler walked over to the firing squad and gestured to the officer. "Is everything ready?" he asked.

"Yes, Reichsführer."

"Let's get on with it, then."

Tristan closed his eyes. This time, there was no way out, no hope of escape. He tensed instinctively, as if his tight muscles might protect him from the biting bullets.

Suddenly, the soldiers presented their rifles as the Nazi flag was unrolled beneath the pediment window, just above Erika's head.

"Music!"

A uniformed marching band emerged from behind the corner of the building playing the Nazi anthem, "Horst Wessel Lied". Tristan opened his eyes. The guns were down, and Erika was standing right next to the SS leader. She smiled at the Frenchman.

Himmler saluted Tristan and walked over to him. He slowly pulled a black velvet box bearing a red swastika from his pocket. The music stopped suddenly, replaced by a drum roll that seemed to last an eternity for Tristan. Then silence again.

Himmler's voice rang out. "In the name of our Führer, Adolf Hitler," he decreed as he opened the box and pulled out a small black metal cross hanging from a dark-coloured ribbon, "I hereby award you the Iron Cross, for services rendered to the Reich . . ."

Tristan felt his mind falter. He wasn't being executed—he was being decorated! With the most prestigious German military award.

Himmler pinned the cross to the lapel of Tristan's worn jacket and added, in a somewhat threatening voice, "And for those you will render still."

50

The two silver lines shimmered in the moonlight, then disappeared in the open mouth of the tunnel. Pressed against the trunk of a pine at the edge of the woods just steps from the tracks, Laure d'Estillac felt her heart begin to pound. The train would be there in ten minutes. Just enough time to set the charge and return to her hiding place. She scolded herself for wasting an hour traipsing through the forest trying to find the entrance to the damn tunnel.

The darkness around her was silent, but her anxiety was reaching its height. There was a sentry box with a searchlight next to the entrance to the tunnel. Everything seemed deserted. There was no light anywhere. According to the map, it was an abandoned German inspection site. She didn't have time to check.

Calm down. Breathe deeply.

She focused on the beating of her heart and cleared her mind. A technique she'd learned from her sabotage instructor at Glenmore Loch, in Scotland.

Above her, an owl hooted from its perch on a branch.

Laure propped her Walther PP6 pistol against the tree trunk and picked up her bag of explosives. She shuddered.

What if it explodes?

What on earth am I doing here, playing resistance fighter when I could be sleeping in my bed?

Her mind started racing again.

Stop being so silly . . . You have to light the fuse. Breathe. Breathe.

She opened the bag in the dark and felt around to make sure everything was there.

Charge, detonator, fuse, pliers. Is that everything? All set.

Satisfied, she left the lighter box on the ground and put the bag on her back.

Go!

Her heart jumped into her throat. The young woman ran as fast as she could, leaving the woods behind. It was only about ten meters to the tracks. She reached the ballast in seconds and lay down at the junction between two tracks. Right where she'd been taught to place her charges. Mechanically, she took out the explosives and stuck them to the junction—the Achilles heel of railway tracks. Now she was running on autopilot.

Her hands were so sweaty, she was having trouble securing the charge. Her fingers trembled. Suddenly the rails started vibrating.

Oh shit! The train is coming. I'll never make it. I have to get out of here.

A quiet rage washed over her. She *had* to succeed. She swallowed hard. This was no time to give up.

She couldn't help but glance towards the tunnel. There was something threatening about the dark opening. It felt like the train might suddenly emerge and squash her on the rails.

Calm down. It's miles away.

She managed to secure the charge, insert the detonator, and tie the electrical wire. As she stood up, the pliers fell from the bag and hit the rails with a loud clang.

She swore under her breath and bent down to pick them up.

Suddenly a white flash appeared in the darkness.

The searchlight on the sentry box flooded the tracks with light. "Halt!"

Laure froze.

"Achtung!"

She heard boots crunching through the gravel.

This is impossible. The post is abandoned.

She felt around her jacket pocket and cursed herself. The pistol! She'd left it in the woods.

A wave of machine-gun fire pummelled the ground around her. "Halt!"

She couldn't move. Checkmate.

Three men came into her field of vision. Three German soldiers in helmets, machine guns aimed at her. She put her hands up, disappointed in herself.

"Eine Sabotage!" shouted one of the men.

"No, I was planting carrots," answered Laure, realizing how unbelievable it sounded.

One of them moved behind her and patted her down. His hands climbed up her thighs.

She kept her hands in the air. Her eyes were full of anger.

"Do you really think—"

A soldier hit her on the back of her head with the butt of his gun before she could finish. She passed out and collapsed onto the tracks.

Laure woke up with a start, her head pounding, and slowly opened her eyes.

A gentle light filled the rococo room she was in. She shot up on the bed to find she was still wearing her combat jacket and rubber-soled work boots. A tall man with a perfectly groomed short beard was leaning against the mantel smoking a pipe and watching her, his eyes filled with curiosity.

"Don't worry. The pain will fade over the next couple of days. I was knocked out twice during commando training at the same centre you attended."

The voice was familiar.

Laure blinked several times. She recognized him, but he'd changed uniforms.

"Commander!"

Malorley walked over to her side.

"The bump will last at least a week, though."

"I don't understand . . . The training centre," she stuttered. "Where am I?"

"In the middle of London. Your instructors brought you here.

You should thank them for leaving your clothes on." He smiled as he cleaned his pipe. "Yes, it's a shame," he continued. "You failed your sabotage exam. You didn't check to see if there were any guards near the tunnel."

"I took too long in the forest."

"The directions were wrong, so you would arrive late. A classic test, designed to measure your reaction to extreme pressure. Time is a luxury we can't afford in war. Follow me. We need to talk."

He helped the young woman stand.

"Where are we going?"

"To my office."

They left the room and walked down a wide corridor. Its walls were covered in garnet-coloured wallpaper and decorated with gold-framed paintings of Greek tragedy masks. There was a thick, high-quality carpet on the floor. Three crystal chandeliers shed a gentle light on the passageway, which led them to a door at the end.

"Wow, no holds barred at the SOE, it seems. Does the Crown pay for your lodgings?" asked Laure sarcastically.

"We're at Prospero's Mansion, a theatre which belongs to a group of friends." Malorley stopped in front of a door on the right, then pushed it open. "Go in and sit down."

She walked into a rectangular wainscoted room of average size with a Victorian desk in the middle. The window, framed by heavy green curtains, looked out over a closed courtyard. A tall, wide mirror occupied the wall space across from it. The décor was minimalist: a console table stood against a wall with a framed photo on top and a painting of a fox-hunting scene hung next to the window.

They sat down across from one another on either side of the desk. Malorley lit his pipe again and looked kindly at Laure.

"How is your training going?"

"With the exception of last night, it's been a ball. Three exhausting weeks of preparations at Brompton followed by two weeks of 'toughening up' at Arisaig House. And let's not forget the skydiving lesson, where I almost broke my neck."

Malorley smiled. It seemed training hadn't quelled her spirits.
"How is it going emotionally?"

"I lost it twice. No, three times if you count the time I slapped a sergeant who was hurling insults at me as I did my push-ups."

He stared at her in silence.

"But I never gave up," she added, a hint of defiance in her eyes. "You seem disappointed?"

"Not at all. I'm impressed. I read the results of your ability to resist Gestapo-style interrogation. Even the toughest guys in the service were dazzled."

"Unlike the other recruits, I have personal experience with SS officers in France. Not instructors dressed up as Nazis."

"Do you think of your father often?"

She lit a cigarette and took a long drag. "What, are you a psychologist now?"

"I don't mean to pry. I just think he would be very proud of you."

"Now it's my turn to ask a question," said Laure, her voice calmer. "Have you heard from Jane?"

Malorley's face fell. "Nothing. I think she must have died in that field, on the spot where the Cathars were burned alive. I prefer to think of her as a martyr rather than being tortured by the Germans."

"I'm sorry."

The phone rang. Malorley picked up, all the while looking right at Laure. He answered yes and no several times, then hung up.

"So, I brought you here to offer you a mission."

"I'm listening."

"Did you hear that Rudolf Hess landed in Scotland last month?"

"Yes, I read about it in the papers, like everyone else. He's being held in the Tower of London and they say he's losing his mind. Even Hitler has declared Hess is a madman."

The SOE officer shook his head.

"That's the official story. In reality, he came to offer peace with England, without the Führer's authorization. It's hard to believe, but England holds a special place in the sinister man's heart. He sees us as stubborn Aryan cousins who have simply failed to understand the Great Reich's civilizing mission. Churchill visited him in secret, to size him up. He left the meeting quite troubled."

"What do you mean?"

"The Prime Minister learned that this high-ranking Nazi official had undertaken his latest mission on the advice of his astrologers, and that Hess has believed in magic and the occult for decades. And that he's not the only one . . ."

"You don't say!"

"Himmler himself subscribes to strange occult doctrines that would send shivers up your spine. But most importantly, Hess told the Prime Minister about the discovery of a swastika in Tibet. A discovery that, according to Hess, led the Germans to declare war a few months later. And that's not all. Hess also knew about Colonel Weistort's expedition to Montségur. He knew exactly what was hidden beneath the Cathar fortress."

"I find it hard to believe that Hitler went to war because of a relic," answered Laure, taking another drag on her cigarette.

"Churchill was sceptical, too. But he's changed his mind."

All traces of sarcasm left Laure's face.

"Following these revelations," continued Malorley, "the Prime Minister ordered Hess be kept under strict guard and that we spread the story about him being crazy. But . . ." He stopped to pull a piece of paper out of a drawer. It bore the War Office seal. He slid it across the desk to the young woman. "He also summoned me to ask me to create a department specializing in the Nazis' occult operations. An equivalent to the Ahnenerbe. Well, a much smaller version, with far fewer resources, unfortunately."

Laure seemed doubtful. "I can't believe your Prime Minister took this nonsense seriously."

"Churchill is a pragmatist above all else. He doesn't believe in magic, but he now knows some of our enemies do. He wants to know what they're predicting so he can counterattack."

"I don't understand. Do you want to send out expeditions, like the Nazis?"

"No. We need to collect all the information we can on their

plans and roll out preventive operations. But first, I need to start thinking like them, and to do that, I need experts."

"Do they exist?"

"I'm setting up a team of researchers specializing in esotericism, magic, and early religions. I must say I've met some astounding people. This morning, for example, I have an appointment with Aleister Crowley, whom a friend recommended. He's had a surprising career. He even managed to open a temple where they worship magic in Cefalù, Sicily, right under Mussolini's nose."

He showed her a photo of a bald man with swollen features—most likely from cortisone use—and a vacant look.

"Charming-looking guy . . . But I don't see what I have to do with all this."

"I'd like to have you with me."

Laure's eyes widened in surprise. "Is this a joke? I'm not an astrologer and I don't tell fortunes. In fact, I'm a hardened rationalist."

"So am I, but the world is full of powerful forces that we don't understand. We reject them on principle just because our minds haven't yet figured out how to integrate them into our reality. Someday they'll be explained. The same way we discovered the secrets of radioactivity, which we talk so much about today. Today's magic is tomorrow's science. And I need you."

She looked at him for a long time, then shook her head. "Thanks for the offer, but I have just one goal: to return to France to fight the Germans."

"Isn't vengeance what drives you? They killed your father."

"So what if it is? Either way, I have no desire to play archaeologist. Why don't you send that traitor Tristan a job offer? I'm sure that if you pay enough he'll be happy to change sides yet again, without any scruples at all."

Malorley relit his pipe and nodded, a sad look in his eyes. "I expected this reaction. You know that your failure last night means you won't be sent to France for at least another six months. And you'll have to take more tests. With me, you'd be sent on missions in occupied countries right away."

Laure massaged the back of her head. The instructors really hadn't held back with the butt of that gun. She hesitated. The offer was tempting and the idea of going back to training was less than enticing. But she was ill at ease with these stories of magic and sorcery. She studied the picture of the fat bald man's lecherous face again. No, she definitely couldn't stomach having *him* for a colleague!

"I don't think so," she said, pushing the photo away. "Good night, Commander."

She stood up and saluted. Malorley did the same.

"As you wish. Return to your room. Tomorrow they'll take you back to your training centre. This is the last you'll hear from me."

She was heading for the door when Malorley called out, "Could you do me one last favour? On your right, there's a pot with several pipe cleaners in it, sitting in the middle of a dessert trolley. Could you bring me one, please?"

"Of course."

The terracotta pot was exactly where he said it was, underneath a large photograph that hung on the wall in an ornate silver frame. She looked at it mindlessly. Six men in combat clothes had posed for the picture, shoulder to shoulder, their eyes tired, their rifles worn cross-body. Malorley was in the middle in a Spanish Republican Army uniform.

"When was this photograph taken?" she asked.

"January 1937. Teruel, in Spain, during the civil war. The Intelligence Service had sent me over to lead an international brigade. Those are the officers from my unit, made up of Frenchmen and Englishmen."

Laure was removing a pipe cleaner when her eyes stopped on one of the men. He was kneeling, his hands posed on the barrel of his rifle. His ironic smile struck her.

"The guy in the picture . . . It's—"

Malorley watched her carefully from behind his desk. "Men from my brigade, like I said. My pipe cleaner, please."

She turned around, her face tense. "Don't play dumb!" she said, placing her finger on the frame. "You know exactly who I'm talking about."

"It's of no concern to you, since you rejected my offer."

Furious, she took the photo off the wall and walked back to his desk to brandish it in his face. "Answer me, Malorley! You knew him all along! He was working for you, wasn't he?"

"Sorry, that's top secret. Like everything else in the files handled by this department. Have a good night, Laure."

"Don't play games with me! You knew perfectly well that I'd see the photograph when you asked me to get your damn pipe cleaner."

He didn't react. "I read your training file. One of your instructors noted your heightened observational abilities. He was right."

Laure d'Estillac stared at the picture. "It *is* him."

The commander took the photo in his hands. "Indeed. He's one of my most effective officers. His name is Tristan . . . Tristan Marcas."

She gaped at him, astounded.

"And the swastika the Germans took in Montségur?"

Malorley smiled.

"But . . . your duel with Tristan in the sanctuary?"

"You're a descendant of the Cathars. You, of all people, should know everything is but an illusion. Tristan had figured out that the mechanism installed by the Cathars was just a trick. It was only there to scare away intruders. It made no difference which of the twin relics he took. The important thing was to give the fake one to the Germans."

"How did he do it?"

"The fake one had a normal cross engraved on the back. A cross for the crusaders, but a symbol of the abyss for the Cathars. That relic was the trick."

"How did he know you were going to attack the cave?"

"Tristan knew he was being followed by our services and that we would meet up with him sooner or later. If we hadn't shown up, he would have hidden the real relic right under the Germans' noses. He would have found a way to send me a message. He's a very resourceful man." Malorley stopped for a puff on his pipe, then continued: "The Nazis left with the fake swastika. We have the real one."

"But they have the one from Tibet, right?"

"Yes. It's a tie for the moment. Good and Evil are neck and neck. And there are two other swastikas to find. That will be our mission. And to find out more about their mysterious origins. We don't know who made them or why they were scattered to the corners of the earth thousands of years ago."

A light went on in Laure's eyes. "So, if they think they have the relic from Montségur, the Germans will become even bolder. They'll do crazier things. They'll want to—" She stopped suddenly as she realized how obvious it was. "They'll open a second front, won't they?"

"When the Germans *feel* invincible, they become vulnerable. And," continued Malorley, delighting in another puff of his pipe, "we have an agent in the heart of the Darkness."

Epilogue

At that exact moment, thousands of miles to the east, history was being made.

On June 22, 1941, at exactly three o'clock in the morning, Hitler's divisions set off to cover more than six hundred miles of front and attack the Soviet Empire. Never before had mankind witnessed such an invasion. Neither Alexander the Great, nor Caesar, Attila, Genghis Khan, Napoleon, nor any other conqueror had ever mustered such a huge army.

On June 22, 1941, exactly one year after France's capitulation, four million soldiers, seven thousand tanks and planes, and half a million horses were set loose on Stalin's doorstep.

On June 22, 1941, the European war became a World War.

For Hitler, the war wasn't just following its course—it came to embody the fullest meaning of the word. All wars are horrible, but this war, led by a failed artist turned tyrant, stands out with a single word: Gesamtkunstwerk. *A total work of art.*

Military victory over Russia would go hand in hand with the planned extermination of populations deemed inferior: mainly Jews, gypsies, and Slavs. For the Führer and his enthusiastic followers, it wasn't the work of evil. Quite the contrary. It was the ultimate fight for the good of the German people, as Nazi propaganda put it.

And since he needed a powerful symbol for this gargantuan undertaking, Hitler himself chose the invasion's code name: Unternehmen Barbarossa.

Operation Barbarossa.

Frederick Barbarossa. Hitler's legendary hero. A name infused with timeless prestige throughout Germany. The mythical emperor of the First Reich, who had set out on his own crusade at the dawn of the first millennium. The emperor who, legend holds, slumbers still in a magical mountain, waiting to be awoken to re-establish the Great Reich.

On June 22, 1941, just a few hours after the summer solstice, the new Nazi emperor had just launched his greatest crusade.

GOOD & EVIL

GIACOMETTI
RAVENNE

TRANSLATED BY MAREN BAUDET-LACKNER

PROLOGUE

Crete
Autumn 1941

They've been waiting for this for so long. Since before they were born. Like their fathers before them. And their fathers' fathers. As far back as the village can remember, they've known it would happen.

They didn't know when, or who, but after centuries of waiting, they know the day has come.

Or rather, the night.

A bloody night.

The five farmers slink silently between the olive trees. In the darkness, olive trees look much like people. They are a similar size and a comparable shape, and even if a tree has been bent or broken by the wind, it can still hide a man.

A man must listen. He must listen to the shadows that never fall silent. They whisper to those who listen out for them. The same word, again and again:

Xeni!

Xeni!

Xeni!

"Invaders."

Warriors from the North, their heads protected by steel helmets, have come to sully their lands and steal the sacred treasure a stranger entrusted to the villagers. A stranger from an ancient boreal nation.

The five farmers are certain that the blond men strutting before their eyes are the barbarians described in the prophecy.

A gentle, fragrant breeze rustles the olive leaves, like a peaceful ancestral melody corrupted by the invaders' presence.

They may not have a name, but the parasites have a sound; the thumping of boots on the earth, of guns jostling in their holsters— the din of imminent war and death. But sometimes death takes another path.

Though still hidden behind the olive trees, the farmers have moved. They need to see now, to know how many invaders there are.

One, two, three.

They observe the barrels of the rifles propped up against the wall, the spark of a lighter, and the tiny sizzling circles of cigarettes. They watch the soldiers become men again. Just in time to die.

The five farmers have been trained to deliver death to anyone who dares defy the rules. Like their fathers before them, and their fathers' fathers.

They are not just farmers, they are Fylaques. Guardians.

All of divine blood. They were born in Crete, the island of honey, the place chosen by Zeus's mother to give birth to the father of the gods.

Fylaques are trained to handle the *kyro*, a dangerous dagger engraved with a red drop of blood, better than any other Cretans. The weapon thirsts for the last droplet of blood in the enemy's body.

From behind the olive trees, the five Fylaques smile as they watch the warriors from the North. The first enemy has just unbuckled his belt and removed his jacket. The heat is stifling. He's not used to it. He and his companions are the children of a cold climate, as cold as their hearts.

Their bodies are pale.

But not for long.

One of the Fylaques steps out of the shadows. He unfolds his *kyro*, the perfectly oiled spring freeing the blade from the horn handle. The metal is coated in charcoal to prevent it from glinting in the light. The others join him, and the atmosphere grows tense.

The invaders have their backs to them. They're working around the well and won't hear a thing. Their ears are focused on the clanging of the bucket against the walls as they retrieve it. They've been thirsty all day and only hear their bodies' cries for water.

They've forgotten they are invaders.

The promise of water drowns out all other sounds.

The first Fylaque emerges further from the darkness.

The head of the pack.

He stands silently, waits for the clang of the bucket against the rim of the well, and strikes.

The *kyro* is so sharp that it slips between the enemy's ribs effortlessly. The pain is so intense that the foreigner doesn't even cry out. He looks up at the stars as if he's never seen them before, then darkness veils his eyes, and he falls silently to the ground. The rest of the soldiers have plunged their hands and mouths into the water. They are deaf to their fate. The blades slide deep into their necks. The last thing they'll notice is the strange taste of the water—the tang of their own blood.

The foreigners are just bodies now. Bodies the Fylaques place around the well in a star shape. They cross themselves, not to ask for forgiveness for what they have done, but for what they are about to do. They turn the corpses over onto their backs.

Each *kyro* pauses just above the victim's sternum, then cuts through the skin, which parts like moist lips.

They plunge their hands inside. Poke around.

When they get back up, a bittersweet smell rises from the ground.

Thanatos.

To truly kill an enemy, you must take more than his life.

PART ONE

Before Hitler was, I am.

Aleister Crowley

This idea of himself as the German messiah was the source of his personal power. It enabled him to become the ruler of 80 million people.

Walter Schellenberg, Hitler's Head of Counter-intelligence.

(From *The Labyrinth*, Harper & Brother, 1956)

I

The horizon disappeared into a lead-coloured sky. A curtain of rain pounded into the silver sea. The Admiralty's forecast was accurate—bad weather always blew in from the southwest. From France. It was only three o'clock in the afternoon, but the harbour master's office had already turned on the safety beacons. The wind was still a breeze, but it would pick up soon.

The port in Southampton—the second largest in the southern part of the country, after Portsmouth—was bustling. Swarms of ships of different sizes moved in and out of the main docks. Since war had broken out, cargo ships and naval destroyers had replaced the legendary transatlantic cruise ships and luxury yachts. The *Titanic* was but a distant memory. No one embarked on holiday from Southampton anymore—now they went to war.

From the bridge of the *Cornwallis*, Captain Killdare watched the cranes dance over the main deck. It was taking forever to load the last crates. The ship should have got underway hours ago. Killdare wanted to leave the estuary as quickly as possible and get past the Isle of Wight, to avoid a possible Luftwaffe raid. Though the bombings had died down since the end of May—Britain had won the battle for the skies, thanks to its Spitfire squadrons—the Germans didn't let them forget they were at war, and regularly launched attacks on British military or civilian targets. Southampton and Portsmouth still received their fair share of fire and shrapnel, and stuck at port, the *Cornwallis* was easy prey for Göring's vultures.

Annoyed by the delay, Killdare picked up the receiver and called the officer in charge of the hold.

"Jesus, Matthews, what are your dockers doing? Do you want to keep us here all night?"

"Just one more crate and we're done, Captain. The actuator on one of the cranes got stuck because of that damn synthetic oil."

"Of course, the oil. Why not blame it on Nazi sabotage, while we're at it? If you want my opinion, the dockers are just taking it easy. War or no war, it's all the same to them."

Captain Killdare hung up, even more irked than before. He'd been in a bad mood for a whole week; ever since his meeting at the shipowner's head office. To his great surprise, the manager of maritime operations for the Cunard Line had asked him to captain the *Cornwallis*, a lightweight cruise ship headed for New York.

A cruise ship! Killdare couldn't stand them.

His speciality had always been cargo vessels. He enjoyed an excellent reputation for getting his merchandise—whatever its worth—safely to its destination anywhere in the world. Shipowners had been vying to hire him since he'd rescued a sinking cargo off the coast of Macao, despite half of his crew having jumped ship.

And now they wanted him to captain the *Cornwallis*. It wasn't even a Class A vessel, like the *Queen Mary*. The *Cornwallis* was to transport industrial equipment to the United States as part of a new strategy implemented by the General Staff. An officer from the Atlantic fleet had explained their reasoning: "The German U-boats hunt in packs across the Atlantic, and only go after military convoys and big cargo ships. Their torpedoes are too precious to waste on civilian transport vessels."

The door to the bridge creaked open as a tall man in a stylish camel-coloured raincoat came in. He held his soft felt hat in his hand. Killdare shot him an angry look.

"Hello, Captain. I'm John Brown," the intruder explained calmly. "Lovely to meet you."

The sailor stared suspiciously at Mr. Brown. He'd been warned of his arrival. A bigwig, according to the Cunard management office. The man was in his fifties, with a thin, pale face—a typical

London bureaucrat, from a ministry or a bank. His name was clearly an alias. It all reeked of trouble. The captain mumbled hello and shook his hand, which was firmer than he'd expected.

"What can I do for you?" asked Killdare in the most dismissive tone he could muster.

"When do you plan to leave?"

"In half an hour or less, I'd say."

"Perfect. One of my subordinates will be on board for this crossing. Please do your best to ensure he's comfortable."

The captain shrugged. "You mean the rude, bearded fellow who smells of tobacco and is inseparable from his metal case? The bloke in cabin 35B? He'll be as comfortable as any other passenger on the upper deck. No more, no less. Now, if you don't mind, I have a ship to ready for departure. I'll pass on your recommendations to my second-in-command. Good day."

The captain turned around, terminating the conversation, and began inspecting the pressure gauges on the instrument panel. A few seconds passed, but Mr. Brown didn't budge.

"Captain, I don't think you understand."

Killdare turned his head, and saw a military card bearing Mr. Brown's photo. *Commander James Malorley, Army Strategic Division.*

"You see, that rude, bearded fellow is my deputy. He's on a confidential mission of the utmost importance to the British government, which is why it would be best for you to make things as easy as possible for him during his stay. Please note that I'm using the conditional only to be polite."

Killdare stood up straight. He'd served four years in the Royal Navy and instinctively grew an inch when confronted with high-ranking officers.

"I apologize, Commander. You should have introduced yourself sooner. I'm a little anxious, with all these Kraut raids. The sooner I'm out of here, the better."

"A network of German spies was uncovered in Portsmouth last week, so I'm wary of lingering ears. I have a letter for you."

Commander Malorley handed him a yellow envelope bearing the Prime Minister's seal. "These are your instructions. Open them when you're at sea. You'll notice that they come directly from the highest authority. Read them carefully. Captain Andrew—the rude bloke, as you call him—will come and explain what it's all about."

"If the mission is so important, isn't it dangerous to get civilians mixed up in it? I have thirty passengers on board. I know we're at war, but using innocent people as a cover isn't very . . . sportsmanlike."

"Do you think Hitler and his friends are sportsmanlike? It's an honourable sentiment, but don't worry about the passengers; they're all professionals who know the risks. Moreover, you'll be escorted by two submarines for the entire crossing. They'll be perfectly discreet, of course, and join you just outside the port."

A siren sounded twice in the bridge, signalling that the ship was fully loaded.

"I see it's time to go. Good luck," said the commander, staring hard at the captain. "If I told you the outcome of the war is in your hands, would you believe me?"

"Given the look of your deputy, I'd bet you a-hundred-to-one. But anything is possible these days, like talking to a military commander who goes by the name of Mr. Brown, or watching Europe march to the orders of a chap with a Charlie Chaplin moustache. I'll get your precious cargo to its destination, even if I have to cross the Sargasso Sea and confront Neptune himself."

The commander gave the captain a firm pat on the shoulder and left the bridge, buttoning up his raincoat tightly. The temperature had dropped several degrees and the damp found its way into his shirt collar.

As he set foot on the wet wharf, the *Cornwallis'* siren wailed across the dock. Harbour employees in mustard-coloured overalls untied the mooring lines and threw them to the sailors swarming on the deck.

Commander James Malorley of the Special Operations Executive, aka Mr. Brown, watched the ship's black stern move slowly away from the dock. How curious that the ship chosen to carry the sacred swastika—the first of four such relics; three others were yet to be retrieved by the Allies—bore the name of the head of the British army during the American Revolution, Lord Cornwallis, George Washington's arch-enemy.

The stench of fuel oil filled the air as the vessel spun around to face the harbour's exit. Deep within the hull, machinery whirred softly.

Malorley glanced one last time at the ship, pulled his felt hat down, and turned towards the harbour master's office, where Laure d'Estillac was waiting for him inside the Amilcar.

He didn't want to admit it, but he was relieved to see the swastika leave for the other side of the Atlantic, thousands of miles away. He and his SOE colleagues had risked their lives to keep it from the Nazis, and many lives had been claimed. Jane's face surfaced in his mind. He could still see the surprised, almost childlike expression on the young agent's face as she was brought down by a hail of German bullets. Her blonde hair shone brightly in the enemy searchlights. She had fallen far away, in southern France, near the Pyrenees. In Cathar Country in a field at Montségur, at the exact place where heretics were burned alive centuries earlier. He hadn't been able to do anything to save her, fleeing like a coward to keep the relic safe.

Malorley could still feel the kiss she'd given him as they fled the castle. A long kiss, as if the brave young woman had known it would be their last.

Big drops of rain soaked the dock. The commander shivered and tightened the scarf around his neck.

The shower dripped down from his hat, blurring Jane's face, leaving him lost in his thoughts. He was a solitary man who'd given up on a normal life. No wife, no children, not even a dog. He lived to do his duty. Not by choice—fate had decided for him by involving him in the quest for the relics. Malorley knew he was a piece on a chess board, and the game's stakes were unclear. A game of chess that had been going on for thousands of years. He had no idea whether he was a pawn or a king, but he was sure that others before him, people from other times and civilizations, had lost their lives and souls to this adventure.

He hastened his step, so as not to be soaked by the time he reached the car on the other side of the dock.

Suddenly, a strident siren rang out over the port. Malorley's blood began rushing through his veins as the muscles in his legs leapt into action. Since the beginning of the war, the reflex had become an instinct, as it had for most British people. Malorley ran along the dock as fast as he could. He only had a few minutes left. This wasn't a ship siren; it was the anti-aircraft defence system. It meant the German eagle was on the hunt. And its cruel presence promised blood, fire, and death.